TWENTY TWELVE

HELEN BLACK

ROBINSON

Constable & Robinson Ltd
55–56 Russell Square
London WC1B 4HP
www.constablerobinson.com

First published in the UK by Robinson,
an imprint of Constable & Robinson Ltd, 2012

A copy of the British Library Cataloguing in
Publication Data is available from the British Library

ISBN: 978-1-84901-475-5 (paperback)
ISBN: 978-1-78033-019-8 (ebook)

Printed and bound in the UK

1 3 5 7 9 10 8 6 4 2

For Andrew

Acknowledgements

This book has been a collaborative effort, as ever, and I owe a debt of gratitude to, if not a cast of thousands, then certainly more than a handful.

My first thanks go to my readers. This is the first book that doesn't feature Lilly Valentine. Thank you for giving me the space for this project.

Next up, a shout out to the Buckman gang. Watching my back of course.

Then everyone at Constable & Robinson. Thank you for letting me take this journey. The next one's a Lilly, honest.

Once again a huge cheer for Lynne McA. Her knack of getting to the heart of what I'm trying to say is uncanny.

To Jon G: massive thanks for advice on all things technical. Why a luddite like me tried to incorporate so much techie stuff is a mystery, but your insights sparked so many ideas, what's a girl to do?

Finally, as always, the biggest dollop of gratitude must go to my family without whom none of this would be possible or have any point.

'Sweet baby Jesus.'

Officer George Stanley wiped a fat sweaty hand across a fat sweaty face.

'Go back to the cruiser and get me a beer from the trunk,' he growled.

Nathan Shaw hesitated. George was the senior officer. Hell, Nathan was barely out of the academy, but drinking on duty?

'Did you hear me, boy?' George shaded his eyes against the sun's dazzle and frowned.

Nathan shrugged and scrambled up the dusty bank to where the cruiser was parked out of view. He popped the trunk and found a plastic icebox nestled between the first aid kit and a carton of surgical gloves. He lifted the lid and let his hand graze the bottles inside. The cold glass was delicious against the pink heat of his skin.

'Get yourself one,' George called.

Nathan smiled. One beer wouldn't hurt. And anyways, who would ever know out here in the August heat? Carefully, he closed the trunk and headed back to George, a Bud in each hand.

George acknowledged him with a nod and reached into his pocket for a bottle opener. 'Always be prepared,' he said.

Nathan forced a chuckle and took a long swig. The condensation on the glass had wet his hand and when he lowered himself to the ground, the gritty earth breadcrumbed his thumb, like a chicken tender. He rubbed it against his trouser leg.

1

'Goddamn waste of time.' George held the Bud against his cheek.

Nathan didn't argue. They'd been here swatting flies and stinking like snakes for six hours straight. He peered at the deserted yard of the Pearsons' farmhouse. 'Are they even home?' Nathan asked.

'Ain't no telling,' said George. 'Reckon Tobias and the boys left before sun up.'

'What about the wife? And the little kids?'

George drained the last of his beer with a sigh. 'Probably inside.'

'Doing what?'

'Cooking, praying, who knows?' said George. 'And more to the point, who cares?'

Nathan squinted through the white heat at the shutters, bleached by the sun and closed tight. 'The Chief thinks they might have illegal weapons in there,' he said.

'The Chief thinks a lot of things.'

'You don't believe it?' asked Nathan.

George blew across the mouth of his empty bottle, the air making one long sad note. 'Ain't about what I believe; it's about what I know. And what I know is that the Pearsons are God-fearing folk who've kept themselves to themselves for the last fifteen years.'

Nathan chewed his lip. George was old school. Voted for Dubya and his daddy before him. If a body didn't bother him, he saw no reason to bother them. But as far as Nathan could see it, illegal guns and children didn't have any business being together.

'I don't see why we couldn't just knock on their door and ask 'em,' he said.

George let out a hoot like an owl. 'And what would you have done if they didn't want to talk to you?'

'Well I don't know.' Nathan scratched his chin. 'I reckon that would have made me suspicious enough to go back to the station for a warrant. To have a look-see around the place.'

'Uh huh,' said George. 'And do you know how to get one of those warrants?'

'Not rightly.'

'Let me tell you, boy, they don't hand 'em out like Christmas cards. You gotta show reasonable cause. You gotta show ev-i-dence.' George spread his arms out wide, to take in their dusty hideout overlooking the farmhouse. 'And that is why we are here.'

Nathan turned and scanned the yard once more. In six hours no one had been in and no one had been out. The scene was freakishly quiet.

'I don't get it,' he said. 'The Chief must be expecting something to happen.'

George pulled at his collar with a doughy finger and breathed a gust of air down the gap.

'Then answer me this. If there ain't been nothing happening up here in fifteen years, what makes you think things are going to get crazy today?'

Chapter One

I hate hospitals.

I know everyone says that.

'It's the smell.'

Well, of course it's not.

I mean, I don't actively like the smell of vomit masked by disinfectant; I wouldn't, you know, swap my Chanel No. 5 for it. But I don't *loathe* it in the way I loathe public swimming pools, or standing in queues, or people who let their dog stick his nose in your crotch and tell you he's 'only being friendly'.

If people are honest about what they truly dislike about hospitals, what makes them squirm, it's the fear of all that pain and death so blatantly and proudly on show. Putting it bluntly, they're shit scared.

With this cheery thought warming the cockles of my heart, you can imagine how delirious I am as I pull up outside Highfields Hospital for the Elderly and Terminally Ill.

'Are you my mummy?'

I try not to wrinkle my nose at the old lady in the Winnie the Pooh nightdress and matching slippers.

She bares her hard pink gums at me. 'Are you my mummy?'

I'm thirty-three and she's a hundred in her stockinged feet. I try not to be offended.

I look around for a member of staff but, as usual, the place is like the Mary Celeste. Back at reception, three women sit behind a wooden desk festooned with fresh flowers and leaflets urging the aged to eat their five a day. They smile with their straight, white teeth.

'Welcome to Highfields,' they trill and direct you to the visitors' area.

But once inside the belly of this beast, you get neither help nor smiles. Take this poor old lady, for instance; why haven't her relatives complained? They can't be happy that she's left to wander the corridors stripped of her dignity and probably her knickers, can they? But what's the alternative? Look after her themselves?

Fat tears well in her eyes. 'Mummy?'

I shake my head and a blanket of hopelessness settles on her shoulders. She opens her mouth in a silent howl. For a second she reminds me of that painting by Edvard Munch.

'Mummy, Mummy, Mummy,' she chants, desperately grabbing my wrist in her bent and swollen fingers.

I try to prise her off but she's surprisingly strong. 'Could I get some help here?' I call out.

No answer. Typical. How much does this place cost a week?

At last I spot a familiar figure stumbling out of a side room. He's more bent than the last time I saw him. He leans more heavily on his walking frame.

'Dad!' I wave at him with my free hand. 'Dad, is that you?'

He shuffles towards me, his breath exploding in raspy puffs. 'Well it isn't George bleedin' Clooney.'

When he finally closes the distance between us, I am startled at the damage inflicted by the last two months in this hellhole. His hair, once thick and curly, is now so thin it barely covers his

5

skull, revealing a smorgasbord of liver spots, moles and itchy-looking warts. I berate myself for not visiting more often, for not being a better daughter.

'What's the matter?' He peers at me. 'Lost my youthful good looks, have I?'

'You've lost weight,' I reply.

'If you saw the crap they serve here, you'd understand why.'

I don't answer. The hospital email me their weekly menu detailing the delicious food on offer: chicken soup. Toad in the hole. Apple crumble.

'Lord knows your mother couldn't cook, but she'd make this lot look like Jamie bleedin' Oliver,' he says.

I smart at the mention of Mum and want to defend her lumpy cauliflower cheese, but I can't do another argument. Instead, I nod at the old crone still attached to my arm.

Dad looks at his fellow patient with what might be pity or sorrow and leans in to her ear. 'Piss off!' he shouts.

The woman screams and scurries away like a beetle.

I've got to hand it to him; even a place like this can't change my dad.

After the slow march back to Dad's room, he settles on his bed. Sun streams through his window. In the glare he looks insectile, the thin sticks of his legs held at an odd angle, the skin of his hands as dry and papery as the wings of a dead moth.

He scowls at me. He hates being here as much as I hate visiting. The irony that this place is where he has ended up isn't lost on either of us. After what he did to Davey, it's almost a bad joke.

'So what have you been up to?' he asks.

'Not much.'

I'm toying with him. I know what he wants but can't resist the perverse pleasure of not giving it to him.

He raises an eyebrow, white whiskers sprouting at wild angles like a catfish.

I open my palms as if there is nothing to tell. Why do I do this? Torturing a shell of a man is pathetic.

'I heard there's going to be a reshuffle,' he says.

He looks so eager, like a child waiting for a slice of birthday cake, hoping to get a bit with a sweet on it. The great Paddy Connolly, darling of the party, champion of the hardworking family, enemy of the unions, brought to this. Sniffing out scraps of gossip like a puppy.

I relent. 'Davison is out.'

Dad nods. 'About time. The man couldn't get a hard-on in a brothel.'

'They say McDonald will get the job.'

'A move from Education to the Foreign Office.' Dad whistles. 'That Scottish bastard always was ambitious.'

I tell him the rest. Who's in. Who's out. Who has the PM's ear. When the old man is satisfied that's he's exhausted the detail, he leans back against his pillow. He closes his eyes, so I drop my own little ingot into the conversation.

'I've been offered something.'

His eyes open, instantly alert.

I hold my hand up to calm him. 'It's not much. Just a junior appointment.'

'Everyone has to start somewhere. Even me,' says the man who became the youngest ever cabinet minister.

I laugh, and for the first time in as long as I can remember he laughs too.

'So where is it?' he asks. 'Health?'

I shake my head.

'Defence?' he says.

'Don't be daft.'

7

'Education?' He gives a throaty chuckle. 'Spent some of the best years of my life in Education under Keith Joseph.'

'It's Culture, Media and Sport,' I say.

Dad stops laughing.

'I guess with my background it seemed an appropriate choice,' I say.

'Your background,' he repeats.

I count to ten in my head. According to Dad, my background is one of politics and power, hailing, as I do, from stock so steeped in the business of government that one of my godparents was the chief whip of the party, the other, Chancellor of the Exchequer.

'I meant my running, Dad,' I say.

He blinks at me.

I try to keep the irritation from my voice. 'I wasn't bad at it, remember? In the 1996 Olympic squad.'

'Yes,' says Dad, but he's no longer interested.

'Actually, I'm pretty excited with the Games coming up. I think I can really bring something to the table.'

Dad doesn't answer. He closes his eyes.

'Try to eat more,' I say and make for the door.

I slam the Mini Cooper into third, stamp on the accelerator and barrel down Shooters Hill Road, glad to put Blackheath and Dad behind me.

I can't believe the old sod still has the ability to make me so angry. I'm a ten-year-old girl again, waving my medals under his nose, only to be asked why I don't do something more con-structive with my time than 'a bit of bleedin' running'.

A black cab pulls out in front of me and I press the heel of my hand against the horn. When I spot a tiny gap in the oncoming traffic I hit the gas and overtake, ignoring the cabbie's proffered middle finger.

'Your dad's a hard man to please,' my mum used to tell me, retrieving the medals from under my pillow.

'I just want to make him proud,' I said.

She wiped the tarnished brass against the leg of her trousers and gave me one of her slow, sad smiles. 'You will, love, you will.'

I thump the side window with the edge of my fist. I refuse to end up like Mum, still trying to do the right thing until the day she died, still dancing to the old bastard's tune.

She never learned that it didn't matter whether she did the waltz, the twist or the bloody cha-cha-cha: Dad is never satisfied.

Well, not me. Not any more. I'm hanging up my jazz shoes.

When the leg gave way and all the doctors could do was shake their heads, I didn't look for sympathy. My running career was over but I got on with my life, didn't I?

The old man didn't disguise the fact that he was relieved I'd stop pissing my life away on the track.

'Mind you,' he told me, 'you'll never make an MP. Too pretty, too indecisive.'

So I joined the civil service.

'That's who really run the show.' Dad winked at me.

And he's probably right, but I've hated every stinking minute of it. The hours, the egos, the backstabbing. Tepid glasses of wine while my smile breaks my jaw.

This job in Culture, Media and Sport is the first thing that has made my blood pump in a very long time. The chance to be involved in the 33rd Olympic Games – here, in London. My town. The chance to reach out and touch, if only fleetingly, something I love.

I force myself to inhale deeply, to exhale through my nose. I will not allow that man to spoil this. The world is bubbling with excitement and I'm going to be at the very heart of it.

'I am calm,' I sing out. 'I am relaxed.'

Shit.

I miss my turn-off for Greenwich and end up in the sludge of Deptford's one-way system.

Miggs was the last to arrive.

Steve and Deano were already in the kitchen, rooting in Ronnie's fridge. Deano pulled out a carton of milk and sniffed it. 'Fucking hell, this is minging.'

He catapulted it into the sink, which was already piled high with greasy dishes and empty takeaway cartons. It landed with a thud, spraying thick white lumps of cottage cheese over the fag ends and cold chips that littered the draining board.

Miggs swallowed down a pang of nausea. He'd stayed in some shitholes in his time but Ronnie's spot was like a Glasgow crack house.

'Got any bevvies?' he asked.

Ronnie didn't even look up. 'Cupboard next to the cooker.'

Miggs helped himself to a warm can of Stella and handed out the rest. He wondered why Ronnie didn't keep them in the fridge, but given the state of it, it was probably for the best.

He took a swig and settled on the sofa where he knew Ronnie slept. A stained sleeping bag lay in a heap in the corner of the room, but the cushions retained the smell of their leader's sweat.

The TV was already on, though the sound was off. Some twenty-four-hour news channel.

Deano took his place next to Miggs. 'You want to get yourself a flat screen telly, Ron,' he said. 'Much better picture than this heap of shit.'

Miggs caught sight of Deano's beefy fingers. Between each tattoo, the knuckles were raw and bloody. How many times had Ronnie warned him not to get into any fights, not to draw attention to himself? 'My brother could get you one for less than five hundred quid. Thirty-six-inch, surround sound,' he said.

Ronnie shrugged. 'I'm not really bothered about all that.'

Deano turned to Steve, who was perched on the arm of the sofa. 'Got you one, didn't he, mate?'

'Put my order in.' Steve flashed the gaps in his teeth. 'Next day delivery.'

'See?' said Deano. 'As good as fucking Currys.'

Sometimes Miggs couldn't believe what a stupid cunt Deano could be. Selling knock-off tellies was a sure-fire way to bring the five-oh crashing down on his head. He flicked a glance at Ronnie, looking for the telltale throb at the temples that would signal the shit was about to hit the fan.

Ronnie and Miggs had known each other since they'd been in care. Miggs was originally from the schemes in Possilpark and had been acquainted with a few hard bastards in his time, but nothing prepared him for the brutality of the kickings wee Ronnie would dole out on an almost weekly basis. Miggs had been on the wrong end of a few batterings himself. Umpteen anger management courses and a spell in the madhouse had made no impact. Violence was simply a part of Ronnie's life.

Luckily for Deano, Ronnie's attention was diverted by the screen. 'Turn up the sound.'

Steve leaned forward and punched the remote control. Some bird was standing outside the Olympic Village in Stratford. The breeze ruffled her jacket to reveal the hint of a black bra.

Deano whistled at the screen. Steve joined in. Ronnie put up a hand and silenced them both.

The presenter was smiling into the camera. She had those straight teeth you always saw on the telly but never in real life.

'An excited crowd is gathered here today to watch the official opening of the Olympic Village, which will be home to more than fifteen thousand athletes from two hundred countries around the globe.'

The camera panned around the village, revealing the rows of spanking new accommodation blocks built around communal squares. A water feature was tinkling pleasantly in the middle. A lifetime away from Miggs's childhood.

In the distance the five rings of the Olympic flag fluttered.

Miggs risked another sideways glance, but Ronnie's eyes didn't leave the screen.

I roar into the car park outside the Village and race over to where the minister is finishing an interview.

Sam Clancy is a consummate performer. When he's done, he sees me and the smile slides off his face. 'You're late.'

'I had to visit my dad,' I say.

Sam's face softens. Even now, Paddy Connolly's name is royalty. 'Where are we at?' he asks.

I pull out my BlackBerry and check my list of things to do. 'The rooms are completely ready,' I tell him.

'You've checked the paperwork? We don't want a re-run of the Delhi fiasco.'

'It's all in order,' I assure him. 'Building regs, health and safety, you name it. There isn't a loose screw in the whole place.'

Sam nods in satisfaction. 'And the Yanks?'

'All booked on flights and ready for a quick photo op at Heathrow.'

'The ambassador?'

I pull a face. The American ambassador is never happy. With anything.

'Still banging on about security, I suppose?' says Sam.

'I danced him through every last detail, even the MI5 assessments,' I say. 'Short of holding the Games in secret, we can't make it any tighter.'

12

Sam cracks a smile. 'You know what they say, Jo – you can't please all of the people all of the time.'

As we're led towards the crowded Plaza, groups of children are pressing their way inside, laughing and pushing one another.

'Looks like we can please some of the people,' I say.

Sam gives my shoulder a couple of taps. 'And that's what it's all about, Jo.'

We make our way inside and I can't keep the smile from my face. The Plaza is fantastic. During the Games this is where the athletes will meet their friends and family, but today we are set up for a conference. Every seat is taken, press and cameramen standing at the sides. I'm glad I wore my new shoes – smart ballerina pumps, the colour of fresh raspberries.

The front row has been allocated to a special school whose pupils have travelled by coach from Bromsgrove so that Sam can make the point that the Paralympics are every bit as important to London as the real deal. A teenage boy with Down's syndrome is giggling loudly, his round features lit up in excitement. The girl to his right sits low in her wheelchair, clapping.

Their teacher puts a finger to her lips to quiet them but they can hardly contain themselves. It's infectious and I laugh too.

See, this is what Dad doesn't get. That politics doesn't have to be all about arguments and meetings that go on into the early hours.

The Olympic Games are about hope and optimism. They send out the message that we should all strive to be the best we can be. Who wouldn't want to be involved in that?

Sam takes to the podium. 'Ladies and Gentlemen, boys and girls, I'd like to welcome you to the 33rd Olympic Games.'

The crowd bursts into spontaneous applause. Even the press corps joins in.

'I'm sure many of you remember the rapturous news that the

UK had been successful in its bid to host the 2012 games. I certainly had a few glasses of bubbly that night.'

A ripple of polite laughter snakes around the room.

'But after the streamers were cleared away, the reality of the task ahead began to set in.' Sam lifts a finger. 'Make no mistake that it has taken years of hard graft and commitment to ensure that everything is ready and in place. It hasn't been easy. The country has been facing difficult times. We've all had our backs against the walls and, to be honest, there have been times when I've questioned whether we could pull it off.'

He pauses and lets his gaze sweep across the audience.

'But ultimately we succeeded because the people of this great country always succeed. We were determined to host a summer of unrivalled sporting achievement which will propel this country into a new era.'

The crowd erupts into cheers and someone throws their cap to the ceiling. The boy with Down's leaps to his feet and punches the air. He takes two steps towards Sam but security block his path.

'It's fine,' says Sam. 'We all want to celebrate, don't we?' He beckons the boy towards him and every camera in the place begins frantically clicking.

Still grinning, the boy looks behind him to the back of the room. Perhaps his mum is there. 'I'm here,' he calls.

I imagine her bursting with pride, snapping away. My mum would have done exactly the same. I hope she's getting a good view.

Then boom.

A flash of light.

An ear-splitting crack.

Black.

Chapter Two

I try to open my eyes but they feel heavy, as if something is weighing them down. I lift my hand to my cheek but I can't feel that either. Am I dead?

I remember a sea of faces. Clapping. Laughing. A boy with a huge smile. Then nothing.

I try to move but I don't know if I'm sitting or standing. I can't feel anything around me. It's as if I'm suspended. As if all around me is air. Hot air. I break into a sweat.

Christ on a bike, am I in Hell?

I know I've been a bit of a twat to my dad, and then there was the time I told that bloke I thought I might be a lesbian so he'd dump me. But are these the sort of sins that warrant an eternal roasting?

I need to open my eyes. I have to see where I am. I let my arms and legs loosen and direct every scintilla of energy towards my face. I control my breathing and concentrate. At last I manage to lift one of my eyelids. Only a tiny slit. But it's enough.

I see black smoke swirling above me and orange flames snaking towards me like tongues flicking back and forth.

I open the other eye and try to take it all in. Sheets of metal are hanging and swinging like branches in the breeze. Rubble and dust shower down. There are chairs scattered everywhere, mangled and broken.

I try to lift my head, ignoring the pain, and I see it. Through the billowing clouds of smog I can just make it out. A flag. Five rings.

Not Hell, then.

And it all comes flooding back to me. I know that sounds like a cliché but that's exactly what it feels like. The sights, the sounds, the smells all pour back into my mind, in a raging torrent. Everything mixed up and violent.

Sam was holding out his hand to the boy, urging him to come up to the podium.

The boy, initially so eager, became uncertain. Sam stepped forward.

Then an explosion that seemed to come from miles away and rush at me with the force of a train. It picked me up and slammed me against the wall. It sucked the air from my lungs, squeezing the life from me.

But I'm not dead.

'What's happening?' I call out.

No one answers. I look around me but there's no one. Where is everybody? 'Is anyone there?' I shout.

Only the sound of roaring, like a wild animal, comes back to me.

'Is anyone there?' I shout out again.

I realise I am lying at the back of the conference room in the Plaza, which means there is a hundred feet of twisted debris between me and the exit. And the entire place is on fire. I have to get out of here now.

I put out my hands and push up. My head spins, making the room tilt. The taste of acid bile burns my throat. I force my chin to keep steady and focus on the horizon, the flag above the door. I can crawl to it. I can make it.

I take a deep breath and the smell of carbon attacks my nose. I cough and spit to clear my mouth. The heat from the flames bears down on me, burning my cheeks.

I can do this. I have to.

I push myself onto all fours and propel myself forward. My hands scrabble through pieces of concrete and shards of glass. My knees follow, pain ripping through me. All I have to do is keep going. One hand in front of the other, then my knees. Every movement taking me closer to escape.

I make it past the ruined stage, the podium completely gone. Out of the corner of my eye I see something white, abandoned on the ground. It's a trainer, the Nike tick still visible. My stomach lurches. I turn my head away and focus on the flag. In less than a minute I will be out of here.

Above me there is a terrible groan. Without thinking I look up. There's a hole in the roof like a gaping mouth, the rafters still attached by no more than a thread. Another terrible heave and a sheet of metal over twenty feet long crashes free. It hurtles towards me and I close my eyes. When it smashes on the ground inches from me I scream. I throw myself forward, desperate to cross the distance to the exit.

I glance up again. What is left of the roof shudders. It's going to collapse and if I don't get out of here in seconds it will crush me. I must run.

Whatever's wrong with me, whatever injuries I have, I must drag myself to my feet and run for cover. If I'm good at anything in life, it's running. A skill that might just save me.

I take all the weight on my hands and push up onto the balls of my feet. I force myself into a standing position and bare my teeth against the pain. I'm already panting as if I've finished a race.

I find my centre of balance and I am ready to go when I hear something else. It could be the rush of the flames or glass smashing in the inferno. It could be the very foundations of the building giving way. Whatever it is I must ignore it and run.

It comes again. I turn to the sound.

'Help.'

It's the girl in the wheelchair. The blast has sent it hurtling across the room and turned it over. She's trapped underneath. Her face is completely black from the smoke. Only her eyes are wide and pale.

I don't know what to do. Surely it would be better for me to keep going and fetch help?

She opens her mouth, which seems impossibly swollen. 'Please. Help me.'

My heart is pounding in my chest, the blood banging in my ears. The roof above rumbles and a concrete slab crashes to the floor, missing me by less than a foot. Clouds of dust choke the air. If I don't get out of here, we'll both die. That's certain.

I focus on the flag. 'I'm sorry,' I say.

'Don't leave me,' she screams.

'I'm going for help,' I tell her.

'Don't leave me!'

Torn in two, I run for the door. Each step is agony but I make it. When I am close enough to touch it, the roof rumbles and begins to shake. This must be what it's like in an earthquake. Everything above you tumbling down. Those people you see on the telly who get trapped for days. The air running out.

I glance back at the girl. Don't, I warn myself.

Too late. I'm sprinting back towards her. With the sky falling in around me, I hurdle over upturned chairs and slabs of concrete.

'I'm coming,' I shout above the din, hoping she can hear me.

When I'm at her side she's crying uncontrollably, her body wracked with sobs. 'I thought you'd left me,' she gasps.

I throw the wheelchair to one side and pull her into my arms. 'I would never do that,' I say.

She throws her arms around my neck and burrows her face into my shoulder. She weighs almost nothing, yet I can hardly lift her. I stagger backwards, almost losing my balance.

There is one last almighty rip and the roof begins to cave. I have seconds to get us to safety.

I tip myself forward and run faster than I have ever run in my life. Faster than all those training sessions and all those races I won. With the girl in my arms I can't pump. With the pain in my head I can't think. It doesn't matter. I barrage through what I've decided after all *is* Hell and I let out a shout from the depths of my belly.

As I burst through the door, the room exploding behind me, I'm still shouting. I don't stop until I am outside and clear. Not until I feel cool drops of rain falling onto my face. Not until a policeman prises the little girl from me.

Then I stop. And I throw up on my shoes.

Deano and Steve were glued to the screen, leaning forward on the edge of the ratty sofa, mouths open, cans in hand, but Miggs kept sneaking a glance at Ronnie. No reaction at all.

The picture showed in full Technicolor every grim detail of the disaster. People were running out of the Plaza building screaming. Blood was running down one woman's face. Miggs wouldn't like to ken how many people were in there. The beer tasted stale on his tongue and he had to force it down. He flicked the ring-pull with his thumb, making a soft metal twang. Ronnie appeared not to notice.

'Unbelievable.' Deano shook his head. 'Totally un-fucking-believable.'

Police cars and fire engines darted across the screen. A helicopter was circling, disappearing in and out of the columns of smoke.

'Turn it over,' said Ronnie.

Steve flicked the button. Every station was running the same story.

Deano jumped to his feet, knocking into Miggs.

'Watch it,' Miggs warned.

But Deano didn't care. He was doing some stupid fucking dance, hopping from one foot to the other. Soon Steve joined him and the two of them pranced around the sofa like the couple of twats they were.

Miggs risked another look in Ronnie's direction. There wasn't even the smallest hint of emotion.

'Tell me this isn't happening,' said the prime minister.

Christian Clement didn't look up from the television screen, watching as the last person managed to stagger out of the burning building. It was that young civil servant. The one who used to be a runner. Clem had met her briefly when he handed over the security assessments. Her face was screwed up in agony as she carried a young girl to safety.

Simon Benning snapped the remote and replayed the scene, finally freezing the scene on Jo Connolly's tortured face. 'This is a disaster,' he said. 'A complete and utter disaster.'

Christian Clement took a deep breath. As one of the most senior officers in MI5 he was used to difficult customers, but Benning, the PM's publicist, adviser and general fixer, was one of the trickiest, slipperiest bastards he'd ever met. Give Clem a Taliban sympathiser any day of the week.

Outside the PM's study a hundred phones seemed to be ringing and three mobiles on his desk vibrated like angry wasps.

'What do I say, Clem?' he asked. 'Was it an accident? Please tell me this was a freak accident.'

'We don't know,' Clem replied.

Benning filled a plastic cup with water. 'Not good enough.'

Clem gave him a hard stare. He despised men like Benning. An unelected suit who spent his time ensuring the red-tops were on message.

'I'm sorry about that.' Clem's tone made it clear he was anything but sorry.

There were lines etched across the PM's face. He'd been a handsome bugger when he'd first got elected. Full head of hair. Bright smile. The worst recession in twenty years, an endlessly bickering coalition government and all-out rioting in the streets had put paid to that.

'It's your job to know these things,' Benning told Clem.

'And I will know as soon as we can get access to the scene,' he replied.

The PM glanced at the TV screen. 'What could cause an explosion that big? A gas leak?'

'Possibly,' said Clem.

'Possibly?' Benning shook his head. 'We can't deal in possiblys.'

Clem was about to explain that certainties were as rare as rocking-horse shit when it came to MI5 when there was a rap at the door, and a woman with an earpiece attached to the side of her head leaned into the room.

'The American ambassador has been on hold for fifteen minutes, Prime Minister,' she announced. 'He says if you don't speak to him in the next ten seconds he's going to jump in a taxi over here.'

The PM shut his eyes. 'What do I do?'

'Tell him the truth,' said Clem. 'Tell him we don't know what happened.'

'You've got to be kidding me,' Benning shouted. 'This is the Olympic Games. The single biggest event in the UK since the royal wedding – and I don't mean Wills and his fucking Waity Katie. Everyone from Barack Obama to the Dalai Lama is due to arrive at any moment and you want the prime minister to say he doesn't know what caused that?' He pointed at the screen. 'Are you completely out of your mind?'

'Are you suggesting he lie?' Clem asked.

'He wouldn't have to, if you were doing your job properly.'

Clem squared his shoulders. For the smallest excuse he would enjoy punching Benning's lights out and screw the pension.

The PM got to his feet. 'This isn't helping.'

Benning opened his mouth to speak again but the PM silenced him with an open palm.

'I'll stall them.' He turned to Clem. 'But you must have a definitive answer for me within the hour. Time is not on our side.'

'My people are on standby at the scene as we speak. As soon as it's safe to go in, we'll get the full picture,' said Clem, then stepped outside the study for the PM to placate a hundred hysterical dignitaries. Not a job he'd have liked to do in a hurry.

The woman with the earpiece strode past him, clipboard in one hand, a burger in the other. The smell made Clem's stomach rumble, but the scales that morning had told him what the doctors had been saying for years – it was time to lose some weight.

When Clem went back into the study, the PM was as pink as a slice of supermarket ham. Clem almost felt sorry for him.

'How's the minister?' he said.

'Not in a good way,' replied the PM.

'Who will take over?' asked Clem. He prayed it wasn't that Scottish bastard McDonald. The man was so conniving he made Lady Macbeth look shy.

'It's got to be someone who can come across well in the press,' said Benning. 'This situation is going to be headline news around the world.'

Clem looked at Jo Connolly's face still filling the screen. 'Hasn't she been running the show behind closed doors?'

'Joanna Connolly couldn't run a bath,' scoffed Benning.

Clem furrowed his brow. 'She was Sam's second in command, wasn't she?'

Benning sighed as if he were having to explain something very simple for the seventh time. 'There is no second in command.

There is no first in command. Downing Street run the show but we needed Sam to do some smiling into the cameras and Connolly was chosen to assist because the public still adore her dinosaur of a father. The daughter's a lightweight but we figured she couldn't do too much damage.'

Clem caught the use of the word 'we' and so did the PM.

'Actually,' the PM interjected, 'I appointed Jo because I thought her background in sport would bring some expertise to the table.'

Benning opened his mouth to speak but thought better of it.

Clem looked again at Jo's face. There was a strong determination there. Fear, yes, but not hysteria – considering she'd just narrowly escaped death. Clem would have paid to see Benning's reactions in the same set-up.

'I'd say that the twelve million viewers watching the news won't think she's a lightweight.'

Benning and the PM turned to the screen as if seeing it for the first time.

'Clem's right,' said the PM.

Benning scratched his chin. 'Connolly, the national heroine.'

I'm still shaking as security rush me into Number Ten. I'm not sure what the hell I'm doing here as we pass the Cabinet Room and I'm bundled into the PM's study. It's cramped and old-fashioned, a velvet sofa in need of re-covering pushed against the wall and the PM squeezed behind the heavy desk in a mahogany chair.

'Jo.' The prime minister gets up. 'Come in, come in.'

He holds out his hand. I go to do the same but I notice mine is black with soot, the knuckles ragged and bloodstained.

'Sorry,' I murmur.

He takes it anyway, covers it with the palm of his other hand. 'I can't tell you how glad we are that you're all right.' He looks me squarely in the eye as he says this.

Everyone agrees that this is what's magical about him. His ability to make you feel important. From the Pope to a hospital porter.

'Can I get you a drink?'

I look up and see Simon Benning hovering over a decanter of brandy. He's what Dad calls a fixer.

To be honest, I don't know if I want a drink or not. One minute I was standing beside an ambulance, the paramedic looking into my ears with a torch, and the next I was being bundled into a black Range Rover with tinted windows and whisked over here. It all feels unreal. As if there's a glass partition between me and the rest of the world. I can see everything well enough, but I'm physically detached.

Benning pours three large brandies. 'Frankly, I think we could all bloody do with one.'

He places a glass in front of me with a smile, but there's none of the PM's warmth in it.

'You're probably wondering why we dragged you over here,' says the PM.

I shrug as if it's nothing.

'Unfortunately, Sam is still unconscious,' he says. 'We have no idea when he'll wake up, and even then . . .' He lets his voice trail off.

So that's it. Sam is being replaced by another minister, who will bring with him his own number two. I'm being sacked. Story of my life. Never quite making it to the winner's podium.

I bring the glass to my lips and take a mouthful. The brandy burns my throat but I take another gulp. Nearly killed and out of a job in the space of an hour. Not bad, even by my standards. I pour the remaining spirit into my mouth, draining the glass. I'm not sure a doctor would approve, but frankly I just want to feel better.

'We'd like you to take over,' says the PM.

I cough and swallow at the same time, brandy shooting up my nose. I splutter into one hand and wipe tears from my eyes with the back of the other. 'Sorry,' I choke.

Benning holds out a pristine white handkerchief between thumb and forefinger. Gratefully I take it and hold it over my mouth until the coughing subsides. When at last I can speak, all I can manage is another apology.

The PM is still wearing a kind smile. 'So what do you say?'

I blow my nose and shake my head. 'It's very generous, but while I'm more than happy to assist I just don't think I'm ready for the responsibility of such a huge task.'

'I think you are,' says the PM.

'But after this?' I say.

'Especially after this.'

Benning crosses his arms and watches me over his beak-like nose. He resembles a bird of prey about to swoop. I realise I'm the doormouse.

'To be honest with you, Jo, the prime minister wanted to give you something bigger in the reshuffle.'

I raise my eyebrows. I was given no hint that I was even being considered for one of the senior posts.

'You might hate me for this, Jo,' Benning continues, 'but I scuppered that for you.' He runs a bony finger around the rim of his own still-full glass. 'The Olympics are the most important thing on the political agenda right now and I thought we needed you on it. No doubt you'll think I held you back, but I won't apologise. You were the right woman for the job and you still are.'

I'm gobsmacked. The PM and Benning both look at me intently and I realise they expect me to say something. I can't. I open and close my mouth like a fish, but nothing comes out.

'The country needs these Olympics to be successful,' says Benning. 'The country needs you.'

My mind somersaults. Is it possible that after all the years of not quite cutting it, Jo Connolly is, at last, of importance?

The PM envelops me with a smile. Everyone matters. Even me. 'Will you take the job?' he asks.

'I'm not a minister,' I say. 'I'm not even an MP. I work in the background.'

'I think you've proved yourself to be much more capable than that,' says the PM.

I can't do it. I'm not cut out for it. Too pretty. Too indecisive. 'Couldn't you appoint a new minister?' I stutter. 'I'd be only too happy to get them up to speed.'

'I don't think that's feasible, Jo,' says the PM. 'I think it would be far better if you headed it up.'

I gulp. Could I really pull it off like he says?

'Come on, Jo,' says the PM. 'Do it as a favour to me.'

'Okay,' I say.

No sooner is the word out of my mouth than Benning stands, whipping a mobile from his inside pocket. 'I'll call Kylie.'

I gulp. Sacha Minogue owns Media Nation. Papers, TV and radio. The man who decides what half the world sees, hears and reads with its cornflakes.

Benning stabs one button. He has Kylie on his speed dial. Of course he does.

'We're on,' he says and hangs up.

The PM gets up, straightens his tie and heads for the door. When I assume he has nothing more to say to me, he turns. The sparkle has left him and in its place I sense a heavy heart.

'Thank you, Jo.' His voice is quiet. 'Thank you very much.'

The door closes behind him and Benning snaps on the TV. I notice the channel is one that belongs to Media Nation.

A posse of reporters has gathered in the street outside Number Ten. When the PM appears they wave tape recorders, cameras and booms at him. His special smile is back in place and the press pack all call out at once.

'Prime Minister, is it true that Muslim extremists are behind this attack?'

'Prime Minister, was the Secretary for Culture, Olympics, Media and Sport killed by the blast?'

The PM puts up his hands in mock surrender. 'The answer to those questions is no and no. My great friend Sam Clancy was very badly injured but I have absolute faith in the medical staff who, as with every patient, are doing all they can.'

Another barrage of questions is volleyed at him but he simply bats them away. God, he reminds me of Dad in his younger days.

'As for the first question, let me be very clear here.' He pauses and straightens up to his full height. 'There is no evidence whatsoever that this tragedy was anything more than a terrible accident. The security services are at the scene, identifying exactly what happened and as soon as they tell me, I will make an announcement.'

I turn to Benning in shock. 'An accident?'

He doesn't take his eyes from the screen, but nods distractedly.

'I'd assumed it was a bomb,' I say. 'A terrorist attack.'

Benning raises an eyebrow. 'Never assume, Jo. We spoke to MI5 before you came over and they were absolutely clear that there is nothing at this moment to support that theory.'

Benning's right – I did put two and two together and make eight.

'A gas leak, perhaps?' I ask.

'That was mentioned during our discussions with MI5,' says Benning. He directs me back to the screen with his finger.

'Will the Olympics be called off?' cries one of the hacks.

The PM shakes his head. 'This country has seen bigger setbacks than this.'

'Who's taking over from Sam?' another reporter calls out.

27

The PM lets a tiny smile seep out. 'I'm pleased to announce that Jo Connolly has agreed to take over the post.'

The buzz through the press pack is incredible. I'm taken aback at their excitement.

'Is she coming out?' they shout.

The PM pushes his palms forward as if he were physically keeping them at bay.

'Give the lady a break,' he says. 'You all know what she's been through today.'

Shouts of disappointment rage through the crowd and the camera focuses away from the PM to the door of Number Ten.

'Come out, Jo,' one journalist shouts. The others laugh, but soon join the fray.

I watch open-mouthed as they chant my name. I turn my head and realise Benning is no longer watching the screen but me instead. I realise too that my mouth is still gaping.

'Well?' he says.

'Well what?'

He stifles a small sigh. 'Do you think you could go out there and give them a few words?'

I laugh, assuming it's a joke, but in the space of five minutes this is the second time I grasp that assumptions are a bad thing in politics.

'Don't answer any questions.' He puts his hand in the small of my back and urges me towards the door. 'Just say how sad you are for Sam, but what an honour it is to take over.'

I almost trip in the corridor as my feet fail to keep up with events.

'You should definitely mention the kid you saved,' he adds and I cringe at the memory of how I almost left her behind.

'What should I say?' I ask.

'That you couldn't stand by and let the girl die,' he says. 'Don't forget to point out that she's handicapped.'

'Disabled,' I murmur.

'What?'

'Society handicaps her,' I say. 'The child is disabled.'

He glares at me. 'Whatever.'

As we approach the door I catch my reflection in a mirror. My face is streaked with dirt, my shirt is torn and bloodied. 'Shouldn't I get cleaned up?'

Benning shakes his head. 'You're going to have to learn very fast, Jo.'

When I step outside a roar goes up and I'm blinded by hundreds of flashes. My heart leaps and I'm tempted to run back inside. The PM welcomes me to him with open arms and I squint and make my way over.

He puts a protective arm around my shoulders and wags a finger at the assembly.

'This isn't the *Today* programme,' he says. 'Jo will give a few words and then she needs to get some rest.'

After more snapping cameras, everyone falls silent. I realise they're expecting me to speak.

'I don't think I could ever have imagined a worse way to be offered this job,' I begin. 'Sam Clancy is a great friend and colleague. He had a real vision for these Games and I only hope that I can do that vision justice. No doubt when he recovers from this accident he'll be straight back to work.'

'So you agree it was an accident?' asks one of the journalists.

I nod. 'Secret services have confirmed it.'

'What about Paddy?' shouts another. 'Will he be pleased that you've turned out to be a chip off the old block?'

I smile politely, wondering indeed what the old man will make of this turn of events.

* * *

Mama's lips move silently as she reads the book of Revelations, her finger tracing the words so she won't miss out a single one. For almost two hours she's sat at the kitchen table, a candle flickering next to her. The house is so hot and still, the girls have fallen asleep, Rebecca sucking her thumb like a baby, though she ain't the youngest.

Isaac wishes he had gone off with his daddy and his brother. They set out at daybreak to get as far as the ridge while the air was still cool. Probably sitting by Old Maple Creek right now, trailing their toes in the cold water, the morning's catch tied to a rope by their feet and hung between two hickory trees.

Isaac's a good fisherman. Better than Noah, who is almost three years older. Bet he could have gotten a couple of catfish if only they'd let him go. Instead, he's been stuck inside all day cus he was sick last night.

He'd pulled on his boots anyway when the others were ready to leave.

'You are going nowhere, young man.' Mama had her hands on her hips.

'I'm fine,' he told her.

'You're running a fever as hot as the pit itself,' she said.

Isaac had appealed to his father. 'I feel all fixed, Daddy.'

'Listen to your Mama, Isaac,' he said with a smile.

Then they left, Noah poking out his tongue as he slung a rifle and rod over his shoulder. Isaac would have liked to rip it right out of his mouth.

When they got to the far side of the yard, Daddy turned back and raised a hand to Isaac, who was skulking in the doorway. 'Remember now, you're the man of the house while I'm gone.'

Chapter Three

I read somewhere that there are over two hundred bones in a human body and this morning I can feel every single one of them. Even the tiny ones in your feet that footballers routinely break before the World Cup. Yesterday I kept going on adrenaline and brandy. Today I ache from the top of my skull to my little toe.

In the shower I have to scrape off the grime and dried blood. I wince as I soap myself down. Tiny pieces of plaster and sand fall from my scalp like shrapnel and collect at my feet. When I'm finally clean I don't move, letting the stream of water wash over me and ease my stiffness.

My mobile rings but I leave it, my face upturned to the warmth of the soothing water. Moments later it rings again.

I groan and regret agreeing to start work immediately. I should have done what the nice paramedic suggested and taken at least a day or two off.

'*Carpe diem*,' the PM had said.

It had seemed a good idea at the time.

When it rings a third time I stumble from the cubicle. I reach for the phone and a searing pain runs across my shoulder blades.

'Aagh!' I shout into my phone.

'Miss Connolly?' It's a woman's voice.

'Yes.'

The woman sounds nervous. 'Are you okay?'

I press my phone between my jaw and my shoulder and lower myself onto the bed. 'I'm fine.'

'Right.' She doesn't sound sure.

I let myself flop back onto my duvet. 'I'm great, honestly. How can I help you?'

She lets out a breath, relieved. 'It's Highfields Hospital here.'

Dad. Shit. I sit bolt upright, pain surging through me again. 'Aaaghh.'

'Miss Connolly, perhaps I should call back later.'

'No!' I shout. 'Please just tell me what's happened.'

'Happened?'

I shake my head, trying to expel the terrible memories of Dad's last stroke. 'Is my father okay?'

There's a moment's silence and I'm terrified that the images of me running from an exploding building will have proved too much. That this time his heart has given out.

At last the woman pushes out another puff of air. 'He's not too bad, actually. Had a good night last night. He just wants a quick word.'

Relief floods over me. My dad is not dead.

'Jo?' Dad barks down the phone.

I can't suppress a smile. 'Hi, Dad.'

'So he put you in charge, did he?'

The miserable old sod hasn't even asked how I am.

'I'm a bit sore, to tell you the truth,' I say.

'What?'

'But thanks for asking.'

He gives a low growl, like a dog who has just been kicked. 'He's a canny bastard, the PM,' he says. 'And I suppose he's still got that bloodsucker Benning at his side.'

I make the torturous journey to my wardrobe and reach in for a clean blouse. 'He was pretty helpful, actually,' I say.

'Don't trust him.'

Dad doesn't trust anyone. Never has done. When I was a kid, we were never allowed to have friends over to play. 'Loose lips sink ships,' he used to say.

'Did you see me outside Downing Street?' I ask.

He gives a noise that means yes.

'How was I?' I ask.

I've watched it at least ten times myself. I thought I did bloody well. I just want to hear Dad say it.

'You're a good-looking girl with a posh voice and you'd just dragged a disabled child from certain death,' he says. 'Even you couldn't screw that up.'

I sigh and fiddle with my buttons, wishing I could just pull on a T-shirt.

'Thanks for the vote of confidence,' I say.

He lets out another growl. What did I expect? A bunch of roses and a kiss on the cheek? This is Paddy Connolly we're talking about. Never look back, never enjoy the moment. Keep moving forward, always forward.

It strikes me how much he must loathe Highfields, where each day resembles the last and the future promises nothing but more of the same. It must be like death by a thousand cuts.

'Any advice?' I ask.

Perhaps if I could involve him more in my career it might cheer him up. We've always had our difficulties, but perhaps we could put them behind us and help each other.

An image flits through my mind. I'm running a tricky problem past him and he is smiling, giving his sage opinion.

'Listen to me, Jo,' he says.

I do. I want to hear fatherly words of wisdom. I want that dialogue we've never had.

'You've dropped lucky getting this job and don't forget it,' he says. 'The PM's Olympic ball nearly fell flat yesterday but he's found himself a new juggler. So don't take your eye off it for a second.'

'You make it sound like life or death,' I say.

'It is, Jo, and if you haven't worked that out by now, you're a bigger fool than I took you for.'

Clem knocked on the door to the PM's study. This wasn't going to be pretty. As requested, he'd sent the findings from the wreck of the Plaza within the hour. Now the shit was about to hit the fan.

The door was opened by a scowling Benning. 'We're not happy with your report.'

Clem all but pushed past him and strode towards the PM's desk. He was leaning heavily on his elbows, his eyes rimmed red, his tie thrown onto the sofa.

'There's no room for error?' he asked Clem.

'There's always room for error, Prime Minister.'

'Well then.' Benning closed the door. 'We can still say this was an accident.'

'That wouldn't be the full truth.'

Benning waved a copy of Clem's report at him. 'We don't know the full truth because you haven't been able to get it for us.'

'It's still early days,' said Clem. 'The scene isn't stable. If we had another twenty-four hours I could be more certain.'

'We don't have that sort of time.' Benning tapped his watch. 'With every second that passes, the Americans are getting closer to pulling out and going home.'

Clem said nothing. Politics was their business, not his.

'The PM has to make another statement this morning and he cannot go on live TV saying this might have been a bomb but you'll have to bear with us,' said Benning. 'If you're still saying you can't be one hundred per cent certain, then we stick with the accident scenario.'

The PM looked up at Clem hopefully. Time to piss on his chips.

'Given the nature of the explosion, I'd say we were almost certainly looking at a bomb.'

'You didn't say that in the report,' said Benning.

'I'm saying it now.'

The PM sighed. 'Who?'

Clem opened his palms. 'I don't know.'

'Come on, Clem,' said Benning. 'You must have some idea.'

Clem felt the muscle under his eye begin to twitch and blinked to release it.

'What's the word out there?' Benning continued. 'The wires must have picked up some chatter.'

Wires? Chatter? The man had been watching too many episodes of *Spooks*.

'Obviously we gather as much intelligence as we can,' said Clem.

'And?' Benning asked.

Clem kept his tone even. 'No one seemed close enough.'

'Looks like someone was close enough, Clem,' said Benning.

Clem imagined the delicious sound of his knuckles landing on this prick of a man's nose. But he knew that his anger was misdirected. It was himself that he was furious with. How had they missed this? They'd been watching and listening for anything remotely threatening the Games. There had been nothing concrete.

The PM interrupted Clem's thoughts. 'Who is most likely?' he asked.

Clem mentally sifted through the organisations keeping him up at night. The ones who moved from talking about action to the next phase. 'Al Qaeda, obviously,' he said.

The PM and Benning groaned. What did they expect? They knew who the current threats were coming from whatever their press releases said.

'That isn't good,' said the PM. 'Not good at all.'

Clem understood that. An Islamist attack would send the Americans back in a nanosecond. Probably the Chinese, too. Might as well call the whole thing off and try not to think of the billions of pounds wasted. The great British public would react predictably and relationships with every Muslim country in the world would be crucified. It would spell the end of the road for this government and its leader.

'Where are the Irish when you need 'em?' muttered Benning.

'I don't suppose it could be a dissident republican group?' the PM asked.

'Not their MO,' Clem replied.

'You must be keeping tabs on someone besides the Islamists,' said Benning.

'Naturally.'

Benning narrowed his eyes. 'Give us a name.'

Clem almost laughed. Did he think he could stand there in his hand-stitched shoes and intimidate someone who had been tortured by the Serbs and the Palestinians and lived to tell the tale?

Once again the PM intervened. 'We just need to consider all the options, Clem.'

Clem paused. He was reluctant to even say the name. 'Shining Light,' he murmured at last.

It was clear that the PM and Benning had never heard of them.

'Anarchists,' he added.

'Anarchists?' Benning couldn't hide his incredulity. 'Didn't they disappear with the Sex Pistols?'

'Who do you think caused all the trouble at the march against university fees? Let me tell you, it wasn't a bunch of middle-class students who stormed the Houses of Parliament.'

'Tell us a bit more, Clem,' said the PM. 'Who are these people?'

'A small group of fanatics. Animal rights activists, disaffected communists, white supremacists.'

'Racists.' The PM rolled the word around his tongue.

Benning's eyes widened. 'Skinheads.'

'Not exactly,' said Clem. 'This is a small but clever group of people who loathe your government and everything you stand for, but I don't think there is any chance of their involvement here.'

'So why were they on your radar?' asked Benning.

'Precautionary,' Clem replied.

'Then you must have thought there was some risk, however small,' said Benning. 'You must have thought it was at least *possible* that they would take action.'

'Anything's possible,' said Clem.

Benning shrugged. 'Then pick them up.'

'There's no point.'

'By your own admission, it's perfectly possible that this group are responsible for the deaths of twenty civilians, children included.'

Clem turned to the PM and looked directly into his tired eyes. 'My instinct is that these are not the people we want.'

The PM took a deep breath. 'Pick them up, Clem.'

Clem ordered a coffee and toast. The smell of bacon frying wafted across the café and he was tempted to get a full English. Sausage, fried bread, mushrooms, the works. Doctors – what did they know anyway?

He was careful not to look over at the group of men in the corner and opened his paper like everyone else. The front page was devoted to the explosion – and Connolly, of course. Poor woman didn't know what a nest of vipers she was diving into.

Clem checked his watch. Any second now, the PM would be informing the world that it might not have been an accident.

By the time the news sank in, Clem and his team were to have Shining Light in custody.

A young woman with startlingly white skin was serving the food, although service might have been the wrong word. Rather, she dumped the plates and steaming mugs of tea in front of the customers with a grunt.

One of the men in the corner let out a shout. Clem looked over. At this point it would have been odd not to.

The waitress had sloshed tea over the laminated table. 'Get us some kitchen roll,' said the man.

She jerked her head towards the counter. 'Get it yourself.'

The man shook his head but he did as she suggested. Clem watched him. Caucasian male, six foot, average build, early twenties, scar on the left cheek. Clem pulled out his iPad and dragged up the file. Bingo. The man was Dean Mantel.

Clem glanced over again, mentally processing the man in the seat next to Mantel. He went back to the file on his iPad. Another match. Stephen Miggs.

With Deano and Miggs in the bag, Clem was willing to bet the other guy was Steve Bentley.

That only left Ronnie X.

The information on the leader of this cell of Shining Light was patchy at best. Unlike the other men, who had led an ordinary life with a trail of paperwork blowing in their wake, Ronnie seemed never to have officially existed. No medical or police records, no membership of any organisations, no driving licence. More importantly, no description. It was as if Ronnie X had invented himself. Still, it would only be a matter of time before the rest of the cell led Clem to him.

'Nice bit of kit.'

Clem looked up. The waitress hovered over him with his breakfast. Her eyes were an odd cross between blue and grey. Almost silver. The contrast against her pale skin was strangely attractive.

Mind you, at his age, two legs and a full set of teeth were attractive.

'Must have cost a bit.' She nodded at Clem's iPad.

Clem smiled and closed the file with his finger. 'Waste of money, really,' he said. 'I only use it for checking the footie scores.'

She let out a laugh and thumped the plate onto the table. Clem caught his toast before it slid onto the sticky plastic and waited for the men to make a move.

Deano and Steve were watching the telly. Some daytime shite that rolled out a string of losers to argue with their girlfriends. Deano was pointing at a poor jakey whose scrawny wee girlfriend was weeping into the sleeve of her tracksuit.

'What a cunt,' Deano laughed.

Miggs wasn't sure if he meant the man or the woman. 'Why don't you two do something useful?' he asked.

Deano curled his lip. Whenever Ronnie wasn't around, he and Steve just messed about. 'Chill out, Miggsy,' he said. 'Don't take everything so seriously.'

But that was the trouble with Deano. He didn't take anything seriously. Miggs was about to give them another lecture about commitment to the cause when his mobile rang.

'Saved by the bell.' Deano winked.

Miggs frowned at him and checked the caller ID. It was Ronnie.

'All right?' he asked.

'No.' Ronnie's tone was even but serious. 'We've got a problem.'

Miggs moved away from the other two. 'What sort of problem?'

'They're onto us,' said Ronnie.

Miggs's pulse lurched. 'Who?'

'Police, maybe MI5. On their way now.'

'Shit.'

Miggs tried to think but his heart was hammering in his chest. 'What about your computer?' he said. 'Your phone?'

'Both with me,' said Ronnie. 'I'll destroy them after this call.'

Miggs nodded and let out a long breath. Nothing to lead them back to Ronnie, that was good. Even if the rest of them got picked up, Ronnie was safe.

Over his shoulder he heard Deano's laughter like machine-gun rattle. It stopped Miggs in his tracks. 'You know Deano will talk.'

'Perhaps.'

There was no perhaps about it. They both knew that if the police pulled the fat fucker, he'd sing like Charlotte Church on Bacardi Breezers.

Miggs closed his eyes. 'I'll sort it.'

There was a pause.

'Are you sure?' Ronnie asked.

'Yes.'

There was another moment of silence, which made Miggs's eardrums throb. 'You can trust me,' he said.

'I know.' Ronnie's voice was low. 'I always could.'

Miggs ran his hands through his hair and blinked back tears. He didn't know what hurt the most, what he was about to do or the knowledge that he would never see Ronnie again.

'Stay strong,' Miggs whispered.

'I will.'

The phone went dead and Miggs knew that in minutes Ronnie's phone would be crushed or burnt and thrown into a skip. It would be as if they had never met.

Another volley of Deano's laughter ripped through the air and Miggs reached for his gun.

Clem leaned against the bus shelter and waited for backup.

After they'd finished their fry-ups, Clem had followed the men out of the café and down Roman Road. The market was in full swing, stalls piled high with fruit and vegetables. A woman covered head to toe in black, only her eyes peeping out from a slit in her burka, was haggling over the price of okra.

The men stopped at a narrow door between a travel agents, the windows covered in posters offering cut-price flights to Dhaka, and a kebab shop. They disappeared inside, leaving Clem to watch a processed piece of lamb perform its pole dance, grease running away like sweat.

The buzzer on the door told Clem it was the entrance to the flat above. That must smell lovely, he thought. He skirted round the back, checking there was no other way out and called it in.

Carole-Ann picked up. 'What have you got?' she asked.

'66A Roman Road,' he said. 'Bethnal Green.'

'Nice part of town.'

Clem laughed. Carole-Ann Bowers was an in-house operative who spent her days scanning the airwaves and coordinating the agents on the street. She was a gargantuan black woman who ruled the back office with a clicking tongue and a will of iron.

'How many?' she asked.

'Three,' Clem confirmed. 'But there could be another one inside.'

'Armed?'

'No way to tell,' said Clem.

'Then let's assume the worst,' said Carole-Ann. 'I can get C Group to you in less than fifteen.'

'Do we need the whole crew?'

Carole-Ann kissed her teeth. 'You want your head blown off, fine. But not on my shift.'

Clem sighed. There was absolutely no point in arguing. 'Tell them not to arrive like the fucking cavalry.'

Carole-Ann let out a hoot of laughter and hung up.

Clem checked his watch and waited. It was never like this in the movies. Brad Pitt and George Clooney didn't spend any time standing around like lemons. They'd be in there now, single-handedly taking the perps down. Then again, they weren't the wrong side of fifty with high cholesterol.

Clem sighed and checked his watch again. He wondered if he would still be able to see the doorway from the baker's on the opposite side of the road. The earlier slice of toast hadn't touched the sides. He was weighing up the option of a ham roll or a croissant when he heard a sound he recognised all too well. Gunshot. From inside the flat.

Clem checked the street but there was still no sign of C Group. He pulled out his phone.

'What's up, Mr Grumpy?' Carole-Ann laughed.

'Where's backup?'

'I told you, they're on their way. Five minutes tops.'

Clem looked up at the window. He thought he saw a figure but couldn't be sure.

'Something's not right in there,' he said. 'I heard a shot.'

'I'll put out a call to all available officers. In the meantime, Clem, keep your head down.'

He didn't answer.

'Under no circumstances are you to go in there without backup.' Her voice was ice. 'Do you hear me?'

'Loud and clear.'

When the second shot rang out, Clem slid his phone back into his pocket and took out his Sig.

He crossed the space to the door in two strides and gave it a push. Locked. He took a step back and shoulder barged it. It didn't give. Clem wasn't surprised. You didn't live on a place like Roman Road without decent security.

From upstairs he could hear shouts. He glanced behind him. Still no sign of C Group. Inside, the argument intensified.

Clem leaned backwards on his right heel and held the gun inches from the lock. He clipped the silencer in place and let off two rounds, the recoil barely lifting his wrist.

Behind him, someone screamed.

'Armed police,' he shouted. 'Stay back.'

He shot another bullet into the lock and the doorframe gave way. Then he heaved himself up the stairs, wishing he were two stone lighter and twenty years younger, until he was outside the flat door. He could still hear the voice from within. A male voice.

'What the fuck are you doing?' the man screamed.

It wasn't an argument. The guy sounded desperate.

Decision time. Let them know he was there or surprise attack. The inside door looked doable. Decision made.

He drew back his right foot and kicked hard at the centre point. The door flew off its hinges, splintering wood.

Inside the shouting stopped.

Clem ran in, his Sig held at arm's length. Swiftly, he clocked the scene. The flat was filthy and the smell of rotting food filled the air. Among the empty cans and wrappers lay a body. A gunshot wound to the head spilled blood and grey matter onto the carpet. The clothes told Clem it was Steve.

He moved to his right towards the tiny kitchen. The man Clem recognised as Deano was backed against one wall, his shoulders pressing into the greasy tiles. His mouth formed a perfect 'O' and he didn't take his eyes from the other man, Miggs, who had a Russian pistol trained on him. It looked like a relic from the days of the Iron Curtain, but it would still do the trick.

'Put it down,' said Clem.

Miggs didn't reply but kept his weapon pointed at Deano.

'If you so much as touch the trigger I will blow your head off,' Clem continued.

Miggs looked at Clem's gun as if weighing up the situation. Deano whimpered and the smell of urine hit Clem's nostrils.

'Please,' Deano pleaded with Miggs. 'You know you can trust me.'

Miggs didn't lower his gun.

'You know my lips are sealed.'

Miggs risked another glance at Clem's weapon and gave an almost imperceptible nod. Then he pulled the trigger.

Deano's head thumped backwards against the sticky wall as the bullet passed through his brain.

Without hesitation Clem fired.

Seconds later, C Group arrived to find Clem standing in a blood-drenched kitchen, a man slumped at either end, another body sprawled in the room next door.

Isaac presses his eye against the chink between the shutter and the window. Daddy can join wood better than anyone so it's mighty small. All the same, Isaac can see the figures out yonder in the scrub.

'Still there, Mama,' he says.

Mama continues to trace the words in the Bible with her finger. 'Blessed is he that readeth, and they that hear the words of this prophecy and hear the things which are written therein.'

Isaac turns to her. 'I should go out there.'

Mama blinks as if he hasn't spoken. 'The time is at hand,' she says.

Rebecca lets out a sob. Even though she's not the youngest and Mama has been predicting the End Times for as long as any of them can recollect.

'I'm just going to ask them what they're doing on our land,' he says.

'You should wait for Daddy,' Rebecca wails.

Veronica-Mae looks up from her rag doll and gives Isaac one of her stares. She may be the baby of the family but she has a way of getting things across. 'He put you in charge,' she says.

Isaac glances across at Mama who, with one finger still stuck to the page, gives him a nod.

TWENTY TWELVE

He's the man of the house and he makes his way to the door. When he slides the dead bolt across it makes the same sound it always does. Thunk. Then daylight streams into the farmhouse. Isaac blinks away the spots it makes on his eyeballs and reaches for a rifle.

Chapter Four

I smile into camera one, face powder making my cheeks stiff. The make-up girl assured me that I would look perfectly normal on the television.

'Just a healthy glow,' she explained, as she removed the tissue paper from my collar. She nodded at the monitor where Toby Scott was already perched on the infamous *Top of the Morning* sofa. 'He even tints his eyelashes,' she winked.

I don't usually go in for make-up. Maybe a dab of lippy for a date. As the crew fiddle with the lighting I banish the thought that we look like the cast of *Priscilla, Queen of the Desert*.

The producer counts us back in from the break: 'Ten, nine, eight, seven, six . . .'

When he gets to five he simply puts up fingers.

Scott opens his mouth wide and wiggles his jaw. I worry he might be about to swallow me.

When the producer's index finger is all that is left to signify one, Scott's face settles into a smile. 'Welcome back,' he says. 'Still with us this morning is the woman charged with seeing the smooth running of the Olympic Games, Jo Connolly.'

'Hi,' I say.

'So, Jo,' says Scott, 'take us back to the moment when you decided to risk your own life to save a disabled child.'

I cringe at the memory of my sheer inability to make a decision. 'I did what anyone would have done,' I say.

Scott pats my arm. 'Most people would have been too scared to do what you did, Jo.'

'I *was* scared,' I say. 'I was bloody terrified.'

Scott and the crew give a polite laugh. 'And what about now?' he asks. 'Can the Opening Ceremony really go ahead this afternoon?'

'Absolutely,' I say. 'This was a terrible accident. It could have happened anywhere. We owe it to those who died to ensure that something they cared about deeply takes place as planned.'

'You're still saying it was an accident, then?' he asks.

'Definitely.'

Scott holds a finger to his earpiece. 'But I'm being told the security services have now found what appears to be a detonator.'

'What?' My tone sounds too sharp.

Scott nods. 'A team managed to get inside the Plaza building late last night and have found what they say is evidence of an explosive device.'

I lick my lips and the taste of lipgloss sugarcoats my words. 'I'm sure this is just a misunderstanding.'

As soon as I've finished the interview I make my way back to Downing Street watching the PM give a live statement. When I arrive, the PM and Benning are waiting for me in the study.

I glare at Benning. 'You told me it was an accident.'

Benning shrugs as if the fact that I've made an absolute twat of myself on national television is of no concern.

'You said MI5 had confirmed it.'

Benning looks down his nose at me. 'Actually, Jo, I said there was no evidence one way or the other.'

I shake my head, furious. 'You gave me the impression it was a gas leak.'

'I made no observation one way or the other.' His tone is cold. 'I simply told you the facts as we knew them at that time.'

I can't believe this is happening. Less than half a day into my new job and I've been outsmarted by a dwarf presenter in tinted moisturiser. My shoulders sag.

The PM puts a warm hand over mine. 'Mistakes happen.'

I want to point out that it was hardly a mistake, that Benning deliberately misled me. But that would make me look like a schoolgirl excusing the loss of her homework. Sorry, sir, but the dog ate it.

'It was a difficult day,' says the PM. 'No one will blame you.'

'So it was definitely a bomb?' I ask.

The PM nods, squeezes my hand.

I sigh. 'What now?'

I can just imagine the fallout. No athletes will risk competing. How could they? I'll be forced to announce the first cancellation of an Olympic Games. My name will forever be linked with the worst failure since the sinking of the *Titanic*.

'Press conference,' says Benning.

I groan. My historic climb-down will naturally appear live, on satellite television.

'What shall I say?'

Benning arches an eyebrow. 'That you're sorry for the cock-up, but it's business as usual.'

I let out a bark of laughter. 'How on earth can it be business as usual? The world's greatest athletes are hardly going to come when they think their safety is compromised.'

The PM and Benning exchange a look.

'No one's safety is being compromised,' says Benning.

I don't know whether to laugh or cry. 'Yesterday I was nearly blown to kingdom come. Safe wasn't how I'd describe it.'

'The risk has been eliminated,' says Benning.

I stare at him, unable to speak.

The PM puts up a hand. 'I think what Simon means is that we have dealt with those responsible.'

I still can't utter a word. Less than an hour ago I was under the impression that I had fallen victim to a freak, yet entirely innocent, accident. Now I'm told that not only were terrorists involved, but that they've been caught.

'When did all this happen?'

'That's not for your ears,' says Benning.

I feel the heat of anger flush my cheeks. 'I think I deserve an explanation.'

Before Benning can answer, the PM leans forward and picks up his phone. 'Show Mr Clement in.'

Clem entered the study. 'Prime Minister.'

The PM smiled at the young civil servant sitting opposite. 'Jo, this is Christian Clement, MI5.'

Clem held out his hand and swamped Connolly's in it. 'We've met.'

The young woman nodded her recollection but looked confused and unhappy.

'Not surprisingly, Jo has asked for an explanation of the events of the last twenty-four hours,' said the PM. 'So I thought it would be better coming from the horse's mouth.'

Clem regarded Connolly. He felt sorry for any poor sucker caught in the middle of this mess, but the fact was she was part and parcel of this government and its machine. Those that live by the sword, et cetera.

'In your own time,' Benning sighed.

Clem ignored him and continued to appraise Connolly.

'Clem,' the PM's voice was searching. 'Please.'

Clem gave a small nod. 'We have been watching a group of extremists called Shining Light. In particular a cell active in London.'

'White supremacists, Jo,' Benning added. 'Very dangerous.'

'This morning I intercepted the cell and two of its four members are now dead.'

Connolly's eyes shot open in alarm. 'You killed them?'

Clem suppressed a smile. Why did the ruling elite remain convinced that their safety could be secured by diplomacy and negotiation? In their narrow little world, they cleaved to democracy and the rule of law like a drowning man clawing at a piece of wood from a shipwreck. Let them try a week in a Kazak jail and see if they still wanted to discuss freedom.

'One of the cell members killed two of his colleagues,' said Clem. 'I had no alternative but to shoot him before he turned the gun on me. He's not expected to live through the night.'

Connolly shook her head as if trying to clear it. 'Why did he kill his own people?' she asked.

Clem shrugged. There was always in-fighting in these groups, those lower down the ranks prepared to do whatever was necessary to gain power and position. Not too different from the world of politics. 'These sorts of people tend not to settle their arguments peacefully,' he said.

Connolly was visibly shaken. She reached for some water, but thought better of it as her hand trembled. Instead she coughed to clear her throat. 'You said three members. What about the fourth?'

Clem blinked. His team were still going through the flat in Bethnal Green, looking for evidence that would lead them to Ronnie X. A letter, an email, a telephone number, even a note for the bloody milkman. So far, nothing. Whoever this man was, he was bloody good. But there was always something if you searched hard and long enough.

'We're on it,' said Clem.

'Now you see, Jo,' the PM interrupted. 'This was a very small group of individuals who can no longer pose a threat to the Olympic Games.'

Benning appeared at the PM's shoulders and hovered there like an unfriendly spirit. 'Think of it as a triumph for the forces of good.'

Back home, I'm still too sore to go for a run, so I opt for the next best thing to soothe my tired mind, and heat a tin of tomato soup. Mum always used this as a failsafe method in times of sadness and adversity. Lost a race? No problem. Failed a maths test? Get a bowl of this down you.

It had been Davey's all-time favourite. So much so, I often wonder if he actively sought out grazed knees and broken hearts just to get his hands on the stuff.

I kick off my shoes, slurp down a spoon of sweet red succour and switch on the box.

The press conference is being repeated on every bloody channel. The sight of my gurning face next to the PM while he explains that crisis has been averted is enough to put anyone off their dinner. I push my soup aside.

No doubt the PM is still on the phone, recanting the story to the leaders of the free world. I'd offered to contact my opposite numbers in China and the States, but Benning had looked suitably horrified. 'Best leave these things to the professionals,' he said. I was too knackered to be offended.

The phone rings.

'Jo? It's Dad.'

'Bloody hell, twice in one day,' I mutter.

'What?'

'Nothing,' I say. 'I suppose you saw the press conference.'

'Bit soon if you ask me,' he says.

'Surely it's better than letting everyone think it was an Al Qaeda attack?' I reply.

He harumphs. 'Sometimes you have to let the hysteria run until you hand over your fall guy. Otherwise it looks a bit bleeding convenient. Still, I suppose there just wasn't the time for that.'

'It's nothing to do with timing and there's nothing convenient about this, Dad. These Shining Light people are the real deal.'

In the background I hear a scream and feet pounding along the corridor. 'What was that, Dad?'

He ignores the question. 'Sounds dodgy to me,' he says.

'Seriously, Dad, I spoke to MI5 myself. They'd been watching this cell.'

'If you say so, Jo.'

'Listen, Dad, everything's going to be fine. You'll see.'

'Holy shit.' Nathan Shaw scrambled for his weapon. 'Someone's coming out.'

George leaned over and pressed a sweaty palm over Nathan's hand. 'Cool your jets, son. It's only the youngest boy.'

Nathan felt his heart thud. They'd been stuck out here broiling like steaks on a barbecue for hours. Now something was finally happening, he felt panicked. 'He's heading over here,' he hissed.

'Well now, that's all right,' George replied, his hand still on Nathan's. 'Probably just wants a breath of fresh air.'

The boy crossed the yard, his work boots crunching in the dirt. He stopped about twenty feet from the place where Nathan and George were hiding and stared straight at them.

'Let me handle this,' said George. He pushed himself up from the ground with a grunt, hauled up his belt and brushed the grit from his trousers. Then he nodded at Nathan and took a step out of the scrub.

The boy didn't move. Or speak.

'Isaac, isn't it?' asked George.

52

The boy didn't answer.

'I know your daddy,' George continued. 'Good Christian man.'

There was a long silence punctuated occasionally by the sound of a coot.

'There's two of you,' the boy finally spoke.

'Indeed there is,' said George. 'Nathan, come on out here and meet young Isaac Pearson.'

Nathan took a deep breath and stepped into view. He could see now that Isaac couldn't be more than twelve or thirteen. He was tall, with a buzz cut, but still a child.

Nathan would have laughed at his unease if it weren't for the rifle Isaac carried across his chest, left hand cupping the barrel, right hand on the butt, a finger curled around the trigger.

'I guess you're wondering what the hell we're doing out here,' said George. He turned to Nathan and laughed. 'To be honest we've been asking ourselves the same damn thing.'

Isaac didn't smile. 'You ain't got no right to be on our land.'

'Don't mean no harm by it,' said George.

Nathan watched the boy intently. He didn't seem frightened or surprised.

'You the police.' It was a statement, not a question.

'Surely are,' said George.

Isaac nodded and moved slowly around them to peer into their hiding place. He caught sight of the discarded beer bottles and threw Nathan a look of disgust. 'You need to leave now,' he said.

Chapter Five

I can't sleep. Dad's words are chasing me into wakefulness. He's wrong. I know he's wrong. After all, I've heard it from MI5 themselves. So why can't I just leave it? I call the nursing home but it goes straight to answer-phone.

Cursing myself, I throw on some clothes and head across town.

Highfields is in darkness. No surprise – it is bloody midnight after all. Most of the residents can't stay awake through *EastEnders*.

I park the Mini and head across the lawns to the bedroom window I think is Dad's. Praying I've got the right one, I rap on the glass with my nail. A minute passes so I tap again, louder.

Inside I hear a groan and the shuffle of feet. The curtains open and Dad's nose presses against the glass.

'Who's there?' he asks.

'It's me,' I say.

'Jo?'

'Yeah.'

'What are you doing here?'

'For Christ's sake, just open up,' I tell him.

It takes him what seems like an age to unlock the window and slide it across. Then he stands there in a pair of stained pyjamas, staring at me.

I push myself up by my hands and swing my legs inside his room in one fluid movement.

'Who are you?' he asks. 'Bleedin' Catwoman?' He laughs at his own joke until I wave him away.

'What did you mean about a fall guy?' I ask.

'Huh?'

'You said you'd have let the hysteria run until you'd handed over your fall guy.'

Dad doesn't answer immediately. He lowers himself onto the bed and wets cracked lips with the tip of his tongue. 'How important are these Olympics?' he says at last. 'On a scale of one to ten?'

I think about the strikes, the unemployment figures, the marches and the riots. The country has been imploding. 'About an eleven.'

'And how disastrous would it be if the terrorists turned out to be Islamists?' Dad asks.

I don't respond. We both know the Americans would be on the first plane home. The whole show would fall apart and the reaction in the Middle East doesn't bear thinking about.

Dad nods. 'This is the last chance saloon for the government and you're still not suspicious when the spooks discover less than twenty-four hours after the event that a bunch of white suprema-cists did it?'

I sigh. It does seem suspicious. But Clem has given assurances. 'You're saying this is all a set-up?'

Dad opens his palms upwards.

I shake my head. Dad is a cynic. He thinks Ghandi had an ulterior motive. If he's right, it would mean MI5 and the PM had deliberately framed and killed innocent people. And that the real terrorists are still out there. That sort of stuff only happens in second-rate thrillers.

'I know how it looks,' I say. 'But this time, you've got it all wrong.'

Dad grunts and gets back into bed. He pulls the sheet up to his chin. With the moonlight pouring across his face, he is so still, he could easily be dead.

Miggs could feel the gear in his system. He didn't know how it got there but the sensation was undeniable. Like being a bairn wrapped in a great big blanket. Not that anyone ever wrapped Miggs in a blanket when he was a bairn, but he could imagine. He let out a moan of pleasure.

Miggs used to do a lot of gear in the old days, before Ronnie convinced him to jack it in.

'It's how they control you,' Ronnie told him. 'Drink, drugs, religion – all the same. Just ways to distract you from the real questions.'

It was spot on. Course it was. Ronnie was always right.

When you're using, you flip-flop between the ecstasy of the hit and the agony of the come-down. You spend your time on the rob, or selling yourself. Far too busy to care who's running your life.

'Stephen Miggs.'

A voice floated towards him from the periphery of his consciousness. He'd ignore it but for the fact that whoever had spoken had used his first name. No one had done that since his last social worker.

'I know you can hear me, so open your eyes.'

Curious, Miggs did as he was told. It was the man from Ronnie's flat, the one with the gun.

'You're awake then?' said the man.

'Aye.' Miggs's voice was barely a low scratch.

'Tell me about Shining Light,' said the man. 'Did you do the Olympic job?'

What job? Miggs hadn't had a job in years. Who'd employ someone like him? A record as long as the tattoos down his arm.

Not that Miggs had been looking very hard. Being a wage slave to some capitalist fat cat didn't appeal. Signing on, Ronnie said, could be a political act.

'The bomb in the Olympic Village,' the man said. 'Was Shining Light responsible?'

Now Miggs understood. This was why MI5 tracked them down. Why the gadge in front of him had come to the flat like fucking Robocop.

He saw no reason to lie. 'I don't know anything about a bomb.'

The man narrowed his eyes and nodded. 'Your cell had nothing to do with it?'

'Cell?'

'You, Deano, Steve.'

Miggs laughed. The idea that those useless twats constituted a 'cell' seemed ridiculous.

'What about Ronnie?' the man asked.

Miggs's smile slipped. Whatever they did to him, no matter how many drugs they pumped into him, he wouldn't give Ronnie up.

Again, he told the truth. 'I don't know where Ronnie is.'

The man tapped his front tooth with his thumbnail. It made a hollow sound. 'You don't deny that Ronnie was involved in the bombing?'

Miggs closed his eyes. Ronnie had never once mentioned a bomb. When they'd watched the explosion on the telly, Miggs had been shocked. He remembered again the presenter, the blood and the black smoke. Then he pictured Ronnie, impassive as usual, giving nothing away.

'I don't know where Ronnie is,' Miggs repeated.

I'm halfway across town when the fuel gauge lights up. The Mini needs petrol. I sigh. It's half past one in the morning and my head is toast. The old man's words have burrowed their way into my skull, nipping me with their sharp teeth.

I consider going back to Highfields, running this whole thing past him again. But what would be the point? He believes this whole thing is a set-up, and I believe . . . well, I'm no longer sure what I believe.

I pull into an all-night garage on the Old Kent Road and jump out. I grab the hose and try to fill her up but each time I squeeze the trigger there's a clunk from the nozzle, then nothing.

I make my way to the shop where an attendant is barricaded inside behind reinforced glass. His ears are punctured by a row of metal studs, as is his nose, lower lip and right eyebrow. A human pincushion.

'The pumps aren't working,' I say.

The guy shakes his head and points to a small microphone.

'The pumps.' I lean into it. 'They're not working.'

'You gotta pay beforehand, love,' he says.

'I don't know how much it will cost to fill the tank,' I reply.

'Gotta guess,' he says.

'What if I don't need as much as I pay you?'

'Come back here and I give you the change, all right?'

'It all seems a bit complicated,' I say.

'Not really.' The guy looks at me as if I'm stupid.

'And what if I don't stop?' I ask. 'What if I pay you ten quid but just keep pumping.'

The guy shakes his head. 'Cut you off, innit.'

Fine. I pass two twenty-pound notes through the metal drawer. 'Can I get a receipt?' I ask.

The guy nods and slides a small white ticket towards me. Carefully, I slot it into the back of my purse. Since the last expenses scandal all receipts are pored over like forensic evidence at a murder scene.

As I go to close my purse, I catch sight of something. It's Clem's card and it makes me stop in my tracks. Rather than Dad, surely this is the man I need to speak to.

I check my watch. It's late but I figure MI5 agents don't work nine to five.

By the time I've put the gas in the tank, I've made up my mind. I jump inside the car and punch the numbers into my mobile.

'Miss Connolly.' He answers on the first ring.

'Call me Jo,' I say. 'I hope this isn't an inconvenient time.'

'I'm at St Barts hospital.'

'Right. I just wondered if I could speak to you about some things I have on my mind.' I pause for emphasis. 'Some concerns.'

'Concerns,' Clem repeats.

'I just want to go through what happened at the Plaza again.'

There's silence on the line.

'Perhaps we could speak tomorrow?' I suggest.

'I'm not sure there's anything else to say, Miss Connolly.'

'It's Jo. Look, I don't want . . . I just need you to answer a few questions.'

More silence.

'Fine,' Clem says at last.

'What time?' I ask, but the line's already dead.

Clem rubbed his mobile against his mouth. Benning had assumed the Connolly girl would make the perfect sap. That she wasn't a patch on her father, just a smiley face to punt whatever story they gave her. Maybe that was the wrong call. Maybe she was a chip off the old block.

He glanced through the window of the private room where Miggs lay, attached to a machine, his head bandaged, hiding the bullet hole that had almost killed him. He was in a bad way. Might not last till morning. Clem needed a confession as soon as possible. Then everyone, Connolly included, could put this thing to bed.

He went to his briefcase, retrieved a small vial of sodium pentothal and headed to the door.

'Don't even think about it.'

Clem looked up, palm still on the door handle, and slipped the vial into his pocket with his free hand. A nurse was staring straight at him, shoulders back, chin cocked.

'MI5.' Clem dismissed her and began to open the door.

'I don't care if you're the bodyguard to the bloody Queen.' The nurse crossed the space between them and pulled the door closed. 'This patient is seriously ill. Doctor Crosby said absolutely no interviews.'

'A brief word,' said Clem.

'Not a chance.'

'You do realise how important this is?'

The nurse narrowed her eyes. 'The most important thing to me right now is keeping that man alive. Shocking as it might sound, this is a hospital. It's what we do.'

Clem gritted his teeth and set off to page Doctor Crosby.

I pull into the car park of St Barts and am stopped by a police officer. The hospital is on high alert due to the Plaza bomb.

'Can I ask your business, madam?'

I show him my department ID. 'I'm meeting security forces here.'

My demeanour brooks no argument and he waves me in. I'm not going to be shrugged off like a minor irritant, not by the police and certainly not by Clem.

The automatic doors open with a whoosh of air and I pass from the cold night into the sterile heat, a blue poster wrapped around

a concrete pillar welcoming me in eight languages. I shudder.
Have I mentioned before how much I hate hospitals?

Even at this time, there are people milling around and a group
of teenagers have gathered in front of the reception desk, pushing into one another, all speaking at the same time. Uniformed
officers patrol the perimeter, keeping a watchful eye.

I glance up at the directions board. Accident and Emergency,
Cardiothoracic, General Surgery, Trauma. The list is endless. It
dawns on me that this is an enormous place and I'm unlikely to
just bump into Clem. I pull out my mobile.

'Miss Connolly.' Again he answers on the first ring.

I don't bother to tell him to call me Jo. 'I'm here.'

'I'm not sure I follow you.'

'I'm at the hospital,' I say.

There's a pause and I steel myself to explain that yes, this is
urgent and yes, I do bloody well need to speak to him.

'Meet me in the café,' he says.

Pleased with myself, I make my way up in the lift, buy a bottle
of Evian and settle at a table facing the door. I take a swig of water
and smile. Dad always calls me a fool for spending money on
something that comes out of the tap for free. 'Too up yourself for
council pop?' All those barbed putdowns stockpiled for maximum
damage.

I take another sip and wait. There's no sign of Clem. No sign
of anyone, in fact. I sit and drink, the silence crashing around me.

Five minutes later, the Evian finished, I check my watch and
mobile. Clem has stood me up. But if he thinks he can shrug me
off, he can think again. I toss the empty bottle in a bin and head
out into the corridor. Another wave of signs hit me. Cardiology.
Haematology. Neurosurgery. Christ knows what most of it even
means.

I need to think this through. Clem is here with a man he shot
hours ago. A man not expected to live. Where would he be?

I recall the signs downstairs and snap my fingers. Trauma. It has to be. You don't get much more traumatic than getting a bullet between the eyes.

I take the lift again and arrive outside the Trauma ward. The reception area is deserted, a half-drunk cup of coffee abandoned, a white doctor's coat hanging limply over the back of a chair, like a sad ghost. At the far side is another set of doors, presumably leading to the patients' rooms. I walk over and try them, but they're locked. I peer through the pane of glass. Two uniformed policemen are standing guard outside the furthest room. No sign of Clem, but this has to be the right place.

I'm about to press the buzzer when a nurse exits the guarded room and hurries down the corridor towards me. As she passes through, I nod and hold the door, hoping to slip inside.

'Staff only,' she says.

I open my mouth to explain but something about the way she has her hands on her hips tells me to shut up.

'Are you with the police?' she asks. 'Or the security services?' She makes quotation marks in the air with her fingers.

'Erm,' is all I can manage.

'Like I told the last one, no one is getting to talk to your fella down there until Dr Crosby says so. You lot might not care if he drops dead, in fact it might suit you given how he ended up in here, but it's not going to happen on my shift.' Her eyes flash. 'Understand?'

'Completely,' I say. 'But I'm not with the police.'

She looks unimpressed. No doubt an explanation of who I actually am and why I'm here won't help the situation. I look around me hopelessly. If I don't come up with something, I'm going to get my marching orders without any answers from Clem. My eyes settle on the chair and the bedraggled doctor's coat.

'I'm Doctor Crosby's colleague,' I say.

The nurse's eyebrows shoot up.

'Given the severity of the patient's injuries he asked me to take a look at him.' As I say the words, I can hear the ridiculousness of it. But I'm desperate. What if the old man is right? What if Clem is feeding me a pack of lies? He's certainly giving me the runaround. What if, I can almost hear the scratchy voice in my ear saying, the man at the end of the corridor conveniently dies?

I take a few steps back, grab the coat and return to the double doors to scan the identity badge clipped to the lapel. Shazia Rashid's pretty brown face smiles up at me. I blot her photograph out with my thumb, thrust out my other hand and beam at the nurse.

She takes my hand and gives it a light shake. 'Can I take your name?' she asks warily.

I blink rapidly, remembering the film forming on the contents of the abandoned cup. 'Kenco,' I say. 'Doctor Kenco.'

'As in coffee?'

'Yup.'

An empty second stretches between us.

'Dark and rich.' I'm gabbling but I can't stop myself. 'And perfect in the morning.' I hear my false laugh and wince. There's no way she's going to fall for this.

She sighs and checks her watch. There are dark circles under her eyes. She's probably been on her feet the whole night and needs all this like a smack on the arse.

At last she moves aside. 'Go on then.' She motions down the corridor with her head. 'But for God's sake, put your coat on.'

I nod and struggle into it. Shazia Rashid must be a size zero because the sleeves finish at my forearms and the stitching groans at the seams. 'Put on a bit recently.' I pat my stomach.

She gives me another withering look, so I duck past her before I can commit any further acts of extreme stupidity.

As I approach the policemen standing guard, I realise I have absolutely no idea what I'm going to do next. All I do know is

63

that I am impersonating a doctor in order to obtain access to a terrorist. And that can't be good.

When I'm at the door they look at me expectantly.

'Doctor Kenco.' I flash Shazia Rashid's badge at them.

'Right,' says the one on the left, swallowing a yawn.

I wait a moment before I understand that there's nothing else they want from me. No complicated procedure for me to prove I am who I say I am.

I push open the door and put one foot inside the room when a voice comes from behind.

'You know who you remind me of?'

I turn. The policeman on the left is wagging a slow finger at me.

'That politician,' he says.

'Oh yeah.' The other copper looks up now. 'The one they put in charge of the Olympics.'

I'm about to point out that I'm not a politician, that in fact, I'm independent of politics, which I think is quite an important distinction, when I remember I'm trying to pass myself off as a doctor to gain access to a terrorist. I smile politely.

'Not a bad thing now she's saved that kid, eh?' the second one laughs. 'You'll get plenty of drinks bought for you down the pub.' He lets out a chuckle and I join in.

'Make the most of it,' adds the first. 'It'll all be forgotten by next month and everyone will be back to wondering who the fuck she is.'

I leave them laughing in the corridor and shut the door behind me. Inside, the room is darkened, only a lamp is on next to a bed where a man is lying, his head swathed in bandages. Wires snake between his chest and arms to a monitor, which lets out a melancholy, rhythmic beep.

There's no sign of Clem.

I take a deep breath. Is this one of the men who tried to blow me up? He looks so small. Pathetic even.

I take a step closer. His face is pale, sprinkled with reddish stubble breaking the surface of the skin. His arms lie lifeless by his sides, covered from knuckle to shoulder in tattoos. I peer at the intricate designs of hawks, guns and swastikas.

Suddenly his eyelids begin to flicker and I'm shocked to find myself looking into his eyes. He blinks three times, as if trying to focus.

'Is tha' you, Ronnie?' his words slur, solidifying around his accent.

I'm not sure what I should tell him, but before I can make a decision, he grabs my arm.

'I didn't think you'd come,' he says. 'Too dangerous.' His unseeing eyes fill with water. 'I told 'em I didn't know anything about no bombing,' he hisses. 'I told 'em I didn't know where you were.'

Still gripping my arm, he tries to lift himself towards me, but can only manage to raise his head an inch or so from the pillow.

'I won't give you up, Ronnie. I'd rather die.'

His chest begins to convulse and he is wracked by a coughing fit. Struggling to catch his breath, he lets himself flop back and releases my arm.

'Remember the orchard, Ronnie? You changed my life – no, you saved it. Now it's my turn to do the same.'

His chest heaves and his throat rattles, and a single tear runs down his cheekbone. Then the alarm on the monitor sounds and the doors crash open.

Chapter Six

Isaac is sweating like a mule as he shuts the door behind him. The girls look up at him, their eyes as wide and their skin as white as a full moon. Mama is still hunched over the book. 'It's the police,' he says.

'What do they want?' Rebecca hisses.

Isaac shrugs. 'Didn't say.'

Mama pushes back her chair and stands. She wipes her hands down her apron.

'They've come for us as we always knew they would.'

Isaac shakes his head. Mama has been expecting the Forces of Darkness for a long time. 'I don't think they mean no harm, Mama.'

A strand of hair has fallen from her plait and she pushes it back with a shaking finger. 'And it was given unto him to make war with the saints, and to overcome them.'

Isaac shakes his head again.

'Are you sayin' you know better than the prophesies, Isaac?' she asks.

'No ma'am, I ain't.'

They hold each other's eyes for a long while, Isaac wishing Daddy were here. He'd kiss Mama's head and tell her to hush. Then he'd go on outside and shoo those strangers off the land like a couple of noisy possums. Isaac glances up at the clock above the range. Daddy ain't likely to be back for more than an hour.

'I just don't reckon it's time is all.'

Mama pauses, her eyes flitting between her boy and the good book. Her voice drops to a whisper. 'And I stood up upon the sand of the sea, and saw a beast rise up.'

Isaac takes a step towards her. 'I know, Mama. I just don't think now's the time.'

Mama blinks, torn in two. Isaac takes another step towards her.

'So if they ain't come for us, what are they doing here?' asks Rebecca.

Isaac could kill her dead. He turns towards her and glares.

'What?' she says, tears tumbling down her cheeks.

Can't she see that he needs to calm Mama down? That he was doing it, too, before she stuck her stupid nose in? He's trying to convey this to her silently when a voice comes from outside.

'Mrs Pearson?'

Mama jumps at the sound of her name.

It's the policeman calling. The fat one.

'Mrs Pearson,' he shouts again. 'We'd like to talk to you for a moment.'

Rebecca runs across the room and throws her arms around Mama's waist. 'Don't do it, Mama. Don't go out there. He wants to make war with us, like you said, I know he does.' She buries her face in the folds of Mama's apron, sobbing.

'There ain't nothing to be afraid of, Mrs Pearson,' the policeman shouts.

Mama automatically straightens her spine and calls back, 'I ain't afraid of you or your master.'

'Mrs Pearson.'

It's the other one now, the one that smells of beer, the one Isaac didn't like.

'We need you to open your door now.' There's something in his voice that makes it clear he isn't asking. He's telling.

'I have to warn you that if you don't open up and come talk to us voluntarily we'll have no alternative but to come in.'

Mama nods as if the matter is at an end and takes Rebecca's shoulders in her hands, pushing her away to arm's length. 'Dry those tears, missy.'

Rebecca lets out a sniff and wipes her nose with her sleeve.

'We always knew this day would come, right?' Mama smiles. She looks at Veronica-Mae, then Isaac. 'Right?'

'Right,' Isaac mumbles.

Sure, he's a good Christian boy and reads his verses each evening after supper. He knows that the Devil is abroad and that one day the righteous will be called upon to fight. But he's always imagined a battle between two huge armies, like the civil war or something. Maybe when he's twenty-five, or even thirty, and his life is pretty much over, he won't rightly mind being drafted to take up arms against the Beast. But like this? In his own yard? With Daddy and Noah away from the farm?

'Come now, children.' Mama approaches them each in turn and kisses their foreheads. 'Today we are the soldiers of the one true God and his only son, Jesus Christ.'

Clem didn't speak as he frogmarched Connolly out of St Barts. What the hell had the stupid idiot been thinking? She worked for the government, for God's sake. And she was high profile now, whether she liked it or not. She couldn't get caught impersonating a doctor.

When they reached his car, Clem released his hold and spoke through gritted teeth. 'Do you want to tell me what you were doing?'

'I needed to speak to you,' Connolly replied.

And sneaking into a police-guarded hospital wing seemed like the logical solution, did it? 'Surely it could have waited?' asked Clem.

Connolly shook her head. 'You were stalling, not telling me the full story.'

Clem sighed. This girl was supposed to be the hero of the hour. Saviour of the Olympic Games. How the hell did she intend to do that from a cell in Holloway?

'I may not be an experienced old hand,' said Connolly, 'but I know bullshit when I hear it.'

'You came this close to being arrested.' Clem held his thumb and forefinger an inch apart.

'Yes,' said Connolly. 'Thank you for getting me out of there.'

Clem was still furious, but there were more pressing things to discuss. He unlocked his car with the remote and it let out a petulant beep. 'Get in.'

Once inside, they both kept their eyes straight ahead.

'The man in the hospital room,' said Connolly. 'Is he dead?'

Clem nodded. A bullet passing through skin and bone would tend to do that to a person. 'Did he say anything?' he asked.

'He said he had nothing to do with the bomb,' Connolly replied.

'In the infamous words of Mandy Rice-Davies, well, he would, wouldn't he?' Clem used enough sarcasm to shame Simon Cowell.

Connolly swivelled in her seat so that she was looking at Clem's profile. 'I thought terrorists were supposed to claim their successes, make sure everyone knows what their cause is all about.'

It was a fair point and one that had been niggling Clem. 'What else did he say?'

She shrugged. 'Nothing very coherent, he just kept going on about someone called Ronnie.'

Clem kept his eyes fixed towards the windscreen. 'What about Ronnie?'

'I don't really know. Just that he'd never give him up.'

'Did he say anything about where Ronnie might be?'

'Nothing,' said Connolly. 'Like I say, he wasn't really with it.'

A moment of silence lapsed while Clem tried to process the facts. He had never really believed that Shining Light were the culprits and having seen the cell and its set-up, he remained unconvinced. The boy, Miggs, was just some no-hoper from the schemes. No way did he have the know-how for something like the Plaza bombing.

But what about the mysterious Ronnie? Nothing had ever been proved but there were suspicions that Ronnie was into some serious shit. Someone who would have all the necessary contacts. And Miggs's face had changed at the mere mention of Ronnie's name. He was clearly not someone to be messed with.

'So do you think this Ronnie person is behind it?' Connolly's voice broke the quiet.

'It's looking possible,' Clem answered.

'Some people might say that's a little bit neat.'

'Then some people would be stupid.'

'Why's that?'

Clem turned so that he was finally looking at Connolly. 'Because it overlooks the small detail that Ronnie is still out there.'

Back at home, I watch dawn break over London; weak, pink sunlight unfurling over the rooftops as I take small sips from a can of Diet Coke.

I had been bloody daft to do what I did. I'd been caught up in the moment, not thinking straight. Now I had a growl of nausea in my stomach from the aftermath of exhaustion and realisation.

Clem had been furious but, fortunately, clearheaded enough to get me out of the hospital. When the alarm had sounded, I was frozen, faced with a clear picture of what I had got myself into. Then the room flooded with nurses and doctors and policemen all barking instructions and talking over one another, until the sister who had granted me access in the first place bellowed at the top of her voice: 'Clear the room. Medics only.'

Clem had grasped his opportunity to get the hell out with me in tow, leaving her to rip open the patient's gown and attach two electric paddles to his scraggy chest. The noise of the current passing through him, throwing his body skywards, had been sickening. I shudder and try to chase the sound from my mind.

But you know how it is when you don't want to think about something. I can almost feel his grip around my arm as he looked into my face, convinced I was his friend. I rub the skin instinctively as his voice rips through me.

'I won't give you up, Ronnie. I'd rather die.'

My stomach lurches so I head into the kitchen in search of food and distraction.

Until a couple of days ago I led a safe and secure life – molly-coddled the old man would call it. He compares my childhood to his and says I've had it easy. Funny how he never considers what it was like when I got injured and my dreams collapsed. Or how I felt about what happened to Davey. That's all swept under the carpet like stale biscuit crumbs.

He says I don't take risks, and he's right. He says I can't make decisions, and he's right. Yet he never asks himself why. Last Christmas I brought him back to my place, cooked a turkey and all the trimmings. Well, I bought it from Marks and Sparks and heated it up. I even put up a tree, for God's sake. We hadn't even pulled a cracker when he started.

'You know your trouble, Jo.' He waggled a gravy-smeared knife at me. 'You avoid unpleasantness.'

'Doesn't everyone?' I laughed.

'Only the weak,' he told me. 'The strong know that to get where they want to be, they have to face the rough as well as the smooth.'

Well, I can safely say I've done that now. In the last forty-eight hours I've witnessed more death and despair than most people see in a lifetime. Including the old man. I almost wish I could go back to my old existence. Almost. The truth is, though, despite everything, I've never felt more alive.

I grab a slice of wholemeal from the bread bin, tear it in two and swallow the first half. It hits my digestive tract like a school bully's thump, but I force down the other half behind it.

For a long time now, I've been running away from life. No more. Whoever Ronnie is, wherever he might be, he is dangerous. He has to be caught. The only man who might help with that is dead and I was the last person to see him alive.

I take another bite of bread and search for a pen. Then I carefully begin to write down everything the dead man said to me.

'He's dead?' The PM looked over his desk at Clem.

'Cardiac arrest at 4.29 this morning,' Clem confirmed.

Benning floated behind the PM like a spectre. 'Not necessarily a bad thing,' he said. 'The dead don't talk.'

The PM sighed and picked up a plastic bottle of water bearing the Olympic flag motif. 'Did he tell you anything before he died?'

'Nothing useful,' Clem replied.

'No confession?' Benning asked.

Inwardly, Clem smiled. Wouldn't that have been handy? Everything wrapped up like a present. Sorry, boys, not today. 'He died before I could administer a proper interrogation.'

Benning shrugged. 'No matter. With all members of the cell eliminated . . .'

Clem bridled. They were talking about people's lives, and not just those who had died. Killing a man, any man, left a mark. A suit like Benning couldn't even begin to imagine what it felt like to watch the light go out in somebody's eyes.

'It's not quite as easy as that, Mr Benning. There's one member still at large,' he said.

He saw the disappointment in Benning's face and couldn't resist adding, 'Possibly the most dangerous of the gang.'

'So apprehend him,' Benning declared.

The PM held up his palms. 'I'm sure Clem is doing all he can.'

Benning barely contained a snort.

'In the meantime, when we issue a press release confirming the death of this suspect do we need to mention the fourth outstanding member?' asked the PM.

'Absolutely not,' said Benning. 'It would cause panic. The Games would never survive.'

The PM tapped his bottle nervously. 'Is that sufficient justification to withhold this information?'

Benning licked his lips as he considered the question, then directed his gaze at Clem. 'If alerted that we're on to him, might the fugitive go to ground permanently?' he asked.

'Ronnie X is already underground,' Clem answered.

'So forcing him deeper still might make him impossible to catch?'

'Very possibly.'

'Then I would say it's a matter of national security that we keep the existence of the fourth member top secret,' said Benning.

Clem almost whistled at the mental gymnastics when his phone vibrated in his hand. He never turned it off, not even during meetings at Downing Street. He scanned the number. 'Excuse me,' he said. 'I think I need to take this call.' He ignored the glare from Benning and turned his body for a semblance of privacy.

'Christian Clement.'

'It's Jo Connolly here.'

'I know.'

'Can you talk right now?'

Clem glanced at the PM. 'Tricky.'

'Right,' said Connolly. 'I just wanted to tell you that I remembered something else that the dead man said to me. It might be nothing; it might not.'

'Where are you?'

'I'm on my way to the basketball arena. Photo op with Team GB.'

Clem glanced at his watch. 'I'll meet you there in one hour.' He hung up. Turned back to the PM. Didn't apologise.

'It's decided, then, that for the time being we will not mention the fourth suspect,' said the PM.

Clem nodded. Of course it was decided.

The PM picked up the remote control and flicked on the television. The Olympic flag fluttered in the breeze above the basketball stadium. 'Are we sure that no one outside these walls knows this information?' he asked.

Clem didn't miss a beat. 'No one.'

Benning narrowed his eyes. 'Let's make sure it stays that way.'

I smile for the cameras in my tracksuit and trainers, basketball in hand. Number Ten sent an advance party including a make-up girl who dabbed concealer over my cuts and bruises. A day ago Benning and the PM couldn't wait to show them off as proof of my heroism. Today we're putting all reminders of any nasty business aside. Another reason why I could never have made a politician: I'd never have been able to keep up.

I try to spin the ball on my finger, dropping it, causing the team to laugh.

'Have a shot, Miss Connolly,' one of the players says.

'Call me Jo.'

'Okay, Jo.' He winks at me. 'Take a shot.'

I bounce the ball to the hoop and score. 'Slam dunk.' I high five each member of the team in turn.

I spot Clem, high in the stadium and make my way towards him, taking the steps two, sometimes three at a time.

'You're fit,' he says.

'Not compared to that lot.' I gesture to the athletes training below us, but I smile because he's right. I feel great. My body is still stiff and sore but I feel energised and happy.

'You have something to tell me,' he says.

I nod and pull out a sheet of paper from my pocket. 'I've jotted down everything I can remember Miggs saying to me. There wasn't much, but I've tried to remember it word for word.'

Clem takes it from me, scanning my messy writing.

'I think this bit is probably the most interesting.' I tap a sentence I've underlined twice:

Remember the orchard, Ronnie?

If Clem is impressed he doesn't show it. He remains straight faced as he folds the paper in half, then in quarters and slides it into his inside pocket.

'I think I might know what it means,' I say.

Clem raises an eyebrow.

'Miggs was Scottish, right? Glaswegian I'd say.'

Clem doesn't answer, so I assume I'm right.

'So I googled orchards in Glasgow.'

'And?'

'There are a few; apples mostly, some pears.'

Clem runs a tongue over his teeth. 'Is this going anywhere?'

'I didn't think so, until I spotted an entry for a parish council newsletter. You know the sort of thing: neighbourhood watch, applications for an extended bar licence for the St Mary's Catholic Mothers' pie and pea supper.'

Clem sighs.

'Then I noticed an entry for a planning application. The local authority wants to change the use of one of their buildings. It's currently housing a debt advisory service but they want to swap it over to a residential unit for young people with drug issues.'

'I'm sure the St Mary's Catholic Mothers are overjoyed about that,' says Clem.

'Not exactly,' I say. 'But therein lies the rub. Until five years ago it *was* a residential unit. Not for drug addicts, but for teenagers in care.'

Clem doesn't respond, which I take to be a good sign.

'And guess what the unit was called?' I'm so pleased with myself, I can't contain a smile.

'The Orchard,' he says, somewhat stealing my thunder.

'It sounds to me like Miggs might have lived at the unit, that he met this Ronnie character in there. What do you think?'

'It's possible.'

'I thought maybe we could check the records, find the details.' I'm on a roll now. 'I mean, I know they'd be out of date now, but it might give us some clue as to how to find him . . .'

Clem puts up a hand. 'Hold it right there.'

My mouth is still open.

'I'm grateful for this, it's a good lead, but you have to leave it to us from here,' he says.

My face falls.

'I was with the PM and Benning this morning,' he continues.

Shit. Is this Clem's way of telling me I'm fired? 'Did you tell them about last night?' I ask.

'Of course not.'

'Thanks,' I whisper.

'I didn't do it for you,' he says. 'But the upshot is they're under the impression that only they and I know about Ronnie, and that's the way they want it to stay.'

I look down at my hands. A moment ago I was elated, taking charge of my own destiny. Now I'm being told what to do like I'm a silly child. Again.

Clem stands to leave, smoothes down his jacket. 'Do you understand what I'm telling you, Jo?'

It's the first time he's called me by my first name.

'Do you understand me?' he repeats.

The feeling of disappointment, familiar and itchy, sticks in my throat.

'Completely,' I say.

Chapter Seven

Nathan Shaw felt the world tilt.

It was as if he was standing right on the very edge, looking down into a heap of nothing. Sometimes, when he was very drunk, he had the exact same feeling and had to hold the bathroom walls to stop himself falling into the bowl. His mother would shake her head and mutter about being more responsible, but his daddy would just laugh and tell her that boys needed to let off their steam. Oftentimes, if the beer made him sick, Nathan would swear off it. Those good intentions didn't make it past Friday night, though. Still, he was pretty sure he wasn't drunk now. Only had one goddamn bottle.

'Nathan, can you hear me?'

He squinted up at the voice.

'You stay with me now.'

It was George, leaning over him, big old flaps of fat swinging around his jaw.

'You listening to me, boy?'

Nathan nodded that yes, he was listening, couldn't do much else with George up in his face.

'You need to press on tight,' said George. 'Understand?'

Nathan smiled, didn't want to admit to the senior officer that he couldn't take his drink. Then his eyes started to close.

'Nathan!'

A hard slap stung his cheek. Hell. He hadn't actually been sleeping, just shutting up shop for a second. Such a hot day. Couldn't George understand that?

George slapped him again. 'I'm talking to you, boy.'

It was the noise more than any pain that forced Nathan's eyes open. When he saw George's face, he knew to keep them open. The old man looked more than frightened. He looked terrified. Like those Halloween masks everyone wore. Nathan had once taken Stacey La Salle to see a horror movie where the serial killer had worn one. She'd laughed every time he jumped. Nathan tried his damned hardest not to, but it was the scariest thing he had ever seen in his life.

Until now.

'What is it, George?' Nathan's voice sounded small and far away.

'I need you to do what I tell you, boy,' said George.

Nathan nodded.

'I need you to press hard on this.'

Nathan followed George's eyes to his hands. He'd seen those hands a hundred times on the wheel of the cruiser. Fingers yellowed by tobacco, a white band of untanned skin peeping out when his wristwatch rode up.

What he saw now made them unrecognisable.

'George?'

They were slick up to his elbows in blood.

'What the fuck's going on, George?'

'No time for talking, son.' He grabbed one of Nathan's hands in his own, the squelch making Nathan gag.

He tried to pull his hand away, but George had a firm grip and forced it down onto Nathan's stomach. Then he took the other and pressed that down on top of it.

'You got to push,' said George. 'Push with everything you have.'

Nathan looked down at his hands, now as covered in blood as George's. Underneath, more was gushing upwards, pouring out like an oil slick.

'Sweet baby Jesus,' said George. 'I'm going to get some help.'

* * *

I step off the Intercity and the late afternoon air feels distinctly colder in Glasgow than it did in London. I wish I'd brought a jacket but there was only enough time to grab my laptop.

I spent the journey gathering as much information as I could. By the Midlands my eyes began to droop and it occurred to me that I should try to snatch a few hours' sleep, but when I closed my eyes, I could hear Clem's warning to leave the investigation to him.

So I went back to the internet.

I cross the concourse and jump in a black cab.

'Where to, sweetheart?' The driver's accent takes me straight back to the hospital room in St Barts.

'George Square,' I reply.

'Right you are.' He pulls out, glancing at me in his mirror, clearly trying to place me.

I know a lot of folk in my position would love nothing better than to chat to the public and enjoy their time in the sun. The old man would never have passed up the opportunity for a blether with a cabbie. Probably would have quoted some nugget he picked up during his next speech. But I'm just not made that way.

I pull out the notes I made on the train and re-read them. The Orchard Residential School opened in 1975, and despite its name was not a school or any type of educational establishment. It was, in fact, residential accommodation for children in care. By 1985 it had become a secure unit housing children with social, emotional and behavioural problems. Or, as the *Glasgow Herald* blithely put it, 'a dumping ground for children that nobody wants'. I bite my lip and refuse to think about Davey. In 2005 it closed, following allegations of abuse. Although the city council refuses to acknowledge the link between its closure and the allegations, there are still ongoing legal cases brought by former residents.

'Okay, sweetheart.'

I look up to see the taxi has already stopped and I wonder if actually I could have walked. The square is not what I imagined. Then again, what did I imagine? Dull grey tower blocks and dirty streets peppered with down-and-outs clutching their cans of Special Brew? Instead, I'm met by a wide public space, accented by flowerbeds full of tulips and flanked by Georgian buildings.

I pay the driver and head towards the City Chambers. I called ahead from the train announcing my approach to Mrs Debbie McAndrews, head of Social Services, who, naturally, had tried to put me off.

'I'm afraid I have meetings all day, Miss Connolly,' she said.

The thing is, I know public servants. I've been around them all my life. They have meetings about meetings. At least half the people there aren't listening. I've done it enough times myself, nodding at regular intervals and pretending to make notes on my laptop, ensuring no one can see over my shoulder and discover I'm actually playing Tetris.

'I understand that entirely,' I said, 'but this matter is extremely important.'

'If you could make an appointment,' she stuttered.

So I pulled rank horribly. 'Mrs McAndrews, I'm charged with ensuring the Olympic Games run smoothly. If I had any space in my diary I would make the necessary arrangements. As it is I need this information today.'

'I see,' she said.

'I must report back to the prime minister tonight.'

Mrs McAndrews greets me outside her office. She's a small, dumpy woman with a tight perm and a plaid skirt. I salute her patriotism considering how badly it suits her.

'Glad to see you, Miss Connolly.' She casts a puzzled smile at my tracksuit.

'Call me Jo,' I beam back. 'Everyone does.' I just pray she hasn't asked herself the bleeding obvious: what has a Scottish children's home got to do with the Olympic Games?

She nods and shows me into her office. Her desk is obscenely tidy – a place for everything and everything in its place.

'You mentioned an interest in The Orchard,' she says.

'In particular a boy who may have stayed there,' I confirm.

'There were a lot of residents there.' Her tone is even but her hand flutters at her neck. 'Is he one of those making a claim against the council?'

I think of Miggs in the morgue, an MI5 bullet through his temple. 'I think that's highly unlikely.'

'Good, good,' she says, as much to herself as to me. 'And I suppose you're not at liberty to explain your interest?'

'Not at this time,' I say. I'm amazed how readily she accepts my implied authority. But didn't I do the same with the PM and Clem? I just assumed they had good reasons.

'Right then.' She turns, all business, to her computer and clicks her mouse, which I notice is the old-fashioned kind, still connected by a cable.

'In around 2005 we began centralising all our records,' she says. 'But of course there are some gaps in respect of the older files.'

The cynical part of me wonders if any of these losses are coincidentally those of former residents suing Social Services.

'What was the name?' she asks.

'Stephen Miggs.'

She taps her keyboard and waits. 'You're in luck,' she says. 'Stephen Miggs's records are here in some detail.'

My heart beats fast. I hadn't anticipated it would be this easy. 'And he was a resident at The Orchard?' I ask.

She scrolls down with her ancient mouse. 'Uh huh. He arrived in 2005 when his last foster placement broke down.'

I resist punching the air. 'Is there anything in his file that might point to him being violent – dangerous, even?'

Mrs McAndrews turns to me and sighs. 'The Orchard was a secure unit, Miss Connolly. None of the residents were sweet wee kiddies.'

I nod my understanding. 'Perhaps you would print off the file and I could look for myself.'

'There's the matter of confidentiality,' she says half-heartedly.

'Stephen Miggs is dead.'

'I see.' She presses the print button on her computer, sending the printer in the corner of the room into life.

I sit in an uncomfortable silence as at least ten pages print out, Mrs McAndrews waiting to catch them like a wicket keeper. When the file is finished she grabs them and holds them out to me at arm's length, clearly desperate for this meeting to end.

'Just one more thing,' I say.

She visibly cringes. 'Of course.'

'I'm trying to find another resident who was probably at The Orchard at the same time as Stephen Miggs.'

Mrs McAndrews's nostrils flare but she heads back to her seat. 'Name?'

'Ronnie,' I say.

She raises her eyebrows.

'I know, I know.' I open my palms. 'It's not ideal.'

She begins tapping once again, her stubby fingers punching hard at the keyboard this time. 'There's nothing for anyone known as Ronnie at The Orchard during the two years Stephen Miggs lived there.'

'How about Ronald?' I ask.

'Nothing.'

It was a long shot, of course it was, but I'm disappointed.

I stand to leave and pocket the information she's given me. I'm not relishing the thought of the journey home. Maybe I'll buy a couple of glasses of wine in the buffet car and knock myself out.

'One second . . .' Mrs McAndrews holds up her hand. 'There

was a Paul Ronald who arrived in 2002 and left in 2005. Not much of an overlap with Miggs. A month or two at best.'

A month was long enough for me. More than long enough.

Clem peeled back the cling film from his sandwich and sighed. Tuna salad on granary. No butter. He opened the car window to release the smell of fish.

He'd spent the day closing down the Miggs story. The PM, or more likely that little toerag Benning, had decided to hold back the news of his death until tomorrow. Today they wanted the press all over the Games. No doubt they'd be chuffed by the pictures of Connolly playing basketball, which had gone viral. You couldn't move on YouTube for montages of her, and the middle-class *Guardian* botherers on Mumsnet had described her as 'our new girl crush'.

Clem shook his head in disgust. Did the PM and Benning really think you could keep everyone quiet? This wasn't North Korea. The stakes couldn't be higher. Every red cent and every ounce of the UK's credibility were on the line and it was warping their sense of reality.

He took a bite of his sandwich and sighed again. Oh, for a bacon roll.

Mouth full, he checked his watch. Ten past five. Just enough time to follow up the intel on The Orchard. Clem had to hand it to Connolly – she'd done a bloody decent job so far of tracking things down. He reached for his mobile, punched in a number and swallowed the dry bread.

'Debbie McAndrews.'

The head of Glasgow Social Services sounded very weary. Clem knew how she felt.

'Good afternoon,' said Clem. 'Christian Clement here. I emailed earlier.'

'Uh huh.' Her voice was heavy. 'Is this about Stephen Miggs?'

Clem sat up straight. He hadn't mentioned any names in his email. 'That's right.'

'I can only tell you what I told your colleague.'

'My colleague?'

'Yes, I gave her a copy of the file,' she said.

Clem couldn't believe what he was hearing. 'Could you confirm the name of my colleague, madam?'

'Jo Connolly,' she said.

Unbelievable.

My taxi pulls up outside a three-storey house with most of the windows boarded over with metal plates.

'Arnsdale Place?' I ask.

'Aye,' says the driver.

This is exactly how I imagined Glasgow. As far as the eye can see are houses and tower blocks, each one as grey as the last, punctuated only by small patches of nettles.

My hand wavers over the door handle as I squint out at the graffiti spray-painted across the pavement.

Robo is a cunt.

Succinct.

A group of boys saunter into view. They wear matching uniforms of nylon tracksuits and scarred cheeks. One is nearly pulled off his feet by a Rottweiler tugging at his chain-link lead.

'Doesn't look like anyone lives in there,' I say.

'Not necessarily,' says the cabbie. 'Windows in Easterhoose get smashed all the time. Council donnae replace them sharpish.'

I don't get out.

The old man would laugh at my reticence. He grew up on an estate in Toxteth. He shared shoes with his brothers, and his uncles settled their scores on a Friday night after a skinful in the working men's club.

'Do you want me to wait?' asks the cabbie.

'If it's no trouble.' I cough away my embarrassment.

He taps the meter ticking away happily. 'Nae bother at all.'

I get out, avoid making eye contact with the local welcoming committee and approach the door. This is the last known address Social Services had for Paul Ronald.

I check the numbers at the door. 22c is on the third floor. I press the buzzer. No answer.

I try again, though I'm pretty sure it's pointless. No one will be living anywhere so derelict.

'Yeah?' A voice comes through the intercom.

I'm so shocked, I'm not sure what to say.

'Is that you, Robo?' a woman's voice asks. ''Cos if you think you can piss me around again, you've got it all wrong, pal.'

I glance down at the graffiti and wonder if this Robo is one and the same.

'Sorry,' I say. 'My name's Jo and I'm looking for Paul Ronald.'

'He hasnae lived here since December.'

'Have you any idea where he moved to?' I ask.

She doesn't answer. Instead, an upstairs window opens and a young woman with her hair scraped back in a high ponytail leans out.

I step back and wave up at her. 'Hi there.'

She looks me up and down. 'You're not from round here.'

'No. I've come from London.'

She looks at me again, then at the waiting cab. 'Hold on,' she says and slams the window shut.

A second later she appears at the door with a toddler on her hip. He peers at me over a bottle of purple juice clamped to his mouth.

'It's kind of you to come down,' I say.

She scratches a scab at the corner of her lip until a pinprick of blood flowers.

'What's it worth?' she says.

'Pardon?'

'What's it worth to know where Paul is?'

It takes me a second to realise she means money.

'Twenty quid,' she says.

'I'm not sure I can—'

'Twenty quid or piss off,' she says. 'Your choice.'

I don't have a choice, do I? I take out my purse and peel off two tens, which she snatches out of my hand.

'Tollcross Cemetery,' she says and begins to close the door.

'What?'

'He OD'd on Christmas Day.'

With that, she bangs the door shut and I hear her muffled footsteps as she tramps back upstairs to her flat.

Rory's intercom flashes.

When he moved into this flat, it had a buzzer. Rory hated the sound. It made his ears hurt. He replaced the buzzer with an electric light. At first he could only find a red bulb, but Rory hates red. It made him ill so he replaced it with a green one.

He leaves his bank of computer screens and checks the video feed. He likes to see who is at the door. He hates visitors. They make a noise and smell of other things he hates. Like onions. And toothpaste.

He checks the video again. Mistakes can be made. The red bulb was a mistake.

He is now sure it is Ronnie at the door.

Rory likes Ronnie. Ronnie doesn't say Rory is weird. Ronnie doesn't say Rory should 'get out more'. Ronnie doesn't say very much at all. And both their names begin with R. Which is good.

Rory releases the door and listens to Ronnie climbing the stairs. Seven steps. Ronnie has taken them two at a time.

'Hey.' Ronnie nods.

Rory nods back.

Then Ronnie holds out an opened family-size bag of peanut M&Ms. Rory likes peanut M&Ms but he doesn't take them.

'No red ones,' promises Ronnie.

'Sure?' says Rory. Mistakes can be made.

Ronnie heads into the kitchen, takes the tray from behind the bread bin and pours out the sweets. Rory checks them carefully. There are approximately seventy-two. No red. He takes the tray, bends from the waist and sucks up an M&M with his lips.

'So what do you know?' Ronnie asks.

Rory knows a lot of things. He knows the rate at which bacteria multiply in an open wound. He knows who invented the laser disc. He knows the square root of 676. But that is not what Ronnie means.

He reaches for his logs. There are five laid out, each detailing different information which he notes in strict rotation every twenty-six minutes. He takes the second, which is Ronnie's log. There are hundreds of entries written in pencil. The time and date is logged next to each of them.

'Busy,' says Ronnie.

Rory nods. Of all the thousands of websites, blogs and databases he watches around the world for Ronnie, five have had increased traffic recently.

'So who's watching us?' asks Ronnie.

When Rory was fifteen he would have looked around the room, expecting to find a person watching Ronnie. But he has had a lot of help since then. He has learned about socialisation and interpretation and empathy.

'Social Services,' he says, pointing to the relevant records.

Ronnie reads them silently, running a finger under the most recent entries. 'What about these?'

'Government,' says Rory.

It is a *golden rule* that he must never tell anyone that he hacks into the systems of the World Bank, all the major credit card companies, the police, secret services and the government. A golden rule has nothing to do with colour and it is not made of precious metal. It is a rule that can never be broken. If Rory tells anyone what he does, he will be sent to a very bad place. Worse than The Orchard.

'Who exactly?' Ronnie asks.

Rory writes down the name of Christian Clement. 'MI5.'

'Who else?'

Rory writes down the name Joanna Connolly, Department of Culture, Media and Sport.

Rory is not good with facial expressions. So many different ones. Some of them impossible to decipher. But he recognises Ronnie's at this moment: surprise.

'Do you know where she lives, Rory?'

Rory writes down the address and Ronnie scans it.

'Thanks.' Ronnie turns to go and Rory panics. He hasn't been asked a question yet he knows there's something he needs to tell Ronnie. He bangs the sides of his head with his fists.

'Hey now,' says Ronnie. 'Enough of that.'

Rory bites his lip.

'Do you have something you want to tell me?' asks Ronnie.

Rory nods.

'Is it about MI5?'

Rory shakes his head.

'Jo Connolly?'

'Yes.' Relief floods over Rory. 'She's in Glasgow.'

Chapter Eight

It's biting cold in the station and I shiver as I watch the departure boards flicker. The next train back to London isn't for another two hours and there's no way I can stand here dithering and hopping from foot to foot until it arrives. I toy with buying myself a coffee to warm myself up but my feet are already leading me to the bar of the Station Hotel.

'What'll it be?' The barman looks up at me, his face flushed and pockmarked.

I check out the bottles of single malt lining the back shelf. Ordinarily I avoid spirits, but this has been no ordinary day.

'Glenmorangie,' I say.

'Double?'

I nod. When in Rome. Amber liquid slips down in a soothing stream.

'Fill her up?' The barman glances at my empty glass.

I look in my purse and discover I'm down to my last twenty. Shelling out for taxis and paying off the girl in Easterhouse has used up all my cash. I'm not going to be able to claim any of this lot back, either.

I put the note on the bar. 'Why not?'

Refilled glass in hand, I pull out my mobile. The battery's low and I don't have my charger. Still, a girl can't be on call twenty-four-seven, can she? I feel the sting of guilt as I think of the old man not being able to get hold of me. He's had so many health problems in the last few years. But I tell myself I couldn't get home any quicker whatever might happen.

I drain the whisky and a wave of fatigue washes over me, seeking out every bone, every joint. Even my teeth feel tired. I'm going to be fit for nothing tomorrow.

The barman eyes me over the craters on his misshapen nose. 'Looks like you need some shut-eye,' he says.

My shoulders slump in agreement.

'I'd bed down for the night, if I were you.'

He's right. It would be better to stay. Get a good night's sleep and jump on the milk train in the morning. I'd be at work by ten, ready for anything they throw at me.

My mind made up, I stumble out of the bar to the hotel reception.

'A single room, please,' I say.

The receptionist is called Iona. Her brass name badge tells me this as it wobbles on her left breast.

Iona checks the computer and smiles. 'Will that be cash or credit card?'

Clem threw his wallet and mobile onto the passenger seat, where they bounced off into the footwell. What the hell did Connolly think she was playing at?

Did she think tracking down terrorists was some sort of girl guide adventure? Clem had seen the public school kids in London pretending to be soldiers, doing their drills for the CCF. Did Connolly think this was the same? Just a bit of fun?

He put the key in the ignition and gunned the accelerator. Bang. He'd left the car in reverse and hit the wall behind. Shit. He'd damn well bill Connolly for that when he caught up with her.

He drove out of the car park and was heading to the airport when his phone rang. He glanced down at it, out of his reach, and thanked the lord for Bluetooth.

'Prime Minister,' he said.

'Where are you, Clem?'

The echo told him that the PM had him on the squawk box. He could picture Benning lingering behind him like a bad fart.

'On my way to Glasgow, sir,' said Clem. 'There's some intel that the outstanding suspect might be up there.'

There was a silence as if the PM did not want to be reminded that an outstanding suspect existed. Sorry, sir, but life doesn't come neatly gift-wrapped and tagged.

'Have you spoken to Jo today?' asked the PM.

There was another little parcel that wasn't half so tidy as it looked from the outside. 'I saw her early this morning at the basketball stadium,' said Clem. 'I briefed her on Miggs's death.'

It wasn't a lie. That was the only time Clem had had contact with her that day.

'She's gone off comms,' said Benning.

Clem grimaced. No wonder Connolly thought she was 007, when everyone around her spoke like they were in a film. 'Maybe she's getting her head down,' he said. 'She's had a rough few days.'

'Absolutely,' said the PM.

Though of course he had no idea just how rough things had actually been. If the PM ever got wind of what had happened at St Barts, Connolly and Clem would both be for the chop.

'No doubt you'll let us know what you discover in Glasgow,' the PM declared.

'Of course.'

Clem hung up and pulled into the airport car park. He flashed his ID, skipped security and boarded the plane. The stewardess smiled cautiously as she showed him to his seat in first class. She would have been told he had special clearance, but no more.

He declined a glass of champagne and buckled his seat belt, cursing Jo Connolly.

There were only three other passengers in first class: a couple of businessmen discussing the bond market at full volume, and a young woman, slumped in her seat, her eyes covered by a pair of dark glasses. Clem thought he recognised her. Actress, maybe, or pop star. As the plane lifted into the sky, the businessmen lifted a glass to one another and a deal worth 'millions'.

Clem growled and snatched up the papers he'd made Mrs McAndrews email to him. Two Social Services files. One for Stephen Miggs; the other for a Paul Ronald. If Clem were in a better mood he would have to give Connolly credit for getting this lot. Particularly the last known address of Ronald. But he wasn't in a good mood.

When the plane touched down, Clem was allowed off while the other passengers were asked to wait a few more moments. He heard the businessmen tutting behind him and imagined the scowl on the actress-cum-pop star's face, but he couldn't give a shit. The stairs had been attached and Clem lumbered down them to the waiting car. Christ, he felt old.

'Sir.' The driver stared straight ahead.

It was dusk in Glasgow and rain spat at the windscreen.

'Easterhouse,' Clem told him.

The driver nodded and sped away.

When I finally kick off my shoes and flick on the television, a picture of me at the basketball stadium fills the screen. I groan and channel hop, looking for something, anything, that has nothing to do with the Olympics. I settle for a re-run of *Only Fools and Horses* – the episode where Rodney and Del Boy dress up as Batman and Robin.

I'm barely horizontal on the bed when I fall into a delicious half sleep. I should take off my clothes but I can't be bothered and instead I wrap my arms around the pillow. I'm not pissed – well a bit, maybe – but it's more than that. It's like I've finally come to a stop. I smile and let myself drift away. David Jason's voice floats in and out of my consciousness. 'This time next year . . .'

Minutes later – or maybe hours, I can't tell – I wake. It's dark and I'm disorientated but I'm disturbed by a noise at my door. A scratching. At first I ignore it, but then it comes again.

A prickle of fear spikes the base of my neck. Is someone trying to get into my room? I lean over to turn on the bedside lamp and blink into the light. My door is shut. I scoot over and check it. Definitely locked.

I listen carefully for the scratching noise but there's nothing. I press my ear to the door but nothing greets me other than silence.

Slowly and carefully I unlock the door. The bombing has made me antsy and I need to know if there is anyone on the other side. The door opens an inch and I peer through the gap. Nothing. I prise it open a head's width. Enough to get a proper look, but I keep my body weight against it in case I need to slam it shut. Nothing.

Then I see the newspaper on the floor. It's *The Times* leading with the story that the terrorist cell has been caught. A mugshot of Miggs that must have been taken years ago stares up at me, eyes hard, scowl tight. He looks every inch the criminal and nothing like the shell of a man I met in hospital. Underneath his picture my own face grins up at me from the basketball court. The PM is quoted as saying, 'Business as usual.'

I sigh with relief. All I heard was a paper delivery. I laugh at my own stupidity and head back to bed, leaving the paper where it is. I need more sleep.

★　★　★

The driver pulled up in Arnsdale Place and Clem wrinkled his nose. Shitsville Arizona.

He got out, his feet crunching on broken glass.

'Wait here,' he said.

At the end of the street a gang of Neds were circling a lamp post, bottles of Buckfast clamped in their fists, ignoring the rain that was now lashing down.

Clem pressed the buzzer hard and kept his finger down until an upstairs window opened.

A girl leaned out. A junkie by the looks of her. 'What's your fucking problem?'

Clem looked up at her, his face slick. 'I need to speak to you,' he said.

'Is this about Paul?' she asked.

Clem nodded and caught the trace of a smile at the corner of her lips. When she opened the door, he spotted the track marks on her arms that confirmed his suspicions.

'You want to know about Paul Ronald?' Her voice had a sneaky edge.

'That's right.'

She cocked her head to one side. 'What's it worth?'

Clem shook his head. Addicts. Always on the make. 'Absolutely nothing,' he said.

Her face fell. Clearly she'd been relying on him for her next fix. 'Fucker,' she snarled and pushed the door.

Clem saw it coming and rammed his foot against the wood. The girl tried to fight him but had little strength.

'Away to fuck,' she shouted. 'What do you think you're on, pal?'

'I just want some information and then I'll leave you alone.' Clem's tone was calm.

'Information?' She was screaming now. 'I'll give you a piece of information. I want you to piss off.'

Behind him, Clem heard the slap of trainers on tarmac. The gang of boys from under the lamp post had relocated. One stepped forward, his skinny white frame swamped by a black tracksuit.

'Everything all right, Charlene?'

'No it's fucking not,' she shouted. 'This bastard's trying to kick the door off.'

The boy looked Clem up and down. 'You're in trouble now, pal,' he said. 'We look after our own in the Hoose.'

Clem didn't answer but kept his foot firmly against the door.

The driver lowered the electric window. 'Problem?'

Another kid at the back hopped from foot to foot, laughing hysterically, completely out of it on drugs or drink or both. 'Aye, there's a problem.' He stuck his head in the window. 'We're gonna fuck you up.'

Glancing at the crazed grin still on the boy's face, the driver punched him hard. There was a wet smacking sound and the boy flew backwards, falling into his mates, blood spewing from his mouth.

In an instant, the others pounced at the car, smashing their bottles against it. The driver tried to put up his window but one of the gang pulled a claw hammer from his pocket and shattered it with one vicious blow. The driver was peppered with glass, small cuts appearing across his cheeks. Another jumped onto the bonnet and began kicking the windscreen.

'See what happens?' The first boy gave Clem a triumphant smile. 'See what happens when you mess with the Hoose?' Then he took out a flick knife.

Clem appraised the scene. Worked out the odds. He had no choices left.

The gunshot reverberated around the night sky. Clem had shot upwards out of harm's way and now had his weapon trained on the boy with the knife.

The boy eyed him with contempt, but stayed put. The blade glistened but he didn't lunge. He might be a headcase; indeed he might have more drugs in his system than Pete Doherty. But he wasn't stupid.

'Feds,' he murmured.

The other boys were silenced and quickly evaporated. The boy with the knife joined them without a backward glance at Charlene, who was still in the doorway, her eyes wide.

Clem nodded at the driver who was shaking shards of glass from his hair. 'Okay?'

The driver licked his finger and stemmed a trickle of blood coming from the bridge of his nose. 'I'll live.'

Clem turned to Charlene, who had let go of the door and was shivering, her arms wrapped around herself. 'Can we talk?' he asked.

She turned and made her way upstairs. Clem followed.

The flat stank of dirty nappies and the culprit lay asleep in a cot, one pink fist clutching a bar. Charlene closed the bedroom door and hurried into the lounge. She began scooping up syringes and empty baggies from the coffee table.

'I'm not interested in any of that,' said Clem.

She smiled weakly and let her works fall back among the over-flowing ashtrays.

'I'm trying to come off it, you know?'

Clem didn't answer.

'But it's hard.' Charlene went over to the window, rubbed at the grime with her thumb. 'This place is overrun with gear.' She looked out into the street. Somewhere in the distance a car alarm was blaring. 'All those years I never even touched the skag 'cos everyone knows it fucks you up, and here I am on the crystal meth.' She gave a shrug and a cold laugh. 'Ironic, eh?'

'Tell me about Paul Ronald,' said Clem.

'Whatever he was involved in had nothing to do with me,' said Charlene.

'I understand that.'

She walked back across the room and reached down onto the coffee table for a packet of B&H. She took one out, lit it and took a deep lungful of smoke.

'So where is he?' Clem asked.

'Dead.' Charlene let out a stream of smoke from her nostrils. 'Overdose.'

'When?'

Charlene took another drag, the end of her cigarette burning brightest red. 'Christmas. He'd been inside and done his rattle. I telt him, when you've been off the gear for a while, you cannae just dive straight back in. You've got to take it steady.'

Clem nodded as if this were sensible and reasonable advice from one friend to another.

'He wouldn't listen,' she said with a shrug.

So this man couldn't be Ronnie X. Nice try, but no cigar.

'Has anyone else been here asking about him?' Clem said.

'Aye. This afternoon. He was never this fucking popular when he was alive.'

It had to have been Connolly. 'Female, white, early thirties?' he asked.

Charlene flicked the ash from her cigarette into the cup of her hand. 'Maybe.'

'Athletic type?'

Charlene shrugged. 'Good-looking and really posh.'

Connolly. 'Right, thank you.' Clem turned to leave.

'You're not going to get the social onto me, are you?' Charlene called out.

Clem looked around the filthy flat. 'Like I said, I'm not interested.'

* * *

Rory holds the mobile phone in his hand. He doesn't like speaking to people on the phone. It's not as bad as speaking to people face to face, when he can smell them and can't concentrate on what they are saying. Or when they move towards Rory with their hand out and he has to move backwards. He hates that.

He taps the keypad and writes a text message. The first text message was sent in 1992 by Neil Papworth. It said 'Merry Christmas'. It was a good invention. Rory presses send on his phone.

From: Rory
To: Ronnie
22.05
Information

Four seconds later his mobile rings. Rory places it at, but not touching, his ear.

'Rory,' says Ronnie.

Rory doesn't speak.

'You have something to tell me,' says Ronnie.

More silence.

'Is it about Joanna Connolly?'

'Yes.'

'What has she done?'

Rory clears his throat. 'She used her Mastercard.'

'Where?'

'The Station Hotel in Glasgow.'

I'm dreaming about Davey. He's called me up and is telling me about a TV show. It's one we both used to love as kids.

'It's Friday. It's five o'clock,' he says, but can't finish for laughing. One of those big Davey laughs that start as a gurgle in the back of his throat but soon turn into a bark that makes his whole body shake. Soon I'm laughing too.

When I hear a noise I ignore it. I want to hold onto Davey. 'Are you okay?' I ask.

'I'm fine, Jo,' he says. 'Don't worry about me.'

I'm not laughing any more. 'I miss you.'

'Don't be sad, Jo,' he tells me. 'There's a tin of soup for our tea.'

I wipe the tears from my eyes. 'What flavour?' I know the answer but I want to hear him say it.

Before he can, I'm pulled back to reality by a sickening pain as I'm thrown onto my stomach, both arms pulled tight behind my back. I try to lift my head but a knee presses hard into my kidneys.

I try to call for help but a hand pushes firmly against the back of my head, forcing my face into the pillow. I shout into the foam, the noise blurring around me. I try to snatch a breath but my mouth is rammed full of my sweat-stained pillowcase. Lungs screaming, I realise I'm suffocating.

I thrash like a fish on dry land, panic running through me. But the assailant is on my back, and with my head and arms pinned, I can do little more than judder. In seconds, I no longer have the energy for even that.

As the oxygen leaves my brain, I see Davey once again, his hand reaching out to me. I'm just about to grab it, when a different hand takes a fistful of my hair and drags my head backwards. My neck is pulled into an unnatural position but I don't care. I gulp down air. As my lungs fight to take in as much precious oxygen as possible, I barely register a sharp sting in my thigh.

When the room begins to sway, I realise I've been drugged. The hand lets go of my hair and my head flops forward, my spine unable to take its weight. The television is still on, a senseless noise in the background.

'Do exactly as I say.'

It's not the TV. The voice behind me sounds as if it has been through a machine. Deep, slow and unreal.

'If you don't do exactly what I say, I will kill you. Do you understand?'

I nod.

'I'm going to stand you up and we are going to walk out of here.'

My entire body has gone flaccid and numb. There's no way I'll be able to walk.

'If you don't do it I will kill you.'

I nod again and allow myself to be hauled upright. A strong arm around my waist prevents me from sinking into the ground.

'If you say one word, I will kill you.'

I know that even if I tried, my tongue would not be able to work its way around a sound, let alone a word. But I'm not going to try. Instead, I concentrate every fibre of my being on putting one foot in front of the other.

For I have learned some key lessons during these last few days. I want to do more with my life. I want to sort things out with my dad. I want to take control of my own destiny. And if I'm going to do any of these things, I must stay alive.

Chapter Nine

Rebecca is screamin' and cryin' and cryin' and screamin'. 'Hush up,' Isaac tells her.

But she ain't gonna stop until her throat gives out.

'I need to think,' Isaac says, more to himself than to any of the others. Yet he can't think. Not with all the noise and the blood.

Mama and Isaac had gone out into the yard to meet the policemen. Him shaking with fear, Mama with righteous indignation.

The fat one stepped forward. 'Mrs Pearson, let's talk about this like sensible folk before things get out of hand.'

There was a light in Mama's eye and Isaac knew she was past talking. She pointed her rifle right at them.

'Ma'am.' The other narrowed his eyes at her. 'You need to give us the guns before someone gets hurt.'

Mama laughed. 'You can't hurt us. God has asked us to be here today.' Isaac gulped hard, hand around his own rifle.

Mama had her finger on the trigger of hers. 'He shall gather together his elect from the four winds . . .'

'Ma'am.'

'. . . from the uttermost part of the earth.'

'This is your last warning,' he said.

Then she squeezed.

Or at least she meant to, but out of nowhere the policeman drew his own weapon and shot her. He was fast. The bullet clipped Mama's shoulder and she stumbled backwards. Yup, he was one fast shot.

But anyone will tell you, even Noah, that Isaac is fast too. Without even lining him up, Isaac fired back. The policeman made an 'oof' sound. Like when someone's punched you good. Then he dropped to the ground, a ripe apple in the fall.

The fat one panicked, dropped his gun and fell to his knees over his friend. Isaac took his chance and dragged Mama back inside.

Now here they are in the dark. Mama on the kitchen floor, her back leaning against the range. She's holding a cloth against her collarbone.

'You all right, Mama?' Veronica-Mae asks.

Mama smiles and strokes her hair. 'Just winged me, darlin'.'

Veronica-Mae looks at Isaac and he tries to smile, but he can see it's a whole lot worse than Mama's letting on. The blood is soaking right through, pooling on the tiles by Mama's side and she's panting hard, like a dog in July.

He creeps to the window and peeps through the chink in the shutters. The fat one has dragged the injured one under the trees and left him there all alone. Behind him, the sun is setting, covering the already stained yard in yet more red. Isaac just prays Daddy gets back soon.

The lights in the hotel staircase seem to flash. It's as if someone is using a strobe and my eyes strain to see the stairs and the handrail. I can hear my steps loud and thudding, the noise crashing in my ears, then it drifts away to silence. My arms are still held in place behind my back, and the hand holding me upright still feels firm.

At the bottom, three fire exits swirl in front of me. I can't say which one is real. We pass into the street outside. It's darker, but the beams from a lamp post skid towards me.

When I was much younger, I went through a clubbing period. Long nights spent dancing in hot warehouses. Most of my friends kicked off the evening with a pill or three, but not me. I was into my running and didn't want to feel like shit the next day. Sometimes, though, when I started yawning around two, my legs beginning to ache, I envied them, still up for it, bathed in sweat, yapping ten to the dozen. Well, if this was how they felt, good for them. I'm struggling not to vomit down my chest.

I'm led to a car and the boot pops open.

'Get in.'

I sway in front of it. I don't want to die, of that I'm sure. But I don't want to get in the boot either.

'I said get in.'

I try to lift my head to look for help, but I can't even manage that. I can't run. I can't shout. 'I can't get in,' I slur.

I needn't worry. The strong arms lift me up and I'm thrown roughly inside. I'm facing inwards, my nose inches from the far side. My knees are bent, my heels touching the back of my thighs. Then the lid is slammed down.

The sound of metal crashing into metal beats across my head and I see stars. I know that's a phrase you read in books without ever giving much thought to what it means. Well now I know. It means that all you can see is ink darkness punctuated by thousands of pinpricks of white light. Like the universe.

The car starts and I take a deep breath in a vain attempt to calm myself. The smell of disinfectant fills my nostrils. Someone has thoroughly cleaned this boot recently. Not a comforting thought.

Clem left Charlene's flat, grateful for a mouthful of fresh air. His emotions towards the poor kid were mixed. Part sadness, part revulsion.

The driver was checking a crack in his windscreen.

'Will it hold?' Clem asked.

'We'll soon see.'

Clem nodded and got in.

'Where to?' asked the driver.

It was a fair question. Connolly had been here hours ago and learned exactly the same as Clem. Paul Ronald was not Ronnie X. What did she do next? Head back to the smoke? He pulled out his phone and called Carole-Ann.

'Hey, Mr Grumpy,' she said.

'I need some information about Jo Connolly.'

'*The* Jo Connolly?'

'One and the same.'

Carole-Ann gave a gravelly burst of laughter. 'Now there's a girl with buns of steel.'

'I hadn't noticed.'

'Of course not,' Carole-Ann chuckled.

'I need to know where she is,' said Clem.

'Do you now?'

They both knew she wasn't meant to access this sort of information without clearance.

'It's important,' he said.

They both knew it went on every day of the week. Their job would be impossible otherwise.

Clem heard her nails tap a keyboard. He'd noticed they were a strange square shape and unnaturally white at the tips.

'She got a return rail ticket to Glasgow,' she said.

'Has she come back yet or is she still in Glasgow?'

'Let me check.'

Her fingers were still tapping furiously. 'Oh yeah, here we go. She used her credit card earlier tonight in Glasgow.'

'Where?'

'You going to tell me why you want to know this, Clem?'

'Ask me no questions, I'll tell you no lies.'

There was a small pause. Carole-Ann insisted on knowing the exact location of her field operatives at all times. She also demanded to know what they were doing. However, she accepted that there were times when it was best for all concerned if that were not the case. 'The Station Hotel,' she told him.

The receptionist swallowed a yawn as Clem approached.

'Can I help?'

'I believe a Miss Joanna Connolly is staying here,' he said.

'I'm afraid I can't give out any guest information,' she answered.

Clem gave a polite smile and laid his ID on the desk. The girl gave him a now familiar look of alarm and intrigue.

'Actually, I recognised her when I made the booking.' She glanced at the front page of the newspaper lying on her desk. 'I didn't let on, of course – that would have been unprofessional.'

Clem reached for the telephone. 'What room?'

'Two three one,' she said.

Clem punched the numbers and listened. Six rings and Connolly hadn't picked up.

'Could she have checked out?'

The girl shook her head. 'I've been on all night. She hasn't been down here.'

Clem let the phone ring three more times.

'She might be asleep,' the girl ventured. 'She was a bit, you know, merry.'

Clem laid the receiver back in the cradle. Was it possible Connolly had passed out? 'Can you take me up to her room?'

The girl squirmed. 'I'm not allowed to leave my post. Mr Radley, the manager, gets annoyed.'

'I'll square it with Mr Radley if I have to,' said Clem.

She smiled and left her station. 'I'm glad to stretch my legs as it goes.' She led Clem into the lift. 'It gets awful boring.'

Clem wished, just occasionally, that the same could be said for his job.

They exited on the second floor and the girl hustled over to the door of room 231. There was a newspaper on the floor, the front page ripped as if someone had trodden on it. The picture of Jo's face had been torn in two.

'That's odd,' said the girl. 'She didn't order a paper.'

Clem kept himself in check. Connolly was probably sprawled on the bed, a rom-com on pay-per-view.

The girl gave three raps with her knuckle. No answer. She rapped again, more quickly. 'Miss Connolly,' she called. 'Miss Connolly.' She looked at Clem, concern knitting her eyebrows.

'Do you have a pass key?' Clem asked.

'Yes, but Mr Radley . . .'

'Forget Mr Radley and open the door.'

She frowned and did as she was told, opening the door with her left hand and reaching in to turn on the light with her right.

They stepped inside. Nothing was out of place. The bedclothes were wrinkled but that was all. Connolly's laptop, mobile and purse were all still on the bedside table. But there was no sign of the woman herself.

The girl checked the bathroom. 'Where could she have gone?' she asked.

Clem was wondering the same thing and glanced again at the items on the bedside table. Something was very wrong.

'Is there a bar? A gym?'

'All closed,' she said. 'Anyway, she would have had to come past reception to get there and I would have seen her.'

'Is there any other way out of the hotel?'

'Only the fire exit,' she said. 'But where would she go without her stuff?'

'Show me,' said Clem.

She gestured out of the room and down the corridor to a door at the far end. Clem jogged over and opened it. The stairwell was cold and concrete. Empty. He hurried down, scanning for any sign that Connolly had been there. At the bottom was the door leading out onto the street. He threw it open and looked outside. Nothing.

Back on the second floor, catching his breath, Clem heard raised voices from Connolly's room. A man with slip-on shoes worn away at the heel was giving the girl a telling-off.

'How many times have you been told, Iona? You cannot leave the front desk.' His hands were on his hips, half hidden by the flesh overhanging his belt. 'It will have to be a warning this time.'

'Mr Radley, no,' she said. 'If you'll just let me explain. I . . . I—'

'There is no "I" in team,' he said.

Clem snorted through his nose. No 'I' in team! Who made this crap up? 'Mr Radley,' he said. 'I think I can help.'

The manager threw Clem a look of disdain. 'And who might you be?'

Clem flashed his ID. 'Christian Clement.'

'MI5?' The man's eyes were wide in his pink face.

'I elicited your receptionist's help. I needed immediate access to this room.'

'I see. May I ask why?'

'No, you may not, and in the meantime I need to borrow her further,' said Clem.

He grasped the girl's elbow and drew her into the corridor. 'Is that CCTV?' He pointed to a camera high on the wall.

'Yeah.'

'Film in it?' Clem crossed his fingers. Half these security measures were all fur coat and no knickers.

'Put it in myself this afternoon,' she beamed at him.

'Excellent.'

She gave Mr Radley a backwards glance. 'Some people say it's a waste of time and money.'

'Some people don't know what they're talking about,' Clem replied.

Rory rocks back and forth, his hands over his ears. He has been doing this for an hour but still has a pain in his chest. A doctor once asked him if the pain felt like having something heavy placed there, but Rory was not able to confirm this as he has never had anything heavy placed on his chest.

He reaches into his pocket and pulls out the string. He holds one end between the finger and thumb of his right hand and drags the thumb and finger of his left hand along the length. When his left thumb and finger reach the end, he drops the other end. Then he drags his right thumb and finger along the length. He repeats this process until the pain begins to ease.

He has had the pain since Ronnie called him.

'I'm sorry,' Ronnie said. Ronnie knows Rory does not like speaking on the telephone.

'It's an emergency,' Ronnie said.

Rory knows what an emergency is. He once cut his hand on a knife and tried to stop it bleeding with a scarf. Four days later his hand swelled up and he kept being sick. Ronnie took him to hospital. When the nurse peeled away the scarf, there was a lot of yellow pus. She said he had septicaemia. This is an example of an emergency.

'I need to come back to your place,' said Ronnie.

Rory didn't answer.

'I'll have someone else with me,' said Ronnie.

That's when the pain started.

★　★　★

Clem looked over Iona's shoulder at the screen. She pressed fast-forward until she reached 21.09. 'This is her arriving,' she said.

Indeed, there was Connolly unlocking the door to her room. She dropped her key and bent to retrieve it, her left hand leaning heavily on the wall.

'Told you she was a bit pished.'

Clem nodded. Connolly did look tipsy. But drunk enough to wander off into the night without cash or phone?

Iona fast-forwarded again until two figures came out of the lift.

'Stop here,' Clem instructed.

Iona played the tape at normal speed so they could watch the couple giggle and kiss their way down their corridor. They paused outside room 231 and Clem tensed. The male nuzzled into the woman's breasts and ran his hands over her arse. Over his shoulder, the woman checked her watch while the man continued, oblivious.

'It's good to know romance isn't dead,' said Clem.

They watched the couple move along the corridor and disappear into another room. Nothing suspicious.

Iona speeded up the tape again, stopping of her own volition when a member of staff in regulation sweatshirt and baseball cap arrived with a stack of newspapers. He went along the corridor, leaving a copy at regular intervals. When he got to Connolly's room, he laid it carefully on the carpet, brushing the door handle briefly as he rose.

'Who is that?' Clem asked.

Iona squinted at the screen. 'Dunno. Could be one of the Polish lads. They say they're over eighteen but some of them are pretty wee.'

'Can you zoom in?'

Iona did as she was asked, but the angle of the camera and the cap made it impossible to get a good look at his face.

Clem asked Iona to move on and the film played until Connolly's door opened. At first just a crack, then finally, Jo herself looked outside. Her hair was dishevelled as she peered up and down. Something had woken her. The newspaper boy in all probability. When she looked down at the newspaper she smiled and shut her door.

'Keep it running,' said Clem.

The tape continued to play for another ten minutes, with no further activity on the second floor. Clem was beginning to wonder if this was a waste of time when the fire exit door opened and a figure emerged. It was the newspaper boy again.

'Why would he come in that way?' asked Clem.

'No idea,' said Iona. 'He shouldn't do.'

This time he moved swiftly and directly to Connolly's room, where he let himself in.

'Shit,' said Iona.

'Shit indeed,' thought Clem.

Another five minutes elapsed and the hotel room door opened. Clem watched in horror as Connolly was led out by the newspaper boy. She was holding her head at an odd angle as she listed to the side.

'She really has had a skinful,' said Iona.

Clem wasn't convinced. The way Connolly was clawing the ground with her feet before each step, and the fact that the newspaper boy's hands were planted behind her back, told a different story. They passed towards the fire exit, the newspaper boy guiding, Connolly stumbling. When they reached the door, Connolly leaned into her companion, pushing the brim of his cap backwards.

'Zoom?' Iona asked, though she had already begun before Clem's answer.

The picture was grainy and blurred. 'It's not great quality, I'm afraid,' she said.

It didn't matter. Clem recognised the face and couldn't believe how stupid he had been.

I wake with the mother of all headaches. It pulses in my temples with an angry ferocity. Each throb like a punch. My arms are still restrained tightly behind my back, all feeling lost.

I open one eye to ground myself and find I am on a green duvet. It smells of soap.

Throughout the long journey in the boot of the car, I fell in and out of consciousness. When I say long, I don't actually know. I was so out of it, I could have been in there minutes, hours, even days. I remember the car stopping and being bundled out. There were some stairs to a flat. After that there's nothing more, so I assume I'm in that flat, though again, I can't be certain.

I move my head, gagging at the pain that movement brings. To the right is a desk, piled high with books. They look like textbooks rather than novels. The wall behind is the same green as the duvet cover. Not similar. Exactly the same. It feels like being inside a pea.

A shadow falls across the desk and I crane my neck to see. There's a man in the doorway. Is this who came to my hotel room and forced me out? He doesn't seem familiar. For a start he's huge – at least six foot and eighteen stone. His face is as round and smooth as a pumpkin. I recall a much smaller arm around my waist. A slighter frame. Though I can't be sure.

The man stares at me without blinking, a thick tongue protruding from between his lips.

'What do you want from me?' I ask.

The man doesn't answer but takes a step closer. I can see now that he has no hair whatsoever on his big pink head, like an obscene oversized baby.

'Did you bring me here?' I ask.

The man shakes his head.

'If you didn't bring me here, then who did?'

The man's lips form a word. He doesn't say it out loud, but I can work it out. Ronnie. My heart lurches. Ronnie X. Criminal. Terrorist.

A vision of the roof of the Plaza falling in on me flits across my mind's eye. I swallow hard, trying to control myself. 'Where is Ronnie?'

The man checks his watch, pressing a button on the side. 'Ronnie has business elsewhere and will come back in thirteen minutes.' He speaks in a singsong voice, as if he were announcing a train arrival.

I struggle to turn and face him but he doesn't move, just stares. It's unsettling but I don't get the sense he means me any harm. Which is more than can be said for Ronnie X. Something tells me that I don't want to wait around for Ronnie.

It's obvious to me now that there's something different about this guy. Whatever it is, I must use it to my advantage and get out of here.

'I need to use the bathroom,' I say.

The man shakes his head.

'Seriously,' I persist. 'If I don't go to the loo, I'm going to pee myself. Is that what you want?'

The man looks aghast. 'No, because that will smell very bad.'

'Yup.'

The man looks around the bedroom in a panic. Everything is neat. Everything smells clean.

'I wouldn't want to make a mess on this duvet,' I say. 'It might even sink through to the mattress.'

The man gasps and begins tapping his forehead with the palm of his right hand.

'Why don't you just help me to the bathroom?' I say.

'Ronnie said you must stay in this room.'

112

'You could get me back in here before Ronnie gets back.'

The man closes his eyes and gives a low moan.

'If you don't take me now,' I press him, 'it will be too late.'

Panting, he shuffles forward, his belly wobbling where his T-shirt doesn't reach his trousers. He pauses by the side of the bed and screws his eyes tight shut again, as if steeling himself. Close up, I can see he has no eyebrows either. He takes a deep breath, his nostrils flaring, then he grabs me by the arm and pulls me off the bed. I hit the floor, jarring my shoulder and banging my hip.

'Hold on,' I shout, but he doesn't.

Instead, he drags me across the carpet and out of the bedroom before depositing me outside the bathroom. He points inside and grunts.

'You'll have to help me up,' I say.

He wrinkles his nose as if he doesn't want to touch me again, then lunges forward and hauls me to my feet. When I'm standing he drops his hand and moves back.

'Could you untie me?' I turn my back to him and wiggle my fingers.

He doesn't reply.

'The thing is,' I say, 'if you don't untie me, then you'll have to take down my trousers and underwear.'

He lets out a feral cry.

'Exactly,' I say. 'You really don't want to do that, do you?'

'No.'

'Can't say I blame you, so just release my hands and I'll do it myself. Then you can tie them straight back up again, can't you?'

'Yes, I can do that,' he says. He doesn't move though, just stares at me.

'What are you worried about?' I ask.

'Your hands will be dirty afterwards,' he says. 'There will be germs present.'

113

'I'll scrub them very well,' I reply, nodding at the bottle of anti-bacterial handwash on the sink. 'I'll use plenty of that, okay?'

'If you touch that, you will transfer your germs,' he says.

I try not to scream. His thought processes remind me of Davey. You could spend half an hour trying to convince my brother that buses were safe, only for him to jump out of an upstairs window.

'I will hold out my hands and you can squirt the soap into them,' I say. 'I won't touch the bottle.'

He pauses, once again tapping his forehead. Time is running out.

'I really need to go now.' I use a whiny voice.

He pushes his tongue back between his lips and moves towards the rope. As he loosens the knot, it chafes the skin on my wrist but I grit my teeth so as not to make a sound.

At last he is finished and takes a step back. He holds the length of rope in one hand, running his other hand along it. Then he changes hands. He watches his fingers intently while he repeats the process. Now's my chance. Sorry, mate, but I don't have a choice here.

I pull back my arm, ignoring the agonising cramp, and punch him. I've never actually hit anyone before and am surprised by the crunch my fist makes as it connects with his nose.

He drops the rope and screams, blood pouring down his mouth and chin. 'You hit me!' His voice is filled with confusion.

Seizing my opportunity, I rush forward, pushing him aside.

'You hit me,' he says again.

I run down the hallway to the door and yank the handle. It's locked. Of course it's locked. I look back at the man, still in the same spot, blood now dripping down his T-shirt and pooling at his feet.

'Where's the key?' I scream.

He doesn't answer.

'Where is the fucking key?'

His eyes flick towards a set of drawers and I wrench the top one open.

'Christ.' There are probably twenty keys in there. 'Which one is it?' I shout, but the man has started rocking back and forth.

I grab a handful and start trying them, flinging them to one side when they don't fit. Didn't he say Ronnie would be back in thirteen minutes? How much time has elapsed? Fear makes me fumble and I drop a small brass key that spins away, coming to a halt under the set of drawers. I fall to my knees and prise my fingers into the gap. It's too small. I push at the drawers, hoping to move them backwards, but they're far heavier than they look. I have to get that key.

I jump to my feet and heave. The damn thing won't budge, but I'm not giving up. I can't. I press the weight of my entire body against it, feeling it give an inch. 'Yes!'

This time, I bare my teeth and howl as I push with all my might. The drawers move. Only slightly, but it's enough. I can see the edge of the key peeking out and I gently slide it towards me.

With shaking fingers I put it into the lock. It fits. I turn it with a sense of elation.

I'm free. I'm getting out of here. Laughing, I fling open the door.

Then I stop dead in my tracks. My way is barred.

It's a woman in her mid-twenties. Tall and slim, she's dressed head to toe in black, the same colour as her hair. Her skin is so white it's almost translucent and her eyes are like fish scales.

'Where do you think you're going, Jo?' she asks.

In that second, I know exactly who she is.

This is Ronnie X.

Chapter Ten

'Are you okay?' Iona eyed Clem nervously.

Clem hadn't spoken for some time. His recognition of Connolly's captor was like a slap in the face. How had he been so blind? As soon as he'd seen the face on tape, he'd recognised the girl on the plane. She'd been wearing dark glasses then, but it was her. The skin, the raven-wing hair. The bitch had been on her way to take Connolly. She'd been sitting feet from Clem the whole journey.

He slammed his fist on the desk, causing papers to scatter and cups to jump. Iona squealed. 'Sorry,' he muttered.

He'd been so caught up in his anger with Connolly, he hadn't been paying attention. He'd dismissed the girl as some C-list celebrity he'd glimpsed in a magazine. If only he'd given himself a second to go through his memory bank he would have known. He would have remembered her and he would have known where from.

It was the café in Bethnal Green. He'd been watching the cell over a greasy table, flicking through information on his iPad. Someone had asked him about it. A waitress. She'd been watching him, checking what he was reading.

'Damn!' He punched the desk again.

Ronnie X had ridden the tide of assumptions made about her and stayed one jump ahead. She was ruthless and violent. That

much was obvious from the Plaza bomb. Now he knew something else about her – she was clever.

And she had just kidnapped Jo Connolly.

I'm flat out on the carpet, my cheek pressed into the weave. In
the split second it took me to understand that the woman in front
of me was Ronnie, she punched me twice in the face, knocking
me to the ground and retying my hands. She is strong and moves
with a deftness I might admire under different circumstances.

When she's satisfied that I'm disabled she moves towards Rory,
who is still rocking and crooning, reminding me of those orphans,
that filled our telly screens after the fall of communism in
Romania. My mum said it was the mark of a civilised society how
it dealt with its young and weak. My dad didn't say anything.

Ronnie doesn't touch him but stands a good foot away, her
hands in the surrender position. 'Can I help you, Rory?' she asks.

He doesn't answer, doesn't even acknowledge she has spoken.

'I won't touch you with my hands.' Her voice is firm but calm.
'I'll use a towel to wipe up all this blood.'

Not a flicker.

'I'll use the towel on the rail in the bathroom,' she says. Then
she moves past me to the bathroom and grabs a green towel.

'You broke his fucking nose, you stupid bitch,' she spits at me
me, her face contorted by anger.

She moves back to Rory and holds out the towel.

He looks at it, then at Ronnie.

'Are you worried about the blood, Rory?' she asks.

'There are bacteria in blood. They multiply on contact with
the air.'

Ronnie nods. 'That's true, Rory, which is why as soon as we've
got you cleaned up, I will place this towel in a plastic bag and
throw it in the dustbin outside, okay?'

Rory looks puzzled. 'Then I'll only have three towels.'

'I will buy another one to replace it,' says Ronnie. 'Then you'll have four as normal. Is that right?'

'I like four,' says Rory.

'I know that,' Ronnie replies. 'So shall I clean you up?'

They gaze at one another, Ronnie patiently and silently holding out the towel.

'Okay,' says Rory.

Ronnie exhales. 'Excellent. Now let's move into the bathroom.'

Rory shuffles in, a trail of blood following him. Ronnie turns to me and pulls out a gun. 'Don't move a fucking muscle.'

I lie still and listen as Ronnie talks Rory through every move.

'I'm putting the towel under the tap.

'I'm going to wipe your face with downward strokes.

'I'm going to hold the towel against the bridge of your nose.'

I have to get out of here. But how? My hands are tied and the door is locked. I breathe through my panic to keep my mind clear.

When they emerge, Rory is bare-chested, his flesh hanging in rolls, skin criss-crossed with stretch marks, his nostrils plugged with toilet paper.

'You should lie down on your bed, Rory,' she tells him.

He stops short and shakes his head.

Ronnie presses her lips together. 'I'll change the duvet cover.'

With impressive speed, she rips off the bedcover I was lying on earlier, and whips on an exact replica.

'Lie down now,' she says, and Rory does as he is told.

When she closes the door, my heart thuds. The look in her eye is one of wild, dark fury. 'I should kill you.' She towers over me. 'I'd fucking enjoy it, too.'

I grit my teeth, anticipating a kick in the ribs. Or worse. Instead, Ronnie strides away to the kitchen. My mind turns to carving knives, but when she returns she is carrying a glass of water.

She pulls me into a sitting position with her free hand, throwing me against the wall. I'm tempted to kick out at her, but I sense she'd just smash the glass in my face. Her eyes glitter as she watches me over the rim.

'You've been trying to locate me,' she says, a drop of water shining on her lower lip.

'No,' I reply.

'Don't fuck with me,' she warns.

'I'm not.'

With a snap of her wrist, she hurls the glass against the wall and it shatters above my head, showering me with shards. 'I said don't fuck with me.'

'Okay, okay.' My heart pounds, the crash ringing in my ears.

'Why have you been following me?' she asks.

'I spoke to Miggs before he died. He mentioned you.'

She narrows her eyes. 'He would never tell you anything.'

'He thought I was you.'

She looks me up and down. 'Not exactly flattering.'

'He was pretty out of it.'

She rubs a knuckle against her teeth, a silver ring rattling against the enamel.

'What did he say?'

'That I – you – should get away.'

Her face is impassive. If she is moved by Miggs's protectiveness, she doesn't show it. 'What made you start digging up old files at Social Services?'

'Miggs mentioned an orchard,' I say. 'I just dug around on the internet until I found a children's home in Glasgow. It seemed like it might fit.'

'Why?'

'Why what?'

'Why bother with all this crap? Tracking us down? Coming to Glasgow? When was the last time someone like you even left

119

Westminster?' There's malice in her voice. 'What makes someone like *you* interested in people like *us*?'

'I was nearly killed in the Plaza bomb.' The vehemence in my voice shocks me. I'm scared shitless, but I refuse to be cowed by someone like Ronnie. 'I've seen up close what people like you are capable of.'

'Why not leave it to your little friends in MI5?' she asks.

I think about Clem, solid and serious. Why didn't I just leave all this to him? Then I picture him with Benning and the PM, and recall all the double dealings, the unanswered questions.

'They told me Shining Light was responsible for the bomb attack and that you were in charge,' I say. 'I wanted to be sure you weren't a scapegoat.'

She leans towards me, her eyes empty, her skin so white she could be one of those left for dead in the stadium. 'A scapegoat,' she repeats.

Then she shrugs. In that shrug I can see she doesn't care. The mangled bodies of children being stretchered away mean nothing. I could kick myself, and the old man for good measure, for all the doubts and soul searching.

'And now you've found me,' she says, 'what do you think?'

'I think I've been wasting my time.'

Clem stepped away from Iona's desk, pulled out his mobile and punched in the number for Glasgow Social Services.

'Debbie McAndrews.' She sounded tired.

'Christian Clement.'

'Oh.' Mrs McAndrews had obviously hoped never to hear from him again. He often had that effect upon people.

'Did any girls stay at The Orchard?'

'For the most part, residential units were single sex,' she said. 'We found there were fewer problems that way.'

Clem could well imagine that a house full of uncontrollable teens with their hormones popping would be a force to be reckoned with.

'There was, however, a short period when government policy overrode good sense,' she continued.

'When was that?'

'2003.'

That would have coincided with Miggs's placement. 'Could you send me the names of every girl that stayed there, and their file?' he asked.

'Fine.'

Seconds later he was scrolling through a short list of names.

Fiona Anderson
Bonnie Fairfax
Ann-Marie Ireland
Catriona Keith
Margaret Lawrence
Lara MacDonald
Veronica Pearson
Lindsay Rae
Chloe Wilson

Nine girls. All troubled, unwanted and damaged. One grew up to become a terrorist.

Where are you?

He read the list again and smiled. Veronica Pearson.

'Hello, Ronnie.'

Ronnie straightens abruptly and stalks back to the bedroom door, which she taps gently.

'I'm going to come in,' she calls.

She opens the door and I catch a glimpse of Rory curled in the foetal position on the bed, his hands covering his face.

'We're going to leave now,' Ronnie tells him.

Rory doesn't move.

'Don't answer your phone or open the door to anyone but me,' she says. 'I'll be back when I've figured this out. Okay?'

'She hit me.' Rory's voice is muffled.

'I know,' she replies and casts me another look of contempt. 'You owe him,' she tells me.

As quietly as possible, she closes the door, then springs towards me. Her movements are more animal than human,

'Come on.' She drags me to my feet and pushes me down the hallway, pieces of glass falling onto my face from my scalp. I blink to protect my eyes.

'Are you going to do as I say, or do I need this?' She extracts a syringe from her pocket.

If I'm going to find a way out of this I must avoid being drugged again. 'I'll do as you say.'

'Good.' She opens the door and leads me outside, her hand keeping pressure on the rope around my wrists. I glance at the deserted street, calculating how long it would take me to run to the crossroads.

'Don't even think about it,' she says and I feel the cold metal of her gun in the small of my back.

There's a car on the street outside and my stomach lurches at the thought of getting in the boot again. 'Please let me sit in the back,' I beg. Panic is starting to rise in my throat.

Ronnie doesn't answer, but checks up and down the street, assuring herself that there is no one around.

'I won't speak,' I say. 'I won't even move.'

She pauses as if she's thinking this through, then moves to the back and opens the boot. She presses a piece of tape across my mouth. 'Forget it.'

The plane was ready for takeoff, engines roaring, when Clem boarded. The other passengers threw him annoyed looks and checked their watches.

His phone rang as he was shown to his seat.

'No mobile phones, sir,' the stewardess told him.

'Safe network,' he informed her and answered the call.

'Hey, Clem.' It was Carole-Ann. 'How's the friendly north?'

Clem looked up at the stewardess, who was scowling at him.

'Cold,' he said.

'Well, I hope you're hauling your ass back here,' she said. 'You're due to see the PM in an hour.'

'Tell him I'm going to be late.'

'Your funeral,' she said.

'Trust me, a funeral would be light relief from the sort of day I'm having.'

'Did you need anything else?' she asked.

'Information on Veronica Pearson, date of birth 6 April 1989.'

'What sort of information?'

'Anything and everything.'

He hung up and waited. Hopefully, Carole-Ann would have something for him soon. In the meantime, he tried to make sense of last night's events. Why had Ronnie risked coming out into the open? Connolly had tried to dig around but had met with a dead end. Perhaps Ronnie was worried that with her connection to The Orchard, it was only a matter of time until Connolly worked it out. Perhaps she needed to know how close Jo had got.

Or perhaps it was too good an opportunity to miss. A kidnapping on this scale would be a coup for small fry like Shining Light.

Another darker thought snaked in. Perhaps Ronnie had just taken Connolly somewhere and killed her, and a bleary-eyed postman would spot her leg poking out of a green wheelie bin this morning.

His thoughts were interrupted by an email from HQ.

To: Christian Clement
From: Carole-Ann Bowers
Re: Little Miss Nobody

No known address, no marriage or death certificate. No tax paid ever. No benefits claimed. No credit cards, no medical records. Not even a poxy driving licence.

It's as if after leaving The Orchard, your girl fell off the face of the earth.

Clem exhaled. This wasn't good at all.

His mood was grey as he got off the plane and made his way over to his car. Then he growled when he spotted the dent he'd made in the bumper. It looked worse in daylight.

When he arrived at Downing Street, the grey clouds turned to black.

'You're late,' Benning, the attack dog, barked.

'I told you I was going to Glasgow.'

Benning waved him away.

'Have you seen the papers?' asked the PM.

Clem clocked the array set out on his desk. Everything from the *Morning Star* to the *Telegraph* was headlining the shooting of Miggs. 'It was bound to be the main story,' he shrugged.

Benning shook his head. 'Unless you've missed it, the Opening Ceremony starts later today. That should have been the main story.'

'I guess the editors thought this was a bigger deal,' said Clem.

'We have to minimise this,' Benning insisted.

'I don't really see how we can.'

Benning rolled his eyes. 'For a start we need you here, Clem. We're telling everyone we've dealt with this. That security is under control. Yet our man in charge of security is away on a jolly.'

Clem breathed out hard. 'Security is the reason I was in Glasgow.'

'You need to be visible,' said Benning.

'I think first and foremost you need me to catch the outstanding terrorist,' said Clem. They might be telling everyone that things were tickety-boo, but that wasn't the full story, was it?

The PM leaned forward. 'How did you get on? Is the outstanding terrorist in custody?'

'And where the hell is Connolly?' Benning groaned. 'She hasn't been seen since yesterday morning and she's not answering her phone. She should be here pressing palms and giving interviews.'

Clem pushed a hand through his hair. 'I'm afraid I've got some bad news on both counts.'

Once again, I can't say how long I've been in the claustrophobic prison of the boot. Even without the mind-bending effect of the drugs, it's impossible to know how time is stretching. Instead, I concentrate on my breathing and assuaging my panic. The engine roars and I feel every bump in the road as my head lifts and crashes back against thinly covered metal.

At last, a different sound punctuates the rush of tyres and my heart swells. A siren. As the car slows and the blare of the siren nears, I almost whoop with joy. It's the police. They've found me.

The car pulls to a stop and I listen intently.

'Can I help you, officer?' Ronnie's voice is syrup.

'Your left brake light isn't working,' says a man.

'Oh dear.' She's a study in concern. 'Is that very dangerous?'

I hear footsteps around the car and imagine her peering intently at the offending light.

'It's not ideal,' the man replies. 'Do you have far to go?'

'Only a few miles,' says Ronnie.

The policeman doesn't know I'm in here and if I don't let him know soon, Ronnie will sweet talk him into buggering off.

'I'd get along home if I were you,' he says. 'But you must get it checked out immediately.'

'I will.'

It's now or never. I can't shout out with the tape, nor can I hit the roof of the boot with my hands tied. Even my legs are bent in an impossible position so I can't lift them and kick out. The only part of me I have any control over is my head. I lift it up as far as I can and whack it against the floor of the boot. The pain and noise ring through my skull but I lift my neck and try again. My ear feels as though it has been hit by a hammer.

'What was that?' asks the policeman.

'What was what?' Ronnie asks in return.

'I thought I heard a banging.'

Ronnie laughs and whacks the boot repeatedly. 'This old girl makes a lot of strange noises. Bit knackered, but well loved.'

I lift my head up and crash it against the metal for the third time. I know I won't be able to do it again and hope the policeman has heard me.

In answer, Ronnie thumps the boot lid again. 'Better be off,' she says. 'The sooner I get her seen by a mechanic the better.'

As the engine starts up and we drive away, I know I have made a huge mistake. My chest constricts with fear and I can't force any air into my lungs.

When the car pulls over and the boot lid is thrown open I am gasping for air.

Ronnie hovers over me, her face contorted by anger. 'What the fuck did you think you were doing?'

I'm writhing around like an injured snake. She leans over and rips off the tape. I barely notice the sting as it takes the top layer of skin on my lips with it.

She reaches in and lifts my head until my breathing calms. 'You were banging,' she says. 'I told you what would happen if you messed me around.'

'Couldn't breathe,' I whisper. 'Panicked.'

She stares at me, her face inches from mine, then she lets go of my head, letting it thump back down. 'You'd better pray I drive quickly,' she says and pushes the tape back over my mouth.

When the boot lid crashes shut once again, I know I came very close indeed to pushing Ronnie too far.

I've sunk into a state of semi-consciousness when the car turns sharply to the right. The road disappears beneath me, replaced by ruts and bumps which throw me around like a fairground ride.

Fear bubbles under my skin. Is Ronnie taking me somewhere inaccessible to dispose of me? From what I've seen, she's perfectly capable of forcing me to dig my own grave and tossing me in. The car stops and I steel myself.

As soon as the boot opens it hits me. A shock of cold wind, like the inside of a fridge, carrying with it the tang of salt. Above, seagulls circle, their call a melancholy welcome.

Ronnie pulls me out onto my cramped legs. My knees crack and my feet sink into a patch of grass barely covering the sand beneath. When she pushes me forward, I catch my breath. We are at the very edge of a cliff. Before us, only sky and miles of grey ocean. Waves crash against rocks hundreds of feet below, creating an angry stew of foam that rises and falls, reaching up to us but being dragged down before it can swallow us whole.

Dizzy, I step back, the wind slicing my cheeks.

Ronnie puts the now familiar pressure of her gun on my spine and leads me along the cliff top to a place where the land falls away. We descend into a small valley, battered and flattened by the storms, home to three derelict caravans, their smashed windows boarded up with the sides of packing boxes and black bin liners, secured with tape but billowing in the wind like sails.

Ronnie shoves me towards the one perched on the edge, its paint pitted with rust, metal panels shaking, wheels replaced by piles of bricks. She pulls out a key, opens the door and pushes me inside. The metal steps clang under me and I enter the darkness.

Out of the direct assault of the elements, it feels warmer, though the walls still shudder with each violent gust of wind.

I recall an ex-boyfriend who lived almost on top of West Hampstead train station. During rush hour the flat rattled with a seismic force that threatened to roll us out of bed. He was cute, as I remember, and funny. Heavily into indie music, cooking and me. I'm not sure now why I left him. Something to do with a weekend away in Devon with his friends and my usual inability to commit. I hope he's found someone who appreciates him.

There's a small pop and a gas lamp bathes the caravan in a weak, jaundiced glow.

I gulp as I take in the ripped upholstery and the mould on the rug. Ronnie has her back to me as she locks the door, revealing the gun sticking out of her waistband.

This place is so deserted no one will ever find me. But what am I doing here? What does Ronnie want? And staring at the gun, I wonder why I'm still alive. At last she turns, the sickly light making her skin yellow. She bares her teeth at me and I shiver.

'You're probably wondering why you're still alive,' she says.

★ ★ ★

Isaac keeps guard at the shutters. Outside the forces of evil have gathered. At the edges of the yard and in the undergrowth beyond, policemen are crouched, rifles trained on the farmhouse.

'How many?' Mama's voice is real weak.

Isaac counts. One, two, three, four . . . like the grains of sand on a beach.

'Fifteen,' he says. 'Maybe more.'

Mama slumps forward in her pool of blood. So much blood. Even Rebecca has stopped her crying, horrified by the amount of it.

'You okay, Mama?' Veronica-Mae asks.

Mama tries to lift her head, but doesn't have it left in her. 'Though I walk through the dark valley of death,' her voice is fading, 'I will not be afraid . . .'

'Mama?' Veronica-Mae shakes her.

She falls to the side, her eyes rolled back in her head. All three children hold their breath until the silence is broken by someone calling to them through one of those bullhorns.

'Lay down your weapons and come out now.'

The fat one is long gone, replaced by someone who ain't even from these parts. He's been hollering at them for over an hour. Mama said she weren't likely to take orders from a damn Yankee.

Isaac glances over at her lifeless body. She ain't got nothing to say no more.

'What do you think, Isaac?' Veronica-Mae looks at him with those wide eyes of hers.

'What do you mean?'

'Did we oughta do what he says?'

Mama would say no to that. But Mama can't help now. Isaac has to make the decision.

'If we don't, Mama's gonna bleed out and die,' says Veronica-Mae.

It's true. If she ain't past saving already.

'And then they're gonna come in and shoot us all,' Veronica-Mae says.

Rebecca starts blubbing again. 'Let's do it, Isaac. Please. I don't wanna get shot.'

Nor does he. He nods and presses his mouth to the shutter. 'All right then, we're coming out.'

There's a commotion outside. A buzz of talk and movement.

'Is that you, Isaac?' the policeman asks.

'Yes, sir.'

'Can I speak to your mama?'

'She's out cold, sir,' he calls back. 'She needs a doc real bad.'

There's a pause filled with more muttering. 'The paramedics are already here, son,' he says.

Isaac doesn't know what a paramedic is, but he wants this to be over with as soon as possible so he ain't going to argue. 'All right then, we're going to come on out now.'

'Hold on, hold on.' The policeman sounds panicky. 'We need to explain how this is going to happen.'

Isaac and his sisters look at one another and shrug. Surely they're just going to open the door and step out into the yard?

'I need you to follow my instructions carefully,' the policeman says.

'All right,' replies Isaac.

'First, I want you to come out slowly, one by one. Slowly. Do you understand me?'

'Yes, sir.'

'And I need you to be unarmed with your hands on your heads.'

'Okay.'

'If the officers see your hands move they will open fire, do you hear me?'

'Yes.'

'Right then, let's do this.'

With that, Isaac leads his sisters to the door. He opens it and blinks into the dusk. The air outside is cooler and smells of purple Heal-All. Fireflies dart past. He puts his hands on his head, mindful of the patches of sweat under his arms. Then he gestures to his sisters to copy him.

Soon, they are standing in the yard in a row, elbows out wide. Three policemen in special uniforms, not the regular kind, walk towards them, shotguns pointing right at their heads. Rebecca sobs. Veronica-Mae purses her lips, trying not to let the tears come. Isaac does the same.

'They're just checking we ain't got our guns, then they'll put theirs down,' he says.

Suddenly there's a noise from the left, dry twigs cracking, boots on dusty earth.

'Daddy!' Rebecca screams.

The policemen turn towards the noise, their sights now on Daddy. Noah lets out a shout, reaching for his own weapon.

'Daddy!' Rebecca screams again and flies off towards him. Veronica-Mae takes two steps after her.

'No!' Isaac shouts.

Too late.

The police open fire, bullets searing through the air. Rebecca falls, the nape of her neck an open mess of blood and bone. Noah fires back, until he too drops to the ground.

Veronica-Mae stops in her tracks, and spins back to Isaac, her arms out to be scooped up.

The look on her face is the last thing he sees before a bullet passes through her shoulder and into his chest.

Chapter Eleven

I look around me for something, anything, to cut my binds. Ronnie left five minutes ago and I don't know how long I have before she returns. She's left me with my wrists tied behind my back and my ankles bound together. My mouth isn't taped, but given the location of the caravan and the shrieking of the wind outside, I could scream for the next week and no one would hear me.

The window frame to my right looks old and rusted. It might be sharp enough to cut through the length of rope wound repeatedly around my hands. If I can just get to it.

Before she locked the door behind her, Ronnie told me not to move. 'I can't think of one good reason why I haven't killed you already,' she said. 'So don't give me an excuse.'

She meant it, too. Something in her is dead and she would happily do it. Not happily, no – that's the wrong word. Draining the life from me wouldn't give her pleasure, but it wouldn't cause her pain either. She wouldn't feel anything, and that is an infinitely more frightening thought.

I watched her open the fridge and take out a small bottle of water. She took a drink and grimaced. 'It's warm,' she said.

I was so thirsty my tongue was stuck to the roof of my mouth. 'What are you going to do with me?' I asked.

She didn't reply but took another snatch of water. The lights began to flicker, casting her face in shadow. She remained as if transfixed, then slipped towards a gas canister in the kitchen, her movements strange and unearthly. A trick of the light.

'Almost empty,' she said and disconnected a black rubber tube, plunging the room into darkness.

It took a moment for my eyes to adjust. I blinked and saw Ronnie bent over the canister, pulling it onto its edge so she could roll it to the caravan door. Deftly, she pulled at the lock with one hand remaining on the metal side of the canister, then kicked the door so that it swung out. In seconds she had it outside and I could hear the clunk as she pulled it down the steps.

Something told me Ronnie had been here and performed this manoeuvre many times before. In a heartbeat she appeared again with a different canister, pushing it in front of her. She was almost inside when a gust of wind howled, making the caravan shudder and the door slam shut, catching her left shoulder. She didn't cry out but her face told me the blow had been hard. Once she had the canister in place she reconnected it and the lights came on with another pop.

Ronnie stood upright, rotated her injured shoulder and winced. She turned her back to me and shrugged off her leather jacket, exposing a tight black vest beneath. I gasped. There was a red welt. But that wasn't what grabbed my attention.

It was the scar. The skin from the nape of her neck to her left bicep was a mass of scar tissue, the flesh pulled and puckered in a swirling pattern that drew me in.

Then she replaced her jacket and turned back to me, her eyes hot. 'I have to go back to Rory,' she said. 'Check he's all right.'

'Are you going to leave me like this?' I gestured to my feet bound together.

Her face didn't move. She crossed the room, pulled open a drawer and rummaged inside. There was a torch and Ronnie flicked the switch with her thumb. Nothing. She cast it back into the drawer. Then she moved aside a packet of Senior Service cigarettes, a book of matches and a board game. I could read the cover of the yellowed box and see it was Twister. It was as if a family in the seventies was still in residence.

At last she found what she wanted; a transistor radio. The battery-operated sort. She twiddled the dials until she found a signal. The sound of tinny music filled the caravan, interrupted by electric crackles.

'Don't want you to be bored,' said Ronnie. Then she left.

Alone now, I know I have to try to free myself. I don't know why she hasn't put a bullet in my head; perhaps she wants to torture me beforehand. Whatever the reason, I'm not going to stick around to find out.

I shuffle along the bench to the window frame. Once I'm there, I push myself to my feet, wobbling precariously. I hold my body rigid until I'm steady, then try to lift my arms to the same height as the window frame. My bones crack as I raise my clasped fingers behind me. I've always been fast but never flexible and my muscles soon begin to burn. I turn my head, trying to see how far I have to go and realise I need to lean forward to help things along. I grunt with the effort and tip from my waist. Please let it be enough.

Bingo. I feel the cold of steel on my knuckles. The corroded edge rakes my skin. It's sharp. This will work. It's got to.

Gently, I place my wrists on the frame, not wanting to shift myself off balance, and begin a left to right wriggle, laughing at the rasp of metal against rope. I keep going until the ache in my arms and chest is unbearable, then I stop to breathe. I stretch my neck backwards to check my progress but it's impossible to see. The rope feels looser, but is that just my imagination?

I go back to work, rubbing back and forth, praying the fibres are coming away. I don't know how long this will take. Or how long I've got. Got to go faster.

I move in a frenzy, swaying from the hips to increase the pressure and speed.

There's a smell in the air, a bit like burning. It must be the rope. I must be nearly there.

I picture the material fraying under the friction.

'Come on,' I yell, using my thighs now, then my knees and feet. Every part of my body is dancing as I drag the rope across the frame.

Too late I realise I've lost my centre of gravity. I'm pitching to the left, my weight transferring to one foot, then the side of that foot. I try to rebalance, throw myself to the right. I end up crashing to the floor, my mouth and nose taking the first hit.

Fuck. Face down on the stained rug, I can smell the iron tang of blood and feel it seeping out of me.

'It's a beautiful day, here at the Olympic stadium,' a voice spills out from the radio. 'And outside, the crowds are already forming for the Opening Ceremony, which promises to be this country's finest hour.'

I groan and wonder what the hell I plan to do now.

'We need to cancel the Opening Ceremony.'

The PM and Benning froze, open-mouthed, and stared at Clem.

'We don't have a choice,' he said.

There was a second when no one spoke, then Benning slammed his fists down on the PM's desk. 'Are you out of your tiny mind?'

Clem pressed his lips together.

'Have you any idea how long this thing took to plan?' Benning shouted. 'No? Well, let me tell you. Six years. Six long years. And every minute of those six years was building up to this afternoon.'

Clem didn't respond.

'And have you any idea how much it's cost? Again, let me enlighten you: four billion pounds.' There were flecks of saliva at the corners of Benning's mouth. 'The country is on the verge of bankruptcy here. Have you seen what happens when the banks lose confidence in a country? Just look at Ireland or Spain or bloody Greece. There is no fucking way the Opening Ceremony isn't going ahead.'

'Have you any idea how many people might die if we proceed today?' Clem's tone was calm. 'Eighty thousand is a conservative estimate.'

Benning let out a roar and swept an empty coffee cup onto the floor. Clem watched it bounce, the handle snapping off.

'Is it a credible threat?' the PM asked.

'This group, Shining Light, was responsible for the Plaza bomb and their leader is still at large,' said Clem. 'I'd class that as credible.'

'Do we really believe this bunch of no-hopers was responsible for the previous attack?' Benning's face was contorted. 'You said yourself, Clem, that it was highly unlikely. You had grave doubts.'

Clem nodded. He had had doubts. A lot of them. But then Ronnie X had proved herself a dangerous and resourceful individual.

'I thought this was just a raggle-taggle bunch of crazies,' said Benning. 'You certainly neutralised them without too much trouble.'

Clem smarted. Shooting people was hardly trouble free. 'Ronnie X is different,' he said.

Benning rolled his eyes. 'With a name like that, I'm not sure I can take any of this seriously.'

'Her real name is Veronica Pearson and she has kidnapped a senior civil servant, your blue-eyed girl, from right under our noses,' said Clem. 'I think that demands we take her seriously.'

'Is it possible for us to deal with this in a different way?' the

PM asked. 'Increase security to a level you're comfortable with, Clem?'

Clem considered this, then shook his head. 'Too risky.'

'What sort of things could we do to reduce that risk?' asked the PM. 'In theory?'

'We could change the status to the highest alert.'

'Consider it done,' said the PM.

'We could double, no treble, manpower at the scene.'

'I'll authorise that immediately,' said the PM.

Clem sighed. 'The risk would still be too great, sir. My advice remains the same. We must cancel the Opening Ceremony.'

Rory likes being on his own.

'Don't you get lonely?' his social worker asked every time they met. She was called Imelda and she smelled like dogs. 'Everyone needs friends,' she told him.

Rory would put his hand over his nose and mouth so he didn't have to breathe in the air between them.

He once caught sight of the file Imelda had made about him. It said he was 'nonverbal'. This means that Rory doesn't speak. Which isn't correct. Rory does speak. Just not to Imelda.

He settles in front of his computers and concentrates. That's one of the best things about being alone. He can concentrate. When there are other people around, Rory gets confused. The smell and the noise make his head hurt and he can't focus on anything.

Rory often wonders what it would be like if everyone on the planet died and only he was left. It would have to be a virus to which only he had immunity. It would also need to be a fast-mutating virus in order to kill everyone before a vaccine could be found.

Statistically this is very, very improbable. But he would be able to go to the library or the park without his head hurting.

Actually, Rory would like it if Ronnie also had immunity to the virus. He likes Ronnie. And Hawk. Rory likes Hawk. But the statistical probability of the only three humans to display natural immunity to the virus being Rory and two people he knows and likes would be incalculable.

He cleans his keyboard with an antibacterial wipe and taps in a website address. It's one he visits several times a day, but he ensures the favourite function is empty and cleans his online history after each use: www.platformnow.com.

Rory's nose hurts as he navigates his way through the site. There are news articles about taxes and government and guns. He doesn't open them but clicks onto the forum. There are lots of topics. Rory estimates that there are approximately forty, listed in alphabetical order.

He hovers the cursor over the 'M's, until he finds 'Militia'. It is always busy in Militia. Inside the topic, he checks which threads are the most active and chooses the one with the most recent activity.

Topic	By	Replies
Should militia groups oppose tyrannical governments?	**Gunshot**	**36**

Gunshot is a prolific poster, sometimes starting ten or more threads a day. The first response is from TheTimeForTalkIsOver:

TheTimeForTalkIsOver   **At 10:37**
You said it, brother.
This government and most other world governments have been subverted. They no longer represent us but seek to enslave us.
It's time for action.

Gunshot   **At 10:42**
By taking up arms?

TheTimeForTalkIsOver   **At 10:46**
By any means necessary.

Rory scrolls down the posts, skim-reading. Everyone will agree
with Gunshot. Everyone always agrees with Gunshot. Finally,
Rory finds what he's looking for.

Hawk   **At 11:15**
Each of us needs to stand up and be counted before the
New World Order brings us to our knees.

Rory hopes Hawk is still online and starts his own post to find
out. It took him three days to decide what to call himself. His
name has been Rory all his life. The other things people have
called him he doesn't like. By the end of day three, he chose
R1234.
He finishes his message and posts it.

R1234   **At 11:21**
I am here.

Then he waits. His nose is blocked and he wants to blow it but
he's frightened it will start bleeding again.
In less than one minute someone replies.

Hawk   **At 11:21**
Hey man, how are you?

R1234   **At 11:22**
Someone punched me.

Hawk   **At 11:23**
No way. Did you punch them back?

R1234   **At 11:24**
No.

Hawk   **At 11:25**
Listen to me. You have to learn to protect yourself, man. If
you don't then others will try to hurt you. Attack is the best
form of defense.

Hawk is correct. For as long as Rory can remember, people have
said bad things to him and hurt him. Gently, Rory touches his
nose. He wants it all to stop.

I manage to roll onto my side, but the pressure on my already
aching shoulder is too great. Instead, I settle back onto my stomach, with my face turned sidewards, my cheek pressed into the
floor. At least the cold air can circulate around my swollen nose
and lips. Thank God Ronnie didn't tape my mouth this time or
I'm certain I would suffocate.

When she gets back I'll have to pretend I fell. But will she
believe that? I'm nowhere near where I started and the rope
around my wrists will tell its own story.

A leaden desperation consumes me. Why is this happening
to me? All I wanted was to do something useful. To be good at
my job. To make the old man proud. I groan at the thought of
him and how he'll react if I'm found dead in some ditch. He'll
probably be embarrassed that I allowed myself to get into this
position.

The radio continues to fizz and crackle in the background. 'With
less than two hours to go, the queues are building here at the

stadium,' says the presenter. 'And I'm standing here next to a little lad who's been waiting patiently. What's your name, young man?'

'Tyrone,' says the boy, who sounds around five.

'And who are you hoping to see today, Tyrone?'

'Usain Bolt,' he says, lisping the s.

'And why's that?'

'He fast.'

The presenter chuckles and begins to chat to a group of school-girls from Bermondsey.

The whole world is waiting for the beginning of the Games. Surely someone has noticed I'm missing. The PM, Clem, my dad? Surely they'll be trying to find me?

Clem knew he should be out there looking for Connolly, but right now he had to concentrate on ensuring the Opening Ceremony was secure. Those bastards at Downing Street had overruled him, as he'd known they would. And now he had to do whatever it took to safeguard the ceremony. He made his way straight to HQ and called an emergency meeting of everyone on site.

'The top priority as of this moment is the Opening Ceremony of the Olympic Games,' he said.

Groans rippled around the room. Large events were the province of the police.

Clem held up his hands. 'There is a real threat of an imminent terrorist attack.'

That shut them up.

'What are we looking at, Clem?' asked Carole-Ann.

He pushed a memory stick into a laptop and a smart board on the wall behind him sprang to life. 'Shining Light,' he said. 'Small cell. Dean Mantel, Steve Bentley, Stephen Miggs.' Clem clicked a key and photos of Deano, Steve and Miggs filled the screen. 'All dead.'

He clicked another key and a picture of each dead body appeared, the first two in situ at the flat, blood and brains splattered on the walls. The third was of Miggs dead in his hospital bed, head bandaged, his eyes lifeless. Civilians often screamed at images such as these. Hell, Clem had known normal coppers faint at autopsy stills, but his audience were agents. This was water off a duck's back.

'Dead men don't blow things up, the last time I checked,' said Carole-Ann.

Clem pressed another key and a picture of Ronnie X taken from the CCTV footage at the Station Hotel filled the room. Her eyes were like lead.

'The group's leader is still at large,' he said. 'And make no mistake, she is very dangerous.'

'Is she likely to have recruited fresh blood?' asked Carole-Ann.

'There's no way we can know that,' said Clem. 'So we have to assume yes.'

Carole-Ann spoke again. 'If we spot her, what are our orders?'

'Disable and capture,' said Clem. 'We need Ronnie X alive.'

A few murmurs rumbled around the room. Taking terror suspects alive was never easy, not if you wanted to avoid getting your own head blown off.

'I know, I know,' said Clem. 'But she's taken a prisoner and we need to know where she's being held.' He pressed the keypad and Ronnie's face was replaced by another.

'You are shitting me,' said Carole-Ann.

'I wish I was,' Clem replied and tapped the smooth cheek of Jo Connolly.

At the stadium, Clem's heartstrings tightened. Crowds were already forming, with groups of children gathered in packs, chattering like monkeys. He put his radio to his ear. Everyone on the ground was pitched into the same frequency, and Carole-Ann was listening in back at base. 'Everyone in position?' he asked.

The resounding response was affirmative.

Clem passed through the security gates and nodded to the operative. 'Everything under control?'

'Yes, Clem.'

He patted the X-ray machine installed moments ago. 'No one gets in without a full body and bag scan,' he said.

'Roger that.'

'It's going to take time,' said Clem. 'You got enough manpower?'

The operative gestured to a band of security guards hovering in the background drinking tea from polystyrene cups.

Each entrance had the same set-up. He checked them all.

'What happens if we do catch a suspect?' asked the operative on the south stand.

'Are your men armed?' he asked.

'With batons and mace,' she replied.

'And you?'

She pushed her coat aside to show the holster of her handgun.

'Okay then,' said Clem. 'You detain if at all possible.'

'What if it's a suicide job?' she asked.

Good question. Clem paused. It was the worst-case scenario. 'Begin procedure 42.'

The woman's face remained straight but Clem spotted the gulp in her throat. Procedure 42 was a system designed to ensure terrorists and other dangerous individuals were stopped before the threat escalated. Shoot to kill was acceptable.

'No chances,' said Clem. 'No mistakes.'

The girl nodded.

Satisfied the entrances were under control, Clem moved into the stadium. In each row of seats an operative was slowly working from left to right, checking each nook and cranny with a detector. High above, the sound of helicopter blades lacerated the air as the police made endless surveillance sweeps.

Clem's radio crackled into life. 'How's it looking down there, Clem?' asked Carole-Ann.

Clem rubbed his chin. The thudding in his chest was subsiding to an insistent knock. 'We're getting there. What's happening at your end?'

'I've got Malik and his team scouring the wires for any chatter.'

'And?'

'And sweet FA so far.'

'That's not good,' said Clem.

'Of course it could mean that nothing is going to happen today,' she said.

Clem grunted. It was entirely possible that Ronnie had nothing planned for today. That she knew the risks were too great. 'What about the screens?' he asked.

'I'm patched in to every camera in a three-mile radius.'

'Three miles isn't much.'

Carole-Ann sucked her teeth. 'That's over a hundred cameras. Do you know how much footage that is?'

'You sound like Benning.'

'And you're gonna get a kick in the tush when next we meet.'

Clem laughed. 'So what can you see?'

'There's a lot of peeps out there,' she said. 'We're sweeping everyone for our girl.'

'Isn't that like looking for a needle in a haystack?' asked Clem.

'I'm using digital recognition. The programme is checking every face to see if it matches our Ronnie.'

'She might use someone else,' said Clem.

'Sure, so I've got a team looking for anything or anyone that looks sus.'

'Is that a technical term?'

'Uh huh. We look for shifty eyes and fake beards.'

Clem laughed again. He knew Carole-Ann would have her best profilers on the job. For the first time that day, he felt as if he had a handle on the situation.

Most of the nurses in the hospital are fine. They don't say much, but if Isaac is in a lot of pain they might put a cool hand on his arm and give some medicine or a jab.

Nurse Mary-Joan is an exception. If there's a meaner woman on this earth, Isaac ain't met her. If he needs help to sit up, she'll jerk him so the hot wound in his chest jars.

If he can't feed himself, she'll knock the soup spoon against his teeth.

One day he woke up from a dream with a jump. This happens a lot. Isaac drifts away, the noises around him bending and stretching like a string of gum, until he can see and hear Mama and Pa and Noah and Rebecca and Veronica-Mae as clearly as if they were standing at his bedside. Sometimes they're all sitting round having supper, Noah braggin' and Pa telling him to hush up while they help themselves to some of Ma's stew with big yellow bricks of warm corn bread on the side. Then, as if someone has reached inside the dream and caught him by the collar, he's dragged back.

'Nightmare?' she asked him.

Isaac was surprised, 'cos Nurse Mary-Joan ain't never seen fit to speak to him before, so he just nodded yes.

'I heard that nightmares come from inside our hearts,' she said.

Isaac thought she was probably right. He always seemed to be dreaming about the family.

'Thing is, I heard something else too.' She looked over her shoulder as if she had a secret to keep, then bent over so Isaac could see the whiskers on her top lip. 'I heard you ain't got no heart.'

He watched her now, outside the ward, laughing with the policemen that are always stationed there. Sometimes she brings them coffee and maybe a piece of pie. She never brings Isaac a piece of pie.

When she enters his room, her smile drops away like a pebble in water. She smoothes the blanket over him, tugging just a little too hard so he rocks from side to side. He doesn't give her the satisfaction of knowing how much it hurts.

'A little bird told me something today,' she says.

Isaac refuses to react, stares straight ahead.

'About your sister,' she says.

He can't stop himself from flinching.

'Veronica-Mae, is it?' she asks.

When Isaac doesn't answer she turns away, humming to herself. He has no choice but to speak to the poisonous old hag.

'Is she all right?'

Nurse Mary-Joan glances back at him, her lips one white line of tightness. 'Well now, she's fine, considering.'

Isaac lets out a sigh of relief.

'Been discharged, actually,' Nurse Mary-Joan continues.

Isaac's mouth drops open. 'Did she go home? To Mama?'

'Oh no, child.' Nurse Mary-Joan gives a tinkle of laughter, showing every last one of her yellow teeth. 'Your mama is dead.'

Chapter Twelve

I'm still on the floor of the caravan, the radio playing in the background. I keep hoping the police are going to arrive any second and save me, but I'm not some character on the telly. Even if anyone has noticed my disappearance, they will have no idea where I am. Christ, *I* don't know where I am.

A sudden scraping at the door makes my heart leap. Ronnie? The noise comes again and I grit my teeth.

Then comes a caw. Not Ronnie. A seagull. I have a fleeting memory of a holiday in Brighton. Me and Davey, both less than ten years old, sitting on the white pebble beach, throwing chips from a polystyrene tray for the birds. Some of the gulls swooped down and managed to catch the chips in their beaks mid-flight. Davey applauded them like a demented cheerleader.

I've got to get out of here. I can't just give up.

I glance at the door. It's rusted and flimsy, the lock from a bygone age. Would a kick force it open? I wriggle along the floor on my belly and lie in front of it, then I tense my stomach muscles and flip myself onto my back. If I scoot towards it, I can bend my knees and get some force into my legs.

Taking a deep breath, I hear the crowds on the radio and bring my knees into my chest, then kick out with all my strength. I thank God for all the time I've spent at the gym as my feet thud against the door, rattling it in its frame. I pull my knees in again and brace myself for another go.

Crack. The blow strains the lock. One more and it will break, I know it will.

I steady myself. I need to concentrate as much energy as I have into my next attack.

Bang. The lock splinters just liked I banked on and my chest sings. But my elation is short-lived – I had been expecting the door to fly open, letting in a rush of salty wind and sunlight. Instead it remains shut.

I nudge it with the sole of my foot but it doesn't budge. The lock is in two pieces, but something else is holding the door shut. I press harder, not feeling any give. Something behind the door is jamming it closed.

I drop my legs to the floor. Ronnie has barred my escape route from outside.

Rory lets Ronnie into the flat. Ronnie is empty-handed. She told Rory she would bring another towel. Rory can't see a towel.

'Sorry,' she says. 'I haven't been able to go to the shops yet.'

Rory likes having four towels. One on the towel rail in the bathroom. One in the top drawer in his bedroom. One in the wash. And one spare. With three towels the schedule doesn't work.

'I'll get you one as soon as I can,' says Ronnie. 'Okay?'

'When?'

Ronnie sighs. This means she is frustrated with Rory. Imelda always told Rory that his 'inflexibility annoys people'.

'You know things are tricky right now, don't you, Rory?'

'I'm sorry,' he replies. He is not sorry for wanting the towel, but he is sorry for his inflexibility.

'Don't worry about it,' she says and glances at the screens. 'Any mention of me?'

Rory grabs the log, relieved that Ronnie is no longer annoyed. He hands the list to her. There are hundreds of entries. Rory hasn't been able to keep up. He clicks into the secure website he has hacked and points.

'Who?' asks Ronnie

'MI5.'

'Where?'

Rory clicks to a Sky television station. He hates television. Even on mute the pictures make his eyes hurt. He squeezes them shut while Ronnie checks the scene of the crowds gathering outside the Olympic stadium.

'You can open your eyes now, Rory.'

He does so and immediately clicks away to Platformnow.

'Are you sure they can't trace anything on your PC?' asks Ronnie.

Rory is very careful. He has built a clean machine, taken a ghost of it and stored it on a partition in his hard drive. He cleans it, checks it and double checks it every day.

'Yes,' he says.

'What about anything coming back to you?' she asks.

Rory has set up his own access points piggybacking off other wireless networks in his area. He shakes his head.

'I worry about you,' she says. 'If they catch you they'll put you away, you know?'

'Away?'

'Prison or hospital,' she says. 'You'd hate that, wouldn't you?'

'I'm not ill,' says Rory.

'Not that sort of hospital,' she says. 'Look, I just want to know that all this is secure.'

Rory runs through his security in his head. He has done this a thousand times. Mistakes can be made.

'Is it?' she asks.

'It is secure,' he says.

Ronnie smiles at him. 'So,' she says, pointing at Platformnow. 'You're still in touch with Hawk.'

Rory blinks at the screen.

'What do you talk about?' she asks.

Rory shrugs. They talk about all sorts of things. Time, space, computers, guns.

'Please be careful, Rory,' she says. 'He's an extreme person.'

Rory doesn't know what this means.

'He can be dangerous. You know that, don't you?' she says.

Rory points to the log. 'They say that about you.'

The crowds streamed into the stadium and took their seats. First tens, then hundreds, then thousands.

Clem watched the flow of people. Any one of them might be carrying a weapon or a bomb. They were easy to make, even more easy to conceal. The London nail bomber had cobbled together homemade devices with nails, screws and pieces of old scissors before letting them do their damage in a pub and on the streets.

'Hey.' Carole-Ann's voice fizzed across the airwaves.

'Talk to me,' said Clem. 'What do you see?'

'Nada.'

'Keep looking,' he said.

Clem thought he heard the trace of a sigh from the other end. He was being hard work and he knew it.

'Shit,' Carole-Ann shouted.

'What?' Clem tensed. 'What's happening?'

'I'm not sure,' she said.

'Be sure. Be very, very sure.'

'Security have a guy,' she said. 'The X-ray's gone off.'

'Where?'

'Entrance to south stand.'

Clem ran, pushing through the advancing crowd. 'Oi! Watch it,' a man holding a Union Jack shouted. Clem ignored him and made for the south stand entrance. The sound of screaming told him he was in the right place.

A young male, around eighteen years old, was standing by the X-ray machine clutching a rucksack to his chest.

The female operative Clem had spoken to earlier had her gun drawn and pointed at him. Clem felt for his own weapon. There were people all around trying to retreat but for many there was nowhere to go. A bottleneck was forming behind and Clem could hear the panic rising.

'Put the bag down,' the woman said, her voice loud but clear.

The young man shook his head.

Clem watched him carefully. The lad was breathing heavily, obviously scared. And yet there was something odd about him. Something not quite right.

'Put it down now.' The woman raised her voice a notch.

The lad took a step back.

'One more move and I will have to shoot you,' she told him.

Clem's hand snaked around the handle of his Sig and gently he removed it. The area was too constricted. Too many civilians. If there was a bomb in the bag, everyone in the vicinity would be killed. Mentally he calculated the risk.

'Bag. Down. Now.' The operative was shouting, one eye closed, her stance making it clear she was ready to offload at any second.

Clem readied his own weapon. Someone behind him gasped. The sound attracted the attention of the terrorist and he looked at Clem quizzically, his head cocked to one side.

'Neither my colleague nor I will miss from this range,' Clem said. 'Do you understand?'

Something in the boy's eyes told Clem that he didn't. Not really. 'We don't want to shoot you,' said Clem. 'We just want you to put down the bag.'

The boy's lips moved as if he were repeating Clem's words.

'That's right,' said Clem. 'Just put the bag down and everything will be fine.'

'Fine,' the boy echoed. 'Everything will be fine.'

Clem nodded and pointed to a spot on the floor where the boy could place his rucksack.

The boy looked at the ground and smiled. Then he bolted. Like a wild animal out of a trap, he leapt backwards, turning in midair. With the rucksack still in his fists he dashed through the entry tunnel towards the stadium.

Panic broke out around Clem as the crowd scrabbled to get out of his way.

The operative turned to Clem. He nodded. Procedure 42. Both agents released their loads into the boy's back.

There's another noise at the caravan door. I pray it's another seagull, but there's a cough and I know it's Ronnie. There's a pause, and then the scrape of metal as she moves whatever was barricading the door. As soon as she opens it, she'll see the lock is broken. And then she'll kill me.

I'm still on my back in front of it and I'll be the first thing she sees. There's a chance she might be shocked. That element of surprise is all I have. I must use it to my advantage. If I kick out quickly and hard enough, I might be able to knock her off balance. She'll be at the top of the steps and perhaps she'll fall backwards. What I'll do then, I have no idea, but my options are limited. I pull my knees into my chest and wait.

When the door opens I catch sight of her white face, those eyes taking in my position, working out what's happened. I take my chance and kick her as hard as I can, connecting with her thighs.

She grunts and, as I'd hoped, loses her footing. She grasps for the doorframe but her fingers slip as she crashes backwards out of sight. I hear the clang as she thuds down the steps.

'Motherfucker!' she shouts.

I ready myself to go again, legs bent, feet upward. When she reappears in the doorway, I kick out again. The impact is strong. The sound of my feet against her legs is sickening, enough to break a bone. This time, though, she's ready. She absorbs the shock, her knuckles white as she refuses to release the doorframe.

I jam my legs towards her again, determined to send her flying. This time I don't connect. Instead she dives up and over the attack, crashing on top of me. With my hands pinned underneath me I can only try to shake her off, but she's like a terrier, her grip secure.

She's straddling me now, her hands pushing into my shoulders. Her eyes bore into mine and her fingers move around my throat. I gag and gasp for air, arching my back to buck her off me.

Then I hear gunshots. They're coming from the radio. There's screaming and shouting. Instinctively, we both turn towards the sound.

'I'm here at the south gate,' the presenter's voice is staccato with panic. 'There's a problem here. A young man has been shot by the police.' More screams fill the air.

'He's on the floor and there is blood everywhere,' the presenter is panting. 'The police are standing over him. They're searching his coat and bag. Oh my God, oh my God.'

Sirens screech and something incomprehensible is called over the public address system.

'I think they're looking for a bomb,' says the presenter. 'I think they've caught a terrorist.'

Something in me snaps. Another attack. How many innocent people was Ronnie hoping to hurt this time? Hundreds? Thousands?

'You bitch,' I cry, and head-butt her, my forehead cracking the bridge of her nose.

She flies backwards, her blood splattering across my face and chest.

I'm shocked at my actions, at what my rage and revulsion have made me capable of. But I don't care if she kills me, or how she kills me; I just want her to know what a disgusting excuse for a person she is. 'You're an animal!' I scream at her.

She recovers quickly, ignoring the gash on her nose. She reaches into her pocket, pulls out her gun and points it at me, panting. She's aiming right between my eyes. At this range I won't stand a chance but I'm past that.

'Go on, then,' I say. 'What are you waiting for? You've been wanting to kill me all along, so why don't you just do it?'

She takes a step closer.

'This is what you do, isn't it? Kill people? How many did you kill at the Plaza? Or don't you bother to count? And how many did you hope would die at the Opening Ceremony?' Sweat streams down my cheeks. 'You must be disappointed that your plan hasn't worked. Not enough innocent people dead. Not enough children lying on the ground.'

Ronnie looks down at me, her eyes vacant.

'You're a fucking monster,' I rage at her. 'So just do your worst.'

She blinks once, then lowers the gun to her side.

Dear Veronica-Mae,

I don't know if you got my last letter. My lawyer Bert says he passed it along to the welfare people but I don't know as I trust him what with him working for the government and being a Jew and all.

Anyhow, this is my second letter, which is pretty surprising seeing as how I never was one for my books. Mama always did say I'd do anything bar my Bible studies.

I'm still in the hospital. I don't know exactly how long I been in here, but it seems like weeks and weeks. I feel better every day but the doctors say I've still got a long ways to go.

Bert told me that if the bullet hadn't have passed through you first then I'd be dead, so I guess I owe you some thanks for that.

To be honest, although I rightly hate it here, I'm not looking forward to getting out either to face everything that needs facing. That probably makes me a coward, huh?

I reckon by now they told you about Mama and Noah and Rebecca. Bert says they had a proper Christian burial and that a lot of folks showed up, some of them from as far away as Texas. I can't say I understand why anyone would go to the funeral of a body they don't know, but I'm glad all the same.

Well I guess I'll leave it here and say goodbye. If you can, write back and tell me where you're at.

Your brother,

Isaac

PS. Daddy ain't been allowed to get in touch cus of some court order. Bert says I'm to concentrate on myself and not worry about him. Thing is, that just makes me worry all the more.

Chapter Thirteen

I lie quietly on the floor, watching Ronnie, who is crouched in the corner, her head on her chest, her arms covering her head. She looks smaller than before, as if she's shrunk in the wash. I have no idea what's happening. All I do know is that I'm still alive.

At last she looks up at me. There are no tears staining her cheeks, but for the first time there is something in her eyes. Something living.

'It had nothing to do with Shining Light,' she says.

'What?'

'All that stuff.' She waves at the radio. 'It had nothing to do with us.'

'Why should I believe you?' I ask.

She shrugs and looks away.

When she moves towards me and pulls me up in one swoop, I'm shocked again at her strength. She throws me back to the bench and I flop onto it, my reserves of energy spent.

She removes a bottle of water from the fridge, nodding as she checks its temperature against her forehead. When she has taken a drink, she holds it out towards me.

I shake my head. I am unbelievably thirsty, but I need to get this straight. 'MI5 told me you were responsible,' I say.

She puts the bottle back to her lips, speaks around the plastic neck. 'MI5 talk shit.'

I watch the skin of her throat bob as she swallows and I lick my parched lips. She wipes her mouth with the back of her hand.

I shake my head. I can't do this again. 'They had you under surveillance before any of this happened,' I say. 'They knew about your activities.'

'Then they know we're not about hurting innocent people.'

I can't keep the hint of sarcasm from my voice. 'So tell me, then, what are you all about?'

She screws the top back on the bottle and slides it into the fridge. I try to encourage enough saliva to swallow.

'Shining Light is against oppression,' she says. 'We fight the state, the media who keep them in power. We fight the multinationals who don't give a shit about anything but profit.'

'High-minded stuff,' I say. 'But does it justify violent attacks?'

A small smile plays around the corners of her mouth. 'We only attack those directly responsible.'

I screw my eyes closed. None of this makes any sense. It just isn't possible.

'Think about it.' Her voice is near and when I open my eyes I find her sitting on the bench next to me, uncomfortably close. 'Didn't it seem just a tad too convenient to you that everyone in the cell was killed before any real investigation could take place?'

I push Dad's words about scapegoats to the back of my mind. 'You're still alive,' I say.

'For how much longer? Don't you think they'll kill me as soon as they find me?'

I think about Clem for a second and I suspect she's right. 'They told me you were white supremacists.'

'Bullshit.'

'I saw Miggs's arms; they were covered in swastikas and other racist crap,' I say.

She nods. 'Miggs was really fucked up by your precious system. You know, the one that was supposed to protect kids like him?

157

He was damaged and angry and went looking for redress in all the wrong places.'

'Until you led him onto the path of righteousness.'

'I don't lead anyone anywhere. If they want to join me then that's up to them. I'm honest about what it might cost them.'

'You don't sound like you care that any of your friends are dead,' I say.

'Care? I wasn't their fucking social worker. They were freedom fighters. They knew what we were up against. They knew the risks.'

Then she gets up and retrieves the water. She doesn't ask this time, just holds it for me to drink. I'm done fighting and gulp it down. I don't know who or what to believe and I hang my head it hurts so much.

'You need to sleep,' Ronnie says. 'And so do I.'

She reaches to a cupboard and pulls out two blankets, brown and itchy, the sort you imagine they hand out in police cells. She gestures for me to lie sideways on the bench and when I do she covers me. The fabric scratches and smells of damp bank holiday weekends but I can't keep my eyes open.

As I drift off into sleep, the last thing to cross my mind is a question. If Ronnie isn't responsible for the terrorist bombs, who is?

The look on the operative's face was a mixture of horror and relief.

'First time?' Clem realised he didn't know her name.

'Yes,' she said.

He could tell her it got easier, which would be true, but only because you never got back what you lost after that first kill. Clem decided the girl didn't need to know that.

'We did what we had to do,' he said.

'Yes,' she replied.

When his mobile rang, Clem was glad.

'You got a name for me?' asked Carole-Ann.

Clem wiped the blood from the student card he had fished out of the dead boy's pocket.

'Thomas Frasier,' he told her. 'Date of birth, eighth of May 1994.' He waited for a second while Carole-Ann ran the name through the computer.

'Clean,' she said. 'No previous convictions, no links to any terrorist organisations.'

'Have we been watching him?' asked Clem.

'Nope.'

'Is there anything at all?'

'Just an address in south London.'

Twenty minutes later, Clem was parked outside an end-of-terrace town house in Greenwich. The door was primrose yellow, recently painted by the looks of it.

There had been no alternative but to kill Frasier, despite him being possibly the only lead to Connolly. Clem's only hope now was that something or someone in this house would provide a clue to Frasier's actions. He signalled to his backup that he was ready to make his move and silently they moved in.

Two years ago E Group had raided a house a few miles east of here. The suspects had decided to go down with the ship and had the place booby-trapped. One agent died and another lost both his legs.

Clem led half of the team to the door; the other half went around the back. He checked the countdown on his watch and at four seconds gestured for the officer with the ram to take his place. He lifted three fingers. Then two. Then one.

Bam. The ram battered the door, knocking it off its hinges, splintering wood. At the exact same moment the back door suffered the same fate.

From inside, Clem heard a scream and trampled over the broken wood towards it.

'Security services,' he shouted, gun at arm's length.

In the sitting room a middle-aged couple were huddled on the sofa. The television was on, the chaos that was now the Opening Ceremony at full blast.

'On the floor,' Clem yelled.

The couple looked at one another in confusion.

'Get down on the floor.' Clem moderated his volume. 'Hands on the back of your necks.'

Clem watched their uncertainty as they did as they were told while all around them agents rushed through the house, checking each room.

'All clear, Clem,' the team leader called from the hallway.

Clem nodded his thanks. 'Does Thomas Frasier live here?' he asked the couple.

'Yes.' The man's speech was muffled as he spoke into the carpet.

'He's our son.' The woman lifted her head, anxiety overcoming caution. 'Is he okay? Has something happened?'

Clem glanced around the scene. A coal-effect gas fire flickered on the 'light only' setting. A tank of tropical fish sat in the corner, the residents swimming endless circles around a plastic shipwreck. Instinct told him these people knew nothing of their son's activities. A tang of nausea tickled his throat.

'Please,' the woman begged. 'Just tell us Tommy's okay.'

Clem coughed and put his gun back in its holster. 'Why don't you get up?' he said.

The man rose first, brushing non-existent dust from his trousers, then helping his wife to her feet. 'Would you mind telling us what on earth's going on here?' His words were stern but his tone couldn't quite conceal his fear.

'I need to see your son's room,' said Clem. 'Could you show me the way?'

The woman took a step towards Clem and put a hand on his arm, blue veins protruding through the skin. 'What's happened?' she asked.

Clem knew that if he told them their son was dead, he wouldn't get the information he needed. The deceit made him wince, but it was necessary. 'Thomas has got himself into trouble,' he said. 'We need to check his belongings.'

'Is it that girl?' Tears shone in the woman's eyes. 'Has he been bothering her again?'

'The bedroom, please,' said Clem.

Mrs Frasier pursed her lips and led Clem upstairs, her husband trailing after them. 'He doesn't mean anything by it.' She leaned heavily against the banister. 'He doesn't realise.'

Clem counted the family portraits lining the ascent. Eight in total. A record of Thomas Frasier's life from birth to death. The last photo showed him as he had been earlier that day. Smooth skin, hooded top, lost look.

'Tell her we're really sorry,' said Mrs Frasier. 'Tell her he doesn't mean any harm by it.'

They paused on the landing outside the first door. A 'No Entry' sign had been pinned to it.

Mrs Frasier pushed the handle and stepped inside. 'Bit of a mess,' she clucked, reaching down to scoop up a towel from the floor.

'Please don't move anything,' said Clem.

Her hand floated in midair, fingers shaking.

At first glance the room looked like any teenager's, all discarded socks and half-eaten bowls of cereal, but closer scrutiny told a different story. A *Star Wars* poster was tacked to the wall; a stuffed giraffe sat on the windowsill.

'How old was Thomas?' Clem asked.

'Was?' Panic shook Mrs Frasier's voice.

'How old was he at his last birthday?' Clem asked.

'Oh. Right. I see.'

'Eighteen.' Mr Frasier spoke from the doorway. Clem saw reality beginning to dawn on him, drawing his features down. 'This has nothing to do with Tommy pestering that girl, has it?' he asked.

'He wasn't pestering her,' said Mrs Frasier. 'He just likes her and he doesn't understand why he shouldn't.'

'Be quiet, Marion,' said Mr Frasier.

Clem breathed hard. 'Did you see your son this morning?'

'Yes.' Mrs Frasier's voice was small. 'I made him his breakfast like every morning; then he went off to the centre as usual.'

'Centre?' Clem asked.

'Portman Row,' she replied. 'It's a centre for education and training and what have you. For youngsters like Tommy.'

Clem raised his eyebrows.

'Our Tommy's not like other kids,' she told him. 'He's special.'

Mr Frasier sighed and shook his head. He appeared to have aged years in the last few moments. 'What Marion's trying to tell you is that our son has learning disabilities.'

Ronnie nudges me awake with her foot.

I blink at her and struggle to sit up. 'How long have I been asleep?' I ask.

'Almost two hours.'

I groan. I feel like I need another twenty at least. Ronnie, on the other hand, seems refreshed. She slides into the kitchen area, pulls out a box of cereal and tears open the inner plastic wrapper with her teeth.

'I'm leaving,' she says, scooping out a handful of flakes and stuffing them into her mouth. She stares into the middle distance as she chews and swallows. 'They'll put everything they've got into finding me,' she says. 'Sooner or later they'll do it. Then they'll kill me.'

She strides back to me, the cereal box swinging in her hand. She presses it to my lips. 'Eat.'

My stomach growls as she shakes cereal into my open mouth. 'Wouldn't it be better to give yourself up?' I choke slightly on the dry flakes. 'You could prove you had nothing to do with the bombing.'

Ronnie shakes her head. 'I'd be dead before I got to the police station.'

Though I hate to admit it, I suspect she may have a point. 'Where will you go?' I ask.

'I know some people,' she says. 'One in particular. If I can get to him, he'll keep me safe.'

I can't imagine who would be able to hide a refugee from MI5, but if such people do exist, I'm damn sure Ronnie will know them. 'Will you let them know I'm here?' I ask.

She cocks her head to one side, puzzled.

'Once you've got away,' I say. 'Or they might never find me.' I don't need to say that I could die in bloody agony in the meantime.

She doesn't answer and closes the cereal box. Even if she were to leave it for me, how long would I last? I once saw a telly programme about some women in Ireland who decided to kill themselves for God. One of them wrote a diary and it detailed how horrifying their end had been as their bodies ate every last morsel of body fat and muscle to try to survive. 'You could do it anonymously,' I say.

'Do what?'

163

'Let them know where I am. I could give you my dad's number if you don't want to call the authorities.'

'I'm not calling anyone,' she says.

Panic hits me. 'But you said you weren't into hurting innocent people.'

She stifles a laugh and I understand my error. To Ronnie I am no more innocent than Clem. I am part and parcel of the establishment and everything she hates.

'Don't worry,' she says. 'You're not going to die in this caravan.'

'How can you be sure? It could be too late by the time they track me down.'

She pulls me to my feet and takes out a hunting knife, the steel blade glinting. I shrink away from the serrated edge. I'm not going to starve to death after all. Ronnie moves towards me, her eyes wide. Then she cuts the binding around my ankles.

'You're coming with me,' she says.

'Dear God, what went wrong, Clem?' The shadows under the PM's eyes were like purple bruises.

'Why didn't you stop this attack?' Benning hissed.

'We did stop the attack,' Clem replied.

'In full view of the watching press,' said Benning. 'Jesus, could you not have taken the boy aside? Dealt with it in private?'

'He was carrying a bomb,' said Clem. 'The loss of life could have been catastrophic.'

Benning sighed. 'It's a disaster. The Olympic Village is in meltdown. The athletes are desperate to leave but daren't get on a plane and every Tom, Dick and fucking Harry is demanding a statement.'

Clem's jaw dropped. If Clem had been able to apprehend Frasier and put a bullet in his brain on the QT, Benning would cheerfully have proceeded with the Opening Ceremony and kept the whole incident quiet. He didn't know why he was surprised, actually.

'There wasn't any way of knowing if Frasier was a lone wolf,' he told them. 'There could have been more bombers. However things panned out, we would have had to cancel the Opening Ceremony.'

'We could have made that decision ourselves. Instead we've been left with no choices,' said Benning.

Clem felt spots of heat in the apple of each cheek. 'There were no choices.'

'There are always choices,' said Benning.

The PM put up his hands. 'I know you mean well, Simon, but Clem's right; we couldn't take the risk.'

'This will ruin everything we've worked for,' said Benning. 'All those years slogging around the opposition backbenches. Everything we've sacrificed – gone.' He snapped his fingers. 'They'll hang you out to dry.'

The PM placed a hand on his. 'Then so be it.'

'What? Throw away what we've achieved?' Benning was incredulous. 'Just give it to the other lot on a plate?'

'We can't put politics above safety.'

Benning tried to pull away his hand but the PM grabbed it and held it firm, then he turned to Clem. 'Let's see what we can salvage,' he said. 'What do we know about the boy?'

'Thomas Frasier. Eighteen. Still living at home with his mum and dad,' said Clem. 'He suffered moderate learning difficulties.'

'A retard?' Benning barked. 'You couldn't even manage to catch a fucking retard?'

Clem didn't bother to point out for the second time that he *had* caught Frasier.

'Anything known about him?' asked the PM.

Clem shook his head.

'Then we say there was no bomb,' said Benning. 'We say this was a terrible mistake.'

'Like Jean Charles de Menezes?' asked the PM.

'Exactly,' Benning replied. 'We say there was no bomb and the event is back in business.' He turned to Clem. 'Who shot the boy?'

'Myself and another operative,' said Clem. 'Katriona Land.'

'Young?'

Clem nodded.

'Excellent.' Benning's eyes began to shine. 'She's inexperienced; she was in a difficult situation. She truly believed Frasier had a bomb.'

'She thought she was saving the lives of hundreds,' added the PM.

Clem growled. Yet again he was being asked to lie, only this time Katriona Land was about to be hung out to dry. 'She *did* save the lives of hundreds,' he said.

Silence fell upon them and Benning's eyes flickered.

'Did she see the bomb?'

'No,' Clem replied.

'Did anyone see the bomb?'

Clem had seen it. Just as clearly as he could see the line drawn in the sand in front of him. He had a choice to support his PM or a fellow officer.

'I know what you're thinking, Clem,' said the PM. 'That this is all so very wrong. And you're probably right, but in my position I have to look at the bigger picture. Sometimes I have to do things for the greater good. You, of all people, must recognise that.'

When Clem looked back over his career, he saw a catalogue of wrongful detentions, cover-ups, torture, even murders, that he had undertaken in the pursuit of national security. It was an accepted part of any operative's job.

'And at least this way, the poor boy's parents can believe he was an innocent victim,' said the PM.

Clem already knew in his heart of hearts that neither Benning nor the PM gave a flying fuck about Mrs Frasier. But he'd met her. It shouldn't, but it did make a difference.

'So I'll ask you again, Clem.' Benning leaned forward. 'Did anyone see the bomb?'

'No one saw it,' said Clem and felt something inside him break.

Back in his car, Clem's mobile rang. He checked the caller ID and sighed. Of all the people he didn't want to speak to, Carole-Ann was probably at the top of his list.

'Yep.' He lowered the window to let in some air.

'What's happening?' she asked.

'Let the Games begin.'

'You're shitting me,' she replied.

Clem only wished he was. 'We keep security watertight at every venue,' he said.

'And the Frasier kid?'

'Go through everything. I want to know everything he did and said in the last six months. If he took a piss, I want the details.'

'We're already taking apart his laptop.'

'And?'

'Clean so far.'

'Keep at it,' he told her. 'Tommy didn't wake up one morning and decide to become a terrorist. Someone got to him.'

'Grooming?'

Clem let out a long, slow breath. There was some intel that a number of suicide bombers in Palestine had had learning difficulties. Easy prey for the recruiters. But that was on the West Bank, where years of hardship and oppression meant anyone prepared to give up their life for the cause was feted. Martyrdom was an honour whatever the mental age of those involved. Could Ronnie X really be involved in something so despicable?

'Let's just get this job done,' Clem sighed.

'What about Connolly?' asked Carole-Ann. 'With Frasier dead . . .'

'I know,' said Clem and hung up. There was now nothing more imperative than finding Ronnie X.

The cliff-top path is still deserted. Nothing to my left but foam-crested waves as far as the eye can see. Ronnie has given me no choice. I am going with her.

The wind whips my ears and I can smell the seaweed. My hands are still bound, but it feels so good to walk freely. I look out to sea and watch the clouds scud across the horizon.

'Okay?' Ronnie has to shout above the howling weather.

I nod and we continue.

At last we come to a small bay formed in the rock by a thousand years of crashing rollers. We scramble down a rocky incline, Ronnie helping me. Her footing is sure, the hold on my arm strong. At the bottom, we wait by a wooden jetty, the old planks held together with blue twine.

'Why are you taking me with you?' I ask.

Ronnie stabs at the sand with the heel of her boot, like a gardener making an impression with a spade. 'I might need a bargaining tool,' she says.

I blink back my lack of comprehension.

'If they close in on me, I'll need something they value,' she explains.

'Me?'

Ronnie shrugs. 'They won't want you dead.'

I imagine Benning and the PM. 'Frankly, I'm not sure they'll be that fussed.'

'In that case,' Ronnie laughs, 'I'll just use you as a human shield.'

For a moment I laugh too, then I wonder if Ronnie would

168

indeed put me between a bullet and herself. An hour ago I would have put money on the answer, but everything's more complicated now.

In the distance, the noise of an engine punctures the air and Ronnie cups her hand above her eyes. When a small fishing boat chugs into the bay she nods to herself. It pulls up at the end of the jetty, its rusted hull bobbing in the choppy waters. A man in black waterproofs appears on deck, his face almost covered by a thick beard, a cigarette dangling from his lips.

Ronnie calls out to him in a language I don't understand. Gaelic, I think. He gives a one-word reply and she begins to make her way along the creaking planks.

'Come on,' she tells me and I try not to slip on the green undercoat of algae.

At the end, Ronnie takes a leap aboard, catching the man's out-stretched hand to help her. She gestures for me to follow and holds out her own hand alongside the man's.

I take a step, then hesitate. What if I refuse? Would Ronnie kill me in front of a witness? The man watches me over his fag, a plume of smoke rising towards his eye. Somehow I can't see him intervening on my behalf.

I glance behind me. I could run. Even with my hands tied, I'm fast.

'Do you reckon you'll make it up the cliff without me?' Ronnie asks.

I sigh. The way back up is steep, the rocks jagged. One false step and I would fall hundreds of feet.

'The only other way out of here is to swim,' she says. 'Do you think you can manage that? It looks pretty rough out there to me.'

The man squints through his smoke and growls something at Ronnie.

'Better decide now, Jo. Connor says he's leaving with or without you.'

I leap aboard.

'That's my girl,' says Ronnie.

I don't reply. She may think she has me beat but she's wrong. I'm biding my time, waiting for the right moment. And when it comes, I'm getting away from her, no matter what.

Inside the boat, the cabin is spartan. A bunk bed with two sleeping bags, a stove in the corner, a small flame licking around a steel kettle.

Ronnie hands Connor a stained envelope, which he opens. I watch him as he thumbs a wad of cash. Satisfied, he says something to Ronnie. She checks her watch and replies.

He barely looks at me, seemingly not in the least bit curious as to what I'm doing there, hands tied, nose and mouth bloody and bruised. Finally he leaves and the boat turns, then sets out to sea, rolling and tilting.

Ronnie pushes me onto the bottom bunk, staggers over to the stove and pours black liquid from the kettle into a small cup. She fishes in a tin for sugar, stirs in two spoonfuls and drinks the cup down in one. Then she repeats the procedure and brings it over to me.

'Tea,' she says. She holds the cup to my lips, the liquid burning the ragged flesh.

'Ow,' I yelp.

She rolls her eyes. 'Just drink it.'

I take a mouthful. It's strong and sweet and seductive. I finish the cup. 'Where are we going?' I ask.

'You'll see.'

Bert wipes a handkerchief across his forehead and takes a seat. 'What happened to your face, Isaac?'

Isaac's hand flies to his cheek. It feels swollen under his fingers, like a ripe peach. He can hear the throaty laugh of the sheriff down the hallway 'Slipped and fell?' *he replies.*

Bert stuffs his handkerchief back in his pocket and nods. 'Dangerous place, police cells.'

Ain't that the truth.

Early that morning the doctor told Isaac he was fixed up, so he got dressed in some old jeans Bert had left for him. He wonders what happened to the clothes he was wearing when he got shot.

'Now don't you look nice.' *Nurse Mary-Joan smiled at the gap between the hem of his trousers and his feet where his bony ankles were displayed to the world.* 'All dressed up and nowhere to go,' *she said.* 'Now hold on a minute, you do have somewhere to go.'

Then she called the police officers who had stood guard all those weeks and they came in and told him he was under arrest, brought him straight over to the jailhouse and slung him in the pen.

Bert fiddles with the pin in his necktie. It's silver with a small green stone. It reminds Isaac of something Mama used to put in her hair.

'Did they ask you anything yet?' *Bert says.*

Isaac nods.

'What did you say?'

'Nothing.' *Isaac knows all about the Constitution and the Fifth Amendment. Mama done drill them with all that stuff almost as much as the good book.*

'Good boy,' *says Bert.* 'Now soon, they're going to take you to the courthouse and ask you how you plead. You just leave everything to me.'

'Yes, sir.'

'Call me Bert, please.'

Isaac nods but he knows he ain't going to do that. He's always been taught respect for his elders, and anyway he don't hardly know Bert. 'Did you hear anything about my sister?' *he asks. It's been near two weeks since he wrote Veronica-Mae and he hasn't had a reply.*

'I'm afraid not, Isaac.'

171

'*What about Daddy?*'

Bert scoops up his papers. '*We'll talk about that after the hearing, okay?*'

'*Okay.*'

Bert taps on the door for one of the officers to let him out. '*Is there anything else I can help you with, Isaac?*'

'*Just get me out of here, sir.*'

Chapter Fourteen

Spray hits the small window of the cabin, obscuring the view, although there is precious little to see. The last time I looked, the only thing I could see was mile upon mile of grey water. Now night has fallen and there's nothing but black out there.

Ronnie stares out anyway, occasionally dipping her finger in the sugar tin then sucking it. With her face still, she seems less angry, less deadly. There's still something electric about her, but it's not as forbidding. She's almost human.

'Why do you work for the government?' Out of the blue she turns to me, pinning me with those eyes the colour of bullets, hatred seeping out from every pore. 'And don't give me any shit about wanting to make a difference.'

I can't see any point in lying. 'My dad was a famous secretary of state.'

'The great Paddy Connolly,' she says.

'Great indeed.'

'I guess when that's your starting point there was never any danger of you working in Tesco.'

I toy with asking how the hell she got involved with Shining Light, but suspect it did have everything to do with wanting to make a difference.

'They fuck you up, your mum and dad,' she says. 'They may not mean to, but they do.'

I sigh and complete Larkin's poem. 'They fill you with the faults they had and add some extra, just for you.'

The cabin door opens and Connor enters. He speaks to Ronnie around another filterless cigarette. She answers him, then pulls me to my feet. 'First leg of the journey is over,' she says.

We make our way onto the deck, Ronnie steadying me with one hand, holding the rail with the other, as the boat sails in the grey dawn towards a small island. When it stops at the end of another wooden jetty, Ronnie jumps off. There's a gap of a couple of feet between the boat and the first plank. The water swirls and froths in the void. If I slip, I'll almost certainly be sucked under.

'Faic tuson,' Connor growls at me.

I don't need to speak his language to know he's telling me to piss off.

'I wouldn't wait to be told twice,' says Ronnie.

So I jump, fall forwards and slam face down onto the jetty, the sea splashing my cheek through the gaps. Ronnie pulls me upright and waves to the boat as it sets off back to sea. I swear I see a smile on Connor's face.

Then she strides away across the beach, leaving me to trot after her, seawater dripping down my chin. We climb a bank of dunes, our feet sinking out of sight, sand coating the bottoms of our legs, and pause at the top.

There's a field of patchy grass and weeds, a short strip of tarmac laid down the middle. At the very far end of the black strip is a two-seater biplane painted in khaki camouflage.

'You have got to be kidding me,' I say.

Ronnie presses on, leaving me standing and gawping. There is no way I am getting on that plane.

Valerie Maynard's tissue had disintegrated, leaving a flake of white paper on her top lip.

'I just can't believe it,' she said for the tenth time. 'How could anyone think Tommy was involved in anything criminal?'

'That's what we're looking into,' said Clem. He took a surreptitious peek at his watch. He'd already sat with the head of Portman Row Centre for half an hour. He needed information and he needed it fast.

'His mother must be devastated,' said Valerie.

Clem didn't want to head in the direction of poor Mrs Frasier. 'I understand there was some trouble with a girl,' he said.

Valerie wiped a fresh tear with the back of her hand. 'He fell in love. These young people might not be as quick as you and I, but their bodies work perfectly well. Hormones racing around like any teenager.'

'She wasn't interested?'

Valerie gave a wry laugh. 'They never are. Not in boys like Tommy.'

'He didn't take no for an answer, I hear.'

'Tommy thought if he kept pestering her, she'd agree to be his girlfriend, so he went to the café where she worked every single day and asked her out,' she said. 'You've got to give him ten out of ten for persistence.'

'She didn't go to the police?' Clem asked.

Valerie shook her head. 'She came to see me and I explained the situation. Nice girl, actually; Polish.'

'Apart from that, did Thomas have much contact with anyone outside the centre?'

'I doubt it,' she answered. 'He came here every day like clockwork.'

The noise of laughter filtered down the corridor outside as two young adults with Down's syndrome chatted and joked with one another. Clem could well imagine that for people like Thomas Frasier this was a place of acceptance. A place he could be himself. 'You'd have to check with his mother,' Valerie added.

Clem smiled but knew that Mrs Frasier was in a very dark place, and that he would be the last person she would want to speak to.

The Shaking Cow was a clean coffee and milkshake bar on the corner of Portman Row. The sound of the cappuccino steamer filled the air.

Kasia Borki smiled sadly at Clem from the other side of a window table. 'I saw on television about Thomas.' She pronounced his name the Polish way, emphasising the 'O'. 'It very shocking.'

'It is,' Clem agreed.

'You think here in UK, it cannot happen like that. The police here don't shoot people.'

'Can you tell me about Thomas?' Clem asked.

Kasia looked out of the window. 'He like small boy.'

'He began to make a nuisance of himself,' said Clem.

Kasia waved her hand. 'Is nothing.'

It could go one of two ways. There were those who were too well brought up to speak ill of the dead. And those who couldn't wait to dish the dirt.

'Serious,' she said. 'Is not important.'

'What did he actually do, Kasia?'

She groaned, clearly not wanting to say.

'Kasia?'

'He come in every morning and ask me to be his girlfriend,' she said. 'He ask me for kiss.'

'You didn't feel comfortable with that?'

She shrugged. 'I go to centre and Mrs Maynard apologise to me.'

'And he didn't bother you any more?'

'No.'

'He stopped coming into the Shaking Cow?'

'Oh no, he still come every morning.'

Clem raised his eyebrows.

'He very polite, he no trouble. He just come in, order his drink and use computer.'

'Computer?'

Kasia pointed to the row of computers along the back wall. 'This internet café.'

Ronnie opens the plane's door and gestures for me to get in.

'Forget it,' I say.

'Fair enough.' She shrugs. 'You're in the middle of nowhere, without food or water and your hands are literally tied behind your back.'

'I'll take my chances,' I tell her.

'Good luck with that.'

As she clambers into the cockpit, the first spot of rain hits my face. I look up into the grey skies and strain at the bindings round my wrists but they don't give a millimetre. The rain gets faster and I shout out my frustration at the growing storm. How long could I realistically survive out here?

I make my way to the tiny plane as the engine starts up and the propeller begins to whir. Ronnie doesn't look at me as I slide into the space next to her. A clap of thunder rocks the runway.

'Nice day for it,' she says.

'Fuck off,' I reply.

The engine rattles like a decades-old lawn mower, making the cockpit vibrate as Ronnie checks the dials and switches – of which there are alarmingly few.

'You do know what you're doing, I suppose?' I ask.

'It's been a while,' she says. 'But yeah. Like riding a bike.'

I swallow hard. I don't like flying at the best of times and always listen to every creak and groan for signs of system failure, gripping the armrests as if that alone is keeping the wings in place. But this is something else.

She reaches down to a handle on her right and yanks until there's a click. This is immediately followed by a noise outside.

'What was that?' I ask.

'Wing flaps going down,' she says.

'Is that meant to happen?'

'Better than them falling off.'

She leans towards another black handle on the control panel and pushes it up. The plane judders forward into the wind and rain. As it gains speed I take a deep breath.

'Relax, Jo,' Ronnie tells me as we reach the end of the tarmac and she pulls back on what looks like the steering wheel.

Suddenly the nose of the plane lifts and we leave the ground. 'Attagirl,' says Ronnie.

We lurch through the clouds, shuddering from side to side and as the plane banks steeply to turn, I fully expect us to fall out of the sky. The wind buffets us from side to side, shaking me to my bones. I glance out of the window and the ground is an alarming distance beneath us.

'The pilot has now switched off the seat belt signs,' says Ronnie and reaches behind her for a cool box, which she dumps on my lap. 'The cabin crew will shortly be passing through with the drinks trolley.' She snaps the top from the cool box. 'Would madam care for beer or wine with her meal?'

'How about a parachute?' I say.

She flips open a carton of apple juice and holds it out to me. I open my mouth and let her pour. Then, with a half smile, she peels a banana, breaks it in two and shoves one half into my mouth, where it squelches on my tongue.

'What I don't understand is how you've arranged all this,' I say. 'Who are these people who just let you use their boats and planes? They must realise that what you're up to isn't strictly legal.'

'Jo, Jo.' She pats my knee. 'You of all people must know every-one has a price.'

'What do you mean?'

She shrugs. 'Deep down you knew Shining Light had nothing to do with the bombing.'

'I didn't know.'

'Okay then, you must have had your doubts.'

I can't deny that.

'But you kept them to yourself. Why was that?' she asks.

I don't answer.

'You wanted the big job, to make the great Paddy Connolly proud,' she says. 'And the way to get that was to keep your mouth shut.'

'It wasn't like that,' I protest.

'No?'

It stings. Did I want it all so badly that I let myself be taken in? 'But how do you know which people to ask? Not everyone would be willing to break the law.'

She shrugs. 'I've done some bad shit and I know some bad folk.'

A reminder, again, that Ronnie isn't one of the good guys. I'm disproportionately grateful when turbulence whacks the plane, air thumping the wings, interrupting the conversation.

When the sky is calmer, Ronnie rummages in the cool box again and extracts a packet of peanut M&Ms. 'Rory loves these,' she says.

'Rory?'

'The guy you thumped on the nose.'

It all seems like a long time ago. So much has happened; time seems to stretch.

'Is he okay?' I ask.

She opens the packet, pours the contents into her lap and separates out the red ones. 'He'll live.'

We eat the sweets, Ronnie popping one in her mouth, then one into mine.

'My arms are killing me,' I tell her. 'Can't you untie me?'

'Isn't that what you said to Rory?'

'That was different, I was trying to get away. There's not exactly anywhere for me to go right now.'

'Not a chance,' she says.

I sigh and close my eyes.

Krish Sharma bent over the computers confiscated from the Shaking Cow while Clem hovered in the background.

'He knows what he's doing, doesn't he?' Clem asked.

Carole-Ann gave a theatrical sigh.

'I mean, how old is he? He looks about twelve.'

'For heaven's sake, Clem. Calm down. This could take a long time.'

'I don't have a long time,' Clem retorted.

'Do you know how much data there is to retrieve on those PCs? How many people use internet cafés?'

'But we know Tommy was in the Shaking Cow each morning between nine and ten,' Clem said. 'Kasia told me she could set her watch by him.'

Carole-Ann's eyebrows shot up. 'Kasia? Tommy? Since when are we on first-name terms with witnesses and terrorist suspects?'

'All I'm saying is it narrows things down.'

'You already told us this,' said Carole-Ann. 'Twice.' She shook her head at him, the beads in her hair making a gentle jangling sound, like a wind chime on a summer's night. 'When did you last eat, Clem?'

'What?'

'Have you eaten anything today?'

'Yeah. No.' Clem raked his hair. 'Maybe.'

Carole-Ann put a hand on his arm. She wore a thick silver band on her thumb.

'You need food, right now.' She led him to the door. 'I will call you as soon as we find anything.'

His stomach growled. He'd assumed the gnawing nausea was stress or guilt or whatever. Thinking about it, it could just be plain old hunger. Somehow the thought was comforting. 'Now you mention it, sausage and beans could really hit the spot.'

She shooed him away and he headed across the road to a Turkish-run caff where everything came with chips. Back in the day this had been a favourite haunt of the team. Happy times taking the piss over steaming mugs of tea. Then a couple of the gang left, wanting a proper life with a family, a mortgage and a dog. He'd mocked at the time, calling them lightweights. Then another couple of them died, caught up in some undercover operation that went tits up. Clem had squared it away. Things like that happened in MI5, all part of the deal.

'Long time no see, boss.' The now grey-haired owner greeted Clem with a wide, warm smile. 'You don't come in often enough.'

Clem patted his stomach. 'Doctor's orders.'

'What do they know?' The owner wagged his finger. 'My father smoked all his life, ate a yarimca every day. You know what this is?'

Clem shook his head.

'Deep-fried dough. Lived to eighty-three. What can I tell you?'

Clem chuckled and ordered shish kebab, chips and salad. His consultant would at least approve of the cucumber. As he waited for his food, he looked around the tables full of young people. Some of them would be working for the service. He probably passed them every day. Like Krish, they all seemed unlined and unscathed.

His mobile rang as the owner slid a plate under his nose, the smell of spiced lamb and fried potato tantalising. 'Carole-Ann.'

'Sorry to interrupt, but I thought you'd want to know,' she said.

Clem eyed his food longingly, a chip between his thumb and forefinger. 'What have you got?'

'Krish thinks he's found out what Frasier was up to.'

'I'll be right back.' Clem turned to the owner of the café. 'Can I get my order to go?'

The old man laughed. 'Where do you think you are? San Francisco?'

'I wish.'

Clem peered over Krish's shoulder, so close he could smell the young man's aftershave. It was one of those androgynous ones that supposedly worked for either sex and smelled of soap and lemons. Sometimes Clem thought he belonged to another century.

'What on earth is in there?' Carole-Ann pointed to the paper bag clutched in Clem's fist. 'It smells revolting.'

'Kebab and chips,' Clem replied. 'And salad.'

Carole-Ann wrinkled her nose.

'What can you tell me?' Clem patted Krish on the back.

'I checked and double checked those three.' The younger man pointed to the computers at his feet. 'Memory, history, hard drive, you name it, but there was nothing.'

'Nothing?' Clem asked.

'Well, obviously there was something. Hundreds of people use the café and access the internet on these PCs,' said Krish. 'But there was nothing important. No patterns. Nothing to interest us.'

'So why am I here?' Clem rubbed his stomach, desperate for food.

Krish tapped the PC on the desk in front of him. 'Because this baby has an interesting story to tell.'

'I'm in no mood for *Jackanory*, son.'

'Excuse me?' Krish had clearly never even heard of *Jackanory*.

'Clem, would you just let Krish finish?' Carole-Ann said.

'Fine.'

'Okaaaay . . .' Krish spoke slowly, unsure of himself, until Carole-Ann gave him an encouraging nod. 'Until a few days ago, this computer was used every morning at five past nine like clockwork. That would give our suspect time to arrive, order his drink, then get to work.'

'Can we be sure it was Tommy?' asked Clem.

'Not one hundred per cent,' Krish responded.

'But it would be one hell of a coincidence if it wasn't him,' said Carole-Ann.

Clem liked facts and hard evidence; he didn't like supposition, although he'd been forced to do a lot of it today.

'Assuming it was him, what was he actually doing on the net?' asked Clem.

Krish smiled. 'That's where it gets really interesting. Our suspect logged on to the same website each day.'

'What website?' asked Clem.

'Looking for ladies dot com.'

Clem coughed hard. 'Come again?'

Krish tapped some keys and the computer came to life. 'It's a chat site where guys go to look for women.' The graphics were bright as photos of blondes with glossed pouts and large breasts filled the screen.

'Don't you have to pay for those kinds of sites?' asked Clem.

'Free month's trial,' Krish replied. 'He signed up as a temporary member, called himself Darth Vader.'

Bloody hell. Clem needed to sit down. 'Who did he chat to?'

'On the first day, he's deluged by offers of company,' said Krish. 'But the girls soon work out that he's not offering hard cash.

Look.' Krish handed Clem a printout of an exchange that had taken place at the end of June.

From **Ebony** On 28 June 2012 at 9:29
Hi Big Boy
We like to give all new members a warm welcome, DV.
So do you want to come and play?

From **Darth Vader** On 28 June 2012 at 9:31
Do you want to be my girlfriend?

From **Ebony** On 28 June 2012 at 9:33
You don't waste any time, do you? I like a man who knows his own mind.
How about we have a little chat, then work out some business?

From **Darth Vader** On 28 June 201 at 9:34
I really want you to be my girlfriend.

'It goes on like that with a couple more girls', said Krish, 'until this one arrives.'

Krish handed up another printout of the profile page of a girl calling herself Petal.

'Is this real?' Clem drummed the picture of a pneumatic brunette with the tip of his finger.

'Nah,' Krish replied. 'Cut and pasted from the internet. The thing with Petal, though, is that she's not put off by our suspect's cack-handed attempts; she just plays along.'

Clem held out his hand for the latest sheet.

From **Petal** On 28 June 2012 at 9:48
I like *Star Wars*. Which is your favourite?

From **Darth Vader**   On 28 June 2012 at 9:50
Return of the Jedi.

From **Petal**   On 28 June 2012 at 9:52
Oh I love that one too. Hans Solo is so cool.

From **Darth Vader**   On 28 June 2012 at 9:53
Will you be my girlfriend?

From **Petal**   On 28 June 2012 at 9:55
Well we do seem to have a lot in common. And I do need a
boyfriend. Why don't you tell me some other stuff you like?

From **Darth Vader**   On 28 June 2012 at 9:56
I have to go now.

From **Petal**   On 28 June 2012 at 9:58
Well make sure you come back here tomorrow and I'll have
an answer for you.

'Let me guess,' said Clem. 'Petal becomes Tommy's girlfriend.'

Krish nodded. 'Within a couple of days they're swearing
undying love for each other and planning a date.'

'Tell me they don't meet up.'

'Sorry.' Krish shrugs. 'Here's the conversation.'

Clem's hands were shaking as he read the last communication between Tommy Frasier and the person grooming him on
the net.

From **Petal**   On 26 July 2012 at 9:40
I can't wait to see you. I am going to bring chocolate and
sweets. What sort do you like?

From **Darth Vader**   On 26 July 2012 at 9:43
My favourite is Mars Planets.

From **Petal**   On 26 July 2012 at 9:46
Oh I love Mars Planets.
I think we were made for each other.

From **Darth Vader**   On 26 July 2012 at 9:48
Can I kiss you?

From **Petal**   On 26 July 2012 at 9:51
Only if I can kiss you first.

Clem screwed up the paper and threw it across the room, unable to stomach the sick manipulation. 'Do we know where they met up?'

'Outside Stratford tube station,' Krish told him.

'There will be CCTV,' said Clem.

'On it.' Carole-Ann was already moving back to her desk.

A heap of hands and faces push against the row of jail cells. All trying to catch a glimpse of the new boy.

'Fresh meat!' someone screams. 'Fresh meat.'

There's a roar as every prisoner on the landing starts hollering and whistling and banging their cups against the bars.

Isaac hesitates. He knew this was going to be real bad. The judge up at the courthouse didn't even look up from his stack of papers as Bert asked for bail. Bert could have been ordering a cheeseburger and fries for all the mind the judge paid. And when he sent Isaac to juvie pending trial the look on his lawyer's face said it all.

'Go on, boy.' The jailer behind Isaac nudges him in the back with a baton. 'Don't be shy.'

Isaac takes a step onto the landing, his head hanging like a kicked dog, trying to avoid eye contact.

'Meat, meat, meat,' someone chants.

Isaac concentrates on putting one foot ahead of the other, carrying his blanket and tin cup. He hears someone to his left hawking up good, then feels the wet slap on his cheek. Soon everyone joins in and spit rains down on him, landing in his hair, on his clothes, on his skin. He turns away and edges to the balcony. A net is strung across to stop folks from throwing themselves off. God help him, he knows it's a mortal sin and all, but right now, he can see why a body would want to kill himself.

At last he is at his cell door and steps inside, grateful when the door behind him clangs shut. Then he sits on his bunk and breathes.

Hours pass and the lights go out abruptly. Isaac lets his eyes grow accustomed to the shadows. When the moon was low, it could grow real dark in the farmhouse. Isaac was never afraid. He'd listen to the wind in the trees and the coyotes howling. Tonight, there are noises from all sides as the other boys shout out.

'New boy, y'all better watch your step. I'm a-coming for you, ya hear me?' one screeches.

'Not if I git there first,' shouts another.

And they laugh while Isaac shivers on his bunk.

'Looky here, I got something for you, new boy,' shouts the first boy.

A plastic bag flies through the air, whipping through the bars of Isaac's cell door. It lands at Isaac's feet with a plop.

'Present for y'all, new boy.'

Isaac gags. He can see through the bag that there's a great big turd inside.

'Quiet,' another voice rings out.

The boys grumble.

'I mean it. The next prisoner to make a sound loses all privileges for a week.'

Isaac's heart thumps in his chest. Mama always said you couldn't trust anyone in a uniform. 'They got their own agenda,' she warned. Maybe

187

she was right, but at this moment Isaac is glad to see the prison officer at his door, baton in his hand. If his agenda is to make everyone hush up and to keep Isaac safe, then that's okay by him.

'You all right, son?' The officer nods at the bag, stinking on Isaac's floor.

'Yes, sir.'

The officer gives a tight smile and relief pours over Isaac.

'Tell me something, son,' he says.

'I'll try, sir.'

'Is it true that you're a cop killer?'

Chapter Fifteen

I wake when the plane jolts, smacking my head against the window. I don't remember drifting off and, without thinking, I lift my hand to rub the injured spot and my fingers probe my scalp for a lump. I sit bolt upright and thrust my hands in front of my face. I'm not dreaming. My wrists are unbound.

'Calm yourself down, Jo.' Ronnie's own hands rest loosely on the controls. 'You'll give yourself a heart attack.'

The rope has been cut, the ragged ends dangling at my elbows. I untangle what's left, throw the remnants at my feet and massage the welts in my skin.

Ronnie has her lips pressed together, the knife in her right palm. 'Can I trust you, Jo?'

'That's a strange question with that pointing in my direction.'

'I used it to cut the rope,' she says. 'But I could have used it to cut your throat.'

'You still could,' I say.

She wags the blade at me. 'At last you're starting to see sense.'

The plane drops and my ears pop. We are sinking through the sky.

'We're coming in to land,' Ronnie tells me.

The descent is steep and we almost plummet, a side wind buffeting us and my teeth grinding. The wings shudder and the sound of clanging metal fills the cockpit.

'Gonna be a bumpy one,' Ronnie shouts above the noise.

I'm thrown around in my seat, smacking my head first against the window, then to my left, elbowing Ronnie in the shoulder. Her eyes darken, their silver light turning to storm clouds. For a second, I consider doing it again. Harder. If I aimed for the side of her head I could probably knock her out. But who would land the plane? I check outside and the grey swell of the Atlantic Ocean yawns at us. I don't fancy a watery grave.

The plane skids across the sky, bouncing into the air pockets, and Ronnie's hands tighten around the controls, her knuckles white, as she tries to keep us straight.

'We're going down too fast,' I say as the waves threaten to lick our landing gear.

Ronnie doesn't answer but I can see the sinews of her neck straining.

At last the engine emits a terrible groan and we thump down, careering to the left, the brakes shrieking. Then there's a bang and we come to a stop, whiplashed forward then back into our seats.

'Shit,' I say.

Ronnie nods, panting, her hands still clutching the controls. I take it that was a close one.

'What now?' I ask.

'We're going to meet someone who will help me,' she replies.

'Then what?'

'Then nothing. I'll go my way and you'll go yours.'

I laugh. 'As simple as that?'

'With any luck,' she says.

Thus far luck hasn't featured highly. I've been blown up, kidnapped, drugged, punched repeatedly in the face and threatened with a gun. No one on the planet has the faintest idea where I am, including me.

Without another word, Ronnie opens her door and slides outside. The clamour of the ocean rocks the cockpit and I have to fight the wind to open my own door. When I jump down, my feet land in wet gritty sand and as I round the plane I have to climb to stand with Ronnie. By her side I can see we've landed on a long expanse of beach, a sand dune bringing us to our violent halt. In front of us, the impossible wall of angry sea attacking white chalk stacks that we must have missed by inches, behind us moss green hills rolling up to meet the black clouds.

The caravan Ronnie left me in felt isolated but compared to the scene before me it might as well have been in a Center Parcs. I feel as if I'm standing at the very edge of the world.

'Welcome to the Outer Hebrides,' says Ronnie and begins to make her way up the steep incline, away from the beach.

Clem swallowed the last piece of lamb kebab and sucked the grease from each finger, his lips making five wet smacks.

'That stinks,' said Carole-Ann.

'You were the one who sent me out for food,' Clem retorted.

'Not for something that smells like Pedigree Chum.'

Clem waved away her protests, propelled the bag into the bin and stifled a burp in the palm of his hand.

'How about that Krish, huh?' she asked. 'Dynamite stuff he retrieved from the PC.'

'Not bad,' said Clem.

'For a twelve-year-old.'

'Are you here to bait me? Or do you have anything to tell me about the CCTV?' Clem growled.

She pulled a face and led him to her desk. 'This is Stratford underground station.' She gestured to three screens, each showing the entrance from a different angle.

'Why so many cameras?' asked Clem.

'You been there?'

Clem snorted a laugh. It was a rough neck of the woods.

'Here comes Frasier,' she said, and three images of Tommy appeared, from above, front and side. He was holding something.

'What's that?' Clem asked.

Carole-Ann zoomed in. It was a teddy holding a heart. The food in Clem's stomach churned.

They watched him wait, looking up and down the street, occasionally behind him into the station. His excitement was palpable.

Moments later, someone approached him. He was at least six foot, wearing a hat and dark glasses, a rucksack slung over his shoulder. Clem doubted very much that his name was Petal. He spoke to Tommy, his body language relaxed, a hand touching the boy's arm. He threw back his head and laughed and Tommy joined in. Then he reached into his back pocket and pulled out a phone, which he showed to Tommy.

'What's the betting it's a message from Petal?' said Carole-Ann.

Clem felt anger flush his neck and he raked at his collar.

'She can't make it, but she wants to meet her new boyfriend at the Olympic stadium,' said Carole-Ann.

With a hideous inevitability they watched Thomas Frasier take a ticket from the stranger and, finally, the rucksack. The man helped Tommy secure it on his back. As the man turned to leave, he waved. Beaming, Tommy waved back. Then they watched Tommy wend his way out through the crowds.

'I've checked CCTV all the way to the stadium,' said Carole-Ann. 'We could track him almost continuously.'

'Did he look in the bag?'

'No.'

Clem slumped onto Carole-Ann's desk. Tommy had had no idea what was in the rucksack. He'd thought he was on his way to meet the girl of his dreams. When he'd been stopped at security, he'd panicked. Wouldn't anyone with two guns pointing at their head?

'There was no other choice,' said Carole-Ann. 'You had to do it.'

Clem closed his eyes and let his head droop. She was right. There had been no other choice. The boy was making a run for it with an IED. Whether he was aware or not, he was a danger to everyone around him and had to be stopped. But that didn't make it any easier.

'What about the guy?' he asked. 'Can we ID him?'

'Face recognition has drawn a blank,' said Carole-Ann. 'But we're using all the CCTV in the area to see if we can find out where he went.'

'Do whatever it takes and hunt him down,' said Clem. 'We have to stop this bastard.'

As I clamber after Ronnie, I can make out a red pickup truck at the brow of the hill. Ronnie continues towards it but her pace slows as a grizzly bear of a man gets out.

She stops about ten feet away from him, staring through the driving rain. When I catch up, I stop too.

The man is wearing a checked shirt buttoned all the way up. Straggles of shoulder-length hair are tucked behind his ears and topped with a baseball cap, rivulets of water running from its peak. Almost too casually, he has a rifle strung across his shoulder by a leather strap.

'Ronnie?' he asks.

'Uh huh,' she says.

'Who's that?' He nods at me.

'A friend,' says Ronnie.

'Hawk isn't gonna like outsiders coming onto the island.'

'I'll square it with Hawk,' she says.

The man pauses for a second, as if weighing up what to do. 'All right.' He drops the back of the pickup. 'Get in.'

Ronnie pulls herself in and takes a place at the back, on a tyre island among a pile of dirty, sodden rags. I heave myself after her and sit among a selection of saws, hammers and screwdrivers, with my back to the side.

The man slams the flap shut and leans over to me. I'm thrown back by the stench of his body odour. 'Got a name?' he asks.

'Jo. You?'

The man scratches his armpit with a hand so large he could use it to paddle a canoe. 'Tiny.' He walks back around to the driver's side, guns the engine and shoots off, skimming the hill top, leaving Ronnie and me to hunch ourselves against the deluge.

If I thought the boat and plane journeys were uncomfortable, it becomes clear that they were merely preparation for this truck ride. As we head out at speed, we are rattled and rolled along a road that's more pothole than track, all in the vicious force of the storm. Ronnie scratches through the various old blankets and coats until she finds two baseball caps and throws one to me. It feels greasy to the touch and smells of week-old milk.

'This is no time to get precious, Jo.' She slips on her hat. 'It's going to be a long one.'

I glance up at the sky, my eyes scrunched against the downpour and slap it on my head. Ronnie can't resist a chuckle.

Mile upon mile of green-brown turf whizz past, the horizon lost in a waterlogged mist, until we slow and pull to the right. As one, Ronnie and I lean over the side to see what's happening and are met with a view of a dilapidated cottage, its white stone walls crumbling, the thatched roof balding.

'Well, I'll be . . .' says Ronnie and jumps over the side of the truck, landing with barely a sound.

Tiny gets out of the cab and eyes up Ronnie, who is standing legs akimbo, staring at the cottage, shaking her head with a small smile. She turns to Tiny, catches him leering at her and the smile falls away to nothing. 'What?' she barks.

'Nothing.' He slopes into the cottage.

I stretch a leg over the side of the truck and let myself fall with an awkward thump onto my hands. I wipe off the mud down my tracksuit trousers and peer into the darkened doorway.

Tiny exits the cottage, a lit cigarette dangling from his mouth. In his left hand he carries a four-pack of beer, in his right a four-pack of Coke.

'What'll it be?' He holds up the drinks.

Ronnie reaches out and takes the soft stuff.

'Works for me,' he says and gets back in the cab.

Ronnie sweeps into the truck like a gymnast and opens up the flap for me. I'm only just inside, one foot still in midair, when Tiny grates the gears and floors the accelerator.

We take our places in the same spots and Ronnie hands me a can. It's so wet I almost drop it. Ronnie opens hers and almost finishes it in one go, then swirls the remnants around the bottom of the can, making a hollow tinkling sound. I pull the ring on my own can, releasing the gas with a pfft sound and take a long swig.

'I don't suppose you want to explain how this,' I hold up the can, 'found its way into that old place?'

Ronnie shrugs. 'They arrange for someone from one of the other islands to leave provisions from time to time.'

'Why?'

'Look around you, Jo. Do you see any shopping centres?'

I check my surroundings. Rolling wet hills as far as I can see, punctuated only by grey rock. The nothingness of it all makes me dizzy and disorientated and I have to close my eyes. When I open them, Ronnie is looking into the distance, as if there's something there waiting to be discovered.

'Who's Hawk?' I ask.

'What?' She tears herself away.

'Hawk,' I repeat. 'Tiny mentioned someone called Hawk. He said he didn't like outsiders. I assume that's who you're going to meet.'

'Yes,' she says.

'So who is he?'

She gives me a sidelong glance. 'We go back a long time. He owes me.'

'In the same way I owe Rory?'

'Something like that,' she replies and goes back to her vigil.

Rory stares at the video feed to his front door. It has been twenty-five hours and forty-two minutes since Ronnie left. She said she would bring a replacement towel as soon as possible. Rory wonders whether more than twenty-five hours and forty-two minutes could be considered 'as soon as possible'. He knows that this is not an exact amount of time and that different people mean different things by it.

It's like when Imelda used to tell him she would visit 'in a day or so'. This sometimes meant three days, sometimes four. On one occasion it meant nine days because 'the arseholes at head office' wouldn't approve her travel expenses.

Ronnie knows Rory hates inaccuracy. She also knows there are only three towels. There is no spare. If an emergency should occur, such as a power cut, he will be forced to abandon the schedule.

He taps the side of his head to stop it hurting and watches the video feed for a further four minutes. At last, he moves away, back to his bank of computers. Platformnow.com is very busy. A lot of posters are discussing a boy called Thomas Frasier who was shot by the police at the Olympic stadium.

Rory checks three threads.

Topic	By	Replies
Do the feds think we're fucking idiots?	Gunshot	69

I don't know if any of you guys are watching this shit happening in England, but shooting a kid in the back?

SecondAmendment At 16:21
They're saying it was an accident.

Gunshot At 16:22
Bullshit.

Freedomfighter At 16:25
Here in the US there is one fatal shooting a day by the police. That's 365 a year.
Police say they're catching criminals, but how many of those people are really political targets?

Gunshot At 16:28
We live in a police state, brother. Government-sponsored terrorism.

SecondAmendment At 16:30
Remember Sean Bell? They shot him over forty times.

Gunshot At 16:32
Remember Waco? Seventy-four men, women and children were murdered so that the New Order could show its authority.

Rory's heart gives a little flutter at the mention of Waco. This is a reference that will always bring Hawk into the discussion. Rory assumes he has the word on alert. He waits two minutes.

Hawk   **At 16:34**
And let's not forget they televised the whole massacre to
instil fear into the people so they wouldn't take action and
fight.

Freedomfighter   **At 16:35**
I'm too scared not to take action, man. I don't want my kids
looking over their shoulders.

Hawk   **At 16:37**
Our brothers and sisters in England need to know we're with
them.
They need to stand up against the might of the state and
we'll stand alongside, shoulder to shoulder.

Rory would like to communicate with Hawk. Ronnie told him
Hawk was dangerous, but Rory wonders if that is true.
  People lie.
  It took Rory most of his childhood to understand this fact. His
mother said she loved him, but that was a lie. Imelda said she
would help him, but that was a lie.
  Ronnie told him she would return with the replacement towel
'as soon as possible'.

R1234   **At 16:40**
I am here.

Hawk   **At 16:41**
Hey, man, I've been thinking about you a lot. How is your
nose?

R1234   **At 16:42**
It hurts.

Hawk   **At 16:43**

You need to put ice on it, man.
I've had a lot of bust-up noses in my time and ice is the
only thing that will bring it down.

Rory sticks out his tongue. If Hawk is dangerous, how come
people have punched him on the nose?

R1234   **At 16:44**

Who did it to you?

Hawk   **At 16:45**

It's a long story.
I had to leave home when I was fourteen and there was no
one to look out for me.

R1234

I had to leave home when I was twelve.

Hawk   **At 16:46**

Then you understand what it's like, man.
No family to look out for you. No friends to watch your back.
You get picked on.
A bloody nose is the least of your worries, right?

Rory remembers the torture inflicted by the kids at The Orchard.
How they hid his shoes and spat in his cereal. How they threw
lit matches into the hood of his parka on the way to school. How
Josh McGreavy stamped on his hand until every finger except the
smallest was broken.

R1234   **At 16:48**

I understand.

★   ★   ★

'I am telling you in no uncertain terms that the boy has been abused.' The doc is standing with her hands on her hips, the way Mama used to when she was good and mad.

The prison officer shrugs. 'Jail does strange things to a body, especially boys. They do all sorts of weird shit to themselves.'

Isaac is in the hospital bed in the very far corner, but he can hear every word.

'Three deep anal fissures,' she says.

'Like I say, with no girls around there ain't no telling what they'll get up to.'

The doc leans forward. She may only be five foot nothing, but she means business.

'The boy has been repeatedly raped,' she states.

The officer flicks Isaac a look. 'He say that, did he?'

'He didn't need to. The injuries speak for themselves.'

The officer rubs his nose with his knuckle. 'The way I see it, there ain't no evidence,' he says.

The doc crosses her hands over her chest. 'I won't let this rest. A prisoner was seriously hurt while in your care. If you won't take action, then I'll go to your superior officer, and if he won't listen, I'll go to the governor.'

'Thing is, Miss Mulholland . . .' he begins.

'Doctor Mulholland.'

'Right, right.' The officer nods. 'The thing is, you've only been here a couple of weeks.'

'What has that got to do with anything?'

'Well now, when you've been here as long as I have and got the same experience, you'll understand the procedure,' he says.

'Procedure?' The doc makes quotation marks in the air. 'You're telling me there's a procedure for dealing with the brutal rape of a child while in the custody of the state?'

'There's a procedure for everything that happens in jail,' he tells her. 'Including allegations of criminal assault.'

'Well, I'm all ears.'

The officer looks over at Isaac again and he can see the hatred burning in the man's eyes.

'First the victim has to make a complaint,' he says. 'And from what you tell me, the prisoner has not done so. Without a complaint there is no victim, and without a victim there is nothing for me to investigate.'

'That is ridiculous!' the doc shouts.

The officer throws up his arms and lets them slap his thighs. 'My hands are tied, miss.'

He leaves the hospital wing, a small smirk on his lips, and the doc smacks the side of her head with a fist. Then she takes a deep breath and makes her way over to Isaac's bed.

'I guess you heard all that?' She fiddles with the chart attached to the metal frame.

Isaac nods.

'I don't suppose you'll tell me who did this to you?' she asks.

He doesn't answer.

The doc sighs and sits on the bed. Even though she does it real gently, a pain shoots through Isaac almost as intense as his shame.

'I know you're scared,' she says, 'but if you would just give me a name I can help you.'

I look away. If I wanted to tell her, I couldn't. There are just too many to recall.

Chapter Sixteen

The truck winds its way up the rugged terrain, endlessly twisting and turning. The hillside is little more than a green smudge on either side. The rain slows to an insistent drizzle and the clouds lighten.

As we reach the summit the truck slows and we pass the remains of another stone building, though the roof of this one has long since collapsed. The left wall is flanked by a small garden of gravestones, many having given up their fight against the elements and gravity. Only one stands proudly erect, seemingly impervious to time, its Celtic cross facing us in challenge. Ronnie makes a sign of the cross. An unthinking gesture. I'm about to say she doesn't strike me as the religious type when she holds up a hand to stop me as Tiny cuts the engine. She points across the graveyard.

'What?' I ask.

'Hush.' She puts a finger to her lips and continues pointing.

I follow the line down her arm and into the trees. At first all I can make out are boulders and moss and tangles of gorse. Then I see it. A hare. He stands tall, sniffing the air, his head and ears proud.

The driver's door opens slowly and Tiny eases himself out, a rifle in his right hand. Soundlessly, he steps forward and brings the gun to his shoulder, looking down the sights.

Horrified, I realise he's about to kill the defenceless creature and I stand and cup my hands around my mouth. 'Go on,' I shout.

The hare starts at the sound. Then the ring of Tiny's bullet echoes through the sky. The hare falls backwards, his legs cycling in the air, a high-pitched squeal coming from his mouth. Tiny runs to him, takes aim above his head and fires. The hare's legs thud to the ground.

'What the hell do you think you were doing, Jo?' Ronnie hisses.

'It's not right,' is all I can manage.

Ronnie shoots me a look of disgust. 'Do you eat meat?'

'Yes,' I murmur.

'Then don't be a fucking hypocrite,' she says. 'All you did was make sure the animal suffered when he didn't need to.'

She jumps over the side of the truck and makes her way to Tiny, her boots swishing in the wet grass.

Tiny bends forward with a grunt, picks up the dead animal and throws it into the back of the truck where it lands inches from my feet. The bullet wound to the head is small and clean, a neat hole between the eyes. The wound to the flank, however, is ragged, the hare's fur ripped open and spewing blood.

'Lucky for you he didn't get away, city girl,' says Tiny, a raindrop shivering under his nose. 'Otherwise I'd have had to shoot you.' He lets out a hoarse shout of laughter that releases the drop of water. I watch it fall onto the hare's back with a gentle plop.

'All right then.' Tiny nods in approval, wipes a slick of blood from his hands down his jeans and gets back in the cab.

'Don't do anything else stupid,' Ronnie warns me.

Carole-Ann had followed the trail of the man who gave Tommy the rucksack to a ground-floor flat in Leyton.

Clem was parked on the street outside, waiting for backup, when he spotted a man in his rearview mirror. No hat or dark glasses, but something in his manner was familiar.

He punched at his speed dial.

'Are you there?' asked Carole-Ann.

'Yeah, and I think our man has just arrived.'

Clem watched him turn off the street at the gate and pat his pocket for keys.

'The flat is registered to a Paul Ronald,' said Carole-Ann. 'I've spoken to the landlord and he described his tenant as mid-twenties, slim build, sandy brown hair.'

The description fitted. 'It's him,' said Clem. 'And for a man who died on Christmas Day, he's looking remarkably perky.'

Clem got out of the car and arrived at the gate as the man put his key in the lock.

'Paul Ronald,' he called out.

The man turned to the sound of Clem's voice.

'I need a word,' said Clem.

The man hesitated for a second, assessing the situation, then opened his front door and dived inside. Clem leapt forward and, as the man tried to slam the door behind him, got a hand to it and prevented the deadlock catching.

'Armed police!' he shouted, but knew it was meaningless. The man had already worked it out.

Clem took out his gun and stepped inside. The hallway was a mess of trainers, bags and recycling boxes overflowing with glass bottles and jars. Carefully, Clem stepped over the detritus, weapon held out in front of him.

He knew he should wait for backup and the bomb squad. He remembered the guys blown to smithereens by booby traps. Christ, this was like bloody Groundhog Day.

He stood very still and listened. There was a scrabbling sound through the partition wall. There was no direct access from the hall. In order to get to it, Clem would have to go through another room, presumably the living room.

He nudged the door with his foot. He was right about the layout, but the term living room was a complete misnomer. Everything in here spelled death. A battered sofa was covered in tins of peroxide and measuring jugs. Wires were scattered across the floor, tangled up with pliers, screwdrivers and rolls of gaffer tape. The glass coffee table tucked in the corner was littered with nails, screws and razor blades. Clem thought of poor Tommy Frasier carrying his payload and checked his revulsion.

The noise came again, from behind a closed door on the far side. Clem cocked his finger around the trigger of his weapon and crept towards it. Then he opened it with his foot and stepped inside.

As Clem had suspected, it was the kitchen and the man was standing on the draining board, his back to the door, struggling with the locks on the window, clearly about to attempt his escape.

'Put your hands on your head,' Clem instructed.

The man froze.

'I'm armed,' said Clem. 'Put your hands on your head and turn around slowly.'

The man did as he was told and gulped at the sight of Clem's gun trained on him.

'Get down from there,' said Clem. 'Slowly. Very slowly.'

The man crouched on the draining board, washing-up water pooling around his trainers, then made a small jump onto the floor, the rubber of his Nikes making a soft squelch.

'Stay exactly where you are,' ordered Clem and he made his way around the man, reaching into his pocket for hand restraints.

'Leave your right hand on your head and put your left behind your back,' said Clem. The man obeyed and Clem secured the plastic restraint around his wrist.

In a moment, Clem would have the man under control. It

would be tempting to beat him to a pulp when he was helpless. After all, he had taken advantage of Tommy's vulnerability. But Clem wouldn't do that. Instead he would take him back for interrogation and make him squeal.

'Now bring your right hand down slowly,' Clem instructed.

As if in slow motion, the man let his arm fall by his side. Clem reached for the hand, ready to bind it to its mate.

Without warning, the man snatched it away and dived towards a drawer.

'Don't move,' Clem shouted, but the man's hand was already inside. Then he spun back to face Clem, brandishing a kitchen knife. A ray of sunlight coming through the window made the steel sparkle.

'Don't be stupid,' said Clem.

The man's forehead was covered in a sheen of sweat and his hand shook.

'That is no match for this gun,' said Clem. 'So why don't you just put it down?'

The man shivered.

'I don't want to have to shoot you, but I will.'

The man's shoulders slumped as if he knew the game was up. In the time it would take for him to strike at Clem, a bullet would be twice as quick, and at this range the damage inflicted would be fatal.

'Throw it in the corner,' Clem indicated with a jerk of his head.

The man looked defeated and let his hand fall; then he stood, head flopped onto his chest, knife held loosely in his palm. 'It wasn't supposed to be like this,' he said.

'It never is, son,' Clem replied.

The man looked up at Clem, eyes glassy with tears. 'I'm sorry,' he said as he plunged the blade into his neck then dragged it across his throat.

★ ★ ★

The summit crossed, we make our way down the other side, the truck at a sickening angle as Tiny snakes in and out of rocks, barely slowing to avoid collision.

When we arrive at a stream flowing across our path, he ploughs on through, water splashing up from the tyres, splattering Ronnie and I. The droplets are freezing on my skin and I wipe them away with the back of my sleeve, my teeth chattering.

'Just be glad it's summer,' says Ronnie. 'It's stupidly cold up here in winter.'

I almost laugh. 'How far?' I ask, hoping we don't have to make our way to the bottom.

'Not all the way,' Ronnie chuckles.

In fact it's only ten minutes or so when the clouds break and a weak shaft of sunlight finds its way to us as we rumble into a clearing with four crofter's cottages clustered together in a small valley.

A German Shepherd leaps from a doorway and bounds towards us, barking, teeth bared. As we come to a stop, the dog leaps up, paws on the side of the truck, fangs sharp and snapping inches from me.

'Down, Hero,' Tiny shouts. 'Down!'

The dog takes his paws from the truck, but his eyes don't move from me as he emits a growl from somewhere deep in his throat, his tail down, ready to attack.

'Bloody dog,' Tiny says and I notice he hasn't left the cab.

A man comes out of the furthest cottage and lets out a whistle. Hero turns and runs back to him and I feel Ronnie tense besides me.

The man pats the dog, orders it to stay and walks slowly towards us. Ronnie stands and shields her eyes with the palm of her hand. When he's ten feet away, the man stops and stares.

He's wearing faded jeans and work boots and his shirt hangs open despite the sharpness of the wind. His torso is completely hairless but covered in tattoos and scars. Even his neck and the left side of his face are inked with a constellation of blue stars. He rubs distractedly at a pierced nipple. It's impossible to tell what he's thinking because he's wearing a pair of mirrored shades. Like those ones you see in telly programmes from the seventies. He has a rifle in his right hand.

'Hi, Ronnie,' he says at last. His accent is American, the slow intonation of the Deep South.

'Hello,' she replies.

'Is that who I think it is?' He waves the rifle in my direction.

'Uh huh,' says Ronnie.

The man pauses for a second, then spits in the dirt at his feet. 'You shouldn't have brought her here.'

'I needed an insurance policy,' she says.

He shakes his head then spits again, leaving a trail of saliva dangling from his chin. He wipes it away with his forearm.

'Come on now,' Ronnie calls to him. 'I brought you a present.' She points down at the hare lying on the floor of the truck. The blood from its wounds has started to congeal and flies buzz around its nose, mouth and arse.

The man wanders over and peers inside, then looks up at Ronnie. She smiles at him, her eyes glittering. 'Go on then,' he says. 'I expect you and your friend need to clean up and get a drink.' Then he turns and walks back to the cottage.

'It's good to see you,' Ronnie shouts.

The man stops in his tracks and his head droops before he half turns to her. 'And you,' he says, then disappears inside, slamming the door behind him.

Tiny leads us past the cottages to the far side of the clearing and the foot of the next hill.

'Over yonder,' he points to the top, 'you'll find a cabin. Should be a free room in there.'

Then he lopes back to the truck and lights a cigarette.

We make our way up until we can peer down into the next valley and find a log cabin nestling in the shadows.

'Home sweet home,' says Ronnie and trudges down towards it.

The porch is littered with empty bottles and Ronnie kicks her way through into the dark interior. The smell inside reminds me of changing rooms at school. The unmistakable stink of sweat, unwashed clothes and shoes. It's exacerbated by the gloom, which seems to lock the odour in. There are windows, but the glass is filthy and outside the green slopes hem us in. The walls and ceilings are made of thick dark wood, which acts like a cocoon.

I hear a match strike and watch Ronnie's face illuminated in its flame, before she lights a collection of candles on a rough wood table. She takes one, melting it onto its saucer holder and wanders through to the next room. There, there are two bunk beds, filthy blankets rumpled on each, and an overflowing ashtray spills out onto a low bedside table. Nailed to the wall is a flag. It's a tricolour of red, blue and white with a red star placed in the centre.

Ronnie leaves the room, shutting the door behind her, and goes next door. This room is smaller, with only enough space for one bunk bed. It seems empty.

'Looks like we're home,' says Ronnie and throws her leather jacket and cap onto the top bunk. With her back to me, I once again catch sight of the scar on her shoulder.

When she turns, I busy myself taking off my trainers. I can feel the crunch of dirt on the soles of my feet but I don't care. I wiggle my toes, grateful for the freedom.

'I was shot,' she says.

I don't look at her, but I nod. I thought that must be the case.

'By the police,' she adds and wanders out of the bedroom.

I follow her back into the first room, where the candles are now dancing on the table. Ronnie is rummaging in a fridge in the corner of the room. She pulls out two bottles of water and hands one to me.

'The guy with the dog,' I say. 'Is that Hawk?'

'Yep.'

'And he's the one who's going to help you?'

Ronnie nods.

'He didn't look very keen.'

She shrugs.

'Are you sure he'll do what you want?' I ask.

'I told you.' Ronnie takes a drink. 'He owes me.'

'What did he do?' I ask. 'Or more to the point, what did you do?'

'Let's wash up,' she says and makes her way outside to a water butt by the side of the cabin. She takes off the lid and squints inside.

'No spiders in there, are there?' I joke.

'Gotta make sure,' she says.

I cringe and peek inside. 'Looks okay.' I go to reach in.

Ronnie bats my hand away. 'Don't put your filthy paws in clean water.'

She reaches around the back of the butt and finds a ladle attached by a chain. She dips it in the water, scoops some up then pours it over one hand before switching sides. Then she takes another scoop and pours it down her back with a shiver.

She hands me the ladle and I follow suit, first washing each hand carefully, then splashing some on my feet. Finally I pour a couple of scoops over my head, rolling my neck in ecstasy.

I'm interrupted by voices coming from the other side of the hill and the sound of boots crashing through the grass. Three men appear at the summit, each wearing a camouflaged combat jacket and carrying a gun. They stop dead when they see us.

'Hawk put us in the spare room,' Ronnie calls out to them.

They mutter to one another in a language I don't understand.

'Serbs,' Ronnie whispers.

They make their way to us, stopping feet from the porch. 'Where you come from?' asks one.

'England,' says Ronnie. 'London.'

They speak excitedly among themselves, nodding and laughing. 'What's happening there is good, yes?' says the man. 'The bombing has been effective, yes?'

I open my mouth to tell him that, actually, it's been a fucking tragedy, but Ronnie elbows me. Hard.

'It's been very effective,' she says.

They move inside the cabin and the two that clearly can't speak English smile at me and give me the thumbs up. I return the gesture, feeling sick to my core.

When they're out of sight Ronnie puts up her hand to me. 'Don't say it. I want to get out of here and you want to go home, right?'

I nod.

'Then don't cause any more problems, Jo. Please.'

Dear Veronica-Mae,
This is the fourth time I've written and I still don't know if my letters are getting to you.

Sometimes I think maybe you get them, but you're too busy with your new life to reply.

Bert says you been placed with a new family and I wonder if you want to put me and everything else behind you.

I hope that's not so, cus right now I need every friend I got. The only person here who was prepared to give me the time of day was the doc on the hospital wing. And she got herself transferred someplace else without even saying goodbye.

At night when I close my eyes and try to say my prayers, nothing comes. I concentrate real hard but all I can hear are the sounds of the jail around me. I don't know what Mama would have to say, but it seems like even God has abandoned me. I can see how that sounds like blasphemy but bad things happen here all the time and He ain't given me no protection.

The trial is next week and that's the only thing that keeps me hoping. I have to trust that the jury will understand that I only shot that policeman because he shot Mama first. I never meant nothing like that to happen.

Bert says the main problem is the stack of guns we had in the farmhouse. He says the prosecution are convinced there was a plan to take up arms, that we intended to kill any police that came onto our land. I explained to Bert that we was frightened of the Devil, that we thought we were the righteous soldiers of Christ. He calls this 'brainwashing' and says he'll tell the jury that I wasn't in my right mind. To be honest, I'm real scared about standing up in the courthouse and talking about it all. Bert says I just have to tell the truth.

I'm going to say bye for now and beg you to write back. Even if it was just a postcard with one line on it, I'd be grateful.

Your brother,

Isaac

Chapter Seventeen

There was a cocktail party in full swing at Number Ten. The sound of a harpist playing in the corner mingled with the tinkle of laughter and crystal. A waitress passed through the guests with a silver tray of canapés, each spiked with a miniature Olympic flag.

When the PM caught sight of Clem, he broke off from his conversation with the American ambassador and made his way over, glass in one hand, a nibble in the other.

'You have no idea how tough this is, Clem,' he said. 'Everyone is freaking out about the shooting. If they ever found out . . .' He looked at his bite-sized chunk of mozzarella, tastefully speared to a cherry tomato, and sighed. 'Drink?' he asked.

'No thank you, Prime Minister,' said Clem.

'Do we need some privacy?'

Clem eyed the guests. The great and the good from all around the world. Each celebrating the first day of events at the Olympics, being manipulated by the Downing Street team into talking about something, anything, other than Thomas Frasier. None of them must ever find out what had been in that rucksack, of that Clem was certain. 'I think that would be best,' he said.

The PM signalled to Benning and the three of them made their way to the PM's study and closed the door.

'Any news on Connolly?' asked Benning.

Clem shook his head.

'I suppose no news is good news,' said the PM weakly.

Clem could have pointed out that the first twenty-four hours in any kidnap case were crucial. That the chances of finding a victim alive after that point became ever smaller. But what would be the point?

'So why are you here?' asked the PM, glancing at the door and the noises coming from the reception beyond. His unflappable manner was needed in the other room.

'I thought you'd want to know that we discovered the man who groomed Thomas Frasier and handed him the bomb. He was using the alias of a dead man from Glasgow.'

Clem paused before presenting the crucial piece of information. 'Thomas didn't know what was in the bag.'

He waited for the PM's reaction to the news that an innocent civilian had been killed, but the PM said nothing.

'Is he in custody?' asked Benning.

'Dead,' said Clem. 'He took his own life rather than be arrested.'

The PM and Benning exchanged a look. No words were spoken, but Clem could hear the message loud and clear.

'Is that everything?' asked the PM.

'Yes, sir.'

The PM nodded and crossed the room. With his hand on the door handle he turned back to Clem. 'Did you manage to catch any of the events today?'

Clem blinked. 'Sir?'

'The heats of the diving were particularly impressive.' The PM made a downward motion with his hand. 'I should think we'll take a place on the podium.'

Clem watched, astonished, as the PM went back to the party, Benning scuttling after him, leaving Clem to stare at the open door.

★ ★ ★

It was after ten when Clem let himself back into HQ. The place was quiet. He should probably go home and get some rest but he didn't think sleep would come. The nagging suspicion that he had misread things jabbed him gently yet insistently in the back.

He had taken Benning for the villain of the piece. A fixer. A manipulator. Someone who got a kick from hanging on to the shirttails of power and would do anything to keep his grip. The PM had seemed tired and frustrated, but essentially decent. Sure, he wanted the Games to go well, and was willing to take some risks, but there was a line.

Now Clem wondered if he hadn't just seen what he wanted to see. His dislike of Benning and his ilk had coloured his judgement, clouding the truth. The PM didn't want the games to go well. He needed them to. Someone like Benning would survive another day, fix things for someone else when the smoke cleared, but not the PM. His career would not outlive an Olympic debacle. He allowed Benning to play the bruiser, to think the unthinkable, to say the unpalatable, while all the while smiling and smoothing the kinks. Did he really give a shit about Tommy Frasier or Jo Connolly?

'Clem?'

He looked up and found Carole-Ann standing at his shoulder.

'We have to find Ronnie X,' he said.

Carole-Ann held up her hands. Each of her nails was painted with a tiny Union Jack. 'Give us a break, Clem; we're trying. Border patrols, Interpol, you name it. But she's clever. Very clever.'

'People don't just disappear without a trace,' said Clem. 'There's always a trail.'

She sat on the edge of his desk, her bulk making it creak. 'Ronnie's just too good to leave one.'

Clem fired up his PC. 'Ronnie might be, but there's always a loose link.'

He clicked on the CCTV footage outside Stratford underground station. The grainy image of Tommy taking the rucksack once again punched him in the guts.

'This guy.' Clem tapped a pen against the face of the man calling himself Paul Ronald. 'He's our link.'

'We can't be one hundred per cent sure that the attempt to blow up the Opening Ceremony is even connected to Shining Light and the first attack,' said Carole-Ann.

'Maybe not,' Clem replied. 'But we can be sure there's a connection to Ronnie.'

'How?'

'The name he was using belonged to a dead man from Glasgow,' said Clem. 'A man who spent time in the same children's home as Miggs and Ronnie. Don't you think that's too much of a coincidence?'

Carole-Ann shifted her weight and the desk juddered. 'Do you think Ronnie gave the fake ID to our man?' she asked.

'Maybe.'

'And you think he would have known where she might be?'

Clem nodded.

'There's only one problem with that theory – he's not exactly able to tell us,' she said.

'She would never have told him anyway. Probably hasn't told anyone,' Clem answered.

'So how the hell do you intend to find her?'

'By following each link in the chain until I reach the end.' He tapped the screen again. 'This man had some form of contact with her, however indirectly. We need to know who else he was in touch with.'

'There was Frasier, for a start,' said Carole-Ann. 'If we're assuming our dead guy was Petal.'

'Do we have a computer?'

She shook her head.

Clem groaned. 'Another bloody internet café?'

'Seems likely,' she said. 'And there are eight in the vicinity of the flat where you found him.'

'Eight?'

Carole-Ann chuckled. 'It's a busy neck of the woods.'

I lie on my bunk, wrapping the sleeping bag tightly around me. My wet clothes are cold and uncomfortable against my skin. I shiver.

Beyond the bedroom door, the Serbs laugh and shout. Every so often, one of them slams his hand onto the table and the others cry out. The smell of pungent cigarettes sneaks under the door and I imagine a rowdy game of cards is in full swing.

'What sort of place is this?' I ask Ronnie.

She bends over the side of the top bunk. 'Wake up and smell the coffee.'

'But what are those guys doing here?'

Ronnie's mattress creaks as she turns over. 'Work it out for yourself, Jo.'

I try to work it out, but cold fudges my brain. Whatever's going on here is definitely illegal. Trafficking, perhaps? Are the guys outside being held here until they make the next leg of their journey into the UK in the back of a container lorry? The old me wouldn't have wanted to know and would have concentrated on the fact that I'll soon be out of here and on my way home. But I'm not the old me, am I?

I'm wondering who Hawk is and what his connection is to Ronnie, when there's a knock at the door. Ronnie sits bolt upright and I do the same, banging my head on the underside of her bed.

'Yeah,' she calls out.

The door opens and the English-speaking Serb takes a step inside. 'We eat now, if you are hungry.'

Ronnie swings her legs over the side and nods at me to leave the room. The table next door is indeed scattered with playing cards and coins, but there is no food.

'We go to the cottages,' says the Serb.

It's dark outside now and they each take a torch. I follow the beam of one, crashing into the water butt as we pass through the blackness. Suddenly the sky opens up as we scale the hill and a million stars twinkle at me. Without any light pollution, they dazzle into infinity.

The smell of wood smoke fills the air and I can make out the glow of a small bonfire in the valley below. As we near, I see Tiny stirring an iron cooking pot, suspended over the flames, a cigarette dangling from the corner of his mouth, a beer in his hand.

The Serbs greet him and Tiny nods at them. 'Evening, lads.'

There are several plastic buckets on the ground filled with drinks. 'Beer?' the Serb asks me.

'Thanks.'

He tosses a bottle to me and hands one to each of his friends. They remove the tops with a twist of their teeth and spit them into the fire. I think of the thousands I've spent at the orthodontist.

'Here.' Ronnie takes my bottle and opens it with a Swiss army knife.

Soon others appear from the cottages like wraiths, their out-lines blurred until the firelight solidifies them. They take their places in front of the fire, chatting in low voices and drinking.

A man with a goatee and black bomber jacket displaying a skull and crossbones intersected with a lightning bolt reaches into the fire to light his cigarette. 'You just get here?' he asks me.

'Yes,' I say. 'You?'

He shakes his head and takes a long drag. 'Been here over a month. Good place.'

'Yeah?'

'Fucking A.' He waves his cigarette at me, the end burning red. 'I've been around, you know what I'm saying, and this is the real deal.'

A hush falls over the group as the door to the furthest cottage opens and Hawk steps out, Hero at his heel. A chemical smell escapes and I rub my nose.

One of the Serbs calls out to him, beer held high. Hawk nods, locks the door behind him and makes his way over. Still wearing his sunglasses, he stops to chat with some men at the far side.

Beside me, I feel Ronnie's muscles tighten. It's the same reaction she had in the back of the pickup truck. If I didn't know better, I'd say she was nervous.

He makes his way to us and stands in front of Ronnie. 'You got everything you need?'

'Yeah.'

Then he turns to me. 'You?'

I'm distracted by the eerie reflection of my face in his glasses and don't answer immediately.

'You deaf?' he asks.

'No, no. Everything's just fine,' I say.

He stares at me, which is bloody disconcerting given I can't see his eyes, until I look away and he moves on.

'Don't worry,' Ronnie whispers. 'He won't hurt you.'

'How can you be sure?' I ask. 'Ah yes, I remember now – he "owes you".'

Somehow this isn't much of a comfort. I've seen Ronnie's own body language change when Hawk is around.

'Grub's up,' Tiny calls to a murmur of appreciation.

Plates are handed around full of a rich brown stew and hunks of what looks like potato, the edges blackened by the fire. I take a mouthful of dark, smoky meat and swallow it down.

'What is this?' I ask.

Ronnie points her spoon to the step of the nearest cottage where the hare's skin has been discarded.

My stomach flips but I'm too hungry and the food is too good to worry.

After supper, we each take another beer and someone begins playing the harmonica. Tiny is now cross-legged on the wet grass, his cheeks sucking in and out as he plays an old Woody Guthrie tune.

Hawk looks straight across the fire at Ronnie and nods. The tension between them is electric and lasts until the man with the goatee begins to sing along. He has a throaty baritone that suits the song.

'Time to go,' says Ronnie and drains her beer.

I do the same and we head back to the cabin, stumbling up the hillside without a torch.

She lights a candle and brings it into our room.

A thousand questions race around my head, but once on my bunk, my eyelids droop with food and beer and exhaustion.

'Just tell me one thing . . .' My words slur into one another.

'Go to sleep, Jo,' she says, and blows out the candle.

Clem was waiting outside Oliver's Sandwich Bar and Internet Café when the streetlights went out. Dawn scorched red across the London skyline. It was going to be a nice day.

At last a man in his late forties arrived, reaching for a key on a chain attached to a belt loop.

'Are you the owner?' Clem asked.

'Manager,' the man replied.

Clem flashed his badge. 'Can we go inside?'

'What's this all about?' asked the man as Clem guided him through the door with a firm hand in the small of his back.

Clem glanced at the row of computers. 'I'm afraid I have to take those.'

'They're completely legit. I have all the paperwork to prove it.' The man set off to the counter. 'I'll get it for you now.'

'It has nothing to do with where you bought them, sir. They're part of an ongoing enquiry, or at least the information contained in them might be.'

'You've got to be kidding me.' The man's face crumpled. 'This is what brings in half of my business. Foreign students, emailing home over a cheese toastie.'

Clem was already signalling a team to collect the PCs. 'With any luck we'll have them back to you by the end of play today,' he said.

Back at HQ, forty-three computers were lined up on the floor. Krish and four look-a-likes stood around listlessly.

Clem could smell the stale beer from the doorway. 'You lot must have had a skinful last night.'

Krish looked up sheepishly. 'We went out for my birthday, ended up in some club.'

'How old were you?' asked Clem.

Krish opened his mouth to answer but the words became tangled in a mournful burp.

Clem held up his hand. 'Actually, I don't want to know because – frankly – I don't care.'

A lad in a pink polo shirt, collar up, let himself flop into a seat with a groan.

'For fuck's sake,' Clem muttered and snatched up his mobile. 'Carole-Ann, could you do me a favour and bring in tea, coffee, toast, doughnuts and whatever else it takes to bring this sorry shower back into the land of the living.'

Moments later, Carole-Ann returned, pushing a trolley laden with drinks and food. Krish and his friends fell upon it like gannets. Only collar-boy skulked around the edges.

'Coffee or Coke?' she asked him.

'I try to avoid caffeine,' he said.

'Hear this, babe – you're this far from an official warning.' She held her thumb and forefinger an inch apart. 'Now get something down you and don't vex me.'

He grabbed a can and two croissants and went back to his seat.

As they all chewed and slurped, Clem approached the smart board. 'Listen up, everyone.' He pressed a key and Tommy's face appeared on the screen. 'This is Thomas Frasier, a young man with learning difficulties.' He pressed another key and the man calling himself Paul Ronald appeared alongside. 'And this is the evil bastard that convinced Thomas to carry a bomb into the Opening Ceremony, getting him killed into the bargain.' He played the CCTV clip outside Stratford station.

'I thought there was no bomb,' said collar-boy.

'That's the official line for the punters,' said Clem. 'And I don't have to remind anyone here that we are all subject to the Official Secrets Act, do I?'

Silence greeted Clem. Good enough.

At last collar-boy put up his hand. 'Can I ask a question, sir?'

Carole-Ann tried to stifle a laugh. These kids were brilliant at what they did, but Christ on a bike, this was MI5, not sixth form.

'By all means,' said Clem.

Collar-boy wiped croissant crumbs from his skinny jeans. 'I was just wondering how that guy did it?' He coughed back his embarrassment. 'I mean, how do you convince someone to carry a bomb for you, even if they do have learning difficulties?'

'Good question,' said Clem. 'Fortunately, the last time your man Krish worked for me he wasn't this hungover.' The group laughed politely. 'He discovered that Tommy joined a website called LookingforLadies.com. For all intents and purposes it's an internet knocking shop, but our Tommy didn't know that. He thought it was a place to find a girlfriend.'

Clem strayed from the board to the trolley and found the plates empty. He helped himself to a polystyrene cup of black coffee. 'And that's where he met Petal.' Clem clicked to the avatar used on the website. 'Petal convinced Tommy she was in love with him and they arranged to meet up. Only when Tommy got there, Petal couldn't make it and this man arrived with a rucksack.' The clip played again.

'We're assuming that man is Petal?' asked collar-boy.

'We are,' said Clem. 'And I want to know everything there is to know about him.'

'For a start, we know he was a member of LookingforLadies,' said collar-boy.

Clem nodded. 'Which is why Carole-Ann is in charge of more than just feeding you lot.'

Carole-Ann moved among them, handing each of them a printed sheet. 'I contacted the hosts of the website and asked for Petal's history,' she said. 'This is it. When she joined, when she logged in, what she said, who she said it to.'

'Basically, it's her chatting up potential victims, and mostly getting nowhere fast,' said Clem. 'There's nothing else that would be useful to us.'

'But if we know Petal was online at specific times, we can search around those times for other activity,' said collar-boy. 'It might lead us somewhere.'

Clem nodded. It was interesting how the one who had looked like the biggest pain in the arse was turning out to be the most on the ball. 'Which is why I've brought in this little lot.' Clem pointed to the PCs. 'There's a good chance Petal used local internet cafés to ensure everything stayed clean.'

'If we can just find the right one,' said Krish.

'No,' said collar-boy. 'Petal won't have just used one.'

'Thomas Frasier did,' Krish replied.

'He was just the patsy,' said collar-boy. 'Petal knows what's what. He will have used different cafés, different computers, different times. Less chance of being spotted by staff; less chance of leaving a trail.'

'Exactly,' said Clem. 'Which is why I need a team of you to search this lot fast. Anything at all that you think might be even vaguely interesting, bring to Carole-Ann or me.'

The techies drained their cups and set to work, splitting the computers, ordering their tasks.

'Since you greedy bastards wolfed every last scrap of food, I'm getting some breakfast,' said Clem. 'Call me if – no, when – you find anything.'

I'm woken by the sound of voices and I stretch in my bunk. For the first time since we arrived I'm not cold. Not warm either, just comfortably cool.

Through the window I hear the Serbs at the water butt, chatting, before they head off. Then a stillness. No traffic, no planes. In London there is no time of day without buzz and movement. In the dead of night, sirens blare. You tune it out, so it becomes like white noise. God I miss it. Outside, the silence is deafening, crashing on top of me. I sit up to breathe.

'You okay?' Ronnie asks from above.

'Just need a bit of fresh air,' I say and make my way outside.

The inky denseness of the previous night has been replaced by a murky grey as the sun tries to raise its head. Everything is covered in a film of dew and I enjoy the tingling dampness on the soles of my feet. My clothes have dried and I smell like I slept in an attic.

Ronnie appears in the doorway, hands me a bottle of water and a flapjack. 'Want to take a walk?'

I pull on my trainers and we head out and up. When we reach the top of the hill, daylight arrives and the skies come alive with gulls calling and wheeling. A butterfly lands on a leaf inches from my foot, close enough for me to see the veins through its parchment wings.

I turn to tell Ronnie and notice she has a rifle slung on her shoulder. 'Just in case,' she says.

Just in case of what? Just in case MI5 turn up? Or I try to leg it? I take in the hills rolling into the distance and the ocean stretching into grey infinity. Neither scenario seems likely.

We reach two streams intersecting one another, water babbling, splashing against rocks coated in a moss so vivid green the intensity makes me lightheaded. Ronnie washes her hands in the flow and wipes them down her jeans.

'Not too far now,' she says.

'Where to?' I ask.

She heads off. 'You'll see.'

The climb becomes rough, the carpet of grass turning to stone. We have to pull ourselves up rocks by our hands. The jagged edges jab me through the rubber soles of my trainers. At last we reach a peak and scrabble up. At the top, I realise we have reached our destination and it takes my breath away.

Far below us lies a loch so vast and still and magical it is as if nothing has moved for a thousand years. Mist rises up in a royal blue haze to meet the morning sky. I don't think I've ever seen anything as beautiful.

'How deep is it?' I ask.

'I don't know if anyone's ever measured it,' Ronnie replies. 'They say there are kelpies in there.'

225

'Kelpies?'

'Shape-shifting creatures who drag their victims down and drown them.'

I laugh.

'Would you risk it?' Ronnie asks.

I look into the water, ice clear yet impenetrable. 'Not a chance,' I say.

We sit and watch the sun move through the sky, eating our flap-jacks. Birds of prey soar above us, and the mist slowly evaporates. Eventually we set off back to the cabin.

Hawk is waiting for us. 'Where've you been?'

'Up the crag,' says Ronnie.

He chews his lip and scratches the back of his neck.

'What's that?' Ronnie points to a spot of blood in the crook of Hawk's elbow.

He covers it with his hand. 'Snagged myself on a branch.'

There's a pause filled only with the sounds of the forest.

'I'm going to get you somewhere safe in a week or so,' he tells Ronnie.

'Why so long?'

Hawk looks at his fingers, now smeared in blood from the cut on his arm. 'Got something going on.'

'What?'

He rubs his hand down his jeans, leaving a red smear. 'Something big. Been planning it a long time and you wouldn't want to jeopardise that now, would you?'

'Of course not,' says Ronnie.

'In the meantime,' he points to the cabin, 'Mi casa, tu casa.'

When Hawk leaves, I slump onto the porch. A week. I thought this might all be over today.

Ronnie looks distracted, kicking at stones.

'Don't you think the police are more likely to find us if we hang around a week?' I ask.

'Jo, look around you. There are no police here,' she says.

'Someone might call them.'

'Who?'

'I dunno,' I say. 'A passerby.'

Ronnie sighs. 'The island is uninhabited; there are no passersby. It's just us chickens.'

'What about the people who left provisions?' I ask.

Ronnie shakes her head. 'They're not the sort of folk who will call the police, believe me.'

I feel a huge sense of foreboding. Ronnie has put herself and me entirely at the mercy of Hawk.

She crouches on the ground and puts her head in her hands.

'Ronnie?'

She doesn't answer.

'You said Hawk owed you,' I remind her.

'He does.'

'He's not acting like someone who owes you anything. Can you trust him?'

She looks up at me and I expect a tirade of abuse. Of course she can fucking trust him. She can trust him with her life. Why else would she have come here?

Instead she says, 'I want to take a look in Hawk's place.'

'Why don't you just ask nicely?'

She gives me a wry smile.

I take a deep breath. Hawk has been very careful at keeping his cottage out of bounds, locking it every time he leaves. And apart from him I haven't seen anyone going in or coming out.

'Whatever he's mixed up in, I'm pretty sure he doesn't want us to know anything about it,' I say.

She tilts her head, her eyes wide. From her position on the ground and mine on the porch, she seems even tinier than usual. 'I need to know,' she says.

'Why?' I shake my head. 'Soon we'll both be out of here and start our lives again. I have to get back to London and you have to get away somewhere safe.'

'I need to know.' Ronnie swallows. 'I need to know he's okay.'

I throw my head back and laugh. Hawk is clearly a grade-A nutter. Mad, bad and dangerous to know. He's holed up in the arse end of nowhere, surrounded by an international gang of gun-toting God knows what.

'You're worried about Hawk?'

Ronnie nods slowly. 'Goes with the territory, I guess.'

'Why?'

'He's my brother.'

The collar of the shirt Isaac's wearing chafes real bad and for two pins he would change it, but Bert says it's important to give the right impression to the jury. Each day he brings Isaac a clean one, and a necktie too.

At the start of the week, he gave Isaac a big old smile, told him not to worry. 'Son, you leave this to me now.' He seems to enjoy being in the courthouse, chewing the fat with the other lawyers.

The judge seems like a reasonable body. Bert stands real tall when he talks to her and she listens to him and nods. Isaac hopes she does the same to him.

Isaac is led over to the witness stand and asked to take the good book in his right hand, then he swears before God that he will tell the truth. And he does.

He tells them how on that day there were two policemen hiding on their land. That he went out to talk to them and saw them drinking beer. He explains how he went back inside and would have stayed there but for the constant hollering for them to come on out.

'So I went with my mama to tell them to get off our land,' Isaac says.

'And what happened?' asks Bert.

'There was kind of an argument between one of them and Mama.'

'Did you say anything?' Bert asks.

'No, sir.'

'Who fired the first shot?' asks Bert.

Isaac pauses. He wants to get this straight.

'To be honest, Mama cocked first, but the policeman beat her to it.'

'So it could have been your mama or the policeman?' Bert asks. 'But not you?'

'Definitely not, sir,' Isaac says.

'What happened next, Isaac?'

'Mama fell back hurt, blood everywhere, so I shot the policeman.'

'Why?'

Isaac rakes at the collar with his finger. 'I thought he might shoot Mama again, or maybe me.'

'Did you believe he wanted to kill you?'

'Hell yeah.' Isaac gulps at the jury. 'I'm sorry.'

Bert holds up a hand. 'Don't apologise, son. I'm sure we can all appreciate how difficult the situation was. Why don't you explain to the good folks here what was going through your mind?'

'Lots of things, sir. For one, Mama said that the End Times had come.'

'And you accepted that?'

Isaac shakes his head. 'I wasn't sure. But then when the policeman shot her, I thought it must be true.'

'So you thought the policemen were the servants of the Devil?'

'Yes, sir.'

'And what did you think they had come to do?'

'I thought they had come to kill me and my family.'

Bert turns to the jury. 'And if you consider it, that wasn't too far from the truth, was it?'

Chapter Eighteen

I sit for half an hour on the porch trying to straighten out my thoughts. Ronnie crouches opposite, her head back in her hands.

Hawk is Ronnie's brother. I'd suspected something between them, something more than extreme politics.

'Where is Hawk from?' I ask.

'Alabama.'

'You too?'

She nods.

'How did you end up in the UK? Glasgow of all places?'

'I was adopted and my new family emigrated to Scotland,' she says. 'It didn't work out.'

'Why not?'

'Everyone thought I needed a new life, to start afresh,' she explains. 'But bad shit stays bad shit. It doesn't change just because you try to leave it behind.'

I catch my breath as I think of Dad and Mum and Davey. 'And Hawk?'

Ronnie shakes her head slowly. 'Left all alone, drowning in that sea of bad shit.'

Her face is stricken with guilt and I understand every last wretched drop of it.

'Let's do it.' I get to my feet.

Ronnie knits her brow.

'Let's try to find out what the hell your brother is hiding.'

We walk through to the valley, as if we're doing nothing more important than enjoying a stroll. 'See anyone around?' I whisper.

Ronnie shakes her head but I'm not taking any chances.

I nod at the cottage furthest from Hawk's. 'You check that one and I'll take this.'

I jog over to the nearest cottage and rap my knuckles against the door. When no one answers, I let myself in to check each room. Every single flat surface seems to be littered with ammunition. There's even what looks like a hand grenade on top of the fridge. When I'm satisfied there's no one home, I wait for Ronnie to finish, then signal for us to approach Hawk's place.

We stand at the door, glancing left to right. 'Everything looks clear,' I say and I try the door.

It's locked. Of course it is. It was never going to be that easy. 'Knife?' I suggest.

Ronnie pulls out her Swiss army knife and extracts one of the implements.

'I thought that one was for peeling oranges,' I say.

She pulls a face and inserts it into the lock, twisting and turning it, listening intently. 'Goddamn double bolt,' she says, bending so her ear almost touches the lock. At last there's a click and Ronnie smiles.

I swallow hard and scan the clearing for signs of life. The closer Ronnie gets to success, the more nervous I become. If Hawk catches us, or if anyone else catches us for that matter, I suspect they'll shoot us first and ask questions afterwards.

There's another click and the door opens. 'I'll go in; you keep watch,' says Ronnie.

I nod. 'Give me the rifle,' I say.

231

She opens her mouth to protest.

'You're not going to need it inside, are you?' I ask. 'But if any-one arrives out here, I might just have to use it.'

'Have you ever used a gun, Jo?'

I've never even held a gun before. Not a real one. I once went paintballing on a team-building weekend but I don't think that counts. 'Just give me the gun,' I tell her.

Reluctantly, she hands it over. It's much heavier than I thought it would be. The way Ronnie swings it around you'd never know how solid it is. The wood of the butt is smooth to the touch, the barrel cool.

'I'm going in,' she says and disappears inside.

That chemical smell I'd noticed the previous night escapes again. I survey the valley from left to right, keeping watch for any-one returning.

'Anything?' Ronnie calls from inside.

'No,' I shout back.

'With any luck they're all training.'

'For what?' I ask.

Ronnie doesn't reply but she doesn't need to. I must be stupid not to have worked it out before. The men, the weapons, the secrecy. It all adds up at last. I grip the gun more tightly, terrified by what I've just worked out.

Out of the corner of my eye I catch a shape in the distance and I snap my head towards it. My pulse quickens as I strain to see. A bird glides across the sky on a thermal. Is that what I saw? It looked bigger.

I bring the rifle up to my shoulder and look into the sight, bringing the edge of the horizon closer. There it is again. A dark mass. A boulder, perhaps? I hold my breath and curl my finger around the trigger. The boulder moves.

'Ronnie,' I hiss over my shoulder.

No reply.

Without taking my eyes off the shape, I take a step backwards and push the door open with my foot.

'Ronnie.'

She still doesn't answer.

I take another step into the cottage and am hit by a wall of toxic fumes that makes me bend at the waist, spluttering. Tears spring into my eyes and I have to blink to clear my vision.

When I've recovered myself enough to stand upright, I find Ronnie motionless at the door to what must be a bedroom, seemingly transfixed. Gagging, I make my way past a table piled high with hundreds of packets of over-the-counter cold and flu pills. On the floor are twenty or more bright yellow bottles of antifreeze.

Ronnie still hasn't moved and when I reach her, I can see why. There are no bunk beds in the bedroom. Instead, there is a Formica table weighed down with oversized glass vials set on camping stoves. An intricate set of tubes runs from their mouths to hooks on the ceiling and down into plastic containers on the floor.

'What the fuck are you doing in here?'

Ronnie and I both spin to the sound and find Hawk in the doorway, his weapon pointing right at us.

Carole-Ann tracked Clem down in the car park, squatting by the boot of his car, rubbing at the dent in the bumper with a handkerchief.

'What happened?'

'Don't ask,' said Clem. 'Have they found anything?'

Carole-Ann see-sawed her hand. 'Sebastian has a theory.'

'Sebastian?'

Carole-Ann mimed putting up her collar.

Collar-boy was called Sebastian? Well, that was about right.

Clem straightened up, his knees giving an almighty crack and sighed. 'This had better be good.'

Sebastian was surrounded by balled pieces of paper when Clem arrived. The mess he had created in less than two hours was incredible.

'I'm told you have a theory.'

Sebastian turned from the PC, pen lodged sideways in his teeth and nodded.

'We've all been checking the times when we know Petal was logged in at LookingforLadies.' He spat the pen out. 'A few of us have found him.'

Krish nodded his agreement, as did a young woman with a bees' nest of blonde hair knotted loosely on top of her head.

Sebastian patted the PC in front of him. 'For example, this one was used by Petal to speak to Tommy on the twenty-eighth of June.'

Clem grabbed a chair and sat next to the young man.

'The trouble is, our man didn't use this PC for anything else that day,' said Sebastian.

'Are you sure?'

Sebastian shrugged. 'I think so. The user before sent emails back to Australia; the one after was checking out property porn. If you think about it, it makes sense. Our man uses one session to cruise LookingforLadies, then moves on.'

'Always covering his tracks?'

'Exactly,' said Sebastian.

Clem looked around the room at the other computers. There was no way of knowing which internet café he would go to next, or even if he would go straight away. Needles and haystacks sprang to mind. 'So what's your theory?'

'He knows that perpetual motion will keep him safe. He needs to log off and use another computer, maybe go home first, then come out again later that day, use a different café.'

'And?'

'And in reality who could be arsed to do that?' said Sebastian.

Clem shook his head. Only someone so young could come up with something as idiotic as that. 'My long experience of terrorists is that they can be arsed to do all sorts of things,' he retorted.

'Lucky for you, this one was different. He just got himself a coffee and used the next one that became free.' Sebastian pushed his seat along the desk until he was in front of the next PC.

'You are kidding me?'

Sebastian laughed and shook his head. 'He logged out of that one after ten. By half past, he's using this one on the same site.'

Clem rubbed his hands. 'If your theory holds, then all we need to do is check the other computers in the same café, whenever we find Petal looking for ladies.'

'Already doing that,' said Sebastian and pointed at the small girl with the big hair. 'Emily found Petal on the twenty-ninth of June. She's checking the other PCs now.'

Clem gave a wordless sound of satisfaction. It was only a matter of time before they found something.

'What the fuck are you doing in here?' Hawk repeats, the end of his gun only a foot from my forehead.

My fear reflects back at me from his sunglasses.

'I could ask you the same question.' Ronnie's voice is brittle.

I can see right into the barrel; it's like a black tunnel that wants to suck me in.

'Of all the things you could do and you spend your time making crystal meth.' Ronnie raises her voice a fraction. 'You used to want to change things, not become part of the problem.'

Hawk's hand quivers slightly. 'The things we do need to be paid for, Ronnie.'

'By selling drugs?' Her voice takes on the hard edge of anger.

'How do you think the state operates, Ronnie? How do you think it pays for all its armies and police?' He takes a step towards us and I wince. 'Alcohol, cigarettes and gambling, that's how. Fight fire with fire, I say. It's the only way.'

Ronnie points to the door. 'Do those men out there know how you fund all this?'

'They don't ask stupid questions.'

Ronnie shakes her head violently. 'Have you been in the cities? Entire generations have been ruined by drugs.' She's shouting now. 'They've had their lives ripped from them and I can't believe you of all people can get involved in that.'

'Read your history, Ronnie. Governments ruin people's lives,' he says. 'They want us to be poor and miserable so we'll work for the paymaster no matter how little they offer or how dangerous it is. And when there's no work for us to do, they just want to keep us quiet.'

Ronnie steps in front of me so that the gun is almost touching her, then she pushes it down with her hand. 'What about you?' She points to the mark on his arm. 'Why are you using this stuff?'

Hawk lets the gun fall to his side. 'Seeing you again. It made my head break in two.'

'Oh, Isaac,' says Ronnie and puts her hand on his shoulder.

He jumps away as if her touch burns. 'Don't call me that.'

'I'm sorry.'

They look at one another for a long moment.

'You should leave now,' says Hawk.

I for one don't need to be told twice.

The prosecutor is called Mr Stakinsky, which doesn't sound like an American name. He's twice as tall as Bert and three times as wide. He wears his hair slicked over his ears with grease and each day a different colour handkerchief peeps out from his breast pocket.

Today's is cornflower blue.

'Isaac,' he says. 'May I call you Isaac?'

'Yes, sir,' Isaac says.

'Can you tell me about your mama?' he asks.

'What would you like to know, sir?'

'Was she a Christian woman?'

'Yes, sir.'

'Read her Bible?'

'Every day, sir,' I say.

Mr Stakinsky nods and checks his notes. 'You told the court earlier that on the day Officer Shaw was killed, your mama declared that the End Times had arrived, is that right?'

'Yes, sir.'

'Was that the first time she'd thought that?'

Isaac shakes his head. 'Oh no, sir.'

Mr Stakinsky leans against the desk and grins. 'My grandma was just the same. Wasn't a week went by that she wasn't announcing the end of the world.'

Bert gets to his feet and looks up at the judge. 'Your honour, I don't know if my colleague intends to ask a question soon, or if he'd rather take the stand himself.'

The judge nods her head. 'Mr Stakinsky, get to the point.'

He holds up his hands to her then turns back to me. 'What I'm getting at, Isaac, is if your mama made these proclamations regularly, why on this particular occasion did you believe her?'

'On account of there being policemen with guns in our yard, sir.'

The jury chuckle, though Isaac didn't intend to make a joke. It makes a small tic appear at the corner of Mr Stakinsky's eye.

'Let's change tack,' he says. 'Why did your mama and you go outside?'

'The policeman told us to.'

'They wanted to talk to you?' he asks.

'So they said.'

'Why did you take your guns?'

'Mama handed me it.'

'Why?'

'To protect ourselves.'

'From what?'

Isaac shrugs. 'From us getting killed, I guess.'

'You guess?' Mr Stakinsky turns to the jury. 'You went out armed because your mama "guessed" they might shoot you?'

'As it turned out, it was a pretty good guess, sir.'

His whole eye is twitching now. 'Let me get to the bottom of what you're trying to say here, Isaac. The idea that these policemen were the servants of the Devil was your mama's. And it was your mama's decision to arm yourselves. And it was your mama who took the first shot.'

'I don't know what you're trying to say, sir.'

'Seems to me, Isaac,' he goes on, 'you're trying to put the whole blame on someone who's not here today to defend themselves.'

Isaac turns to the judge in panic. 'I would never disrespect my mama. Never.'

'Just tell the truth,' she says. 'Nothing more, nothing less.'

'Where was your daddy when this whole nightmare took place?' asks Mr Stakinsky.

Isaac's throat has closed over and when he tries to speak all that comes out is a squeak.

'Take a drink, Isaac,' says the judge.

Isaac pours himself some water from the plastic jug in front of him, almost dropping the glass because his hands are shaking so bad. Mr Stakinsky raps his fingers on his desk as if Isaac were deliberately wasting time.

'Out fishing with my brother, Noah,' Isaac answers eventually.

'Why didn't you go?'

'I'd been sick the night before, sir,' says Isaac.

Mr Stakinsky gives a low whistle. 'I bet that made you mad. A boy like you needs to be out in the fresh country air.'

'I wasn't too happy about it, sir.'

'I expect you're a good fisherman, Isaac.'

'I do okay, sir.'

'And hunting?' he asks. 'You a good shot?'

'Not bad, sir.'

He wags at finger at me. 'I know pride is a sin, Isaac, but you're under oath here, so why don't you tell us just what a good shot you are.'

'A very good shot, sir.'

'Better than your elder brother?'

'Yes, sir.'

'And your daddy could trust you to protect the family while he was gone?'

'Yes, sir.'

Mr Stakinsky nods and taps his pad of paper with his finger. 'What was the last thing your daddy told you before he left that morning?'

Isaac takes another sip of water. He's played that scene a thousand times in his mind, enjoying his daddy's deep voice, the kind smile on his lips.

'He said he was putting me in charge,' Isaac says. 'That I was the man of the house.'

Chapter Nineteen

I pace between my bunk and the porch, waiting for Ronnie. She didn't follow me back to the cabin and I've no idea where she is. I sit on the steps, still clutching the rifle in one hand, swatting flies from my face with the other.

At midday the Serbs troop back down the hill. The sight of me dishevelled and armed doesn't seem to bother them. 'Okay?' asks the English-speaking one.

I give a nod.

'Good weapon.' He points to the rifle. 'Direct hit possible at very long range.'

I nod again and he shows me his rifle. 'Excellent for sniper.'

I gulp down my horror and smile.

'We train hard today,' he tells me. 'And you?'

'Yes,' I say.

'We rest now,' he adds. 'More practice this afternoon.'

'Good idea,' I mutter and they go inside.

Relief washes over me when Ronnie finally appears. It's not that I trust her, or even feel safe in her company, it's just that at this moment in time she is the nearest I've got to ballast.

'Where have you been?' I ask, jumping to my feet.

'Thinking.'

Jesus, couldn't she have done that at the cabin? My mind has been working overtime since Hawk caught us in his cottage and I've come the same conclusion a million times.

'We need to get out of here, Ronnie.'

She frowns at me.

'I'm serious. The more I think about it, the more I'm convinced that Hawk and the rest of these guys will never let us walk out of here.'

Ronnie shakes her head.

'C'mon. We've just discovered a meth factory in a terrorist training camp.' I raise my voice. 'There is no way they're going to risk us getting out of here to tell anyone.'

'Hawk knows I would never give him up,' she says. 'He trusts me.'

'Maybe he does, but hé sure as hell doesn't trust me,' I hiss, banging the porch rail with my fist.

Ronnie shushes me, finger to her lips and I drop my voice.

'He's not going to let me get off this island,' I whisper. 'I'm part of the establishment and everything he despises. He's going to find a reason to kill me and there's nothing you can do about it.'

Ronnie looks into the distance. This thought has obviously occurred to her too.

'We could leave now, while everyone is resting,' I say. 'Just keep walking until we get back to the beach. The plane must still be there.'

'No,' she says.

'You could fly me back to the mainland and then take off to some place far, far away from all of this.'

'No.' Her tone is final. 'I can't betray my brother.'

'What if he's going to betray you?' I ask. 'What if he plans to get rid of both of us?'

'He would never do that.'

I throw the gun down into the dust.

'You don't understand, Jo,' she says. 'You haven't lost your family like we did.'

'You think you know it all, Ronnie, but you don't.' I point at her. 'You know absolutely nothing about me or my family.' I go back to my bunk, slamming the door so hard the walls rattle.

The group of young techies was flagging. They'd been chained to their desks, searching and checking data for almost seven hours, escaping only to use the toilet and sneak the odd fag. Krish tapped with one finger, his chin resting in his other hand.

'Get this lot down you.' Clem plonked seven cartons onto Carole-Ann's desk.

She waved her hand around wildly. 'Not that crap again.'

'Afraid so.'

He'd nipped over the road and ordered seven portions of kebab and chips.

Sebastian was first up to grab some food and had shovelled half of the kebab into his mouth before he got back to his seat.

'I thought your body was a temple, sunshine,' Clem called after him. 'What with all that avoiding caffeine and what have you.'

Sebastian grinned, his lips greasy. 'Right now I'm so hungry, I'd eat shit on toast.'

Clem laughed and handed around the rest. 'Come on, Carole-Ann.' He wafted an open carton under her nose. 'You know you want to.'

'I know I do not.' She pushed his hand away.

'More for me,' he said and tossed a chip into the air, catching it between his teeth.

'Pig.'

He was about to chuck some salad at her when Emily, the blonde, waved her hand wildly. 'I think I might have something,' she shouted.

There were some groans from the others. Emily had thought something similar at least three times already. The last one had turned out to be a transsexual looking up the Beaumont Society. Only Sebastian made his way over, buoyed, no doubt, by a combination of fat and carbs.

'What is it this time?' asked Krish. 'Dwarves auditioning for *The Wizard of Oz*?'

There was sarcasm in his tone that went beyond ordinary team banter. Clem sensed his nose had been put out of joint by Sebastian and that he would be pretty pleased if his theory turned out to be a crock of shite.

Clem ambled over, food carton in hand. 'Talk to me.'

Emily sifted through a raft of papers, her hair bouncing softly. Stray tendrils escaped and snaked down her back in artful dishevelment. Or perhaps she was just crap at pinning it up.

'I've been searching the five units taken from . . .' she ran her finger down a handwritten list, 'Oliver's Sandwich Bar and Internet Café.'

Clem remembered he'd told the manager he would have the kit back to him by now.

'I've numbered them for ease of reference.' Emily waved at the computers, each marked with a number in bright red lipstick. 'Our man was definitely using them. I've found Petal logged in at LookingforLadies on all of them.'

'Looks like a favourite haunt,' said Sebastian.

'So going by your theory, our guy should have also used them for other stuff, dotting around them,' said Clem.

Emily nodded, her hair threatening to unravel entirely. 'If we look five, no wait, six days after Petal first introduced herself to Tommy, we find them talking again on number three. I've made a transcript but it's not particularly illuminating, just more grooming.'

Clem waved away the offer.

243

'What is interesting is that fifteen minutes after coming off number three, number one is used to look at this,' she continued. Emily used a mouse to enter a website called Platformnow. The banners showed smiling families hunting and fishing in the great outdoors.

'It's an anti-state site,' she said. 'Freedom from government, corporates and the like. Lots of reporting on what they consider oppressive regimes.'

'Including us?'

'Oh yeah,' Emily laughed. 'We're one of the worst. Plenty of talk about bringing us to our knees.'

'How do we know it's our guy looking at this site?' asked Clem. 'I can see that it's tempting to make the connection, but sadly, there are a lot of crackpots out there.'

Emily shifted her mouse again and entered the forum. 'Whoever was using number one didn't just look, he logged on, calling himself TheTimeForTalkIsOver.'

'Pretty apt for someone just about to try to blow up the Opening Ceremony,' said Sebastian.

'It's just a name.' Clem held up his hand, careful not to get carried away.

'I checked some of the things he's posted, and he's a hothead all right,' said Emily.

'Might mean nothing,' warned Clem. 'A lot of people talk a lot of rubbish, especially on the internet.'

'True,' said Emily. 'But check this out.' She handed over a copy of a brief conversation.

TheTimeForTalkIsOver   **At 11:22**
I've found a friend.

Hawk   **At 11:23**
Is he with us?

TheTimeForTalkIsOver   **At 11:24**

He will be.

Emily and Sebastian looked up at Clem expectantly, clearly convinced that this was our man. Clem had to admit it was persuasive.

'We could get Carole-Ann to work her magic,' said Emily. 'Get the full poster history.'

'Somehow I doubt an operation like this will play ball,' said Clem.

'No chance,' said Sebastian. 'Looks like an NFP site.'

'Come again?'

'NFP. Not for profit,' said Sebastian. 'Run for fanatics by fanatics. If they get wind of us sniffing around, they'll tear down the site in an instant.'

'We can't risk that,' said Clem. 'If this turns out to be one of their methods of communication, we need to monitor it closely.'

'Then it's a DIY job,' said Sebastian.

'Looks that way,' Clem agreed.

Emily sighed and looked around the room, each team member slumped over the PCs, surrounded by coffee cups and chips.

Sebastian got to his feet. 'Listen up, people, we've got to go back to the drawing board.'

'You're kidding,' said Krish.

'We need to go through each unit again, looking for this website.' Sebastian tapped a few keys and the banners to Platformnow appeared on the smart board.

Then he glanced at Clem. 'Sorry, I should have let you do that.'

Clem didn't reply. He liked a kid with chutzpah.

Ronnie and I haven't said a word to one another for hours. At first we lay in our respective bunks, tossing and turning, until

Ronnie jumped off hers and stormed out of the cabin. No doubt she's gone for another think.

Not that there's much to think about. Hawk is going to kill us both. Or maybe just me. Either way, Ronnie's not going to do anything to stop him. I'm on my own.

When she returns, she's carrying a candle. I'd barely registered that the sun had set.

'Let's go,' she says.

For a second my heart leaps as it grabs at the possibility that she's changed her mind and we're getting out of here. Then I see her face in the candlelight, the lines between her nose and mouth.

'Where are we going?' I ask.

'To get some food.'

Once again we troop over the hill to the next valley. The Serbs are already at the campfire, talking to Tiny. Soon, everyone arrives except Hawk.

The man with the goatee hands me a beer. I nod my thanks and press the cold glass neck to my lips, but I can't drink. My throat is too tight.

'I'll be going down to England in the next day or so,' he says. 'Anyone you can put me in touch with?'

I gulp. He clearly has no idea who I am. I look around the group and it dawns on me that none of them know. They think I'm one of them and Hawk hasn't told them any different. What would happen if he did? I catch sight of the guns everyone carries so casually, the knives attached to their belts, and I picture the hand grenade I discovered in one of the cottages.

There's a rumble at my side and I realise that the guy with the goatee is still speaking.

'Of course it would have to be good people,' he says. 'People like us.'

He's asking me if I can give him the names of any friendly terrorists. 'Let me have a think,' I say.

'Doesn't pay to be hasty.' He nods. 'Gotta be the right folk. Can't trust someone just because they talk the talk.'

Our conversation is interrupted by the door of Hawk's cottage flying open with such force it splinters against the wall behind. Everyone looks up as Hawk appears in the doorway, bare-chested, a fresh cut across his chest dripping blood. He moves from foot to foot, his shoulders twitching. Hero runs to greet him, but Hawk pushes him away with his foot.

The firewood crackles and smoke rises up into the starry sky, but tonight there's no magic, only tension. Beside me Ronnie exhales loudly enough for me to hear. I push the stew around my plate.

'Something wrong with our good island food?' Hawk walks towards me. 'Not to your fancy London tastes?'

'Not hungry,' I say.

'Right, right.' He's still padding from foot to foot, his head moving from side to side. The blood from his cut is now mingled with the tattoos on his stomach, blurring their edges.

Without warning he bats the plate out of my hands, sending it flying into the fire.

'If you don't fucking want it, don't fucking eat it,' he shouts.

'Hey Hawk, man, calm down,' says the guy with the goatee.

'What did you say?' Hawk gets right into the other man's face.

'I can see you're a little wired tonight is all.'

Hawk throws back his head and for a second I think he's going to head-butt the other guy, but instead he laughs and everyone joins in. Only Ronnie and I keep straight-faced.

'Don't worry about Hawk.' The man with the goatee puts a hand on my arm. 'He's one crazy bastard, but he's good people, you know?'

When the food's finished Tiny takes out his harmonica, but after the first melancholy note, Hawk tells him to put it away.

'Too fucking miserable, man, all that shit about the past.' He stumbles back into his cottage and returns with a ghetto blaster. 'Time to look to the future.' He presses a button and the clearing shakes to the sound of an electric guitar getting faster and faster. He turns up the volume as a voice begins to scream along, the sound reverberating around the hills.

Hawk nods violently to the music, oblivious to the fact that one by one the others are leaving. Only Ronnie and I remain as she watches him across the fire, his skin glowing orange.

'Fuckers!' he shouts into the air.

'Come on.' I pull Ronnie's arm but she resists. 'There's nothing you can do,' I tell her.

She stares at her brother for another minute or two, watching him convulse, until I grab her wrist tightly and drag her to her feet.

'Come on,' I repeat and lead her away.

As we trudge back to the cabin, I know that come what may, I am leaving this place tonight.

The talking's all done and Isaac is just waiting for the jury to return their verdict.

'I think it went well,' Bert keeps saying over and over as he paces up and down my cell.

'What's happening with my daddy?' Isaac asks.

Bert stops in his tracks and looks at Isaac.

'You been telling me not to worry about him, but I want to know.'

Bert nods and sits on the bunk next to him. 'I wanted you to focus on the trial, Isaac,' he says.

'Trial's over now, sir.'

Bert takes a deep breath. 'There's no easy way to tell you this, so I'm just going to come right out and say it. Your daddy's dead.'

Isaac can't believe it. He was sure Daddy hadn't been shot. He remembers Rebecca falling. And Noah. Then a bullet passed through Veronica-Mae into Isaac, but Daddy was alive. 'That's not right,' he says. 'The police took him away.'

Bert puts his hand over Isaac's. 'That's right.'

'Then how can he be dead?'

Bert shakes his head real slow. 'He killed himself, son.'

Isaac snatches his hand away and jumps to his feet. 'That's not true.'

'I'm afraid it is, Isaac. They found him hanged in his cell.'

'Daddy would never do that!' Isaac screams.

'Maybe he just couldn't face another day, son.'

Daddy couldn't face another day? Daddy? What about Isaac? Every moment a living hell, locked up with no air or sky. Every night waiting for them to come to his cell.

'He wouldn't leave me all alone!' he screams. Tears pour down his face. He hasn't cried once since that day. Not about Mama, or his brother or his sister. Not even when the prison officers commit their sins on him. Now he can't stop.

'I'm so sorry, Isaac,' says Bert.

Then Isaac launches himself against the wall and beats it with his fists and his head until blood runs down the bricks. It takes three guards to pull him away and get the handcuffs on.

When the jury are ready to give their decision, Isaac has to go back into court with a bandage around his forehead.

'Stand up, please, Isaac,' the judge tells him.

He feels sick and dizzy now and has to lean his hands on the railing to hold himself up. A woman in the front row of the jury gives him a look full of pity.

'Has the jury reached a verdict?' asks the judge.

The woman stands up. 'We have, Your Honour.'

'And on the count of murder, how do you find the defendant, Isaac Pearson? Guilty or not guilty?'

She glances at Isaac, then turns away. 'Guilty,' she says.

Bert puts his head on his desk but Isaac doesn't care. He can't feel anything at all.

Chapter Twenty

I wait until I'm sure Ronnie is asleep. When her breathing is rhythmic, I steal out of my bunk and creep through the cabin, cringing at each creak and groan of the wooden floor.

I open the door as slowly as I can and step out into the night.

When we came back from supper, I took one of the Serb's torches and hid it under the chair, next to my trainers. In the blackness, I feel with my hand and smile when I find them unmoved. Silently, I put them on and sneak out.

My plan is simply to find my way back to the beach and the plane. I might not be able to fly the damn thing but it must have a radio. I don't know anything about signals or frequencies but I'll just keep trying until I manage to contact someone. Anyone.

Actually, finding the beach will be the hardest part. It's pitch black, the moon at its lowest wane and picking my way will be a challenge. Not impossible, though. The truck must have left tracks that I can follow. And there was a stream as a landmark. I just need to head up, over and then down. And repeat. At some point I must reach the beach.

The neighbouring clearing is silent, the embers of the fire glowing and I skirt as far from the cottages as I can, hoping everyone is fast asleep. I'm almost at the other side when the door to Hawk's cottage opens and I freeze.

I can only just make out his outline in the light given off by what's left of the fire. I hold my breath and tense every muscle, blood beating in my temples. If he spots me, I'll run. I'm fast enough to lose him. But what about Hero? I'm not convinced I can outrun a German Shepherd.

At last, the door creaks shut and I exhale. Nothing and no one are going to stop me now and I hurry up the steep incline, grateful to be swallowed into its darkness. When I'm a hundred feet or so safely on the other side, I turn on the torch and shine it at the ground. It's tough to see where tyres might have made a track with only one beam of light and I tap with my trainers too, hoping to feel a ridge. Eventually, I find a flattened clump of gorse, the stalks ground into the dirt. This must be it.

I shine the torch ahead and there is a definite impression through the grass and moss, veering off to the right. I punch the air in triumph and follow its intricate pattern.

In the cool night air, I increase my pace, breathing deeply through my nose. I'm filled with a sense of hope that keeps my limbs loose, allowing me to move freely.

I hardly dare believe it when the ground evens. Yet my thighs tell me it's true. I must be on the stretch of land that runs the length of the island, separating the inland hills and valleys from the shore. Something crashes into my subconscious and I pause to concentrate. Then I smile. It's the ocean. I can hear the endless roar of the waves calling to me.

Buoyed by the sound, I sprint until something shrieks up ahead, making me jump. When it comes again, I realise it's only an owl. He screeches at me again as if my very presence is heretical. 'Don't worry,' I tell him. 'I'm out of here.'

I run for another five minutes then stop. My body could go on for miles but I need to make sure I'm following the tyre tracks. If I take the wrong route down, I might miss the place I need to be and find myself on the wrong beach or at the top of a cliff I can't descend.

A crushed clump of grass tells me I'm where I need to be, but I bend and feel with my fingers, assuring myself that I can feel the imprints of the tread. Satisfied, I set off again.

My mouth is parched and I wish I'd had enough foresight to take a bottle of water from the fridge. Never mind. I won't let thirst slow me down. I can drink gallons of the stuff when I'm home. I smile at the thought of my flat, with its bare cupboards and un-ironed sheets. First thing I'm going to do is buy a new duvet, one of those filled with real feathers. Imagine how soft it will be. Then I'm going to fill all the shelves and the fridge with delicious food. I might even learn to cook.

I'm still smiling when I hear something behind me. A sigh. I stop and listen. Another sigh, then another, then another. The sound of someone panting. I tell myself it could be an animal, but what animal makes a sound like that? More panting. Louder this time. Whoever it is, they're getting closer.

Could Hawk have seen me in the clearing? Has he been following me all this time? I think of him earlier, manic with drugs and paranoia, his body rippling with pent-up violence. And I run.

Regardless of the tyre tracks, I just head forward, tripping over rocks, almost losing my footing. I won't let him catch me. No way. I dig deep and increase my speed, ricocheting and stumbling. I channel every part of me into escaping.

The beam of my torch catches something looming up ahead. It's large and square: the crofter's cottage where Tiny stopped. I charge towards it. If I can get inside, maybe I'll find a telephone or a radio. It's not likely given the collapsed roof, but if all else fails at least I can barricade myself inside and hide.

I'm only a couple of metres from shelter when my feet become trapped under what feels like a concrete ledge and I'm thrown forward, smashing my head against another hard object.

As I tumble to the ground, my left thigh crashes against a third immovable obstacle. There's a crack and I yelp in excruciating pain. I try to flip onto my back, but my feet are still caught.

I scrabble for the torch and shed some light on my problem. All around me are dark slabs covered in moss, scattered like an outsized pack of cards. Closer inspection reveals faint script etched into the rock. Gravestones. I've stumbled into the tiny graveyard that flanks the crofter's cottage.

As I arc the beam of light I find the culprit on which I banged my head. It's the upright Celtic cross, rune-like markings chasing one another around the upper circle. Instinctively I reach over to trace the unfathomable patterns, but even that small movement sends a bolt of pain through my thigh. I feel as if I've been stabbed. I touch the spot where it hurts the most and my fingers come away wet. In the torchlight I can see the rip in my track-suit trousers and the red stain spreading across the fabric. Shit.

As if things couldn't get any worse, the panting noise is getting closer. I grasp the Celtic cross and pull myself to my feet, blood pouring down to my knee, and limp towards the cottage. Each step is like a hot poker jabbing me, but I have to keep on going.

The footsteps behind me get faster and I try to run. When I reach the door, I don't stop, but career into it with a thud.

I can hear breathing now. Hawk is right behind me. I let out a shout of anger and fear.

My hand scrabbles for the doorknob. I can do this. I can.

The metal of the handle is rusty and won't turn so I step back to force it with my shoulder. Too late I remember the wound in my leg and it gives way beneath me. I throw my arms out as I lose my footing and the torch flies out of my hand, crashing behind me and beating me to the ground. As I follow it, my head meets solid rock again.

When I open my eyes, there's only a blur and a sick feeling in my gut. Someone above me is speaking, but I can't catch the words.

As the world slowly comes back into focus I see who has been chasing me.

It's Ronnie.

Sebastian rapped his cheek with a ruler to keep himself awake. The techies had worked all night and found more postings on Platformnow. It seemed that Petal a.k.a. Paul Ronald a.k.a TheTimeForTalkIsOver kept in regular contact with another poster called Hawk.

Though the language was guarded, it was fairly clear that they were discussing Tommy. In a sick twist of the knife, they'd been in contact in the hours before the handover at Stratford underground.

TheTimeForTalkIsOver　　　**At 3:41**
I'm on my way.

Hawk　　　**At 3:42**
Good luck, soldier, and may God go with you.

'You can go home now,' Clem told Sebastian. The others had already left.

'I just want to check what this guy's up to now,' he said.

Clem understood. He couldn't take his eyes off the site either. If Hawk had been involved in the attack at the Opening Ceremony, what was to say he wasn't planning something similar right now.

'Do you think Hawk knows his friend is dead?' asked Sebastian.

'He must know we intercepted the bomb,' said Clem.

'And he must know Tommy was killed,' said Sebastian. 'It's all over the net, especially Platformnow. He's even been on a thread about it, muttering on about Waco.'

Clem thumbed through his notes. Quite a number of Hawk's posts mentioned Waco. 'Does he mention Frasier or anyone else?'

Sebastian shook his head. 'He was around for half an hour or so yesterday, chatting with someone called R1234.'

'Imaginative,' said Clem. 'What did they talk about?'

Sebastian smiled and yawned at the same time. 'Not a lot. R1234 says his nose is still hurting and Hawk commiserates. They've had pretty much the same conversation for the last few days.'

Clem frowned. Hawk didn't strike him as a compassionate kind of guy. His posts simmered with hatred, not the grandstanding of some members, which made them all the more frightening.

Carole-Ann breezed in, all fresh lipgloss and white teeth. 'Tell me you two haven't been here all night.'

'Okay,' said Clem. 'We haven't been here all night.'

She put her hands on her hips and surveyed the room. The remnants of yesterday's kebab and chips were everywhere. 'It smells like a kennel in here.' She turned to Clem and Sebastian. 'And you two look like dogs. Go home and try to get some rest.'

'We need to keep a track on this one.' Clem flicked Hawk's name on the screen. 'He's definitely still active.'

'I'm on it,' she said. 'Now go and at least take a shower.'

Ronnie shines the torch in my face. 'What on earth are you doing out here, Jo?'

I try to get up but my head is spinning.

'Crashing through these hills at night,' she says. 'Have you got a death wish?'

My stomach lurches and I lean to one side and vomit. 'I had to get away.' I wipe my chin with the back of my hand. 'Otherwise Hawk would have killed me.'

'I know,' she says.

'What?'

'You were right,' she answers simply.

I struggle to a sitting position, taking the weight on my hand. 'Come on, then. Let's get out of here before he notices we've gone.'

'Don't be stupid, Jo.'

'It won't take us long to get down to the beach,' I say.

She puts a hand on each of my shoulders and looks deep into my eyes. 'You won't make it, Jo.'

'I will.'

She shakes her head. 'You're losing too much blood.' She points the torch at my leg to show me the blood pumping out. I stem the flow with my hand, but it pours through my fingers. 'Let's tie something around it,' I say, my vision swimming.

'It's too deep,' Ronnie replies.

'So what's the alternative?'

'We go back,' she says.

I push her away. 'No.'

'We go back and get you patched up.'

'Patch me up here,' I say.

'With what?'

'I don't want to go back,' I tell her.

'Me neither, but it's the only way you're getting out of here alive. We go back, get your leg treated, then we leave at the first chance we get. You have to trust me.'

Do I trust her, though?

She pulls me to my feet and once again I feel her arm around my waist. 'You're freakishly strong, you know.'

'You say the sweetest things.'

I lean heavily against her as we make our way back to camp. When we arrive, the grey dawn is appearing and the bonfire is nothing but a heap of smoking ashes. Tiny is asleep behind the wheel of the pickup.

'Hey!' Ronnie smacks the bonnet with the palm of her hand. He jumps up. 'What the fuck?'

'I need some help here,' she shouts.

He rubs his face with his hands and gets out of the cab. His feet are bare, airing long yellow nails that curl under the pad of each toe. 'Put her in there.' He gestures to the cottage where I found the hand grenade.

Ronnie drags me up the step and kicks the door open. The man with the goatee leaps from the bedroom, gun in hand, wearing nothing but a pair of black Y-fronts.

'Sorry to disturb,' says Ronnie and staggers to the table where she sets me down.

'What happened?' he asks.

'Out hunting,' she replies.

'At night?'

Ronnie shrugs. 'What can I tell you? She's from London.'

She takes hold of each side of the tear in my tracksuit bottoms and rips, exposing a wound in my thigh that looks like a gaping mouth mid-scream.

I let my head fall forwards against the table top with a thud.

'That don't look good,' goatee tells Ronnie.

'No shit,' she says.

The door opens and Tiny appears with a first aid kit, a camping stove and a bottle of whisky.

'Boil some water,' he tells goatee. 'And clean these.'

He rummages through the first aid box and hands over two huge darning needles and a pair of scissors.

Goatee gives me a wink then takes the stove and the implements outside.

'Okay, my friend, I want you to take a big swallow of this.' Tiny helps me sit up and holds the bottle to my mouth. 'I mean a really big one.'

I glance at Ronnie, who nods, so I take a gulp and cough it

down. Tiny claps me on the back and takes a swig himself. 'For luck,' he says.

'Come on, Tiny,' Ronnie says. 'Let's get this over with.'

'All right then.' He reaches into his back pocket and pulls out a pair of pliers.

'Mary, Mother of God,' I say, using my mum's preferred Irish expletive.

'You need to keep very still now, okay?' says Tiny and Ronnie presses me back with a firm hand.

Then goatee crashes through the door. 'Did I miss it?'

'Not yet,' says Tiny. 'Hold her down.'

Ronnie pushes against both my shoulders. Someone else – goatee, I assume – grips my feet. 'Look at me, Jo,' Ronnie says. 'Look right at me.'

'This is going to hurt, isn't it?' I say.

'Only a little.'

I concentrate on my breathing, slowing down my pulse, when out of nowhere comes a pain so intense it radiates from my thigh outwards until every cell in my body is screaming as loudly as I am.

'I got the skin pressed tightly together now,' says Tiny.

Ronnie pushes harder to keep me in place as I thrash, wanting to see what the hell is being done to me. I crane my neck to find that Tiny has clamped together the two pieces of ripped skin with his pliers. It meets in the middle in an ugly ridge.

'Let's sew her up,' he says triumphantly.

'You've got to be kidding me,' I yell.

Surprised by my voice, Tiny lets the pliers fall and the cut opens up, blood spurting like a fountain.

Ronnie turns to him. 'Tiny, didn't you tourniquet it first?' She lets go of my shoulders, whips off her belt and ties it tightly above the wound. Tiny grabs the pliers from the floor and once again prises the wound shut.

They both wait a moment, watching.

'It's slowing,' observes Tiny.

'Good,' says Ronnie. 'Now pass me the needle and thread.'

I float in and out of consciousness until I feel a wet cloth pass over my face and I find Ronnie smiling down at me. 'Good as new,' she says.

'Can I look?'

'I wouldn't, if I were you.'

Tiny passes me three pink pills and the whisky, then helps to prop me up. 'Better get you back to your cabin to rest,' he says.

'She can bunk down in my bed,' says goatee, still in just his pants. 'I won't be needing it.'

'You leaving today?' Tiny asks.

Goatee nods and grins. 'I'll be in London by tonight.'

They carry me through and lay me on the bottom bunk. I feel woozy from the loss of blood, but I need to speak to Ronnie alone so I force my eyes to stay open until Tiny leaves.

'What you said in the woods,' I ask her. 'You did mean it?'

'Hush,' she says, gesturing to the other room.

'I have to know, Ronnie,' I say. 'Just tell me yes or no.'

She glances at the door then nods.

Clem dropped Sebastian outside his flat in Bexleyheath. It was a fair drive from Millbank, but the kid had worked bloody hard.

'Thanks for your help,' said Clem, as Sebastian got out.

'No need. I enjoyed it.'

Clem gave a grunt.

'Seriously,' said Sebastian. 'I'd love to do what you do.'

'Where do you work at the moment?' Clem asked.

'JTAC.'

The Joint Terrorism Analysis Centre was home to a lot of techies.

'If I wanted to transfer over, do you think I would stand a chance?' asked Sebastian.

From what Clem had seen, the kid was not only bright; he also had great instincts. 'I think the bigger question is why you'd want to,' said Clem. 'This is a hard life.'

'But the quid pro quo is that you live in the knowledge that what you do really matters.' Sebastian's face was a mask of seriousness. 'That your actions are directly responsible for keeping people safe, saving lives.'

'I didn't save Tommy Frasier.'

'But you've saved plenty before and tomorrow you'll save someone else,' said Sebastian.

'You make it sound simple.'

'Isn't it?'

Clem smiled and watched the kid let himself in. There had been a time when Clem, too, had seen everything in such clear and uncomplicated terms. When he'd first signed the Official Secrets Act all those years ago, he'd understood his job, and it had nothing to do with protecting politicians.

He leaned forward and banged his head against the steering wheel. Then he got out and rang Sebastian's bell.

'Clem?' Sebastian opened the door with a toothbrush in his mouth.

'Have you got a computer?' asked Clem.

Toothpaste dribbled down Sebastian's chin. 'Is the Pope a Catholic?'

Dear Veronica-Mae,
This will be the last letter I write to you.
  I don't know if anyone told you, but they found me guilty of killing that policeman.

They can't give me the death penalty because of my age, but they needn't worry none; my life here in jail is much worse than ten minutes on a gurney getting a lethal injection.

I wish I could do what Daddy did, but I know that I can't. I wish I could say I ain't mad at him, but I know that I can't. All I can do is try to survive, hour by hour, day by day and hope that one day I can find it in my heart to forgive him.

As for you, I want you to forget all about us. Maybe you've done that anyways, but if you ain't, then I'm telling you that you gotta. Mama, Daddy, Noah and Rebecca are all dead. I might as well be. So you have to concentrate on your new family now and make a new start. You can't be making comparisons, all right? You gotta take them as they is, and put your trust in them.

That's all I got to say.

Your brother,

Isaac

Chapter Twenty-one

Ronnie wakes me with a gentle shake. 'Are you okay?'

My entire left leg feels as though someone has wrapped it in barbed wire and set it alight.

'Yeah.' As I sit up, a wave of nausea breaks over me and I gag. But I have no time to be ill.

'Jo?'

I put up my hand. 'I'll be fine.'

Injury or no injury, there is no way I'm staying here.

'The others are out training,' she says.

'Hawk?'

'He's gone somewhere with Sean.'

'Sean?'

'The guy with the goatee.' She rolls her eyes at me.

How come I'm the only one who didn't know his name? Did he tell me and I forgot? My head is so thick that it's possible. Right now, anything's possible.

'Can you stand?' Ronnie asks.

I clench my teeth and swing my legs off the bed, the rip in my trousers flapping like a tattered flag.

Ronnie grabs a rucksack from the corner. 'I've got water, food and ammo.'

I cry out as I put weight on my feet and stand.

'Are you sure you can do this, Jo?' Ronnie asks.

'Stop with the questions,' I snap. 'I'm sure.'

She nods, leaves the room and I limp after her.

'Here.' She throws me a metal pole from the corner of the room. I catch it in one hand and use it as a crutch.

Before we leave, Ronnie checks her knives are secure, slips a pistol into her back pocket and slings a rifle over her shoulder.

I hold out my free hand. 'Give me a gun.'

Ronnie sighs.

'Now,' I say.

She takes the pistol from her pocket and thrusts it at me. I slip it into my waistband.

'Ready?' she asks.

I nod.

She opens the door a crack, checks outside, then gestures to me to follow. She slides down the porch steps and I hobble after her.

The sun is high in the sky and within seconds sweat is coursing down my back, but we daren't wait any longer before making our escape. Hawk could return at any second.

Once we're over the summit we follow the tyre tracks. The pain in my leg is so intense I have to bite my lip to stop myself from screaming. I put as much weight as I can on my right leg and the makeshift crutch, but when I have to swing my left leg forward, it feels as if the flesh is tearing apart. Given that it was sewn together with a darning needle, it might well be doing just that.

Despite my handicap I find myself ahead of Ronnie, whose head is scanning left, right and behind us. She turns at every sound, her rifle pointed. Anxiety is written large across her face. I realise that Ronnie is frightened of her brother.

'It's okay,' I tell her. 'We'll be okay.'

When we finally make it to the crofter's cottage, Ronnie opens her rucksack and takes out a bottle of water. I lean against the Celtic cross and close my eyes.

'Take a small drink,' Ronnie instructs. 'We have to make it last.'

My hands shake as I put the bottle to my lips and some water sloshes out onto the ground.

'Careful,' Ronnie admonishes.

I ignore her. It's as if everything that once frightened me about her has drained away. Or maybe it's me that's changed. Certainly I feel stronger despite my injuries.

'I bet you rue the day you tracked me down to that hotel in Glasgow,' I say.

She shakes her head. 'You just don't get it, do you, Jo?'

'Get what?'

'You were the one hunting me,' she says. 'You and MI5. You left me with no choice but to find you.'

I look at her now, like a wild animal in the woods, and I begin to appreciate how trapped she must have felt, especially when Miggs died. She wasn't prepared to just wait and see what happened.

'How did things end up this way?' I ask.

'What do you mean?'

'You and your brother. How did it turn out this way, with you on the run from MI5 and him living here, fucked out of his mind.'

'Long story.'

'We've got all day.'

She shakes her head and sets off towards the sound of crashing waves just out of sight. When I catch up to her, she looks at me wearily. 'Do you really want to know?'

'Yes, I really want to know.'

We navigate an area covered in jagged stones and I stumble and swear. While I'm concentrating on finding the smoothest path, she speaks.

'Our family was killed by the police.'

I'm taken aback, but try not to show it.

'How?' I keep my voice as cool as possible.

'Shot.'

I cough. 'Who?'

'My mama, my older brother and sister,' she says.

'All dead?'

'Uh huh.'

'What about you and Hawk?' I ask.

'Oh, they shot us too,' she says.

I glance at the scar on her shoulder and she touches it with her free hand.

'Bullet passed right through me. Two inches lower and it would have gone through my heart,' she says. 'I was nine years old.'

'Why?' I can't believe it. 'Why would they do that to you?'

Ronnie shrugs. 'Must have had their reasons.'

I shake my head. A whole family decimated? Children gunned down in cold blood?

'So now you know,' she says.

I'm so shocked I can't speak. Even the pain in my leg has lessened. When children lose everything to violence, how do they move on from that? The answer is they don't.

We arrive at the stream and Ronnie cups her hands under the flow to drink. Awkwardly, I lower myself down, my left leg held out straight to the side. The water's ice cold and numbs my lips. I take mouthful after mouthful, gulping it down. Then I splash my face and neck.

'When I get home, the first thing I'm going to do is take a shower,' I say. 'For eight hours.'

A smile threatens the corners of her mouth, then she freezes. 'Ronnie?'

She holds up her hand and gets to her feet. I struggle to do the same, stand at her side and listen. She points back to the cottage still visible behind us. I can't see anything moving.

Ronnie taps her ears, telling me to listen. I do, but all I can hear is the sea and the wind. Then something jars. A slight crack and a high whine. Ronnie's eyes dart back and forth until they settle on one spot and she grabs my arm.

I follow her eyeline to the Celtic cross. Something is now standing next to it. An animal. It stands utterly still, ears pricked. Hero.

Ronnie's grip tightens and she mouths, 'Don't move.'

We're locked in our position like statues, eyes fixed on Hawk's dog. He makes the whine we heard earlier but still he doesn't move.

My leg begins to shake. I need to take the pressure off it, transfer my weight to the other. But I can't. A dog like Hero will spot the slightest shift in the landscape. I will my leg not to give out. Not now.

At last, when I think I can't take any more, Hero darts away.

Ronnie exhales and loosens her grip. We've had a lucky escape, but it won't be long before Hero is back. And if Hero is out here, then where is Hawk? We turn to head away as fast as we can, but our path is barred.

'Hello, Ronnie.'

Hawk smiles at us, rifle on his shoulder, eye to the cross hairs.

Sebastian brought Clem a coffee. 'No milk,' he said. 'Sorry.'

Clem took a sip from the chipped mug and winced. It tasted as though there wasn't much coffee either. 'Let's go over this again,' he said. 'We both noticed that Hawk persistently referenced Waco.'

'And Ruby Ridge,' added Sebastian.

'Both incidents where it's alleged that the American police killed innocent civilians.'

Sebastian, who had changed into a turquoise polo shirt, sat at his computer. It was the latest kit and must have cost thousands. Shame he hadn't spared a couple of quid for some proper coffee.

'Almost eighty people died in Waco.' Sebastian clicked on a website called The Truth About Waco and a list of names filled the screen. 'A lot of them were just kids.'

Clem scanned the list of the deceased and their ages. One. Two. Four. Just babies, really.

'A lot of people see it as a wholesale massacre by the authorities,' said Sebastian. 'The subsequent enquiries have been critical about the police tactics used.'

Clem scanned the list again. 'What about Ruby Ridge?'

Sebastian clicked on another website showing an image of a farmhouse. It was in an idyllic location. 'The Weaver family lived here. The place was under surveillance when the father was suspected of trading in illegal firearms. Things went tits up and one of the kids got shot in the back. One of the women was shot in the head while she held a baby.' Then he clicked on an image of Timothy McVeigh, the Oklahoma bomber. 'Hawk wouldn't be the first person galvanised into action by this stuff. McVeigh cited Waco and Ruby Ridge as two of his primary motivators.'

Clem pushed his hands through his hair. He had the feeling that everything Sebastian was telling him had a terrible logic.

'But what I don't understand is why wouldn't Hawk make his point in America?' Sebastian asked. 'Why here in London?'

'That one's easy to figure out. The greatest show on earth just rolled into town,' Clem answered. 'A successful terrorist attack at the Olympics would take place on the world stage. It doesn't get bigger than that.'

'I can see what you're saying; it's just that for these guys it's usually about the Constitution and the right to bear arms and all that shit. They see Waco and Ruby Ridge as a war between the state and the people,' said Sebastian. 'Look, here's another one.'

He clicked into another site called Death At Old Maple Creek. 'The police were on a routine stakeout of the Pearson family. They were, like, super-religious, believed in keeping themselves to themselves. It ended with the mother, fifteen-year-old son and eleven-year-old daughter dead. The other kids were shot too, but survived.'

Clem jumped to his feet, throwing back his chair.

Pearson.

'Clem?'

Pearson.

He pictured the list of girls' names sent to him by Debbie McAndrews. There it was, slap in the middle.

Veronica Pearson.

'Ronnie X is one of those kids,' he said.

'Who's Ronnie X?' asked Sebastian.

Things aren't looking good. Again. I'm handcuffed to one of Ronnie's hands. Her other is handcuffed to the metal frame of the bunk bed. Which is braced to the wall.

Hawk marched us back to the camp at gunpoint, Hero snapping at our heels. Tiny and the Serbs were poking around in the bonnet of the pickup. They looked shocked at the sight of us being forced into Hawk's cottage.

'Got us a couple of traitors,' he shouted to them. Then he handcuffed us in this bizarre chain, locked us in and we heard the sound of the pickup screeching away. We don't know where he's gone, but it's only a matter of time until he comes back to deal with us. With the doors and windows locked, the vapours from the meth factory bubbling only feet away are choking.

Ronnie pulls at the frame, but it's bolted to solid timber. 'Fuck.' She strains until the skin around her wrists bleeds. 'Fuck.'

I look around wildly for anything we might use to prise the bolt free. On the table are the things Hawk took from Ronnie and me: knives and the pistol. I stretch out to them, pulling Ronnie with me, but I can't reach.

'It's no good.' She rattles the handcuff. 'It's no fucking good.'

I reach out again. There's only a foot between the tips of my finger and the table.

'We need something to bridge the gap,' I say.

'Like what?'

I point at the lengths of rubber piping connecting up the bottles of chemicals. 'A piece of that might work.'

'Jesus, do you know how dangerous crystal meth is, Jo?' Ronnie asks. 'Those chemicals are highly flammable. If they come into contact with one another we're in deep shit.'

I take in the evil-looking red stew, the canisters of acid, the bottles of antifreeze.

'The way I see it, we're already in deep shit.'

She thinks for a second, then nods. 'If you climb on my back, do you think you can reach?'

'I'll try.'

With our hands secured to one another's it's going to be awkward. She turns slightly and bends her back forward for me to climb on. When I push my hands into her shoulders for momentum, she gives a sharp intake of breath as I wrench her wrist backwards.

'Sorry,' I say.

'Just do it.'

I jump and Ronnie staggers forward. I have to grip her waist with my knees for balance, sending a pain ricocheting down my leg. She grabs the frame with the hand attached to it to steady herself.

'Okay?' she shouts.

'Yeah,' I say, though I feel as if I might fall backwards at any second.

'Can you reach the pipe?'

I extend my free arm, wiggling my fingers towards the rubber.

'Move up my body, Jo,' she says.

I press my free hand onto her shoulder and pull my legs up, dragging the injured flesh past the waistband of her jeans. I close my eyes against the pain and reach up again until I feel my finger-nail tapping against something solid.

My eyes shoot open. I'm almost there. My finger is touching a piece of orange pipe. If I can just get a fraction higher, I can hook my finger over it and pull it down.

Ronnie begins to wobble beneath me. 'Hurry, Jo. I can't hold you much longer.'

This is it. I imagine every vertebrae in my spine unlocking and my diaphragm expanding. Anything for that extra inch.

As my finger loops over the pipe I shout out in triumph, but Ronnie can't take my weight and collapses under me. We crash to the floor, all sharp elbows and soft ribs. When we manage to untangle ourselves, I'm still holding the length of pipe.

Ronnie looks at me and laughs. Real laughter that makes her shine. 'You did it, Jo.'

Suddenly the happiness falls from her face and she turns. The large glass vial to which the pipe was attached has fallen over, its contents pouring out, dripping onto the floor and pooling side-wards across the table. Towards the naked flame of the camping stove.

I look at Ronnie, she looks at me. 'Not good,' she says.

We have to get out of here right now and the only things that can help are a foot out of reach.

I bend the pipe into a loop and throw it at the table. It hits the side, missing the weapons.

'Come on, Jo,' Ronnie shouts.

I try again, this time getting so close that the rubber hits one of the knives, then bounces off.

I glance at the chemical spill inching towards the flame. In a few seconds we'll be toast. I throw again. This time the loop encircles the pistol. Carefully I drag it to the end of the table where it falls, bouncing across the floor.

'Shit.'

Behind me, I hear a whoosh and feel intense heat on the back of my neck. I throw the loop again, managing to circle the gun. I drag it towards me and grab the barrel.

'Shoot the handcuff,' Ronnie shouts.

'What if I miss? What if I hit your hand?'

The red chemical has caught fire, engulfing the table. The upset vial explodes, showering us in shards of glass.

'Shoot the goddamn handcuff!' she screams.

I've never fired a weapon before but I've seen plenty of films. I point it at the handcuff attaching Ronnie to the bed, curl my finger around the trigger and pull. Nothing.

'The safety, Jo. Remove the safety catch.'

Hands shaking, I click the catch, take aim, say a prayer and fire. The noise of the shot is deafening, so I don't hear the metal ping as it breaks, releasing Ronnie from the bunk. Then she grabs the pistol and shoots the cuff still attaching us to one another. Free at last, we race for the door, more vials exploding behind us. Ronnie gives it one sharp kick and the wood splinters around the lock as it flies from its hinges. The blast of fresh air is welcome, but then I remember what happens when fire meets oxygen.

'Run!' I yell.

I'm at the step when there's a boom. I dive forward as if I were at a swimming pool, taking Ronnie with me as the fireball erupts, engulfing the shack.

I hit the ground hard, flames singeing the back of my hair, then I crawl across the clearing commando-style, half pulling, half dragging Ronnie with me.

At the other side, we get to our knees, gasping for air and retching. Black smoke billows from the shack into the sky and the glass in the windows shatters. I haul myself up and Ronnie after me. Her face is covered in blood and soot. We lean against one another like drunks.

'Let's go,' I say.

Before we can move, the pickup roars into our path.

'It's him,' says Ronnie.

The pickup barrels towards us. 'This way!' I shout and make my way up the hill, hoping the steep bank will slow Hawk.

Ronnie follows me. 'He's still on us.'

I turn. Instead of slowing Hawk, our move seems to spur him on and he careers after us.

'There.' Ronnie points to a cluster of boulders and we scramble up.

The pickup comes at us, tries to brake and skids off out of control, the wheel clipping the boulders, flipping it on its side. We stare at the wreck in horror as Hawk crawls out, the flesh of his chest ripped open, muscle and sinew on display. His sunglasses have cracked and he takes them off and inspects them. When he looks up at us it is the first time I've seen his eyes. They're the same silver as Ronnie's.

'Don't move.' Ronnie points the pistol at him. 'Don't move, Hawk, or I'll shoot you.'

His shoulders heave and he covers his eyes. At first, I think he's crying, but when he moves his hands I can see he's actually laughing.

'Veronica-Mae, you won't shoot me,' he says. 'We're family.'

'I once had a brother called Isaac,' Ronnie replies. 'He would never have done anything like this.'

'Is that the brother you left to rot in prison?'

Ronnie's hand is shaking as she keeps him in her sights. 'I was nine years old, Isaac.'

'And I was fourteen.' Hawk jabs himself with his fist, splattering blood. 'I had no one.'

'I didn't know that,' she says. 'They took me away. They didn't tell me anything.'

'Do you know what happened to me night after night? Do you know what they do to cop killers in jail?' Hawk opens his arms wide as if he's on a crucifix. 'Go on, then. Do it. Just go ahead and shoot me.'

Ronnie's whole body shudders and her breathing is shallow.

Hawk drops his hands to his sides. 'You see, Miss Connolly, she can't do it. It's like the old saying goes, blood is thicker than water.'

They stare at one another, neither moving, until Hawk begins to lower his hand to his waistband. As if in slow motion, I see he has a gun tucked into it.

'Ronnie,' I warn.

'Move another muscle, Hawk, and I will kill you,' says Ronnie. 'I will not let you hurt any more innocent people.'

'What? You'd hurt your own kin to save this piece of shit?' Hawk jerks his head at me.

'It's not her fault she got mixed up in all this,' Ronnie replies.

Hawk throws his head back and gives another roar of laughter. 'Listen to yourself, Veronica-Mae. Making excuses, not taking responsibility. Mama would be ashamed of you.'

I hear Ronnie's breath catch.

'What did she always teach us?' Hawk continues. 'That doing the right thing ain't always easy.'

'And you think she'd say this was the right thing?' Ronnie asks. 'Cooking up meth and training terrorists?'

'We're trying to change the world is what we're doing. I thought that's what you wanted too.'

'I did,' says Ronnie. 'But not like this.'

'Veronica-Mae.' Hawk drops his voice. 'I do believe you have gone soft.' Slowly, Hawk makes for his weapon and Ronnie doesn't move. If she doesn't shoot him, he will kill us first. I watch her trigger finger. Nothing. Hawk's right, she can't do it.

I grab the pistol from her and fire. He drops like a stone.

'Isaac!' Ronnie screams and tumbles down the boulders.

He's lying on his back, his stomach spilling out. Ronnie crouches at his side.

'Why did you never reply to my letters?' he asks. 'If you'd just replied to my letters . . .'

'What letters? I never got any letters,' she says.

He coughs and blood spews from his mouth, then he convulses twice and falls still. Ronnie reaches over and tenderly closes his eyes. A single tear runs down her cheek. When she sees me looking, she bats it away.

'How long have you been here, Isaac?'

'Since I was fourteen, ma'am.'

'And how old are you now?'

'Twenty-six, ma'am.'

The woman nods. She's got that real straight hair that makes you wonder if she don't take an iron to it.

'Do you think you're a different person from the one that came in here?' she asks.

'Yes, ma'am.'

'How so?'

This is the tricky one. One-Two and the other Aryan Brothers have told Isaac all about this question. 'You gotta make the parole board see you're a changed man,' One-Two told him. 'If you gotta lie, then so be it.' Isaac trusts One-Two and the other ABs. They saved his life and took him in. 'Ain't nobody gonna mess with you no more,' One-Two said, as he inked a swastika onto Isaac's bicep.

'Well, ma'am,' Isaac says. 'The boy that came in here thought the police were the enemy because that's what he'd been raised to believe.'

'And now?' the woman asks.

'*And now I can see that they're just honest men trying to do an honest day's work.*'

She scribbles something on her pad of paper and waggles her ankle so that her shoe comes loose. 'I hear a journalist came to see you, Isaac.'

'*Yes, ma'am.*'

'*What did he want?' she asks.*

'*Said he wanted to tell my side of the story,' Isaac replies.*

'*He offer you money?*'

'*I told him I don't want no money and I don't want to tell my story,' Isaac says. 'Truth is, ma'am, I just want to start my life afresh.*'

She smiles and makes another note. 'Thank you, Isaac. I think that will be all.'

Chapter Twenty-two

'Give me the gun.' Ronnie holds her hand out to me.

I'm still in shock that I've killed a man, sickened by how easy it was.

'Give me the gun, Jo,' she repeats and I drop it into her open palm. 'Now help me with the pickup,' she says and walks over to the truck, which is lying on its side, two wheels in the air. She jumps up and uses her body weight to try to right it. I join her and together we manage to tip it sufficiently. It crashes back onto four wheels of its own accord. The doors are full of dents and scrapes and the windscreen is cracked, but Ronnie jumps into the driver's side and turns the keys, which are still in the ignition. The engine coughs and cuts out.

'Come on.' She bangs the heel of her hand on the steering wheel. She tries again and this time it splutters into life. I jump in beside her, pushing aside a checked shirt.

Expertly, she weaves her way through the rocks, up and over the hills.

'Check the glove compartment for a drink,' she says after a while.

I open it and a bottle of water tumbles out. As I hand it to Ronnie, I catch sight of the other contents. Papers, credit cards, a wedge of money and an iPhone.

Ronnie takes a drink and pulls her tongue out in disgust. 'I hate warm water.'

I close the glove compartment and take it from her. 'I'm sorry about your brother,' I say.

'Like I said back there, that wasn't Isaac.'

'Still,' I say. 'He was once.'

'How did you know I wouldn't shoot him?'

'I lost my brother.'

'How?'

'Long story,' I say.

She smiles at me with a deep sadness. 'What was his name?'

'Davey,' I tell her, surprised by how good it feels to say the word out loud. 'His name was Davey.'

Clem and Sebastian arrived back at HQ and Carole-Ann looked up from her bank of computers. 'By the smell of you, that shower didn't involve any soap.

'I need to speak to Veronica Pearson's adoptive parents,' Clem shouted out to an assistant. 'I need to know if they can shed any light on where she might be now.'

'You might want to see this first,' said Carole-Ann.

'It had better be good,' Clem told her.

She kissed her teeth. 'You were the one who said you wanted me to watch this character Hawk.'

'He's been online?'

'About half an hour ago,' she said. 'There was some delay in the feed.'

'Delay? What sort of delay?' Clem asked.

'A technical problem, a glitch in the network,' she said. 'Computers are like that.'

Clem threw up his arms in despair.

'If you knew anything about computers, you'd know that glitches are what they do best.'

'Show me then, woman,' he said.

Carole-Ann clicked into the forum of Platformnow and navigated into a thread called 'Anyone Up For An Image-Sharing Thread?' started by Hawk himself.

Hawk   **At 19:14**

I'm uploading some nice pictures to share with you guys.

Clem clicked the link and it was a photo of Waco, the buildings burning, smoke plumes rising into the sky.

SecondAmendment   **At 19:16**

Good one, man. How do you like this?

The link took Clem to the charred remains of one of the victims of the Waco siege. It was curled into a foetal ball.

Hawk   **At 19:17**

Back at ya, big guy.

There was a photo of the Weaver family outside their farmhouse at Ruby Ridge, squinting against the sun.

Gunshot   **At 19:18**

Can anyone play?

Gunshot's image was the mugshot of McVeigh staring remorselessly into the camera, his serial number on display. What the hell was all this about?

Clem's phone rang. 'Yeah,' he growled.

'Mr Clement?' The woman's voice was soft, with the sugar twang of the Deep South of America. 'This is Nancy Clayton. You asked me to call you about our adopted daughter, Veronica.'

'Oh, thank you so much for getting back to me, Mrs Clayton,' Clem replied.

'I'm afraid it's been a very long time since I've seen Veronica,' she said.

'Could you tell me a little bit about the adoption?' Clem asked.

'Well now, my husband and I wanted children for a very long time but sadly it was not to be, so we applied to adopt.'

'And Veronica was placed with you?'

'That's right. She was orphaned at nine.'

'Were you aware of the circumstances in which she came to lose her parents?'

Mrs Clayton coughed. 'We were not told the exact whys and wherefores but this little girl came to us unable to speak and with a large bullet hole in her back. We did the math.'

'Why did you move to Scotland?' Clem asked.

Mrs Clayton sighed. 'My husband Jim had a brother in Glasgow and Veronica, well, she was always so very angry.'

'You thought a move might help?'

'Uh huh.'

'And it didn't.'

'No. Veronica's behaviour just got worse and worse. Do you know she wouldn't even change her name to Clayton? I said we needed to go to a doctor and get her some help but Jim – he was so old-fashioned, you see, raised in the Deep South on discipline and respect – he said we needed to show Veronica some tough love.'

'What did you do, Mrs Clayton?'

'We put her in a residential unit for children like her,' she said. 'Disturbed.'

'The Orchard?'

'Yes. It seemed like a nice place, not at all what you'd expect. I didn't want to leave her, of course, but Jim said it would teach her to value what she had.'

Clem raked his scalp with his nails. What had these people done?

'Anyway, a few months after she'd been in there we got a letter from Social Services saying she didn't want to come home,' she said. 'I went to see Veronica but she was adamant, so . . .'

'So you left her in there.'

Mrs Clayton didn't reply and a pause stretched out between them. 'We made a big mistake,' she said finally. 'We should never have adopted her. She hated everything about Scotland. And us.'

'I'm sure you did your best,' Clem said mechanically.

'I really did try. Do you know, the only time I ever saw that child smile was when we went on holiday to the islands?'

Clem's heart beat a little faster. 'Where did you go, Mrs Clayton?'

'The Outer Hebrides,' she said. 'A tiny little place. I didn't like it all, but Veronica loved the quiet. She spent hours just walking those hills on her own. There were only a few people living there and I heard they all left in recent times.'

'Do you remember the name?'

'Let me see now, it was such a long time ago. If I recall correctly we had to fly over there in the smallest plane you ever did see. I thought I would die of fright.'

'The name?' Clem interrupted. 'It's very important.'

'Well, it sounded like something you'd call a girl,' she said. 'Tara? No, that wasn't it. Mara, perhaps?'

Clem hung up and ran to his office. He grabbed a thick black book from his shelf and blew off the dust. Then he thumbed the pages until he found what he was looking for and raced back to Carole-Ann's desk.

'Here.' He plonked down the atlas.

She wafted her hand through the cloud of dust.

'I think this is where Ronnie has taken Jo Connolly,' he said.

Carole-Ann peered at the page. 'The Outer Hebrides?'

'Cara.' He circled a small speck with his thumb. 'The island of Cara.'

Carole-Ann sniffed at his puffed-out chest. 'In the meantime, Hercule Poirot, are you the least bit interested in this?'

'What?'

'The website.' Carole-Ann pointed at the thread they'd been reading.

Hawk   **At 19:19**
R1234, if you're out there, man, this one is especially for you.

This time the link was to a photograph of two hands almost touching, an electric current between them.

R1234   **At 19:20**
I'm here.

Hawk   **At 19:21**
Good to see you, friend. I want you to look at the photograph, man. It's from me to you. You got to look deep, man, to see what I'm telling you.

R1234   **At 19:22**
Okay.

'Do you think it's important, Clem?' asked Carole-Ann.

'I don't know,' he said, leaning in to look more closely. 'I really don't know.'

★　★　★

When we reach the crofter's cottage again, Ronnie pulls over. 'I'm going to check if there's anything in there we can take,' she says and jumps out.

When I'm sure she's safely inside, I open the glove box and take out the iPhone. To my surprise I can get a signal so I tap in a number I've memorised.

'Yeah?'

'Clem, it's me.'

'Jo?'

'Call me Miss Connolly,' I say. 'Everyone does.'

'Holy cow, are you okay? Are you hurt?' he asks.

'I'm fine.' I look down at the wound on my thigh. 'I'm in one piece, anyway.'

'Where are you?'

'You'll never believe me,' I tell him.

'Yes I will, Jo – you're on an uninhabited island in the Outer Hebrides.'

'How the hell do you know that?'

'It's my job to know these things,' he says. 'What I need is your exact location.'

I look around. 'I don't know. I'm on a hill not far from the beach.'

'North or south part of the island?'

'Dunno.'

'Don't worry, we'll find you. What about Ronnie?' Clem asks.

'You don't need to worry about Ronnie,' I say. 'She had nothing to do with the bombings.'

'Listen to me, Jo.' Clem's tone is urgent. 'Whatever she's told you, Ronnie is very much involved. She's manipulating you.'

'I don't think so.'

'This is how she works, Jo. She and a person called Hawk orchestrated the entire operation. They used people with learning difficulties, groomed them, then got them to plant the bombs.'

I picture Ronnie with her friend Rory and feel sick. Could it be true? Was she planning to use him?

'We're watching Hawk right now,' says Clem. 'We think he's planning something else.'

'Hawk's dead,' I tell him.

'Are you sure?'

'I shot him myself.'

Ronnie comes out of the cottage, arms laden. 'I have to go,' I tell Clem.

'Jo, you need to stay on the line so we can lock in your location.'

I hang up.

Ronnie swings back to the pickup, opens the door and is about to drop cans of Coke and family bags of crisps into my lap when she sees the iPhone. 'Jo?'

'I called MI5,' I say.

She drops everything onto the ground. 'Why did you do that? I told you I'd make sure you got back.'

'I didn't tell them where I am.'

'It doesn't matter, Jo, they can track phone signals.'

'I'll get out now. You get to the plane.' I slide out of the car and stand opposite Ronnie, cans at our feet. 'Answer me one question,' I say.

'What?'

'Did you have anything to do with the terrorist attacks?'

She groans through her teeth. 'I told you I didn't.'

'What about Hawk?'

She falters.

'Well?' I demand.

'At first I had no idea he had anything to do with it.'

'What about later?' I ask.

'I began to suspect.'

'Did you help him?'

'No,' she says.

'Not in any shape or form?'

She falters again. 'I gave some friend of his a fake ID, but I had no idea at the time what he intended to do; I had no idea about the Plaza bombing and that's the truth.'

I stare at her. Is she lying? I still can't tell. 'What about Sean? Why is he heading to London?' I raise my voice. 'What is he going to do?'

'I don't know,' she shouts. 'Maybe he's taking a holiday.'

'Jesus Christ, Ronnie. Do you think he went to plant another bomb?'

'I don't care!' she screams. 'I just want to leave.'

'People's lives are at stake, Ronnie. You can't just walk away. Hawk was right about one thing. Sometimes you have to do what's right, however hard it is.'

'Fuck you,' she says, gets into the pickup and drives away.

There's a gentle smattering of summer rain as Isaac steps through the prison gates. He puts his face to the sky and lets the drops fall onto his face like tiny kisses.

'Hey, Pearson,' one of the guards calls out. 'We'll be seeing you real soon.'

Isaac shakes his head.

'A leopard can't change its spots,' says the guard. 'I'll give you a month, two at tops.'

Isaac picks up the transparent plastic sack that contains his belongings. Not much to show for twelve long years. He'll throw it all away, first chance he gets. Today is the first day of the rest of his life and he can't wait to get on and live it.

Not far away in the field, a mouse scampers past, his little pink nose twitching. Then out of the sky swoops a bird of prey; his beak fastens around the mouse and snatches him away. Poor thing was no match for the mighty hawk.

Isaac smiles. Yes, sir, he just can't wait to get on with his life.

Chapter Twenty-three

I sit at the side of the road, sipping a Coke, staring at the iPhone. I still haven't called Clem back. Given everything that Ronnie's done, am I really prepared to let her get away? I dial a number.

'Highfields.'

'Could I speak to Paddy Connolly?' I say.

I wait while they fetch my dad. I hear him grumbling before he gets to the receiver.

'Is that you, Jo?'

'Hi, Dad.'

'Where've you been?'

'Long story.'

'Listen, Jo, this is just the time you should be getting yourself known,' he says. 'You should see the amount of coverage the Olympics is getting since this handicapped boy got himself shot. It's twenty-four-seven and you need to milk it for all it's worth, then you might get promoted to something half decent.'

'It's disabled, Dad.'

'What?'

'The person is disabled. It's society that handicaps him.' Dad of all people should know that.

'I don't know what you're bleedin' going on about, Jo.'

Anger swells in me. Why won't he ever recognise what he's done? 'Why did you send Davey away, Dad?' I ask.

'Come again?'

'You heard me.'

He doesn't speak but I can hear his raspy breath down the phone. 'Why do you want to talk about this after all these years?' he asks.

'I've always wanted to talk about it,' I say. 'I just didn't dare bring it up.'

'It's not important,' he says.

'Davey was important.'

'Your career is what matters now.'

'Does it matter more than the truth?' I ask.

He sighs. 'Just let sleeping dogs lie.'

But I can't. I think about Davey every day. I need to know. 'Why did you do it, Dad? Why did you send him away?'

'It was for the best, Jo,' he says at last.

Typical. All about him, as usual. I imagine it was pretty inconvenient for the great Paddy Connolly to have a son with Down's syndrome. Not likely to have a glittering career, was he? That sort of thing could ruin a man's image.

'Best for who?' I ask.

'Best for all of us,' he replies. 'Your mother couldn't cope.'

I do remember Mum spending days in bed and the fits of crying.

'She was depressed, Dad,' I say. 'She needed help.'

'I know that, but the way I saw it, Davey would never be independent, he'd always need looking after and if anything happened to me and your mum, it would fall to you. You had your own life to lead. We couldn't expect that of you.'

'What are you saying?' I feel my chest constrict.

'I'm saying I did it for you.'

'For me?' I can hardly squeeze the words out. 'You sent him away for me?'

'Yes,' Dad says.

Misery sweeps over me and my eyes sting with tears. I think I've known this all along. I've blamed Dad, but deep down I knew.

'I loved Davey, Dad. I missed him every day of my life,' I say.

'I know.'

'When he died in that awful place, I thought my heart would burst in two.'

'Mine too,' he says. 'It was the biggest mistake of my life.'

I can't believe my ears. The mighty Paddy Connolly has just admitted he got something wrong.

'Dad,' I say.

'Yeah?'

'Sometimes you can be a real bastard.'

'I know, kid. I know,' he admits. 'But I'm the only bastard you've got.'

I hang up and contemplate my next move. Staying right where I am doesn't seem a shocking proposition. I'm just considering opening the huge bag of crisps when the pickup screeches to a halt.

'Did you save any of those for me?' Ronnie asks.

'I'm not sharing.'

'Don't like that flavour anyway,' she says. 'Gives you bad breath.'

I haul myself up, my leg killing me, and get in. 'Where to?' I ask.

'We've got a plane to catch.'

Clem paced up and down his office. 'Can we get a trace?'

Carole-Ann shook her head. 'She's hung up again.'

What the hell was Jo doing? Surely she hadn't fallen for Ronnie's bullshit?

Sebastian had fallen asleep at his desk, Hawk's picture thread still on the screen of his PC. Clem envied his ability to shut down and shut off.

'The island's not big. We'll find her eventually,' said Carole-Ann.

'It's the eventually I'm worried about,' Clem replied.

'At least we know she's alive.'

Clem nodded, but he couldn't help thinking that if Jo was still with Ronnie, it might not be for long.

The biplane judders across the skies with me wedged next to Ronnie, my leg at an awkward and painful angle. Ronnie is fiddling impatiently with a dial.

'What made you change your mind?' I ask.

She doesn't look up from her task. 'I think I might know how we can find the guy using Paul's ID.'

'Go on.'

The dial comes away in her hand. 'Goddamn piece of crap.' She throws it behind her.

I hold my breath, waiting for the plane to fall out of the sky without it. When it doesn't, I decide to continue the conversation. 'How can we find him?' I ask.

'When I gave my brother the fake ID, I also told him about a landlord I know who rents out houses for a few days, no questions asked,' she says.

'Isn't that what hotels are for?'

'Too many cleaners, bellboys, maintenance guys,' she says. 'Not ideal if what you're doing is illegal.'

'I thought you didn't get involved in anything illegal.'

Ronnie smiles at me. 'I said we didn't hurt anyone if we could help it. I didn't say any of it was legal.'

I lean my head against the window. I must be mad not to have just waited for Clem to pick me up. 'How did you pass on information to Hawk?' I ask.

'Internet.'

I'm incredulous. 'You emailed each other?'

'Don't be stupid,' she says. 'We'd log into the same websites and chat in the forums. Difficult to spot amongst all that endless crap people talk.'

'Didn't you worry that if someone did spot your conversations they could track you?'

'Internet cafés,' she says.

'I didn't see any of those near Hawk's training camp.'

Ronnie shrugs. 'He went back to the mainland regularly. All he had to do was piggyback someone else's connection. Easy.'

It doesn't sound easy to me. It sounds like a lot of hard work. 'Don't you ever get sick of all this, Ronnie?' I ask. 'Don't you ever crave a normal life?'

She goes back to the controls and I know I won't get an answer.

Rory pours himself a glass of water. An adult male is made up of 60 per cent water. An adult female is 55 per cent. 71 per cent of the world's surface is covered by water. Rory sips his drink and re-reads Hawk's message.

As soon as he clicked on the picture, he knew what to look for. It was obvious.

The last time Rory saw Imelda she sighed at him and said, 'What's obvious to you, Rory, isn't always obvious to everyone else.' He could have told her that what is obvious to everyone else is often mystifying to him.

But he didn't say that because Imelda did not want to know what Rory thought.

Rory did not speak to Imelda.

Rory's glass is empty so he puts it in the steriliser. It is designed for six baby bottles but can only fit four glasses in it.

Rory sits back at his desk and reads Hawk's message for the twenty-sixth time.

R1234, I think by now we are friends.
I need your help.

Please meet me tomorrow outside Stratford underground
station at 11.00 a.m.
Stay off Platformnow. It is no longer safe.
Hawk

Rory checks again where Stratford underground station is. He has
already checked six times. Rory has not left his flat for eleven
months and seventeen days.

Ronnie lands the plane with a thud and I look out of the window. 'Where are we?' I ask.

'Mainland,' she says. 'I'd have liked to get us closer to London,
but it wasn't possible.'

'Too many police?'

She opens her door. 'Not enough gas.'

My stomach rolls at the thought of running out of fuel over
the ocean.

'We're gonna have to drive the rest of the way,' she calls over
her shoulder.

I get out my side and look around another deserted field
doubling as an airfield. 'I don't see any cabs,' I say.

She cups her hand over her eyes and looks into the distance. 'I
called one earlier.'

My sarcastic laughter soon disappears when a battered jeep, the
exhaust making an almighty rattle, comes careering over the horizon. 'What the fuck?'

'Transport.' Ronnie winks at me.

The jeep screeches to a halt only feet from where we're standing and two men get out. They both lean against the bonnet, arms
crossed over thick chests, eyeing me suspiciously. Ronnie moves
towards them, leaving me next to the plane. They speak in low
voices, the men periodically shrugging their shoulders. I check my
watch, aware that miles away 'Paul' is planning a terrorist attack.

At last Ronnie holds out her hand. Thank God they've reached an agreement. One of the men spits on his palm and Ronnie takes it in hers. 'Get over here, Jo,' she shouts to me.

I make my way to them, sweating under the glare of the men's stares. One of them nods at my face.

'What happen?' His accent is thickly Eastern European.

Ronnie smiles. 'You know these famous types. They get work done.'

He raises a bushy eyebrow. 'Nip and tuck?'

'Yup.'

He says something to his friend, who gives something between a laugh and a cough, then tosses a key to Ronnie who catches it in her outstretched hand. We jump in the jeep and she starts the engine. It's been left in gear and we shoot forward, stalling with a groan. The men laugh.

'Very funny,' Ronnie says and flips them the finger.

She gives it another go and guns the engine hard, then we barrel away, spraying dirt at the men.

'Nip and tuck?' I shout above the din of the exhaust.

'I had to say something.'

'And you couldn't come up with anything better than a face-lift?'

'I'm a bit knackered,' she says. 'Anyway, tell me you haven't had anything done.'

'I have not.'

She circles her eyes. 'Not even a little around here?'

'No.'

'A bit of Botox, then?'

I'm furiously indignant. 'No I have not!'

Hooting with laughter, she rams the gear-stick into fourth and heads for the nearest road.

Chapter Twenty-four

The PM didn't smile or get up when Clem entered his study. 'Clem?'

'Prime Minister.'

'What can I do for you?'

Clem noticed that there was a piece of food stuck in his top teeth. 'I've come to ask you to cancel today's events,' he said.

The PM sighed and Benning finally looked up from his BlackBerry. 'Again?'

'I believe there is likely to be an attack today,' Clem told them.

'Haven't we been here before, Clem?' asked Benning.

Clem shrugged. 'I'm afraid the evidence is all pointing to another attack today.'

'And what evidence do you have to support this?' Benning sounded unconvinced.

What was wrong with these fucking people? How many had to die before they took this thing seriously? Clem had met KGB agents with more humanity. 'We've intercepted a message from someone who we believe to be one of the main instigators of the Plaza bombing.'

'And what did this message say?' Benning asked.

'There weren't any words; it was an image posted on a website called Platformnow,' Clem explained.

'An image of what?'

'A valley,' said Clem. 'We believe it to be the location of a terrorist training camp.'

The PM cast a glance at Benning, who raised his eyebrows.

'How long is it since you slept, Clem?' asked the PM.

'I'm fine, sir.'

'One, two, three days?'

Clem sighed. He was tired but this was just part of their usual bullshit. 'With all due respect, Prime Minister, that has nothing to do with the issue at hand.'

The PM leaned forward. 'Actually, Clem, I think it does.'

Clem narrowed his eyes.

'You look exhausted and your judgement seems off the mark.' The PM smoothed his wrinkle-free shirt. 'It's perfectly understandable, of course, given the incident with Thomas Frasier.'

Clem knew exactly what was happening. The PM was using distraction tactics for the fact that he was going to sweep Clem's advice under the carpet. 'We believe the message sender was also involved in the attack at the Opening Ceremony.'

Benning cleared his throat and dropped his voice. 'There was no attempted attack at the Opening Ceremony,' he said. 'The death of Thomas Frasier was a tragic, but sadly avoidable mistake.'

'We believe the message sender was directly involved in passing the bomb on to Tommy,' said Clem.

'You told us, in this very room, that there was no bomb.' Benning tapped the PM's desk. 'You were very specific, Clem.'

Clem shook his head. This was a complete stitch-up. Everyone in this room had known the score.

'Did you or did you not say that there was no bomb?' asked Benning.

Clem bit his lip.

'I'm afraid I've let you down,' said the PM, his voice dripping with concern.

'What makes you think that, Prime Minister?'

'I should have seen how badly you were affected by the death of that young man. The very fact that you began to call him Tommy should have set alarm bells ringing.'

'I'm fine,' Clem repeated.

The prime minister shook his head. 'No, Clem, you're not. You need rest and you may need counselling. Isn't that standard after any officer is involved in a fatal shooting?'

It was in the book that after certain operations that were considered highly stressful, an officer should take four weeks off work and avail themselves of the assistance of the agency shrink. Since all Clem's cases fell within the remit of 'highly stressful', it was hardly practical for him to follow the guidelines.

'I don't need any time off, sir.'

'This isn't a request,' said Benning. 'It's an order.'

'You don't give me orders,' spat Clem.

'I'm afraid you'll find that I do,' Benning replied.

'Listen to me.' Clem leaned across the desk and was gratified to see Benning flinch. 'You are a suit. A pen-pusher. You have no jurisdiction over me or anyone else at MI5.'

'That's true, of course,' the PM interrupted.

'Thank you, sir,' said Clem.

'But I do have jurisdiction and, as of today, I'm suspending you from active service.' The PM's face was firm. 'Do you understand?'

Clem felt as if he'd received a low blow to the kidneys.

'Do you understand, Clem?' the PM repeated.

Clem understood all right. 'Perfectly, sir.'

Nine a.m. on Roman Road and the market is already busy. Ronnie and I criss-cross through the stalls, ignoring the delicious smell of fresh oranges, until we're outside a tatty travel agents. Ronnie presses her nose to the window, peers inside and nods.

The shop is empty, a desk in the corner clear except for a plant in a pot emblazoned with the words 'World's Best Dad'. The leaves are brown and drooping.

An Asian man in a white cotton kurta appears from the back, a steaming cup of coffee in his hand. When he sees me, he smiles, but his face falls when he sees Ronnie. He drops his mug and flees out the back. Like a tiger, Ronnie vaults over the desk after him and I follow.

The man has his hand on the back door but Ronnie pulls him towards her and slams him against the wall. 'Problem, Ahmed?' she asks.

'I couldn't help your friend,' he says. 'I couldn't give him any-where to stay. Not now.'

'Which friend?' Ronnie demands.

'I didn't ask his name.'

Ronnie slams him again. Harder.

'I didn't ask!' the man screams. 'Why would I?'

Ronnie pulls back her fist. 'Don't lie to me.'

The man closes his eyes, waiting for the crunch, but I intervene.

'Describe him,' I tell the man.

'What?'

'You didn't ask his name but you met him, right?'

The man nods.

'Then tell us what he looked like,' I say.

'I don't know,' the man stammers. 'I don't pay attention to such things.'

Ronnie growls and balls her fist in anger but I cover it with my hand. What use will this guy be to us unable to speak through broken teeth?

'Was he white?' I ask.

'Yes.'

'Tall or short?' I ask.

'Tall,' the man says.

'Accent?'

The man shakes his head. 'I'm not sure. Not English.'

'Scottish?'

'I think maybe, yes.'

'What about this?' I prod my chin. 'Did this man have a beard?'

'Yes, yes. Neatly trimmed.'

Ronnie looks at me. He must be talking about Sean.

'Did he say where he was going?' I ask.

'No.' The man begins shaking violently.

'Let him go,' I tell Ronnie. She doesn't react. 'He's told us all he knows,' I say.

Reluctantly she releases him and the man sinks to the floor. 'I cannot do this any more. Can you understand how difficult this is?' He buries his face in his hands. 'I cannot do this any more,' he repeats.

Rory's seat is 22A. He also bought a second ticket and reserved 22B so no one could sit next to him. It has been a difficult journey. Even with his ear defenders, the noise is deafening. He has considered going back, but Hawk is his friend. Hawk needs him.

A woman points at the seat next to him and says something. She has a jewelled ring in her nose, which catches the light and makes his head hurt. She speaks to him again.

The man opposite leans over and yanks off his ear defenders. 'She's talking to you, mate,' he shouts.

Rory can hardly breathe. The noise of the engine, the wheels on the track, the whooshing of the automatic door to the next carriage all mix together.

'Is that seat taken?' the woman asks.

'Yes,' says Rory and goes to replace his ear defenders.

'No one's sat there the whole way down here,' says the man. 'So whose seat is it?'

'Mine,' says Rory.

'What?' the man snorts. 'You bought both tickets, then?'

'Yes,' replies Rory.

'Then have some manners and let the lady sit down. You can see her condition.'

Rory looks at the woman. Condition is the word used to describe an illness. The woman does not look ill.

'Come on, love,' coaxes the man. 'Sit yourself down there.'

The woman smiles at Rory and sits down. She has eight bangles on each wrist and they jangle when she moves. Rory gags.

'Is there a problem?' the woman asks.

'You smell of onions,' Rory says to her.

'A bloody racist as well,' the man shouts. 'You should be ashamed of yourself.'

Rory can't take any more. He pulls his ear defenders back on, pushes past the woman and runs down the aisle. When he gets to the toilet he goes inside. He daren't touch anything because of the germs. Instead, he stands with his eyes closed and waits to arrive in London.

I tap my head with my knuckle and try to think. Ronnie is out of ideas but we must find the guy posing as Paul. 'If we can't find him, maybe we could send him a message,' I suggest.

'How?'

'You said you contacted Hawk via websites. Is it likely he would do the same with Paul?'

Ronnie shrugs. 'I guess.'

'So let's send a message to Paul, pretending to be Hawk, telling him the whole thing is called off.'

'I don't know,' Ronnie replies. 'Maybe they used code words to identify each other.'

'Maybe they did and maybe they didn't,' I say.

Ronnie still looks dubious.

'Look,' I tell her. 'It's worth a try, surely?'

At last she nods.

We head to the nearest internet café and grab tea and toast while we wait for a computer. Then Ronnie looks up a website called Platformnow.

'Do you know Hawk's password?' I ask.

'No.'

'You could make an educated guess.'

'Such as?'

'Your name?' I suggest.

She screws up her face but types it anyway. No luck. Then she tries several other names. 'My family,' she tells me, but none give her access. 'This is hopeless,' she says. 'It could be anything.'

I shake my head. 'Most people use something meaningful. For someone like Hawk it would be especially so. How about where you grew up?'

Her face takes on a pained expression, as if the very memory physically hurts. 'Old Maple Creek,' she says. 'That's where we lived.'

She doesn't need to say it. It was also the place where so many of her loved ones died.

She types in the words 'Old Maple Creek' and is given access to Hawk's account.

We both take a long, slow breath. 'What shall we say?' I ask her after a few seconds. 'We can't just start a thread saying the bombing is off, can we? It has to be something Paul will believe.'

'Let's look at Hawk's last posts,' says Ronnie. She clicks a few keys and is directed to a thread started by Hawk not long before he died. He's sharing images with a number of other posters.

'What on earth's that all about?' I ask.

Ronnie doesn't answer.

'I said what's that all about?' I turn to her. Her skin, freakily pale in any event, has all the colour bleached from it and the light has left her eyes.

'Ronnie?'

She doesn't take her eyes from the screen. 'You said Hawk was using people to plant the bombs?'

I nod. 'Young people with learning disabilities.'

'This is Hawk leaving a message for Rory,' she says.

'What does it mean?'

Ronnie shakes her head, but I understand what she's alluding to.

'You don't think Hawk is using Rory to plant a bomb?' I ask.

'He can't be.' Ronnie speaks slowly. 'Rory doesn't leave his flat.'

'Not ever?'

'Not if he can help it.'

'What if Hawk managed to convince him he was his best friend?'

'Rory doesn't have any friends,' she says. 'I'm the nearest thing he's got.'

'And when did you last check in?'

She shrugs.

'Exactly,' I say. 'If Rory now thinks Hawk is the only person in the world that cares about him, surely he'd be prepared to do him a favour.'

Clem's doorbell was ringing. 'I'm coming,' he shouted, but whoever it was kept their finger pressed down. 'Jesus Christ!' Clem flung open the door.

Sebastian stood there, the collar of his lilac polo shirt obscuring his face.

'You shouldn't be here, lad,' said Clem. 'I'm off the case.'

'I heard what happened and I think it's disgusting.'

'Thanks, but you still shouldn't be here. They'll sack anyone in MI5 who gets in contact.'

'Luckily I don't work for MI5, remember?'

Clem gave a snort. 'You'd better come in.'

Sebastian followed him into the living room. He took in the bare walls, the empty shelves. 'Homely,' he said.

'What do you want, Sebastian?'

'The message from Hawk, I worked it out.'

'What?'

'He told R1234 to look deeply into the picture,' said Sebastian. 'So that's what I did.'

'I don't understand.'

'I looked into the pixels and there it was, a hidden message.'

'Fucking hell, is that even possible?'

Sebastian rolled his eyes. 'When all this is over I am giving you a crash course in technology.' He handed a piece of paper to Clem. 'This is what it says.'

Clem read the brief message, taking in the two important pieces of information.

11 a.m. Stratford station.

Shit.

'What time is it?' asked Clem.

'Ten thirty-five.'

Clem flew out of the door. 'You're a genius.'

302

Chapter Twenty-five

The traffic was hideous. No matter how many times Clem got on his horn or cut up other drivers, he kept getting boxed in.

He checked the clock.

10.48.

He banged his fist on the steering wheel, abandoned his car and ran the rest of the way, one hand clutching his chest.

The pavements around the station were just as crowded as the roads. Groups of people blocked his path so he had to dodge into the gutter. Panting, he checked his watch.

10.56.

He wasn't going to make it. His heart felt as though the PM was squeezing it with his bare hands.

10.58

People were staring at him as he staggered up the road. He didn't care. He had to get there. Sweat pouring down his face, gasping for breath, he stumbled into the entrance of Stratford station. He looked around wildly for signs of anyone with a rucksack.

11.03

Surely the handover couldn't have happened already? Surely he couldn't have missed them? He pulled out his mobile. 'Carole-Ann?'

'Clem, I really can't speak to you.'

Clem struggled to get his words out. 'There's a bomber on his way to the Games.'

'Are you okay, Clem?'

He breathed deeply, trying to regain control. 'There's another bomber on the way to the Games, Carole-Ann,' he said. 'You have to trust me on this.'

She didn't reply.

'The handover took place at Stratford station,' he told her. 'I missed it, but the device must be on its way to the stadium now.'

'Do we have an ID for the carrier?'

'No, but it's going to be someone on their own, someone different.'

'Clem, that's not enough to go on.'

He leaned against the railing. 'Please, Carole-Ann, just look at the screens. He's there, I know he is.'

She said nothing but Clem could hear those fingernails tapping. 'Have the profilers spotted anyone?' he asked.

'Nope.' She sighed. 'Hang on a second, though.'

'What?' he shouted. 'What is it? Carole-Ann, talk to me.'

'It's the face recognition software,' she said. 'It's picked up your terrorist friend.'

'Who?'

'Ronnie X,' said Carole-Ann. 'She's just entered the stadium and . . . shit . . . you will never guess who she's with.'

I look through the crowds feverishly. I thought Rory would be easy to spot, but there are too many people. It's as if the nations of the world have descended on east London, all chattering excitedly in a hundred different mother tongues. Children dart between street vendors selling balloons and vuvuzelas, their parents chiding them gently to stay close by. Somewhere at the back of my mind I know I should be pleased that the event is such a success, but right now I can't let my thoughts wander.

'Rory will hate this,' says Ronnie. 'He just can't operate in this type of environment.'

We dive in and out of the crowds, desperately trying to find him. 'What event do you think Hawk might target?' I ask.

'Track would be the obvious one,' she says. 'The world will be watching Usain Bolt.'

I nod and we begin to make our way across to the stands, trying not to think about how many thousands are in danger. Suddenly, there's a commotion up ahead. A woman is shouting.

'Can't you watch where you're going, you moron?' She's standing with her hands on her hips, a look of disgust on her face.

I catch sight of who she's speaking to. A hulk of a person, his T-shirt too short, fluffy earmuffs balanced on his bald head. 'Rory!' I shout.

We watch him hurry off, the woman still berating him, and begin to give chase when we're stopped by a burly security guard.

'Can I see your tickets, please?'

Ronnie and I look at each other. No amount of clever chat is going to remedy this situation.

'I'm sorry,' I say.

'What for?' asks the guard.

'This,' I say and punch him in the face. As he hits the deck, blood pouring from his nose, we sprint after Rory. 'I am sorry, honestly,' I shout at the guard, but Ronnie pulls me away towards Rory, who has disappeared inside the mammoth aquatic centre.

'Swimming?' I say.

'More damage in contained areas,' says Ronnie. 'Very difficult to evacuate.'

'Would Hawk really be that much of a bastard?' I ask.

Ronnie doesn't answer. It's a stupid question.

We race inside, hit by the heat, the smell of chlorine and the sound of cheering.

It's actually a diving event taking place. The young British superstar, set for a gold, is making his way up the ladder to the high board. The crowd shout out his name. Rory is at the far side, pushing his way past grumbling fans, a rucksack bobbing on his back. When he gets to a spare seat, he squeezes himself in, placing the bag carefully on his lap and jiggling it like a baby. I hold my breath at the thought of the contents.

'What are we going to do?' Ronnie asks.

'For a start you're going to tell me what the fuck is going on.' I spin and find Clem behind me, gun in Ronnie's back.

'I knew you were a wild card, Jo,' he says. 'But this is fucking ridiculous.'

'There's a bomber in the building,' I tell him.

'I know that.' He nods at Ronnie.

'It's not her, Clem. Believe me, it's not her.'

Clem blinks once, gun in place.

'Think about it, Clem,' I say. 'The last person Hawk would use for this would be his sister.'

'Ethical soul, was he?'

I shake my head vigorously. 'I know how it sounds, but Hawk had a twisted sense of morality. His family, or what's left of it, was all that mattered to him.'

Clem doesn't react. I have no idea whether I'm making any inroads. All I do know is that Rory is less than 200 feet away, carrying enough explosive to blow us all to kingdom come.

'Anyway, Hawk had a much better system than risking his sister, didn't he?'

Clem doesn't reply.

'He picked on the vulnerable and convinced them to do his dirty work,' I say.

There's a slight twitch at the corner of Clem's eye.

'See the guy over there?' I gesture to Rory. 'He's the one.'

Clem glances up at Rory, taking in his ear defenders and ill-fitting clothes.

'The bomb's in the rucksack, Clem,' I tell him. 'We have to take action right now.'

Clem looks from Ronnie to Rory and back again, assessing the situation. At last he nods to himself, takes three steps forward, holds his weapon high in the air and shouts, 'Armed police!'

Someone in the crowd screams and soon pandemonium breaks out as people try to move out of Clem's way. He ignores the chaos around him and coolly points the gun at Rory. 'Give me the bag, son.'

Rory screws his eyes closed and hugs the rucksack to his chest.

Clem gives a weary sigh and cocks his finger around the trigger.

'No,' Ronnie begs. 'Please don't kill him.'

'I can't take any more risks,' says Clem.

'Please.' Ronnie's voice catches in her throat. 'Rory's just like the other boy who was shot. He's being used.'

Clem breathes audibly.

'Let me speak to him,' says Ronnie. 'He trusts me.'

A pause stretches between them, then Clem gives a nod.

Ronnie takes a step forward. 'Rory, can you hear me? It's Ronnie.'

Rory begins to rock back and forth.

'You have thirty seconds,' Clem whispers.

'Rory, I need you to give me that rucksack,' she says. 'It's really, really important, do you understand?'

'You said you'd come back,' Rory mumbles. 'You said as soon as possible.'

'This is as soon as possible. It got too crazy, Rory. I had to go away.'

Rory buries his face in the rucksack.

'I can't wait any longer,' says Clem.

Ronnie's face is stricken.

'Let me try,' I say.

Clem raises his eyebrow.

'Just for a second,' I persist. 'Let's try not to spill any more blood.'

Clem narrows his eyes at me, which I take as a yes and step forward towards Rory. 'Do you remember me, Rory?'

He opens one eye. 'You punched me.'

'I'm sorry about that,' I say. 'I was very frightened. Have you ever been very frightened?'

He nods.

'Then you'll understand. I think it was very brave of you to come down here. Were you very frightened on the journey?'

'A man was nasty to me.'

'That was wrong of him,' I say. 'What people don't understand is that just because you're a bit different doesn't mean you're stupid or worthless.'

Rory doesn't answer, but both his eyes are open.

'I had a brother called Davey,' I say. 'He was very different. There were things that most other people could do that Davey found impossible.' I take another step towards Rory, gulping at the thought of what's in that bag. 'But there were things Davey could do that I found completely impossible.' I take another step. 'I bet you can do all sorts of things other people can't, eh?'

'I can remember things,' says Rory.

'There you are, then.' I smile. 'I can't remember what I had for breakfast this morning.'

I take one more step. 'Did Hawk's friend give you the bag?'

Rory nods.

'Do you know what's in it?'

He shakes his head.

'Would you be prepared to give it to me?'

Rory's knuckles go white as he tightens his grip. 'I can't.'

'Did Hawk's friend tell you to keep it with you?'

Rory nods. 'At all times. It's very special to Hawk and I have to look after it until he gets here.'

'Hawk's not coming, Rory,' I say.

He looks pained and makes a noise like an animal.

'Do you understand, Rory?'

'He said he would meet me here.'

'He can't do that, I'm afraid.'

Rory begins rocking again, making his low moan.

'I have to do this now,' says Clem and moves into position.

Desperate, I look around me. There at the bottom of the diving ladder is a pile of towels. I sprint to them and grab one. 'How about I swap that bag for a towel?' I say.

Rory freezes.

'You need four, right?' I ask.

He nods.

'How about it?'

I hold the towel out and Rory releases one of his hands. Slowly I move forward until I'm a foot away from him. 'Take the towel,' I say to Rory.

Unsure at first, he reaches out to it. Once it's in his fingers he pulls it to him and rubs it against his baby-soft cheek.

'Now give me the bag, Rory.'

Gingerly, he lifts it and passes it over. In turn, I pass it to Clem, my hands shaking, and he rushes it out of the building.

As the police and security forces begin to arrive, I grab Ronnie's hand. 'Come on,' I urge her.

'Where to?' she asks.

I don't answer but lead her away.

'What is this place?' Ronnie watches me undo several locks and bolts on a small flat in Westminster.

'My dad's old flat.'

Inside, there's a smell of mould and cobwebs drape from the ceiling. 'It's like Miss Havisham's house,' says Ronnie.

I'm momentarily surprised to hear Ronnie reference Charles Dickens, but the feeling passes as I realise I am no longer surprised by anything Ronnie says or does.

'Dad bought it when he was an MP,' I tell her. 'He used to bring me here sometimes, try to interest me in politics.'

Ronnie noses through the bookshelves at the biographies of all the greats covered in dust. Churchill, Macmillan, Thatcher. Another century. 'Did it work?'

'Not really,' I say. 'I was far more interested in sport.'

'What happened?'

'I got injured.'

'So you went for plan B?'

'Something like that.'

When I started working for the civil service, Dad said I should use this flat, but it never felt right.

'Can I get a shower?' Ronnie asks.

'The water will be freezing.'

Ronnie sniffs her armpit. 'Right now, that's the least of my worries.'

I show her to the bathroom and stand on the landing, listening to the water run.

'Why did you keep this place?' she shouts.

'I dunno,' I say. Why did I keep it? Was I hoping Dad would get better? Was I hoping that one day I'd feel worthy enough to move in myself?

The water stops. 'Any chance of finding a toothbrush?' Ronnie calls.

'Try the cabinet,' I say.

'What?'

I open the door. 'Try the cabinet.'

Ronnie is wrapped in a towel, her back to me, water dripping down her scar. In the mirror she sees me looking at it.

'Does it still hurt?' I ask.

'Sometimes.'

There's nothing I can say so I don't try.

Later we sit at the table eating Cornish pasties I bought from the corner shop. I open a bottle of wine from Dad's collection.

'Very swanky,' says Ronnie, taking a gulp of claret to wash down a mouthful of pastry.

'For a man of the people, my dad always had very expensive tastes,' I laugh.

When the bottle's almost empty, I broach the subject on both our minds. 'What now?'

Ronnie shrugs. 'I should be safe here until it's dark.'

'Where will you go?'

She takes another sip of wine. 'I hear Brazil is nice this time of year.'

'You know, we could go to Clem and explain everything,' I say. 'You had no involvement in any of the attacks.'

'I kidnapped you,' she states.

'Says who?'

Ronnie raises her eyebrow.

'If I don't tell them anything, where's the evidence?' I ask.

She drains her glass and holds it up to the light, letting the last shafts of sunshine bounce off the crystal.

'You don't have to live like this, Ronnie,' I tell her. 'Hawk is dead but you can have a different sort of life. If you want it.'

She doesn't look at me.

'Will you at least think about it?' I ask. 'Promise me you'll think about it.'

She puts down the glass and leans over to hug me. She smells of toothpaste and fresh mountain air. 'You're a real case, Jo Connolly,' she laughs.

Then I feel a sharp sting in my thigh and feel myself fall into blackness.

When I wake, it's dark and my head is pounding. There is no sign of Ronnie. I check the telltale pinprick where she injected me and rub it with my finger.

In the living room, on the bookshelf, next to a huge tome about Paddy Connolly, is a letter. I don't want to read it, and I wait until darkness falls.

Finally, I have to pick it up.

Jo,
It's been one hell of a ride, hasn't it?
But now it's time to say goodbye.
Don't be sad. Don't look back.
The future is ours, Jo, and like you said, we can make it into whatever we want.
Your friend,
Veronica-Mae

Epilogue

Autumn 2012

I smile into the cameras.

'What do you think of the prime minister's resignation, Jo?' one of the hacks calls out.

'He wants to spend more time with his family,' I say. 'I think we can all understand that.'

'Will you throw your name into the ring, Jo?'

I wag my finger. 'I'm not a politician.'

'Come on, Jo,' he shouts. 'The country needs you.'

I smile, jump into the Mini and race off to Brighton.

The hospital receptionist smiles at me with her straight white teeth. 'Nice to see you again, Miss Connolly.'

'You too,' I reply and make my way up to Kingfisher ward.

Rory is waiting at the security door, his eyes fixed on his watch.

'What time is it?' I ask him.

'Eleven oh two and thirteen seconds,' he says.

'That's not bad, is it?'

He looks at me with a frown. 'You're two minutes and thirteen seconds late,' he tells me.

'So not bad?' I ask.

Rory frowns at me and gives one slow shake of his head. 'Not bad,' he says mechanically.

We make our way to his room. For the past few months I've been paying for Rory to have a private room off the ward. He's really made it his own with a pea-green duvet, four white towels and the latest MacBook.

'The doc tells me your therapy is going well,' I say.

Rory doesn't answer. To be fair, I haven't asked a question.

'He says I can take you out for a few hours if you'd like that.'

Rory's tongue protrudes through his lips like a big, wet, pink cushion.

'Would you like that?' I ask.

'Where would we go?'

'How about the beach?' I suggest. 'I know a deserted stretch of sand a few miles from here. Would that be okay?'

'I have to come back for lunch,' he says.

I nod. 'I'll make sure you're back for one o'clock precisely and if we get hungry in the meantime, I've brought a snack.'

I pull out an opened family bag of peanut M&Ms.

'No red ones,' I say.